*more . . .*

## ALSO BY ELIZABETH PETERS

### THE VICKY BLISS SERIES

*Borrower of the Night* • *Street of the Five Moons*
*Silhouette in Scarlet* • *Trojan Gold Night* • *Train to Memphis*

### THE AMELIA PEABODY SERIES

*Crocodile on the Sandbank* • *The Curse of the Pharaohs*
*The Mummy Case* • *Lion in the Valley*
*The Deeds of the Disturber* • *The Last Camel Died at Noon*
*The Snake, the Crocodile and the Dog*
*The Hippopotamus Pool*
*Seeing a Large Cat* • *The Ape Who Guards the Balance*
*The Falcon at the Portal* • *He Shall Thunder in the Sky*
*Lord of the Silent* • *The Golden One*
*Children of the Storm* • *Guardian of the Horizon*
*The Serpent on the Crown* • *Tomb of the Golden Bird*

### AND

*Amelia Peabody's Egypt* (edited with Kristen Whitbread)

### THE JACQUELINE KIRBY SERIES

*The Seventh Sinner* • *The Murders of Richard III*
*Die for Love* • *Naked Once More*

### AND

*The Jackal's Head* • *The Camelot Caper*
*The Dead Sea Cipher* • *The Night of Four Hundred Rabbits*
*Legend in Green Velvet* • *Devil-May-Care*
*Summer of the Dragon* • *The Love Talker*
*The Copenhagen Connection*

# ELIZABETH PETERS

## NIGHT TRAIN TO MEMPHIS

**GRAND CENTRAL**
PUBLISHING

NEW YORK    BOSTON

Copyright © 1994 by Elizabeth Peters
All rights reserved. Except as permitted under the U.S. Copyright Act of 1976, no part of this publication may be reproduced, distributed, or transmitted in any form or by any means, or stored in a database or retrieval system, without the prior written permission of the publisher.

*Cover design by Don Puckey*
*Cover illustration by Stanislaw Fernandez*
*Handlettering by Ron Zinn*

Grand Central Publishing
Hachette Book Group USA
237 Park Avenue
New York, NY 10017
Visit our Web site at www.HachetteBookGroupUSA.com

Grand Central Publishing is a division of Hachette Book Group USA, Inc. The Grand Central Publishing name and logo is a trademark of Hachette Book Group USA, Inc.

Printed in the United States of America

Originally published in hardcover by Hachette Book Group USA
First Paperback Printing: December 1995
Reissued: August 2008

16  15  14  13  12  11  10  9  8

ATTENTION CORPORATIONS AND ORGANIZATIONS:
Most HACHETTE BOOK GROUP USA books are available at quantity discounts with bulk purchase for educational, business, or sales promotional use. For information, please call or write:

Special Markets Department, Hachette Book Group USA
237 Park Avenue, New York, NY 10017
Telephone: 1-800-222-6747  Fax: 1-800-477-5925

# *Acknowledgments*

At the risk of sounding like a giddy young first-published author who thanks everybody except the electrician, I must acknowledge the assistance of many friends and friendly experts in writing this book. I couldn't have gotten myself or Vicky to Amarna without the help of Dennis Forbes, editorial director of *K. M. T (A Modern Journal of Ancient Egypt)*, and that journal's special projects editor, George B. Johnson. They were mines of information and the most congenial of fellow-travelers. Kent Weeks of the American University in Cairo good-naturedly informed me that I couldn't possibly get Vicky away from Amarna via the route I had proposed, and suggested an alternative. Peter Dorman, director of the Oriental Institute's Epigraphic Survey, and his wonderful crew at Chicago House fed me, instructed me, entertained me, and dragged me up and down the cliffs of the West Bank searching for an imaginary tomb. Practically everybody connected with the American Research Council in Egypt amiably endured my pressing inquiries and pervasive presence: Terry Walz, executive director; Mark Easton, Cairo director, and Mark's associates Barbara Fudge and Amira Khattab. To all of them, my affectionate thanks.

The basic inspiration for the book came from an earlier trip to Egypt and the two friends who accompanied me on a Nile cruise. One couldn't ask for more delightful companions than Charlotte and Aaron Elkins, and there is no truth whatever to the rumor that I stole my plot from Aaron. I tried, but he was too clever for me.

The title of the book originated while I was meeting with a group of fellow mystery writers. This group convenes each year, purportedly for the purpose of carrying on professional discussions, and we actually *were* carrying on a professional discussion when I asked plaintively, "What the Hades am I going to call this book?" The answer came, as it usually does, from Sharyn McCrumb. I thought it was a great title, but I failed to recognize the source; my ignorance prompted Sharyn to lecture me on the subject of country-western music and to supply me with various research materials. As a result I am now a convert, which may explain some of the esoteric references in this volume. I would offer a prize to the reader who can spot the most songs, except I'm sure Sharyn would win it.

Sharyn is also the author of "You're a Detour on the Highway to Heaven," in which endeavor she acknowledges some assistance from Joan Hess and Dorothy Cannell. Joan and Dorothy claim the assistance was considerable, amounting to actual collaboration. I have no further comment to make on this subject, except to say that my debt to these writers and the other nonmembers of the organization to which they and I belong is profound.

None of the individuals mentioned is responsible for any errors I may have made in recording the information they gave me. The views expressed are those of the characters, who are, I hardly need say, entirely fictitious. The tomb of Tetisheri is also fictitious. For reasons that should be apparent I could not use an actual, known tomb, so I invented one. (A real tomb of Tetisheri may yet be found, though such an eventuality is, in my opinion, unlikely. If this happens, bear in mind it isn't the same tomb as mine.) The particular Fourth Dynasty cemetery at Abydos to which I have referred is also apocryphal. I think. One never knows what is going to turn up in Egypt.

There are, of course, many museums in Cairo. The proper name of the one to which my characters constantly and carelessly refer is The Egyptian Museum.

Vicky's comments on the problems of conservation faced by overworked and underfunded antiquities organizations are unfortunately only too accurate. The problem is acute; positive, public support is badly needed, especially for organizations such as the Epigraphic Survey, which for many years has concentrated on making accurate copies of fading reliefs and inscriptions. If we cannot preserve all the monuments—and we cannot—we can at least record them before they vanish forever.

## YOU'RE A DETOUR
## ON THE HIGHWAY TO HEAVEN

(To: *Great Speckled Bird*)


When Mama lay a-dyin" on the flatbed,
She told me not to truck with girls like you;
But I was blinded by the glare of your headlights,
And wnt joy-ridin' just for the view.

CHORUS:  You're a detour on the highway to heaven,
            I am lost on the backroads of sin,
            I have got to get back to the four-lane,
            So that I can see Mama again.

Your curves made me lose my direction,
My hands from the steering wheel strayed,
But you were just one more roadside attraction,
It's been ten thousand miles since I prayed.

If you ever get out of the fast lane
And get back to that highway above,
I'll be waiting for you at the tollbooth,
In that land where all roads end in love.

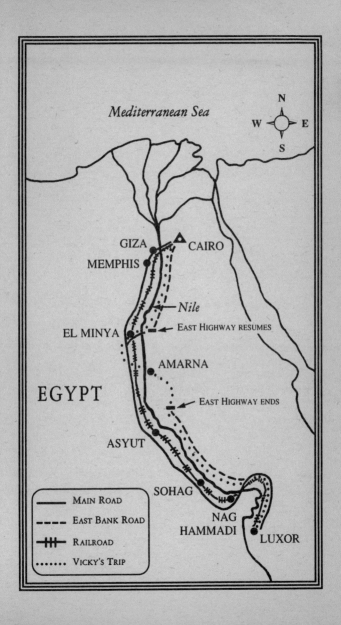

# Chapter One

*i*

The mountain meadow was carpeted with fresh green and starred with small, shy flowers. He came toward me, walking so lightly the grass scarcely seemed to bend under his feet. His hair shone silver-gilt in the sunlight, and he was smiling, and his blue eyes held a look I had seen in them only once before. Trembling, I waited for him to come to me. He stopped a few feet away, still smiling, and held out his hands.

They were wet and red and dripping. I looked from his bleeding hands to his face and saw blood erupt from it in spurting streams, from the corners of his mouth, from under the hair on his temples. Bright scarlet patches blossomed on the breast of his shirt. There was blood everywhere, covering him like a red rain. I stretched out my arms but I couldn't reach him and I couldn't move and the scream I tried to utter wouldn't come out of my throat and he fell, face down at my feet, and the back of his head wasn't golden fair but sticky scarlet and the blood spread out, staining the green grass and drowning the shy flowers and still I couldn't reach him . . .

"Oh God, oh God, oh God . . ." Somebody was whining. It wasn't I. I was blubbering and swearing—or was I praying?

Swearing. "Damn him, damn him!" I reached out blindly in the dark. There was something monstrous and hairy on my bed. I threw my arms around it and clutched it to my bosom.

Caesar stopped whining and began licking my face with frantic slurps. Caesar is a Doberman; his tongue is as rough as a file and about a foot and a half long. He has very bad breath.

"All right, okay," I gasped, fending him off and reaching for the bedside lamp.

The light helped, and so did the sight of my familiar messy bedroom, but I was still shaking. God! That had been the worst one yet.

Caesar's furry face stared worriedly at me. He wasn't allowed on the bed. I must have cried out in my sleep, and the gallant dog had leaped up to my rescue.

Clara *was* allowed on the bed. Caesar hasn't got over the injustice of this yet, but he can't do anything about it because he is terrified of Clara, who weighs approximately seven pounds to his seventy. I think he thinks she is a god. He slobbers with delight when she condescends to curl up next to him, and grovels when she raises a paw. She had retreated from her usual position, on my stomach, to the foot of the bed and was sitting up, eyeing me with that look of tolerant contempt only Siamese cats have fully mastered. In the dark seal-brown of her face her eyes looked very blue.

A shudder twisted through me as I remembered how blood had filled those other blue eyes.

It was the third time that week I had dreamed about John. The first one hadn't been bad, just an ordinary anxiety/frustration dream in which I pursued a familiar form along endless streets only to find, when I caught up with it, that it wore someone else's face. The second . . . well, never mind the details of that one. The metamorphosis of the body I clasped into a scaled, limbless creature that slid slimily through my arms and vanished into darkness had left a nasty memory, but it hadn't awakened me.

I knew the cause of the dreams. My subconscious doesn't fool around; it's about as subtle as a brickbat. I had told myself there was nothing to worry about, even if I hadn't heard from him for over a month, and I had believed it—sort of—until a week ago. Hugging my warm, hairy, smelly dog as a child would clutch a teddy bear for comfort, I remembered the conversation that had forced me (or my subconscious) to admit there *was* something to worry about.

*ii*

"But I don't know anything about Egyptology!" I yelled.

Normally I don't yell when I say things like that. I mean, it's hardly the sort of statement that arouses passionate emotions. But this was the fourth time I had said it, and I didn't seem to be getting the point across.

The two men behind the desk exchanged glances. One of them was my old friend Karl Feder of the Munich Police Department. The other man was about the same age—mid-fifties, at a guess. Like Karl, he was losing his hair and starting to spread around the middle. He had been introduced to me as Herr Burckhardt, no title, no affiliation. If he was a colleague of Karl's he had to be a cop of some variety, but I had only known one other man with eyes as cold as his, and Rudi had definitely not been a police officer.

I knew what they were thinking. It was Burckhardt who said it. "I fail to understand, Dr. Bliss. You are an official of our National Museum, a well-known authority on art history. The Herr Direktor, Doktor Schmidt, has often said that you are his most valued subordinate."

"Yeah," I said gloomily. "I'll bet he has."

Schmidt has a mouth almost as big as his rotund tummy. He is as cute as one of the Seven Dwarfs and not much taller, and if he wasn't so brilliant he'd have been locked up long ago as a menace to society. Not that he's a crook. On the contrary; Schmidt thinks of himself as a brilliant amateur sleuth, the scourge of the underworld, and of me as his side-kick. As Watson was to Sherlock, as Archie was to Nero

Wolfe, so Vicky Bliss is to Herr Doktor Anton Z. Schmidt. At least that's how Schmidt looks at it. My own view of our respective roles is somewhat different.

I said slowly and patiently, "Human beings have been producing works of art of one kind or another for over thirty-five thousand years. Even if you include only the major visual arts and restrict yourself to Western art, you have to start with Stone Age man, proceed through the Egyptians and the Minoans and the Etruscans and the Greeks, to early Christian art and Byzantine and medieval and Renaissance and . . . Oh, hell. What I'm trying to say is that nobody can be an expert on all those fields. My specialty is medieval European art. I don't know—"

"What about the Trojan gold?" Feder inquired. "That does not come under the heading of medieval European art, does it?"

I had been afraid somebody was going to bring that up.

Schmidt refers to the affair of the Trojan gold as "our most recent case." He doesn't often refer to it, however, because it had not been one of "our" most resounding successes. People had been looking for the gold, a hoard of priceless ancient jewelry which had vanished from besieged Berlin at the end of World War II, for almost fifty years. Educated opinion believed the Russians had carried it off to Moscow. Schmidt and I and a few other people had spent several weeks the previous winter following up a clue that suggested it had been smuggled out of Berlin before the Russians entered the city, and hidden somewhere in Bavaria. At one point I thought I had found the hiding place. Turned out I was wrong. Schmidt was still complaining about how I had misled him. Which I hadn't, not deliberately. I had been—well—wrong. Sometimes I *am* wrong.

Not this time, though, dammit. Feder was smirking at me as if he had said something clever. He was correct. The Trojan gold could not be described as medieval art.

I tried again. "That had nothing to do with my expertise or lack thereof. It was pure chance."

"But you recognized, from a bad photograph, that the jewels pictured were genuine. Some degree of expertise—"

"Anybody could have done that!" My voice rose. "The

gold of Troy is famous. Everybody knows about it. Almost everybody ... Let me put it this way, meine Herren; I could not pose as an expert on Egyptian art for more than five minutes without getting caught out. If I understand you correctly, you are suggesting I accept the position of guest lecturer on a Nile cruise. In exchange for a free tour I will be expected to talk at least once a day on some damned temple or pyramid, and be prepared to answer questions from the people taking the cruise, who wouldn't be taking the cruise if they weren't already interested in and informed about the subject. Five minutes, hell! I wouldn't last sixty seconds. Why me, for God's sake? There are hundreds of people who know more about the subject than I do."

"But my dear Fräulein Doktor!" Burckhardt exclaimed. "Look at it this way. Never again will you have the opportunity for such a holiday. This is a luxury cruise; the boat is new, designed for millionaire tourists—suites instead of rooms, gourmet food, the best of everything. Passengers will be admitted to places that are barred to the ordinary tourist, the lecturers are all distinguished scholars—"

He waved a brightly colored brochure at me. I shied back. "That's just the point, Herr Burckhardt. Karl, will you please tell your friend that I am not an empty-headed blond bimbo, even if I do look like one."

Lately I'd been trying very hard not to look like one, swathing my too well endowed torso in loose jackets and my long legs in full skirts that flapped around my calves. I had let my hair grow long so I could wind it into a schoolmarmish bun. Nothing seemed to work. If you are tall and blond and blue-eyed and shaped like a female, some people assume you don't have a brain cell working.

Karl tried to hide his smile. "I warned you this approach would not work, Burckhardt. The lady is very astute. I imagine she already suspects why we are making this request."

I nodded gloomily. It didn't require a high degree of intelligence. The affair of the Trojan gold was only the most recent of several encounters I have enjoyed with the criminal element, if "enjoyed" is the right word. I do not enjoy being shot at, assaulted, kidnapped, and chased across the countryside. I didn't want to do that anymore.

"Something is going to happen on that cruise," I said. "What is it? Murder, hijacking, or just a simple case of grand theft which could easily lead to murder or hijacking?"

"If you will allow me to explain," Burckhardt began.

"That's what I've been asking you to do."

Burckhardt leaned back and folded his arms. "The information reached us via a channel which has proved particularly fruitful in the past. How our agent acquired the information we do not know, but he has never before failed to be accurate. He gave us three facts: first, that there is a plot to rob the Cairo Museum; second, the individuals involved will be on the Nile cruise which starts on November first; third, one or more of them is personally known to you. Now obviously we cannot halt the cruise or detain everyone who has signed up for it. We must have an agent on that boat. You are the obvious choice, not only because you—"

"Wait," I said. My voice sounded quite normal. That surprised me; even though I had half expected it, one of his statements had had the same impact as a hard kick on the shin. "Let's go back over that interesting assemblage of so-called facts, shall we? First, why are you guys involved? Why don't you pass the information on to the Egyptian government and let them handle it?"

"Naturally we have notified the authorities in that country. They have requested our cooperation. Are you familiar with the current political situation in Egypt?"

I shrugged. "Not in detail. Keep it short, will you?"

"I will endeavor to do so." Burckhardt steepled his fingertips and tried to look like a professor. He didn't. "The modern nation of Egypt did not attain independence until 1922. For over a century it was exploited, as some might say, by Western powers, and many of the most valuable antiquities were—er—'removed' to museums and private collections in Europe and America. Anti-Western sentiment is of long standing and it is now being fostered by certain groups who wish to replace the present government of Egypt with one more sympathetic to their religious views. They have attacked tourists and members of the government. If the historic treasures of Egypt were stolen by a group of foreigners—"

"I see your point," I said reluctantly. "Okay. Next question.

Seems to me your information is very fragmentary. Why don't you ask this hot-shot agent of yours where he got it and tell him to dig around for more?"

Another exchange of meaningful glances. "Oh, please," I said. "Don't tell me. Don't tell me this is another of *those* plots. He's dead. Right? Found in an alley with his throat cut? Horribly tortured and . . . I don't believe this!"

"Believe it," Karl said soberly. "We had not wanted to tell you—"

"I can see why. It might have put a slight damper on my girlish enthusiasm for playing Nancy Drew."

"You would be in no danger," Karl insisted.

"And if I believe that, you've got a bridge you'd like to sell me cheap."

"Bitte?" Karl said, looking puzzled.

"Never mind."

"It is true. We will have other agents on that cruise; they will guard you day and night. The moment you have identified the individual—or individuals—in question, they will be placed under arrest—"

"No, they won't."

"Bitte?" said Burckhardt, trying to look puzzled. He knew perfectly well what I meant.

I spelled it out. "You can't arrest people because Victoria Bliss thinks they look like somebody who might once, maybe, have committed a crime. You'll have to wait till they do something illegal. And while you're waiting, I'll be sitting there like a groundhog on a superhighway at rush hour. If . . . they . . . are known to me, I'm also known to them."

"You will be in no danger," Burckhardt repeated.

"Damn right." I stood up. "Because I won't be on that cruise. Auf Wiedersehen, meine Herren."

"Think about it," Karl said smoothly. "You needn't decide now."

I was thinking about it. My acquaintanceship with the members of the art underworld is more extensive than I would like, but there was one individual with whom I was particularly well acquainted. His had been the first name that occurred to me—if it was his name. He had at least four aliases, including his favorite, "Sir John Smythe." I didn't know—I had never

known—his last name, and even though he had told me his
first name was John, I had no reason to suppose he was telling
the truth. He hardly ever did tell the truth. He was a thief and
a swindler and a liar, and he had dragged me into a number
of embarrassing, not to say dangerous, situations, but if he
hadn't come to my rescue at the risk of grievous bodily harm
to himself—something John preferred not to do—I wouldn't
be in Karl's office wondering whether he and Herr Burckhardt
knew, or only suspected, that the "individual" they were after
might be my occasional and elusive lover.

## *iii*

It took me a long time to get back to sleep after that grisly
dream. I was not in the best possible condition to cope with
Munich's rush-hour traffic next morning—short on sleep,
tense with a mixture of anger, anxiety, and indecision. It was
raining, of course. It always rains in Munich when somebody
offers me a trip to someplace bright and warm and sunny.

   I've lived in Munich for a number of years, ever since I
wangled a job out of the funny little fat man who had been
a prime suspect in my first "case," as he would call it.* He
wasn't the murderer, as it turned out; he was a famous scholar,
director of the National Museum, and he had been impressed
by my academic credentials as well as by the fact that I could
have embarrassed the hell out of him by telling the world
about some of his shenanigans during that adventure. We had
become good friends and I had come to think of Munich as
my adopted home town. It's a beautiful city in one of the
most beautiful parts of the world—when the sun is shining.
In the rain, with fallen leaves making the streets slick and
dangerous, it is as dreary as any other large city.

---

*Borrower of the Night.*

When I pulled into the staff parking lot behind the museum, Karl the janitor popped out of his cubicle to inquire after the health, not of my humble self, but of Caesar, for whom he has an illicit passion. I assured him all was well and hurried through the storage areas of the basement, praying Schmidt hadn't arrived yet. I had to go to the museum office to collect my mail and messages; if I didn't, Gerda, Schmidt's hideously efficient and inquisitive secretary, would bring them to me and hang around, talking and asking questions and ignoring my hints that she should go away, and then I would probably hit her with something large and heavy because Gerda gets on my nerves even when they are not already stretched to the breaking point.

I entered the office at a brisk trot, glancing at my watch. "Goodness, it's later than I thought. Good morning, Gerda, I've got to hurry, I'm awfully late."

"For what?" Gerda inquired. "You have no appointment this morning. Unless you have made one without informing me, which is contrary to—"

I snatched the pile of letters from her desk. She snatched it back. "I have not finished sorting them, Vicky. What is wrong with you this morning? Ach, but you look terrible! Did you not sleep? You were, perhaps, working late?"

She hoped I hadn't been working late. She hoped I'd been doing something more interesting. Gerda has one of those round, healthy pink faces, and mouse-brown hair, and wide, innocent pale blue eyes. She is short. I am all the things Gerda is not, and the poor dumb woman admires me and tries to imitate me. She also harbors the delusion—derived in part from Schmidt, who shares it—that men whiz in and out of my life like city buses, only more often. Little does she know. It was questionable as to whether John qualified for the role of my lover—three visits in nine months isn't my idea of a torrid affair—but for the past two years he had been the only possible candidate.

"Yes. I was working late," I lied.

She didn't believe me. "Ach, so. I thought perhaps Herr Feder—"

"Who?" I gaped at her.

She *had* sorted the messages, damn her. She waved two slips of paper at me. "He has telephoned twice this morning. He wishes that you call him as soon as possible."

"Thanks." This time when I grabbed my mail she let me keep it. "We will have lunch, perhaps?" she called after me as I headed quickly for the door.

"Perhaps." If I could just get out of Gerda's office before Schmidt emerged from his . . . I was in no condition to cope with Schmidt that morning. He's even nosier than Gerda.

I might have known it was going to be one of those days. Schmidt wasn't in his office. He had just arrived. When I flung the door open there he was, briefcase in one hand, the remains of a jelly doughnut in the other. Schmidt eats all the time. Jelly doughnuts are his latest enthusiasm, one he acquired from me.

He was wearing one of those trench coats covered with straps, flaps, and pockets—the style James Bond and other famous spies prefer—and an Indiana Jones fedora pulled low over his bristling eyebrows. The ensemble, which indicated that Schmidt was in one of his swashbuckling moods, was ominous enough, but that wasn't what brought me to a stop. Schmidt was singing.

That's how he would have described it. Schmidt can't carry a tune in a bucket, but he loves music, and he had recently expanded his repertoire to include country music. American country music. What he was doing to this tune would have sent the citizens of Nashville, Tennessee, running for a rope.

It was my fault, I admit that. I had heard them all my life, not the modern rock adaptations, but the old railroad and work songs, the blues and ballads. During the Great Depression my granddad had wandered the country like so many other footloose, jobless young men; he bragged of having known Boxcar Willie and John Lomax, and he could still make a guitar cry. I had once made the mistake of playing a Jimmie Rodgers tape for Schmidt. That was all it took.

In addition to being tone-deaf, Schmidt never gets the words quite right. ". . . I sing to my Dixie darling, Beneath the silver moon, With my banjo on my knee." Imagine that in a thick Bavarian accent.

He broke off when he saw me. "Ah, Vicky! You are here!"

"I'm late," I said automatically. "Very late. I have to—"

"But my poor Vicky." He stood on tiptoe peering up into my face. "Your eyes are shadowed and sunken. You have the look of a woman who—"

"Shut up, Schmidt," I said, trying to get around him. He popped the rest of the doughnut into his mouth and caught hold of my hand. Strawberry jelly glued our fingers together. A stream of water from the hem of his coat was soaking my shoes.

"Come and have coffee and tell Papa Schmidt all about it. Is Karl Feder annoying you again? Tsk! He should be ashamed, the old rascal. Or,"—he grinned and winked—"or is it another individual who is responsible for the disturbance of your slumber?"

Glancing over my shoulder, I saw that Gerda was on her feet, leaning precariously across the desk as she tried to overhear. Schmidt had seen her too. Shaking his head, he said disapprovingly, "There is no decent regard for privacy in this place. Come into my office, Vicky, where we can be alone, and you will tell Papa Schmidt—"

"No," I said.

"No what? It was not Sir John—"

"No everything! Nobody disturbed my slumber, no, I will not come into your office, no, Karl Feder is not . . ." I stopped, clutching at the last ragged strands of sanity. Better to let Schmidt think Karl's reasons for calling were personal instead of professional. Or was it? The world was dissolving into chaos around me.

"See you later, Schmidt," I babbled, freeing my hand. "I have to—I have to—go to the bathroom."

It was the only place I could think of where he wouldn't follow me. I locked myself into a cubicle and collapsed onto the seat.

My hand was red and sticky. In certain lights, strawberry jelly looks a lot like fresh blood.

John was certainly a reasonable subject for anxiety dreams. He had more deadly enemies than anyone I'd ever met. Sometimes I was one of them.

When I first ran into him I was trying to track down a

forger of historic jewels.* I had no business doing any such thing; it was a combination of curiosity and the desire for a free vacation that took me to Rome, and some people might have said that it served me right when I got in over my head. John got me out. He had been an enthusiastic participant in the swindle until the others decided to eliminate me, but, as he candidly admitted, chivalry had nothing to do with his change of heart. He disapproved of murder on practical grounds. As he put it, "the penalties are so much more severe."

I never meant to get involved with him. He isn't really my type—only an inch or so taller than I, slightly built, his features (with one or two exceptions) pleasant but unremarkable. I don't know why I ended up in that little hotel in Trastevere. Gratitude, womanly sympathy for a wounded hero, curiosity—or those exceptional characteristics? It turned out to be a memorable experience, and it may have been the worst mistake I have ever made in my life.

Another brief encounter, in Paris, was both embarrassing and expensive. I woke up one morning to find the police hammering at the door and John gone. Naturally he hadn't paid the hotel bill.

So why did I respond to that enigmatic message from Stockholm a few months later?[†] I told myself it was because I wanted to get back at him for Paris, meeting his challenge and beating him at his own game. (That's what I told myself.) It was a relatively harmless little scheme to begin with—he needed me to gain access to an innocent old gentleman whose backyard happened to be full of buried treasure—but it turned ugly when a second group of crooks zeroed in on the same treasure. That was my first encounter with the hard-core professionals of the art underworld, and I sincerely hoped it would be my last. John was a professional, but compared to Max and Hans and Rudi and their boss, Leif, he looked like Little Lord Fauntleroy. They disliked John even more than I did, and from my point of view he was definitely the lesser of two evils, so once again we were forced to collaborate in

*Street of the Five Moons.
†Silhouette in Scarlet.

order to escape. My negative opinion of him didn't change, though, until . . .

It was one of the more lurid incidents in a life that has not been precisely colorless. There we were, trying to row a leaking boat across a very deep, very cold lake during a violent thunderstorm, with an aquatic assassin holding on to the bow and slashing at me with a knife. I had just about resigned myself to dying young when John went over the side of the boat. He was unarmed and outweighed, but he managed to keep Leif occupied until I got to shore. They found Leif's body later. John never turned up, dead or alive. Everybody except me assumed he had drowned. After eight months without a word I began to wonder myself.

The matter of the Trojan gold* gave me an excuse to contact John, through the anonymous channels that were the only ones I knew. To be honest, I was surprised when he responded. He had once told me I brought him nothing but bad luck.

His luck didn't improve. He got me out of trouble a couple of times, and the second rescue resulted in a considerable amount of damage to John himself. This was decidedly against his principles. He had once explained them to me: "It is impossible to convince some people of the error of their ways without hitting them as often and as hard as possible. I simply object to people hitting *me*."

The Trojan gold affair had ended with another event John undoubtedly resented as much as he hated being hit by people. I had taken ruthless advantage of a man who was battered, bruised, and bloody to force him to admit he loved me. He had used the word before, but always in context—Shakespeare or John Donne or some other literary giant. The phrases I had wrung out of him that day were boringly banal and direct. They had no literary merit whatever.

It had been ten months since that momentous event. I had seen John only three times, but almost every week I'd received some message—a postcard or a silly present or a few words on my answering machine—just enough to let me know he was all right.

*Trojan Gold.

The last postcard had arrived at the end of August—six weeks ago. There had been nothing since.

I got up and went to the washbasin to rinse the jelly off my hand. I'd have to leave the museum and call Karl from a kiosk or a café; I didn't want Gerda listening in.

The "individual" referred to in the message from Burckhardt's agent had to be John. He was the only crook I knew that well, and I was one of the few people in the world who knew *him* that well, one of the few who had seen him au naturel, who would probably recognize him no matter what disguise he assumed. He couldn't hide the shape of his hands or his long lashes or . . .

Six weeks without a word. How could he do this to me, the bastard? Love had nothing to do with it. I was inclined to take that declaration of his with a grain of salt, and I had never returned the compliment; but if he meant to end the relationship, the least he owed me was a courteous dismissal.

It had of course occurred to me that John might have planted the message himself. He'd done it before. If that was the case I wouldn't be in danger. John was no killer. ("What, never? Well, hardly ever.") I had known all along I was going on that damned cruise. As Burckhardt had said, it was an opportunity not to be missed.

*iv*

I've never been very good at poker. I quit playing with Karl Feder a couple of years ago. We had agreed to meet at a café. He was waiting when I arrived and before I so much as opened my mouth I saw he was smirking. He had known I'd fall for it.

I said, "Supposing I did agree—I'm not agreeing, but supposing I did—why couldn't I go as a tourist? I don't want to make a fool of myself pretending to knowledge I don't possess."

"Because there is no way you could have saved the money for such a trip," Karl said. His voice was as smooth as the whipped cream on his coffee. (Bavarians put whipped cream on everything except sauerkraut. That's one of the reasons why I love Bavaria.) "Oh, yes, we could invent an aunt who died and left you her fortune, or some such piece of fiction; but who would believe it? Why would you spend your windfall on such a trip? As you said, this is not your main area of interest. No, let me finish." He raised his finger and shook it in grandfatherly admonition. "The story will be that you agreed to replace a friend who was taken ill at the last moment. You are cheating a little, that is understood, but who would not, given such an opportunity? You will be lecturing on— um, let me see. Ah! On medieval Egyptian art! That will be perfect, nicht?"

"Nicht," I said. "I don't know anything about . . . Oh, hell, what's the use? There's just one thing, Karl. Schmidt."

"What about him? Everyone knows he has a fondness for you; he would give you leave of absence for such a chance as this."

"No! I mean, yes, he would, that's just the trouble. He'll want to come too!"

"So? He will not know your real purpose."

"Oh, God." I clutched at my head with both hands. My hair promptly fell down over my face. I had been experimenting with braids that week, and I hadn't quite got the knack of winding them around my head. No matter how many bobby pins I stuck in, the structure had a tendency to collapse under pressure.

Karl began collecting bobby pins from the table while I tried to explain. "Schmidt has the most lurid imagination of anyone I know. Even if I *were* an innocent tourist he'd assume I had an ulterior motive—something romantic, as he calls it. He'll poke his nose into everything and screw everything up and get himself in trouble, and I'll have to get him out of it. If Schmidt goes, I don't. That's flat."

Karl Feder looked thoughtful. He wasn't as familiar with Schmidt's peculiarities as I was, but he had heard a thing or two. "Ah, I see. Well, my dear Vicky, do not worry. We will think of some way of preventing him."

I didn't like the sound of that. "You're not to hurt him, Karl. No hit-and-run or broken legs."

"Would we do such a thing?"

"You might not, but if I read Herr Burckhardt and his crowd aright, they wouldn't hesitate. I'm not kidding, Karl. If you touch a hair of Schmidt's mustache I'll blow the whole deal wide open."

"I believe you," Karl said.

"You damn well better. All right. If you can get Schmidt out of the way, I'll do it. What happens next?"

"We will handle all the arrangements. Your passport is in order, I assume? Good. Visa, tickets, and other necessary documents will be delivered to you within a few days. My secretary will make the appointments for you, but she cannot take the inoculations—hepatitis, typhoid, typhus—"

"Urck," I said. I hate shots. "Is all that necessary? I thought this was a luxury cruise."

"We cannot risk your falling ill," Karl said seriously. He took a thick manila envelope from his breast pocket and handed it to me. "I must ask you to sign a voucher acknowledging receipt of the money. We will supply a medical kit, camera, binoculars, and the like, but I assume a young lady will want to purchase her own clothing and other personal effects."

It was a very thick envelope. Karl's smile was very bland. I sighed. "We have already determined what you are, madam," I quoted. "All that is left is to determine your price."

"Bitte?" said Karl.

"Never mind."

"We will take care of everything," Karl repeated. "You need do nothing . . . Excuse me, what was it you said?"

He knew perfectly well what I had said. He prefers to believe a lady doesn't use words like that.

I pushed my chair back and stood up. "Anything else?"

Karl reached into his pocket again. The object he withdrew was a slick, brightly colored brochure. It had been folded once, lengthwise, to fit in his pocket. He unfolded it and handed it to me.

On the cover, under a tastefully designed title, was a photograph of the Sphinx, with the pyramids of Giza behind it. It was a gorgeous photo; the pyramids were a soft pale gold, the sky above them was a bright clear blue. The smile on the face of the Sphinx has been described in a number of ways—mysterious, enigmatic, contemplative. At that moment it seemed to me that it bore a distinct resemblance to the smug smirk on Karl Feder's face.

v

Two weeks later I sat on a rock at Giza contemplating the real thing. I was trying to avoid the eyes of the Sphinx. It was still smirking.

The actuality wasn't as attractive as the photograph. The photographer must have been a genius or a magician to eliminate other objects from his composition. There were lots of them, all more or less unattractive. Camels (they are not, at their best, handsome animals), tourists (ditto), guides and peddlers in dirty flapping robes, cheap souvenir shops, scaffolding and barbed wire and makeshift, ramshackle bits of fencing and construction. However, only a pedant would quibble about such minor flaws. The pyramids were wonderful. The Sphinx would have been magnificent, marred and scarred though it was, if it hadn't been smirking. Was I enjoying the view? No, I was not.

My arms were swollen and sore from too many shots too close together, but that wasn't what bothered me. The sun was beating down on my head and shoulders, but I didn't mind that. My stomach felt slightly queasy, but it wasn't from anything I had eaten.

Some distance away a small group of people had gathered round an individual who appeared to be lecturing to them. They were distinguished from the other groups that covered the plateau like hordes of locusts by the bags they had slung over their shoulders. Many of the tour groups presented their clients with such bags, so that the bright distinctive colors could help identify lost or wandering members of the group, but there were no colors quite as distinctive as these: broad

stripes of gold, turquoise-blue and bright red-orange, the
shades so often found in Egyptian jewelry. One of the same
bags, trimmed in gold braid and bearing my name, lay on the
sand at my feet.

My eyes went back to the paper on my lap. It was the
passenger list. My name wasn't on it. I would appear, and be
introduced, after the boat had sailed. This was in keeping
with my cover story—that I had replaced a friend at the last
moment. It was also a safety precaution, to keep my presence
from being known in advance. Some safety precaution, I
thought sourly. Well, it couldn't hurt.

Some of the passengers had boarded the boat the day before.
I had gone to a hotel instead and spent the afternoon . . . guess
where?

A few hours in the Cairo Museum for someone in my
profession is like a nibble of fudge to a chocoholic. The place
is stuffed, bulging, overflowing with wonders. I was familiar
with many of them from photographs and films, but there is
no substitute for seeing the real thing. And the "minor" arti-
facts, the ones that weren't so often featured, were just as
beautiful. I stood for ten minutes studying the inlay on a small
box.

Shadowing my enjoyment, however, was my real reason
for being there. The more I saw, the more I wondered why
people like John hadn't already stripped the museum.

I don't mean to criticize. The whole damned country is a
museum, and no one knew better than I how much it cost in
money and manpower just to maintain the antiquities, much
less support additional excavation. Egypt is a poor country,
with a soaring birthrate; there aren't enough schools, clinics,
or jobs, or even food; half of it has to be imported. The
Egyptians were in a particularly ironic situation, since the
hordes of tourists on which the economy depended were
slowly and inexorably destroying the treasures they came to
see. According to one article I had read, visitors to the tomb
of Tutankhamon put out as much as twenty-five pints of
perspiration per day, raising the humidity in the small room
to a point that damaged the paint and the underlying plaster.
The very stones of the Sphinx had been eaten away by pollution and misguided attempts at repair.

The museum was a disaster in progress—dirty, crowded, and dangerously understaffed. Some of the cases looked as if they could be opened with one of my hairpins. There was no air-conditioning or humidity control; the windows were open, admitting dust and the exhaust fumes from Cairo's teeming traffic. When I left, reeling under a combination of horror and artistic overload, I had to pick my way through a group of chattering women scrubbing the floor on their hands and knees, and I found myself peering intently at their faces, looking for familiar features—the shape of a neatly curved ear, the outline of a high cheekbone. That was the sort of disguise that would appeal to John's bizarre sense of humor.

What could he be after this time? His usual modus operandi involved substitution rather than outright theft; this must be something big, so big in size or importance that its absence couldn't be concealed. God knows there were plenty of possibilities, starting with the golden coffins of Tutankhamon.

I had managed to convince myself there was no immediate danger. The tour group was leaving Cairo next day; it would return in three weeks for a longer stay. That must be when he intended to do the job, using the other passengers as camouflage.

That morning I had sent my luggage to the boat and taken a taxi to Giza; I would join the others when they got on the bus that was to take them back to the boat.

I had already spotted John on the passenger list. It had to be he; no one would have a name as ridiculous as Peregrine Foggington-Smythe. He had even had the gall to use a variation of his favorite nom de guerre. Typical of his arrogance and his sometimes dangerous sense of humor . . .

He wasn't a passenger. The list included the names of the staff; Foggington-Smythe was one of the guest lecturers, a distinguished Egyptologist from Boston, author of several books with titles like *Caste and Gender in Ancient Egypt*, whatever the hell that might mean. I wondered how John had convinced Galactic Tours, Inc., that he was the man in question. For all I knew he might be an Egyptologist; he had claimed his specialty was classics, but once or twice he had displayed a fairly esoteric familiarity with matters Egyptological. But I was sure—well, almost sure—he couldn't be the

real Foggington-Smythe. Not that an Egyptologist couldn't
be a criminal; scholars are no more noble than the next man.
But not even John would have time to lecture, write several
ponderous tomes, and carry on a career as a master thief.

Would he?

I looked up from the list to see someone plodding toward
me. One of the bright bags was slung over her shoulder. She
must have spotted mine. She was the type that would notice
things like that—a woman of a certain age, of medium height
and stocky frame, with unblinking gray eyes under heavy
brows. She had to be English; her fair skin was already pink,
though it glistened with sun shield, and she was wearing a
long-sleeved tan blouse and a shapeless khaki skirt that
reached almost to her ankles. She looked familiar, and of
course I knew why; I had seen her type in a number of British
films: the housekeeper, the headmistress, the stocky spinster
who is either the detective or a leading suspect.

She stamped up to me, frowning. Suddenly I felt very
young. Her expression brought back painful memories of my
great-aunt Ermintrude, who had disapproved of everything
about me and had never bothered to conceal her opinion.

"One of us, are you, dear?" she inquired, indicating the
bag. "You must be a newcomer, so I thought I ought to make
certain you know where the bus is and that it will be leaving
shortly; you'd best come along with me, you don't want to
miss it, you shouldn't be alone in a place like this, these
natives will take advantage of an attractive young woman,
my name is Tregarth, call me Jen. How'd ja do?"

I said brilliantly, "Hi."

"And where is your hat?" Jen looked at me severely. "Most
unwise of you to come out without one. You have a nice
color, but the sun is deadly here, you risk heat prostration or
sunstroke."

"I forgot," I said meekly. "I do have one. A hat. I forgot
it."

"Well, don't do it again. What did you say your name was?"

"Vicky. Vicky Bliss." There was no reason for me to be
coy about it. She'd find out in a few hours.

"You are not on the passenger list." Her tone made it sound
like an accusation.

"No. I joined the cruise at the last minute. A friend of mine had to cancel, owing to illness, and—"

"I see." Her face relaxed. The expression wasn't anything like a smile, but it was probably as close as she could come. "Glad to see another young person on board. Most of the passengers are practically senile. My son and his wife will be pleased to have someone their own age to talk to. Not that they . . ." She looked up, over my shoulder, and the change in her face made me stare. So she could smile. "Ah, but here they are. Looking for me, I expect. My dears, allow me to introduce . . ."

I didn't hear the rest of it. When I turned, my ears went dead, the way they do after a sudden change in altitude.

She couldn't have been more than eighteen—twenty, at the outside. Her skin had that exquisite English fairness and her hair was a mass of cloudy brown curls framing her heart-shaped face. I saw that much, and the fact that the top of her head barely reached his chin, and that he had gone dead-white under his tan and that his eyes were as flat and opaque as blue circles painted on paper.

The girl smiled and spoke. My ears popped midway through the speech, and I caught the last words. ". . . call me Mary. This . . ." She tilted her head and looked up at him, her eyes shining. "This is John."

He had himself under control, except for his color; he always had trouble with that. His voice was cool and steady. "How do you do. We'd better hurry; the others have gone on. Mother—"

She waved away the arm he offered. "No, darling. I'm perfectly capable of walking a few more yards unassisted. You look a little . . . Are you feeling well?" His brows drew together, and she said hurriedly, "Oh, dear, I'm fussing, aren't I? I promise I won't do it again. Come along, Vicky, you and I will lean on one another."

She didn't need assistance; she was a lot steadier on her feet than I was. I stumbled along beside her, grateful for the uneven terrain and the heat and the need for haste, since they offered an excuse for the fact that I couldn't seem to take a deep breath. From behind me I heard a murmur of voices and a soft, silvery laugh.

The bus was one of those modern monsters, air-conditioned and enormous. As soon as we had settled ourselves an attendant came round with a tray. "Mineral water?" he inquired softly. "Orange juice? Mimosa?"

It occurred to my numbed brain that mimosas had alcohol of some kind in them. Champagne? Who cared? I grabbed one and tossed it down.

Jen had taken the seat next to mine. Several rows ahead I saw the familiar outlines of a neatly shaped skull covered with fair hair. Mary's head wasn't visible over the back of the seat. She was so tiny.

Have I mentioned I am almost six feet tall?

Maybe it was the alcohol that cleared my head, but I doubt it; the damned thing was mostly orange juice. I turned to Jen—Guinevere? He had told me that was his mother's name. I had assumed it was a joke.

"Guinevere," I said experimentally. My voice seemed to be working.

She didn't question my knowledge. I suppose she thought she'd told me. She couldn't possibly remember everything she said, she had been talking nonstop. Her chin lifted proudly. "We are an old Cornish family. Tre, Pol, and Pen—you know the rhyme? Names beginning with those syllables distinguish the Cornishmen. There is a tradition that Arthur himself was our remote ancestor. My father's name was Gawain, his father's name was Arthur. On my mother's side . . ."

"Mother's side," I repeated, to show I was paying attention. I waved at the steward. Guzzling my second mimosa, I lost the next few sentences.

". . . only a distant connection with Egypt, really. So, when I decided to marry, I chose a cousin in order to carry on the family name. Poor Agrivaine. I didn't see a great deal of him; he was always running off to some war or other."

"Agrivaine?"

"That was what I called him. He had been christened Albert, and I believed his friends referred to him as—as Al. So common! It was he who insisted on calling our son John. I wanted to name him Percival or Galahad."

I choked on my drink. Jen gave me a hearty slap on the back. Her brow clouded. "Oh, dear, I hope I didn't offend the dear boy. Men are so sensitive about weakness, you know, and I promised myself I would stop fussing over him, especially now that he has a wife to look after him, but he was so ill last winter . . . A skiing accident, and then pneumonia. He seems quite fit now, but I worry."

"Skiing accident," I repeated, like a parrot. I guess it could have been described that way. John wasn't the world's greatest skier, and he had fallen flat on his already damaged face while he was trying to reach the spot where a very unpleasant individual was about to do unpleasant things to me before finishing me off permanently. However, the worst of his injuries had resulted from the hand-to-hand fight that followed his arrival and from the avalanche that had followed the fight. I had not known about his subsequent illness, but I wasn't surprised to hear of it. If he had stayed in bed for a few days instead of sneaking off the first time I left him alone . . .

Fortunately Jen didn't notice my abstraction; she was perfectly happy to carry the conversation. I sat slugging down champagne and orange juice while Jen went merrily on, telling me how she had feared her dear boy would never settle down—"he is so attractive to women"—about the whirlwind courtship—"he didn't bring her to meet me until a few weeks ago"—and about their insistence that she join them on their honeymoon.

"Honeymoon," said the parrot.

"Yes, they were married last week. Such a lovely ceremony, in the family home, with only their close friends present . . . Of course I refused when they first suggested I come along, but Mary was so insistent, and John assured me she would be deeply wounded if I did not agree. Naturally I mean to stay out of their way as much as possible."

I don't remember what else she said.

The others had checked in the day before, so I didn't have to wait unmercifully long before a steward was assigned to show me to my room. I was vaguely conscious of its elegance—a long curved window, with a small railed balcony beyond, a private bath. My suitcases had been arranged at the foot of the bed. I got rid of the steward and collapsed into the nearest chair.

Sometimes, especially in the middle of the night when you

wake up and stumble sleepily through a darkened room, and stub your toe or bang your elbow, it takes several seconds for the pain to reach your sluggish brain. I had managed to keep it at bay for much longer than that.

# Chapter Two

*i*

A badly bruised ego can hurt just as much as a broken heart. When one is young and stupid and romantic and vulnerable, one is inclined to confuse the two. I was none of the above, except possibly stupid, but God knows I had made that mistake on a number of occasions.

Not this time, though. Shock, anger, humiliation, shame— to mention only a few of the emotions that boiled inside me— had been responsible for my reaction. I must have managed to conceal it from Jen; she hadn't seemed to see anything unusual. I only hoped I hadn't betrayed myself to John.

I pulled myself to my feet. The cocktail hour would begin shortly and I was supposed to attend. It would be my first public appearance, my first chance to connect faces and forms with the names on the passenger list. A waste of time, since I had already found the "individual" I had been asked to identify, but I'd have to face him sooner or later and I was damned if I'd let him know how badly he had shaken me.

The accommodations lived up to the advertisement. In addi- tion to the twin beds there was a couch long enough for even me to stretch out on, and two comfortable chairs. The bathroom had not only a shower but a tub (not quite long enough for me to stretch out in, but few of them are), and the dressing table was lined with fancy bottles bearing the labels of a famous French cosmetician. Methodically and mechanically I unpacked, showered, and settled myself at the dressing table, ready for action. Usually I don't bother with much makeup, but I planned to use every speck of artificial assistance I could get that night. I wanted to look gorgeous, cool, calm, and indifferent.

With luck I might manage the last three, anyhow. My hands were still unsteady; I tried to calm myself by recalling all the dirty, low-down tricks John had pulled, but my mind kept wandering off the track, remembering . . .

Remembering times like the Christmas Eve we had spent in the abandoned church, huddling close to the feeble fire while a blizzard raged without, drinking tea made in a dirt-encrusted flowerpot with a crumpled tea bag from the hoard I carried in my backpack. John had laughed himself sick over the contents of that backpack, but he had been hungry enough to eat the crumbling gingerbread and the squashed chocolate bar. He had played Bach on a tissue-covered comb, and when I couldn't keep my eyes open any longer he had sat up all night holding me in his arms to keep me warm, and patiently feeding the tiny fire . . .

I didn't need blusher. My cheeks were bright red. I went to work dulling the flush of anger with foundation and covering up a few lines that hadn't been there last time I looked.

There had never been a commitment or even a promise. But it is, to say the least, disconcerting to kiss someone good-bye after he has made tender, passionate, skillful love to you, and have him show up with a brand-new wife the next time you meet.

He hadn't set me up for that shock, though. His pallor might have been due to rage, consternation, or fear, but it had been genuine. He hadn't expected to see me.

I selected a dress and slid into it. It was black and slinky, with long sleeves and a neckline that plunged lower than Aunt Ermintrude would have approved. I filled in some of the space with a heavy (faux) gold necklace and pendant, stuck a couple of gold-headed picks into the hair coiled at the nape of my neck, and stood back to study the effect.

My cheeks were still flushed. I would have to claim it was sunburn. Jen had warned me about wearing a hat, hadn't she?

A delicate chime of bells sounded and I started nervously before I realized that it was the summons I had been waiting for. It was five minutes before five, time for the opening reception and cocktail hour. Some of the guests had come on board the day before, but others, like myself, had joined the cruise later; for the first time they would all be together, inspecting me as I would be inspecting them. I don't often suffer from stage fright, but my fingers froze on the doorknob and I had to force myself to turn it.

I plunged out into the corridor and found myself in the arms of a strange man who had emerged from the room next to mine. My timing was perfect, but the strange man was not; he was a good six inches shorter than I, and I had an excellent view of his balding cranium, across which a few strands of hair had been arranged with pathetic optimism. Clutching me to his stomach, he staggered back into the grasp of another man who was as tall and thin as he was short and pudgy. After a brief interval, which seemed to last a lot longer than it actually did, we got ourselves sorted out and began a chorus of apologies.

"My fault," I said. "I should have looked before I leaped."

"I do beg your pardon," said my first encounter simultaneously. He began to laugh merrily. "Allow me to introduce ourselves. I am Sweet and this is Bright."

The tall, thin man bowed. He had a nice thick head of hair. It slipped a little when he inclined his head.

"Bliss," I said. "Victoria Bliss."

Sweet chuckled. "It was meant to be!"

"What?" I said.

"Bright, Sweet, and Bliss!"

"Oh," I said. Sweet beamed. Bright beamed.

The corridor was too narrow to allow us to walk arm in arm, so we proceeded single file, with Bright leading the way and Sweet following me. They managed it very neatly. In fact, the whole business had been carried out with consummate skill; if I hadn't been on the alert I would never have spotted them.

Burckhardt had refused to tell me how I could identify his agents. "It is a matter of security, you understand," he had said solemnly.

"It is a matter of my neck," I had pointed out.

"Fear not," said Burckhardt. "They will make themselves known to you."

Well, they had, and very deftly at that. I would not have expected subordinates of Herr Burckhardt's to have such crazy senses of humor. The cleverest part of the performance had been when Sweet pressed me close, and the hard object in his breast pocket had jabbed painfully into my ribs. A bruise was a small price to pay for that kind of reassurance.

The central lobby, into which the corridor led, was magnificent. I hadn't been in a fit state to take in the details earlier; now I admired the lush greenery in the center, the miniature waterfall that tumbled through it, the soft chairs and sofas and little marble-topped tables scattered around. Bright and Sweet swooped in on me, one on either side, and led me toward the stairs.

The lounge, or saloon, occupied the entire front section of the boat. Curving windows gave a magnificent view of the city, its high-rise hotels and minarets and bridges blossoming with lights, and glass doors opened onto the deck. Waiters were circulating with trays of glasses. The beverage of choice that evening appeared to be champagne. Since I do not care for champagne, and since I wanted to get rid of Sweet for a few minutes—he had been talking incessantly, about God knows what—I accepted his offer to get me something else from the bar.

Bright and I settled down at a table. He smiled bashfully at me and tugged at his grizzled mustache, which was as luxuriant as his hair. Either it was real or the fixative was more effective than the stuff he used on his head.

I inspected the other guests with unconcealed interest. They were doing the same. There were only thirty of us, and we would be in close company for several weeks.

I had been warned that this crowd would probably dress

more formally than was usual on such cruises. People who are embarrassingly rich like to show off. My mail-order cocktail dress looked pretty insignificant next to the designer gowns many of the other women were sporting, and the dazzle of diamonds dimmed my faux gold locket. Many of the men wore tuxes or dinner jackets.

Jen and her new daughter-in-law were sitting at a table on the other side of the room, with two other people—a married couple, I cleverly deduced. The woman's pink hair matched her dress and his bald head. When she caught my eye Jen waved and gave me a tight-lipped smile. John wasn't with them, but as I returned Jen's wave he came sauntering toward their table, as infuriatingly casual as always. He looked very much the bridegroom, with a flower in his buttonhole and a matching crimson cummerbund. Catching me in mid-wave he raised an eyebrow, nodded distantly, and sat down with his back to me.

Sweet returned with a glass of chablis and a man stepped up onto the podium in the center of the floor. At the sight of him I forgot Bright, Sweet, *and* John. The tux set off his lean body and broad shoulders, but he ought to have been wearing flowing robes and a snowy bedouin headdress that would frame his walnut-brown skin, hawklike nose, and sharply cut features. His black eyes were fringed with lashes so thick they looked artificial.

A chorus of involuntary sighs came from every woman in the room. Some of them looked old enough to have seen the original Rudolph Valentino film. I wasn't old enough, but I had read the book. I have read every soppy sentimental novel ever written. To look at her, you wouldn't think my sharp-tongued, practical grandma had an ounce of romance in her soul, but she owned all the old novels. In her day, *The Sheik* had been pretty hot stuff. " 'Ahmed, mon bel Arabe,' she murmured yearningly," I murmured yearningly.

"I beg your pardon?" said Sweet.

"Sssssh," I said.

His name wasn't Ahmed, it was Feisal. His accent suggested he had been educated in England. The underlying traces of his native tongue gave his velvety baritone a fascinating touch of the exotic.

"I am your leader and your devoted servant, ladies and gentlemen. I will be with you on the boat and on shore, wherever you go. You will come to me with all your troubles, questions, and complaints, and I will pass them on to your crew, which I now have the honor to introduce."

He presented the captain, the purser, the doctor, the chef, and a few others; I lost track of what he was saying as I studied the blonde at the next table. Her eyes were fixed in a glassy stare and she seemed to be having trouble breathing. It might have been her corset. She had to be wearing something formidable under the white, draped silk jersey; it molded, not moving flesh, but a substance as rigid as concrete.

I caught a name and returned my attention to Feisal. "Dr. Peregrine Foggington-Smythe, our expert on Pharaonic Egypt," he announced.

So there were parents cruel enough to saddle a kid with a name like Peregrine. If I had seen him from a distance I might have taken him for John—briefly. He was a stretched-out, washed-out version of the Great John Smythe—taller and skinnier, with ash-blond hair and pale blue eyes. He informed us with magnificent condescension that he would be lecturing on Sakkara, the site we would visit the following day, as soon as Feisal finished his introductions.

He stepped back and Feisal, whose face had frozen into a look of barely contained dislike, turned on the charm again as he presented Dr. Alice Gordon, who would be delivering the lectures on Hellenistic Egypt. Dr. Gordon rose and raised her hand but remained modestly in her place at a table near the back of the room. She was a plump little woman with a mop of unkempt graying brown hair and thick glasses.

The boat was certainly overloaded with experts, or at least with Ph.D.'s. When my name was announced I followed Dr. Gordon's example, rising and subsiding without comment but with a modest smile.

I was the last of the staff to be introduced. A babble of conversation broke out as several of the crewmen started setting up a slide projector and screen, and Sweet exclaimed, "So it's Dr. Bliss? We are honored! I have always been fascinated by Islamic art. Tell me—"

I got quickly to my feet. "If you'll excuse me, gentlemen,

I'm going to sneak out for a smoke before the lecture starts. Don't move, I'll be right back."

Several other sinners followed me. Smoking wasn't allowed in the lounge during lectures, and it was only permitted in a small walled-off area at other times. I was rather proud of myself for having realized that this habit, which is approximately as socially acceptable as spitting in public, might come in handy if I needed to extricate myself from a sticky situation. Avoiding the other lepers, who were clustered defensively at the rail, I walked on till I found myself alone.

But not for long. "Permit me," said a too-familiar voice. A lighter materialized in front of me. The hand holding it was equally familiar, though it wasn't as well-tended as usual. The knuckles were scraped and rough. He must have run into a pyramid or something. Or slammed his fist into something? Maybe I had shaken that cultivated cool of his, as he had shaken mine. I'd have loved to think so. Taking a firm grip on my temper, I inhaled, coughed, and turned.

"Where's Schmidt?" he asked.

I had assumed he'd want to have a private word with me, and I had carefully composed sarcastic (but very cool) replies to the questions I thought he'd ask. Waste of time. I should have known he wouldn't start out with anything as obvious as "What are you doing here?" Caught off guard, I told the truth. "Uh—in Amsterdam. Some rich Dutchman is considering offering the museum his antique-jewelry collection."

"Oh, jolly good," John said, not so enigmatically. His eyes moved from my face to the V of my dress. Reflexively my hand closed over the locket.

John's lip curled. It was one of his better sneers. "Don't bother switching it on."

"I already did. How did you know?"

"It's a tasteless trinket, my dear. Not your style."

I bit my lip to keep from swearing. He was fighting dirty, hitting below the belt where it hurt the most. Had he seen the thin gold chain under the heavier chain that held the locket? Almost certainly. But it had been a shot in the dark; he couldn't possibly know I was wearing the little enameled rose he had given me, because I had tucked it securely down under, out of sight. That trinket was not tasteless; it was an exquisite

example of antique Persian goldsmith's work. I wasn't wearing it for sentimental reasons. I was wearing it because I
didn't want to leave it lying around where someone might
see it.

John's eyes shifted. "You're on the wrong track, Vicky,"
he said softly. "I don't know what imbecile impulse persuaded
you to join this cruise, but I strongly suggest you accept my
assurance that it is nothing more and nothing less than it
appears to be."

"A romantic honeymoon?" I inquired evenly.

"With the girl who swept me off my feet," said John.

He had seen her coming and pitched his voice so she would
hear the last sentence. Laughing, she slid her arm through his
and leaned against him.

"Isn't he a dear? Sorry to disturb you, darling, but the
lecture is about to start."

John gave me a smile that went nowhere near his eyes.
"That's just an excuse. She doesn't approve of my habits."

Mary shook her head. "I don't approve of your smoking,
no. It's so dangerous."

"Not nearly so dangerous as certain other habits," said
Mary's husband.

I declined Mary's invitation to join them, claiming I wanted
another cigarette. The only drawback was that I had to let
John light it for me and pretend not to notice his amusement
when I tried to inhale without turning purple. After they had
gone, I unclenched my left hand. My nails had left dents in
the skin of my palm.

I missed the first few minutes of Foggington-Smythe's lecture, which turned out to be a smart move. He was the most
boring speaker I have ever heard. My interest in the development of the pyramid form is decidedly limited, but he could
have made a lecture on pornography (with slides) dull.

When the lights went on, several people snorted and started
and blinked. Not my new friend Jen; bright-eyed and full of
vim, she headed straight for me. She was wearing a salmon-
colored silk frock that would have looked absurd on any
female less superbly indifferent to the opinions of womankind;
the uneven hem waved around her ankles.

"I had no idea when we met that you were a distinguished scholar," she cried. "You don't look like one, my dear, you are far too young and attractive."

"Thank you," I said, since that is just about the only way one can respond to a dubious compliment of that sort. I assumed it was meant as a compliment.

The others were drifting toward the doors, except for a few presumed archaeology buffs, who had gathered around the lecturer. "Won't you join me for dinner?" Jen asked. "There is no assigned seating, you know; I do think that's an excellent idea; it gives us a chance to make new friends and change about if we like. I'd love to have you tell me all about yourself."

I rather doubted that. Nor did I feel I was quite up to munching my way through six courses in the company of the lovebirds.

"I'd like to, but—" I indicated Bright and Sweet, who had punctiliously risen to acknowledge her arrival.

"Yes, I know Mr. Bright and Mr. Sweet. That will be splendid; four of us will complete the table." She gave me a conspiratorial wink. "I don't want my dear children to feel they are obliged to entertain me all the time."

Relieved of that anxiety, I was pleased to agree. Not that I had much choice; Jen had taken my arm, in a grip as firm as that of a prison guard. I had realized early on that she was one of those women who will get her own way by one means or another, and I wondered whose idea it had been to make the honeymoon a ménage à trois. Surely not John's. Unless he was ruthless and unprincipled enough to use his own mother and his bride as a means of diverting suspicion?

We wended our way down the stairs to the lowest deck and the dining room. The decor reminded me that this wasn't just any old cruise; there were fresh flowers on every table, and a row of wineglasses at every place. A waiter led us to a table for four and presented us with menus stiff with gilt print. The napkins had been folded into intricate shapes; I was reaching for mine when the waiter whipped it out of my grasp and spread it neatly across my knees. I tried to look as if I had expected it.

Sweet and Bright took forever deciding on an appetizer; I

had already ordered so I had leisure to inspect the room. The murals covering the walls were copies of famous tomb reliefs—not scenes of death and judgment, but bright, cheerful depictions of birds and animals and scenes of daily life. The one on the wall next to our table showed two pretty Egyptian maidens with long black hair and diaphanous robes, playing musical instruments. The third pretty maiden wasn't wearing anything except a few beads. Sweet goggled appreciatively at her.

Jen was speaking to me. I turned to her with an apologetic smile. "Sorry, I was admiring the murals. They are excellent copies, aren't they?"

"Morbid," Jen said decidedly. "Pictures from tombs are not suitable for a dining room."

Her lips had tightened and her brows had drawn together. It was a forbidding expression, and I remembered a comment John had made about his mother: "She looks like Judith Anderson playing a demented housekeeper." The wild surmise that entered my mind was equally demented. Ridiculous, I told myself. Chicanery isn't hereditary.

Sweet had finished ordering. "But Mrs. Tregarth, the paintings show the Egyptians' enjoyment of the pleasures of life. What could be more appropriate for such an occasion as this?" Jen turned The Look on him; he swallowed and said, "People are much more interesting though, aren't they? Tell us about yourself, Dr. Bliss."

"I will if you will," I said coyly. "What business are you in, Mr. Sweet?"

He manufactured nuts and bolts. Very special nuts and bolts, for a specific kind of machine. Don't ask me what kind. I was no more interested than Mr. Sweet appeared to be. After rattling off a description of the process, he explained that he and Mr. Bright were partners in business as well as in their passion for archaeology. "When we heard of this cruise we knew it was an opportunity not to be missed," he said enthusiastically. "To see so many sites that are normally closed to tourists, and of course the pièce de résistance—the tomb of Queen Tetisheri. We are the first visitors to behold the restoration of the paintings. The work has taken years—"

"And a great deal of money that might have been spent on more worthy causes," said Jen, with a loud sniff.

"Mr. Blenkiron has contributed munificently to a number of worthy causes," Sweet protested.

"That is a matter of opinion," Jen said. An opinion, her expression made clear, that she did not share.

"Is he here? Which one is he?" I swiveled around.

"Don't stare," Jen said.

My head snapped back into position. It was pure reflex—shades of Aunt Ermintrude. Sweet gave me a wink and a knowing smile. "We are all staring," he said amiably. "It's only natural, Mrs. Tregarth, that we should take an interest in our fellow travelers. For long weeks we will be together in a little world all our own, separated from our friends and families, thrown together in an artificial intimacy. Which of these strangers is to be cultivated, which to be avoided? Will some of these passing encounters result in lasting friendships, or even in—er—more intense relationships?"

"You have quite a gift for words, Mr. Sweet," I said. "Are you sure you aren't a famous writer in disguise?"

Sweet laughed. "Alas, no. We do have a well-known writer with us; she is traveling under her own name, but she has made no secret of her pseudonym. No doubt she means to make copy of us all! Mr. Blenkiron is the tall, dark-haired gentleman at the table under the painting of the fellow spearing fish."

Jen had given me up as a bad job and was devouring smoked salmon, so I proceeded to stare to my heart's content.

The activities of most excessively wealthy individuals bore me to tears, but Blenkiron was an exception. Unlike some of his billionaire peers he shunned publicity; he didn't attend fund-raisers or hoity-toity social functions, or hobnob with politicians and rock stars. He didn't give interviews, or even get divorced. I knew his name because he had been a generous and unobtrusive supporter of many cultural enterprises—the rebuilding of the Uffizi Gallery in Florence after a bomb blast, the conservation of the water-rotted monuments of Venice, to name only a few. His chief interest, however, was ancient Egypt. I had read of the restoration of Tetisheri's tomb, and

I admit that the prospect of visiting it was one of the few plus entries in an otherwise negative agenda. To see the famous paintings restored to their original freshness, with the film of grease and grime removed and the damaged sections repaired, would be a unique experience.

I had expected Blenkiron to be older. There was gray in his hair but it was only a sprinkling of silver against dark brown, and the lines in his face, fanning out from the corners of his deep-set eyes and framing a long-lipped flexible mouth, were those of good nature and maturity. He too was inspecting his fellow passengers; catching my eye, he nodded and smiled.

"The person on his right is his secretary," Sweet informed me in a conspiratorial whisper.

The person wasn't a blond female but a bald male. I couldn't see his face, since he had his back to me.

"Who's the other guy at the table?" I had a pretty good idea. He resembled all the lean, lined heroes of western films and his dinner jacket didn't fit quite right.

Sweet rolled his eyes. "Bright and I have dubbed him The Bodyguard."

"How clever of you," I said.

By the time we had finished (five courses, not six), Sweet had identified some of the other passengers for me, and supplied capsule biographies for many of them. The blonde in the tight corset was a Mrs. Umphenour from Memphis (Tennessee, not Egypt), who had taken the cruise to console herself for the death of her third husband. The misanthropic reader alone at a nearby table was a German surgeon who specialized in urology. What he was doing on the cruise Sweet could not imagine; he was not a friendly person and he appeared to be only mildly interested in Egyptology.

I sincerely hoped he was not interested in medieval Islamic art.

Jen had eaten her way through all five courses and was looking a trifle bloated by the time we prepared to return to the lounge for coffee and after-dinner drinks. Sweet announced he and Bright would have to deny themselves that pleasure, since the group was to leave for a shore tour at seven the next morning. "You young ladies can do without sleep," he said, with a gallant bow, "but if Bright and I don't get our eight hours we are good for nothing."

Bright nodded and smiled. He hadn't said a word.

Jen took me by the arm. I winced. John had mentioned that his mother was a dedicated gardener; I had no idea that form of exercise could develop such formidable muscles. I don't like being manhandled, even by women, so I said, "I'm a little tired myself. I think I'll skip the coffee."

"But it's included," Jen exclaimed.

Bright and Sweet had faded away. I was on my own. I let her tow me toward the stairs. Not until she had settled us at a table and waved imperiously at a passing waiter did I remember I had an excuse to escape.

"I'm going out on deck to have a cigarette," I announced, rising.

Again that imperative hand closed over my arm. "No need for that, my dear. We'll move to the smoking section. You should have told me. Waiter!"

"But you don't—"

"I do indulge occasionally. My son smokes," Jen said, as if that were justification for any evil habit. (*Any* evil habit?)

The sinners had gathered in a railed-off area near the open doors. Among them, I was surprised to see Mr. Blenkiron. His secretary was not with him, but he was surrounded by Mrs. Umphenour and her fur coat. It was the biggest damned coat I've ever seen, some sort of long, silky white fur I couldn't identify in the dim light; she had tossed it over her shoulders and it appeared to be eating Blenkiron.

Jen dragged me to a table as far from the pair as she could get. "Disgusting," she muttered. "Her husband not dead a month and she's already looking for number four."

I took out a cigarette. I supposed I had to smoke the damned thing.

Jen accepted one when I offered it. She also had brandy (included). She was decidedly glassy-eyed by the time the newlyweds turned up. They must have been strolling the deck. Mary's hair was bewitchingly windblown.

"Still at it?" John inquired of his mother, as the waiter delivered another glass of brandy.

Jen giggled. "Darling, you're such a tease. What will you and Mary have? It's all—"

"Included," John finished. He held a chair for Mary but remained standing, an inimical eye on his maternal parent. "The doctor warned you about your spastic colon."

"Delicate stomach," Jen corrected.

"You'd better take some of that ghastly medicine," her son said resignedly. "I watched you at dinner. You were shoveling it in like a stevedore."

"Darling," Mary said. "Aren't you being a little rude?"

"He's just teasing," Jen explained, rummaging in her bag. "And taking good care of his old mum. I will take a dose, right this minute. I brought the bottle . . . I thought I had . . . Oh, never mind, it can wait. I feel quite well."

"I'll get it," John said. "Give me your key."

She handed it over and he left. He hadn't acknowledged my presence except by a brusque nod.

"He's so thoughtful," Jen murmured.

"What does your son do for a living, Mrs. Tregarth?" I asked.

Mary gave me an odd look. The question had been somewhat abrupt, but Jen was in no condition to notice nuances, and John was obviously her favorite topic of conversation.

"Why, my dear, I'm surprised you haven't heard of him, since his line of work is so closely related to yours."

I inhaled involuntarily and burst into a fit of coughing. Jen slapped me on the back and went on, "He began in a modest way—a little shop in Truro—but his business has expanded at such a rapid rate that he has just opened an establishment in London. I am informed that he is regarded as one of the most reputable authorities in all of England."

"Don't tell me," I wheezed. "Let me guess. Antiques?"

"And works of art."

"Of course." Gasping for breath, I covered my face with my hands.

"There's plenty of this revolting stuff to go round," said John. "Would you care for a nip?"

I fumbled for a napkin and looked up. He stood over me, one eyebrow elevated, both lips curling.

"Darling," Mary said reproachfully.

"It's all right. I just inhaled the wrong way." I wiped my eyes.

John handed his mother a bottle filled with a virulent pink liquid. "Here you go, old girl. Would you care to try one of my cigarettes, Dr.—er—Bliss, isn't it? Yours appear to be a trifle too strong."

## ii

By the end of the evening I had managed to meet most of the other passengers. Jen had been guilty of unkind exaggeration when she described them as senile, but "elderly" wouldn't have been inaccurate; the majority of them had to be at least seventy.

One of the exceptions was Suzi Umphenour, the bleached blonde from Memphis (Tennessee). I hadn't expected to like her, but I did, perhaps because she cheerfully admitted that she had joined the cruise only because it was hideously expensive and very exclusive. "All my friends in Memphis were green with envy," she had declared with naive satisfaction.

"Then you aren't interested in Egyptology?"

She emitted a fat chuckle and grinned, displaying an expanse of expensively capped teeth. "I'm interested in men, honey. Young men. All my husbands were old and boring. I figure now I'm entitled to a little fun. There aren't as many cute guys on this trip as I'd hoped, but some of the Egyptian boys are kind of sweet, don't you think?"

I agreed that they were, and left Suzi closing in on Feisal.

By the time I got back to my room I was tired enough to die, but I knew I was too uptight to sleep, so I went out onto the balcony. The lights of the city glowed like jewels against the dark—diamond white, ruby and emerald and sapphire. The night breeze was cool, and if it was polluted—there was no "if" about it, in fact—I didn't notice.

The worst was over, I told myself. I hadn't lost my temper or my dignity, and there was no danger of my doing so now—

not when I had him dead to rights, under my thumb and in my power.

I had replaced the tiny tape reel in my gold locket, but the old tape was still on the table. It was supposed to be in the little safe under the dressing table.

Every suite had such a safe—not an ordinary lockbox, but a specially designed safe with a specially designed key that could not be reproduced by an ordinary locksmith. I'd heard of luxury hotels that provided such a service, but never a cruise ship. However, this was a special ship in every way, and people who were rich enough to take the cruise probably expected such amenities.

We had been warned that if we lost the key the safe would have to be drilled open, at our expense, since there was only one. In my case that wasn't true. At least one other person had a key to mine. I was supposed to leave messages in it and he—she—it?—would communicate with me in the same way.

Nobody would be entering my room that night. The door was equipped with enough hardware to stop a tank. People were nervous about traveling in Egypt, and this was only one of many additional security precautions our management had provided. My mysterious ally wouldn't open the safe until after I had left the room the following morning. I could leave the tape anytime before then.

There was nothing on that tape that could be of use to Burckhardt and his pals. John hadn't admitted anything, except that he and I had known one another before.

But that conversation might be enough to identify him to other people who knew him only by one of his innumerable aliases. My acquaintance with Sir John Smythe, et cetera, ad infinitum was a matter of record in the police departments of at least three countries, and I didn't doubt that Interpol was one of the organizations involved in this investigation.

I sat with my elbows on my knees and my chin propped on my hands and tried to think clearly. That mysterious message of Burckhardt's had been rather vague. Maybe his informant had been mistaken. Even hot-shot secret agents are mistaken sometimes. Suppose that for once John was on the level. He had a job—a nice, honest job—and a nice little wife. Maybe he *had* turned over a new leaf. Maybe he *was* trying to go straight. He must realize that he'd have to find a new profession before arthritis and/or the cops caught up with him, and surely he wouldn't involve his mother and his bride in one of his forays into crime.

A voice from the not-so-distant past jeered, "And if you believe that, you are as innocent as a new-laid egg."

So maybe I was. I'd rather be innocent (translation: stupid) than vindictive.

He had told me once that he loved me. Only once—and I had badgered him into saying it, at a time when he was too battered and bruised to fight back. I owed him for those bruises, and for a couple of other times when he had risked his precious hide to get me out of a nasty situation. Perhaps he had meant it at the time. Perhaps he had only said it to shut me up.

If I betrayed him now I would stand accused, if only by my own conscience, of revenging myself on a man who had wounded my pride and my vanity. My initial protest to Burckhardt was still valid. Even if I identified John as the thief and swindler half the police of Europe were looking for, they couldn't arrest him on my word alone. From what I had heard about the Egyptian security forces, they weren't always too scrupulous about legal formalities, but John was a British subject, protected by the noble code that proclaims a man innocent until proven guilty. I believed in that code, even if it did seem at times to give crooks an unfair advantage.

There was no hurry. The tour wouldn't return to Cairo for three weeks. If John did mean to have a shot at the museum I'd have to turn him in, there was no question about that. But I could afford to wait a little longer.

I decided to go to bed. A book I had brought along, on the medieval mosques of Cairo, had my eyelids at half-mast before I had read two pages. At that rate, I'd never become an expert on Islamic art in time to lecture on the subject. Cheer up, Vicky, I told myself; you may not have to. Once they put the handcuffs on your ex-lover, you can pull out. With a clear conscience.

## *iii*

The horrors of rising at dawn, an activity I try to avoid, were mitigated by the handsome, dark-skinned youth who tapped at my door less than a minute after the chimes had wakened me. I was in no condition to appreciate him, but I certainly appreciated the tray he carried. After two cups of coffee and a cold shower I was ready to face the day.

I made it to the dining room ten minutes before the tour was to leave. Breakfast was buffet-style; there was still plenty of food on the table, but only a few people lingered in the room. One of them was the German urologist, still hunched over his book.

My professional colleagues were gathered in one corner. I deduced that they were waiting for me; as I contemplated the lavish spread, trying to decide what to eat, Feisal rose and joined me.

"An embarras de riches, is it not?" he said, giving me a dazzling smile. "I don't recommend the eggs Benedict; they are a trifle overdone."

"I'm late, I know," I said. "All I want is a roll and—"

"No, no, take your time. Sit down and relax, I will select something for you."

I joined my "colleagues" and we shook hands all around. Foggington-Smythe graciously informed me that I could call him Perry, and returned to his breakfast. Alice Gordon gave me a friendly grin.

"It's difficult to get used to this schedule," she said. "One is tempted to linger in the saloon, but dawn comes all too soon. How nice you look! Very professional."

I had tried to control myself with Burckhardt's money, but I hadn't been able to resist the safari outfit. The pants were modestly loose—we had been warned not to offend Egyptian sensibilities by wearing scanty or skintight garments—and the jacket had more pockets than a shoe bag. It made me feel like Amelia P. Emerson, but when I saw Alice's calf-length cotton skirt and casual shirt I realized I had made a fool of myself. Professional archaeologists didn't dress like that. Not these days, anyhow.

"I resisted the pith helmet," I said with a sheepish smile.

Alice let out a booming laugh. "You shouldn't have. Why not enjoy yourself?"

Feisal returned with a loaded plate. I buttered a croissant and began eating. Perry (I wondered if I would ever be able to call him that) pushed his plate away. Having concluded the primary business of the morning, he was ready to give me his attention.

"I look forward to your lectures, Dr. Bliss," he said solemnly. "I confess I have not read any of your publications—"

"It isn't actually my field," I said. I had known this would happen, and it would have been a waste of time trying to fool these people. "I—uh—I cheated a little bit."

Perry frowned. "In what way?"

"Don't be such a stick, Perry," Alice said easily. "I don't know what strings you pulled to be selected for this cruise, but I wasn't exactly forthright either. My specialty is New Kingdom literature. There are at least a dozen people who know more about Ptolemaic temples than I do. But I'd have cheerfully murdered all of them to get a chance of living like a millionaire for once in my life. This is a far cry from the Hyde Park Holiday Inn."

Feisal laughed. He really was gorgeous—even white teeth, glinting dark eyes—and he had a sense of humor. "A pity one can't claim bribes as legitimate business expenses, isn't it?"

"I always do," I said.

Perry looked blank. "Really," he began.

"Time we were off," Feisal said. "Forward!"

He bustled us out. The antisocial reader remained.

Alice fell in step with me. "I'm sure you were warned about lecturing on site. You can answer questions, but only licensed Egyptian guides are allowed to lecture."

"There's very little danger of my breaking that rule," I assured her.

She laughed and gave me a friendly pat on the arm. "Some

of these people don't know the difference between the nineteenth dynasty and the nineteenth century; if they back you into a corner, just refer them to me or Perry or Feisal."

The passengers had assembled in the lobby. I joined the fringes of the group—which, I was sorry to see, included the Tregarths. Avoiding them, I found myself standing next to Suzi Umphenour. She hailed me like an old friend, and I studied her in consternation. She had ignored the guidelines about dress, and was attired in a jumpsuit that clung lovingly to her posterior and bared her arms, shoulders, and cleavage.

"Don't you have a jacket?" I asked.

"It's on the chair." She gestured carelessly. "But I don't see why—"

"You'll get a horrible sunburn. If nothing worse."

"Feisal said If I didn't wear it somebody would drag me off behind a pyramid and rape me," Suzi said hopefully. "He's such a bully."

Feisal overheard, as she had meant him to. Frowning masterfully, he handed Suzi her jacket and hat, and ushered us down the gangplank.

"Let's sit together," Suzi said. "And have some girl talk. I adore men, but sometimes it's a terrible bore having them cluster around."

"I seldom have that problem."

"Oh, now, honey, you're just being modest. You know, if you'd spruce yourself up a little bit, you'd be real attractive."

We took our places on the bus. By the time we reached the site my ears were ringing. Suzi had made helpful suggestions about my hair—"those little picks you have stuck in your bun are right cute, but you ought to let your hair hang loose instead of pulling it back"—my makeup—"you ought to wear eyeliner, honey, and a darker-color lipstick"—and every article of clothing I had on. She had also analyzed, with devastating accuracy, every man on the boat. Feisal was the sexiest, but that Tregarth man had a certain something; a pity he was newly married.

I was determined to dump Suzi at the earliest possible moment but first I made her put on her jacket—a billowing big shirt of gauze so fine it did very little to fend off possible rapists—and her hat, a broad-brimmed straw that tied under her chin with a huge bow à la, I suppose she thought, Scarlett O'Hara. Then I fled. We had been told to stick with the group, but I figured that didn't apply to me, and by that time I didn't give a damn if it did. I don't like listening to lectures, I'd rather wander in happy ignorance.

Taking my guidebook from my bag, I headed toward a corner of the enclosure, where massive walls of pale limestone towered high above my head. Solitude was impossible to attain; there were a dozen different tour groups present, clustered around their guides like flies on spilled sugar. I fended off a few importunate vendors of souvenirs and services and found a relatively quiet spot and a rock on which to sit.

It was still early; shadows lay cool and gray across the pale sand. The sky was a brilliant blue. Rising up against it, soft gold in the sunlight, was the Step Pyramid—the earliest example of monumental stone architecture, over four thousand years old. Worn and weathered, simple to the point of crudeness, it had more than sheer age to stir the imagination; there was something *right* about it, the slope and the proportions and, above all, the setting. One of my beloved medieval cathedrals would have dwindled in that immensity of sky and sand. This was a dream trip all right, a trip I had hoped to take one day. But I'd have traded the luxurious suite and the fancy food for an ordinary tourist excursion. How could I concentrate on pyramids and tomb paintings when my stomach was churning and my nerves were twanging like Granddad's guitar strings? My eyes kept wandering from the carved lotus columns of the Southern Colonnade to the people gathered around Feisal.

I forced my eyes back to the guidebook and read a long paragraph about the Sed festival, but if you want to know what it was you'll have to look it up, because I've forgotten everything except the name. Many of the fallen columns and walls had been restored, with original materials, and there was now enough to indicate how impressive the structure must have been in its prime. The slender fluted columns and gracefully curved cornices had a classical elegance. I was staring dreamily at them when I saw Jen heading in my direction.

I bent my head over the book, hoping she wouldn't join me. I didn't want company, especially hers. For a couple of minutes I had actually been enjoying myself.

She passed fairly close to me but she didn't stop. Fumbling in her bag, she disappeared from sight behind a low wall.

What could she want back there? It was unlike her to wander off alone. She hadn't looked her usual energetic self, her steps had been slow and dragging.

I got to my feet and followed.

The space was dark and shadowed. Jen was sitting on the ground, her open bag beside her. "Jen?" I said uncertainly. "Are you—"

She turned a blank, gray face toward me and toppled over onto her side.

# Chapter Three

I yelled. At its loudest my voice is the equal of any Wagnerian soprano's, in volume if in no other quality. My call for help was answered sooner than I had dared hope; apparently I hadn't been the only one to observe Jen's sickly look. First on the scene was her devoted son, with Mary close on his heels.

Jen had resisted my attempt to lift her, curling herself into a ball with knees raised and arms clasped over her midsection, but when she saw John she made a gallant effort to smile.

"Just my silly old tummy," she gasped. "Don't worry, darling, I'll be fine in a minute."

Her face was now green instead of gray, and sticky with perspiration. Mary knelt by her with a little cry of sympathy.

"Mother Tregarth!"

"Get out of my way," John said brusquely. I didn't know whether he meant me or his bride. Mary assumed it was me. As she bent tenderly over Jen, the latter was violently and messily sick. Mary stumbled to her feet and backed off, her face twisted with disgust.

John hoisted his mother into his arms and put her down again a few feet away. Contemplating the spots on my brand-new outfit I said, "Oh, shit," took a handful of tissues from my pocket, and began wiping Jen's face.

"I do admire a woman with an extensive vocabulary," John said under his breath. "Don't just squat there, fetch the doctor."

"I'll go," Mary said quickly. "I'm sorry, darling, I . . . I'll go."

When they returned they were accompanied by several of the other passengers, moved by kindly concern or morbid curiosity. It's not always easy to tell the difference, I admit. I felt fairly sure it was the latter emotion that had moved Suzi to join us, but I was willing to give Blenkiron the benefit of the doubt. "What's wrong?" he asked.

Jen demonstrated. I had hoped she would throw up on John, but he managed to avoid it, supporting her head and shoulders so she wouldn't choke. She kept on heaving, poor thing, although she had obviously got rid of everything in her stomach.

I hadn't paid much attention to Dr. Carter when he was introduced the night before, except to hope devoutly I would not require his services. He was a particularly unnoticeable man—middle-aged, middle-sized in both height and girth, with a bland, pink face.

"Just a case of the pharaoh's curse," he said, with that infuriating blend of condescension and jollity some doctors mistake for a soothing bedside manner. "Relax, Mrs. Tregarth; we'll get you back to the boat and—"

"No." John didn't look up. "I want her in hospital. The boat has moved on, we're as close or closer to Cairo."

"Now, son, there's nothing to worry about. This is a common affliction, and the infirmary is—"

"Moving steadily south, among other disadvantages," John said, in his most offensive drawl. "My mother is not a young woman, Doctor, and she has had difficulties of this sort before."

Carter started to fuss, and Blenkiron murmured, "Mr. Tregarth is right, Ben. It would be foolish to take chances. Perhaps the bus can take her to Cairo and then return for us?"

His voice was soft and hesitant, but when you are rich you don't have to yell to get your point across.

"Just what I was about to suggest," Carter exclaimed.

Jen was too weak to resist. She looked awful, her closed

eyes sunken. "Wouldn't an ambulance be better?" I said anxiously.

Blenkiron directed a smile in my general direction. "The back seats on the bus fold down into a cot, Vicky. She'll be far more comfortable there, and safely in Cairo by the time we could get an ambulance out here."

John scooped his mother up and walked off, followed by Mary and Carter.

"Wow," said Suzi, staring. "He's stronger than he looks, isn't he? The old lady must weigh a hundred and sixty, and he's practically running."

Since I knew exactly what she was thinking I decided to ignore this. Since Blenkiron did not know, he responded. "One can understand his concern, though I'm sure it's unnecessary. Many travelers get some kind of digestive upset. It's nice to see a young man so devoted to his mother, isn't it?"

"He's not so young," I said.

"Had you known him before?"

I recollected myself. Blenkiron's question had been casually disinterested, but the gleam of avid curiosity in Suzi's eyes warned me that she was the kind who thrives on scandal. "No," I said.

"I don't believe we've met formally," Blenkiron said. "First names are easier and friendlier; mine is Larry."

He looked younger and more relaxed in a sweat-stained shirt open at the throat and a pair of wrinkled khaki pants. I noted with sympathetic amusement that he was wearing a pith helmet. The darned things *were* practical, shielding the head and neck from the deadly rays of the sun, and heavy enough to resist the tug of the constant north wind.

"I believe this is your first visit to Egypt?" he went on, looking down at me and offering me his hand.

I let him pull me to my feet. He was still looking down at me; not many people can do that. A part of my mind I try to ignore assessed the breadth of his shoulders and his flat stomach and decided he wasn't at all bad for a man of fifty-odd. And he was a multimillionaire. Or a billionaire? What's a few million more or less? I thought tolerantly.

"Does everyone on the boat know I'm a fraud?" I asked.

"Now, Vicky, don't call yourself names. You have quite a reputation. I read your article on the Riemenschneider reliquary with great interest."

"I'm flattered. But I don't know a damn thing about Egyptology," I admitted, with one of my most winning smiles.

"Would you like me to show you around? I'm only an amateur, but I know Sakkara fairly well."

It was one of the most fascinating mornings I have ever spent. Sakkara is a very complicated site; there are several smaller, ruined pyramids in addition to the Step Pyramid, which is surrounded by a maze of subsidiary buildings, temples and courtyards, corridors and chapels. There are underground structures whose function is still unclear, and a lot of private tombs built for high officials. The larger of these mastabas, as they are called, are mazes in themselves. One has thirty-four separate rooms in the superstructure and a tomb shaft below. I had given the guidebook a hasty perusal the night before and ended up with my head stuffed full of miscellaneous, unrelated facts. Larry made sense of it all.

"You've missed your calling," I said, as we left the temple complex. "You ought to be a guide."

He looked absurdly pleased at the silly compliment. We were getting on like a house afire, I thought complacently. No wonder the poor man fled from women like Suzi; he must be sick of being relentlessly pursued. All he wanted was to be treated as an intellectual equal, to be admired for his brains instead of his money. I could sympathize with that, though in my case it wasn't money that distracted admirers from my intellectual achievements.

"It's easier to simplify a complex subject when one is an amateur," he said modestly. "Shall we have a look at one of the mastabas before lunch? As an art historian you are probably familiar with the reliefs."

"I remember some Old Kingdom reliefs—they were wonderful, very delicate and detailed—but at this moment I couldn't tell you which tomb they were from. There was one of a baby hippopotamus . . ."

"You're probably thinking of Mereruka." Larry took my

arm. "But some of the other tombs are equally remarkable. We'll see which is least crowded."

They were all crowded, at least to the eyes of someone like me, whose definition of too many people is three, but Larry said, "Never seen so few people here at this time of year. Tourism is down, people are afraid of terrorists. Nice for us, but unfortunate for the Egyptian economy."

I got to see my baby hippopotamus, who was ambling along through the river reeds apparently unaware of the huge crocodile right on his heels (if hippos have heels). He had no cause for alarm; his devoted mum had grabbed the predator and was in the process of biting it in two.

The photographs I'd seen hadn't done the carving justice. To an eye accustomed to Western sculpture the reliefs had a simplicity that verged on naïveté, but the more I studied them the more I realized that that impression was deceptive. The technique was sure and skilled and highly sophisticated; only an ignoramus or an observer who was unable to put aside his unconscious prejudices would have undervalued them.

Larry absolutely agreed with me and told me how clever I was to have reached that conclusion. We were having a lovely time when I heard shuffling footsteps and a familiar voice. "That's Feisal, surely," I said.

Larry looked at his watch. "He is right on schedule. It's later than I thought. The time has gone very quickly."

He gave me a meaningful look. I probably simpered.

The first to enter the room was the tall raw-boned man who had been at Larry's table the night before. He had been following us at a discreet distance all morning, and he continued to be tactful, staring off into space until Larry murmured, "I don't believe you two have met. Dr. Victoria Bliss—Ed Whitbread."

"'Morning, ma'am." Ed whipped off his hat—a broad-brimmed white Stetson—and bowed.

Despite the stifling heat he was wearing a jacket. I thought I knew why. He was a good three inches taller than Larry, which made him almost six-five. I sincerely hoped that Larry had convinced him I was a friend. I wouldn't have wanted him to think of me as an enemy.

Led by Feisal, the others crowded into the room. Larry faded discreetly away as Suzi headed toward me, shoving bodies out of her way with good-natured impetuosity. "I wondered where you'd got to," she said. "How'd you do that?"

"Do what?"

"You know." She gave me a grin and an elbow in the ribs. It was a surprisingly sharp elbow to belong to a woman so well padded elsewhere. "It sure didn't work when I tried it. You'll have to tell me how you—"

"Quiet, please." Feisal clapped his hands like a teacher calling a class to order. "We have only fifteen minutes, there is another group waiting. The reliefs in this chamber . . ."

He was a good lecturer, crisp and witty and, so far as I could tell, absolutely accurate. I had a hard time concentrating, since Suzi kept whispering and nudging me. After a while Feisal broke off and fixed a stern eye on her. "Suzi, you are a bad girl, you do not pay attention. Come here and stand by me."

Giggling happily, Suzi obeyed. Feisal caught my eye and lowered one eyelid in a discreet wink.

The sun was high and hot when we left the tomb and set out across the uneven surface of the plateau. Sunlight bleached the sand and rock to a pale buff; though the distance wasn't great, several of my companions were puffing and complaining by the time we reached our destination.

The bus was waiting. I collapsed into a seat with a sigh of relief and accepted a glass of water, tinkling with ice, from a smiling waiter. Not for us the crowded rest house where ordinary tourists ate and drank, risking not only discomfort but the pharaoh's curse; the seats had attached trays, like those on planes, and we were served chilled wine and food on fine porcelain. Even as I thought how easy it was to accustom oneself to such luxuries, my scholar's conscience reminded me that the exhaust was pouring out pollution that gnawed away the very stones of the pyramids.

As soon as everyone was settled, Feisal addressed us. "Some of you know that one of our friends was taken ill this morning. You will be glad to hear that Mrs. Tregarth is now comfortably resting in a Cairo hospital . . ."

I didn't hear the rest. One word had forced its way through the layers of stupidity that enrobed my brain.

Cairo. The Cairo Museum was in Cairo. Take it slow, Vicky, slow and easy; you obviously aren't up to complex reasoning. Right. No question about it. The museum *was* in Cairo. And now John was too.

Not only was he in Cairo (where the museum was) but his departure had been sudden, unexpected, off schedule. I had told myself I had three more weeks. I should have known—damn it, damn it, I should have known!—that John never stuck to schedules and that the unexpected was his stock-in-trade. The mere sight of me would have warned him that someone had got wind of his scheme. He wouldn't abandon it, not John, not until he had to; he'd change his plans, catch me off guard, find an excuse to get to the scene of the crime ahead of schedule, a nice valid excuse like . . .

Poisoning his own mother?

It seemed a trifle extreme, even for John.

All the same. . . .

I blundered up out of my seat, squeezing past the tray with its load of china and glasses. Bright and Sweet were a few rows ahead of me; I could see Bright's thick, brown expensive hair over the top of the seat. They beamed a welcome, but I didn't wait for an exchange of greetings.

"It's a shame about Mrs. Tregarth, isn't it?"

"Very sad," Sweet said cheerfully. "But Feisal says she is on the road to recovery. It should be a lesson to us all, you know; the poor dear lady was constantly overeating. That is epecially dangerous when one is unaccustomed to strange food and water."

Bright nodded vigorously. He probably wouldn't have spoken even if he had been able to, but in this case he wasn't; he had just shoved an entire stuffed egg into his mouth.

"Right," I said. "I wonder how long they'll stay in Cairo. Where the—" I managed to stop myself. Larry, in the seat across the aisle, was watching me with a bewildered smile.

"Let us hope she will be able to join us again soon," Sweet said. "A pity to lose part of such a delightful trip."

I tried again. "Especially when it's also a honeymoon. I suppose her son will stay *in Cairo* with her?"

"I suppose so." Sweet gave me a puzzled look.

I got a grip on myself and turned to go. "Well. See you later."

"We will meet in a pyramid," Sweet called after me.

I inserted myself into my seat and picked up a sandwich— nothing plebeian like cheese or chicken, but a masterpiece of shrimp and chopped egg yolk and some mysterious sauce. Sweet and Bright didn't appear to be concerned; in fact they had both looked at me as if I were losing my feeble mind. Of course, I told myself; they were professionals. Like the others they had heard of Jen's illness. They might not know John was the man they were after, but they'd be on the alert for anything unusual. They probably even knew the Cairo Museum was in Cairo.

I can't say I enjoyed the remainder of the tour of Sakkara, even though Feisal was at his most eloquent and Alice stuck with me most of the afternoon. She was good company, knowl-edgeable and yet unassuming, with an unexpectedly wicked sense of humor. Watching Suzi, who had attached herself to Feisal, she said with a grin, "Looks as if she's going to settle for youth and beauty instead of cash. Larry will be relieved, he looked like a cornered rabbit last night."

"He's a very nice guy," I said. "Larry, I mean. Do you know him well?"

"Nobody knows him well." Striding briskly, her hands in her pockets, Alice looked as fresh as a woman half her age. "I'd met him once or twice; he's truly dedicated to archaeology and very well informed. But I was surprised to find him on this trip, he's a very private person. Of course the highlight of the cruise is the reopening of Tetisheri's tomb and that has been his major interest for over three years. He's probably hoping to persuade the other filthy-rich types on board to support similar projects."

She stopped, waiting for the others to catch up, and I said, trying not to pant, "He's not with the group this afternoon. Trying to avoid predatory females?"

She caught my meaning. "Not you. You made quite a hit. In fact, he sidled up to me and asked me if I thought you'd like to accompany him this afternoon—he's gone off to see the Eighteenth-Dynasty nobles' tombs, which aren't open to the public."

"And you told him I wouldn't? Hell's bells, Alice, how am I going to catch myself a millionaire if you interfere?"

Alice laughed. "Don't blame me. He talked himself out of it before I could reply. Honest to God, I felt like a high school student counselor trying to convince some bashful kid it was okay to ask the cheerleader to a dance. But," she added, with a shrewd glance at me, "don't get your hopes up. He likes you because you treated him like a human being but I don't think he's interested in matrimony."

"Neither am I."

"Sensible woman."

"Why didn't you go with him? This tourist stuff must be boring for you."

"My dear, I'm on duty. Anyhow, I never tire of the tourist stuff. I haven't been inside the Teti Pyramid for years."

"Is that the next stop? I'm getting confused," I admitted.

"No wonder. We're cramming an awful lot into one day. The brain overloads. You don't have to go inside if you don't want to."

"I think I won't. Go ahead, I'll sit here and admire the view."

All but the most energetic were beginning to flag, after a long morning and a large lunch. Some had stayed on the bus, others wandered off in search of souvenirs, of which there was no dearth. Only a dozen people expressed an interest in the interior of the pyramid. Among them were Bright and Sweet and the large square woman who had been pointed out to me as a famous novelist. No one could have accused her of treading on Egyptian sensibilities; she was draped from shoulders to shins in flowing robes, with a scarf wound wimple-style around her large square face. Her features were vaguely familiar, but I couldn't remember where I'd seen them, and I thought I would have remembered that face. Not many famous lady novelists have perceptible mustaches.

"What's her name?" I whispered to Alice.

"Louisa Ferncliffe. But she writes under the name of Valerie Vandine. Ever heard of her?"

I had. I had even, for my sins, read a couple of her novels. She was one of Schmidt's favorite authors. Schmidt only reads two types of fiction: hard-boiled mysteries featuring lean tough detectives, and torrid historical romances featuring helpless voluptuous heroines. Violence and sex, in other words. I studied the massive form ahead of me with disbelief. The woman must have an incredibly vivid imagination. The sexual gymnastics she described in such interesting detail would have been physically impossible for someone built like that.

So that was why she looked familiar. The photographs on the backs of her books had omitted the mustache and the lines scoring her forehead. A couple of chins had been airbrushed out too.

"Her heroines are all tall and slim and blond," I muttered.

Alice chuckled. "It will be interesting to see how she gets a tall slim blonde into a novel about ancient Egypt. She's gathering material for one, I understand."

Louisa tilted her head back and inspected the crumbling side of the structure. "Where are the Pyramid Texts?" she demanded.

Feisal had almost certainly heard dumber questions; he said patiently, "Inside the pyramid, Miss Vandine. Are you coming?"

Instead of answering she turned her back on him and addressed Alice. "Are you?"

"I had intended to, yes."

"In that case I will accompany you. I want to have some of the texts translated; to hear echo, in the air of the tomb chamber, the magical words of protection." Throwing her arms up, she intoned, "O gods of the underworld, greet this pharaoh in peace! O heavenly guides, bring down the wrath of Anubis on all who would violate this tomb!"

That was too much for Feisal. "I'm afraid there is no such text, Miss Vandine."

She looked him up and down and back up again. "How would you know? Dr. Gordon is an expert—"

"Not on the Pyramid Texts," Alice said. Her face was flushed, though not as darkly as Feisal's. She went on, very quietly, "Feisal's doctoral dissertation involved a comparison of Pyramid and Coffin Texts. He is a graduate of Oxford and the University of Chicago. I believe I won't accompany you after all. The air is rather . . . close inside."

After the group had gone in I said, "Well done, Alice. Firm but ladylike."

"Too ladylike." Alice took off her hat and fanned her hot face. "She didn't get it. There are always a few like that in every group. I don't know why I bother; bigotry and rudeness are unconquerable."

"With his qualifications, why is he working as a guide?"

Alice shrugged. "Jobs are hard to find. I shouldn't have to tell *you* that."

"You're right." The memory of how I had wangled my own job made me squirm uncomfortably. Blackmail would be too harsh a word, but . . .

"His father is a low-level bureaucrat," Alice went on. "Hardly more than a glorified clerk. He has sacrificed all his life so that his son—the only son—could have a professional career. The pressures on Feisal have been enormous, as you can imagine."

"Yeah. People are pretty much the same everywhere, I guess."

"In some ways." Alice grinned at me. "And very different in other ways. Let's have a look at a few of the other mastabas, shall we? If you like reliefs, some are quite lovely. Or would you rather visit the Serapeum? It's a little distance, but—"

"I'm not really all that keen on deep dark places."

I spoke without thinking, and after I had done so I was sorry I had let down my guard, even with someone as friendly as Alice. She didn't pursue the matter, just nodded.

By the time Alice had finished showing me around I had begun to think more kindly of dark sunless places. I wasn't the only one who was weary, sweat-stained, and red-faced when we assembled at the bus. The group that had been inside the pyramid looked as bad as I felt. Apparently they had enjoyed themselves, though. Sweet rhapsodized about Feisal's lecture, and Bright kept nodding and grinning. I was happy to observe that Louisa's veils were in tatters. Somebody must have stepped on her hem.

As I reclined in air-conditioned comfort, sipping my iced drink, I tried to concentrate on the exotic scenery gliding

past—the Step Pyramid, golden in the afternoon light, green
fields of alfalfa and vegetables, barefoot children smiling and
waving as we spoiled foreigners passed—but my mind was
a jumble of disconnected impressions. "The Step Pyramid is
two hundred and four feet high . . . He likes you because you
treated him like a human being . . . O gods of the underworld,
greet this pharaoh in peace . . . The poor woman was constantly overeating . . ."

Jen hadn't been faking. Some unpleasant evidences of that
still clung to my clothes. Would John really go to that length
to carry out his plans? I felt reasonably certain the Cairo
Museum was still intact; if he'd laid plans for an event to
take place three weeks hence, they couldn't be changed so
quickly. Anyhow (I kept telling myself) I had now done my
duty as a good little spy. Sweet and Bright knew John was
the one they were after. I had been as direct as I dared; they
couldn't have misunderstood the message. It was out of my
hands now; I hadn't volunteered to defend the museum with
six-shooters in hand.

The first person I saw when I walked up the gangplank
was John. He was leaning on the rail, cigarette in hand. Fair
hair becomingly ruffled by the breeze, shirt as fresh and clean
as new-fallen snow, he surveyed the dusty, sunburned, limping
crowd with kindly condescension.

"Much better," he called, in response to a question from
someone—Feisal, I think; it certainly wasn't from me, I was
speechless. "No cause for concern, the doctors said." He
turned eyes as blue and expressionless as cornflowers on me
and added, "I felt certain you'd want to know at the earliest
possible moment."

Whereupon he vanished, leaving me a prey—as Louisa
Ferncliffe might have written—to a torrent of passionate,
conflicting emotions. Chief among them was fury.

I plucked Suzi out of the group waiting at the desk for their
room keys. "You'd better see the doctor about that sunburn,"
I said abruptly.

She looked surprised. "Is it that bad? It doesn't hurt."

"Your back is bright red." That was a slight exaggeration,
but she was bright pink all over the parts that showed.

My forceful personality (or something) prevailed; Suzi allowed herself to be towed away.

Carter earned his passage; he was on call twenty-four hours a day, ashore and on land, but the only time when one could count on finding him in the infirmary was after the tours returned, when he would be available "to attend to any minor injuries incurred." I hadn't liked the sound of that; however, after seeing the rough terrain and feeling the heat of the sun, I could understand why people might be in need of attention for a variety of "minor" ailments ranging from sunstroke to twisted ankles. The infirmary was an impressive setup, spotlessly clean and very well equipped, including a locked cabinet that presumably contained drugs.

While Carter was inspecting Suzi, I asked about Jen. "Not a damned thing wrong with her except overindulgence and a touch of the usual virus," was the irritable reply. Apparently the doctor's amour propre had been seriously ruffled. I could guess by whom. "She managed to persuade that officious son of hers to go on with the cruise, which he finally consented to do, after inspecting the hospital and interrogating the entire staff."

"So you all came back together?"

"Yes. If you ask me, Mrs. Tregarth was relieved to be rid of him and looking forward to a few days' peace and quiet. All right, Suzi, you're in fine shape, if you'll permit me to say so; use this ointment tonight and cover up for a few days."

So that was that. Unless one of the hospital staff was a stooge of John's, he hadn't had a chance to speak to anyone. I hoped.

I hadn't left a message in my safe, but I found one there when I opened it. It was short and succinct. "Please report soonest."

I screwed up the paper and tossed it into the wastebasket. If Burckhardt wanted to be so damned mysterious and security-conscious he could damn well wait till I was good and ready. Anyhow, I had reported, to Sweet and Bright.

I hadn't realized how tired I was until I got in the shower and let the nice hot water flow over my aching body. It was tension rather than exercise that had stiffened those muscles;

I'd been on edge all day. Considerate of John to reassure me at the earliest possible moment . . . Damn his insolence!

Dress that evening would probably be informal, I decided, slipping into a cotton skirt and sleeveless shirt. Everyone else would be tired too. The schedule was really fierce, and tomorrow would be another full day, with tours to Meydum and the Faiyum. I found myself looking forward to Tuesday, when we were supposed to cruise all day. I hadn't had time to enjoy my little balcony or explore the amenities of the boat, which included a hairdresser, shop, gym, and pool.

However, when I arrived at the saloon in time for Happy Hour I found the others discussing the change in schedule which had been posted on the bulletin board. Meydum and two other scheduled stops had been postponed till the return trip. We were to sail immediately for Amarna.

Most of the group didn't seem to care, but a few were complaining bitterly—the elderly couple from San Francisco because they were habitual complainers and Louisa because she wanted to use Meydum as the setting for her new novel. "This will disrupt my writing schedule fatally," she declaimed. "I had promised my impatient publisher to have at least fifty thousand words written by the time we reach Luxor. But now—how can I begin? My imagination cannot take fire until I have seen those magnificent ruins."

I suspected Louisa was thinking of two other ruins. Meydum had never been a city, just a huge cemetery. How could she set an entire novel in a graveyard? Love among the mummies? That one had already been done. Seeing my colleagues gathered at a table nearby, I started toward them, figuring they would know the reason for the change in plan, but then I saw Larry beckoning me. He was sitting by himself in the smoking section. Whitbread and the secretary, whatever his name might be, were at another table.

We exchanged raves on the activities of the day and then I asked, "Do you know why the change in schedule?"

"It has to do with the water level" was the prompt response. "This is one of the largest boats on the river; it can't get through the locks at Asyut, which were designed for smaller vessels, if the Nile is low. There won't be a problem going upstream, but I gather there is some concern about the return voyage."

We had been left strictly alone until then. Tact, consideration for Larry's obvious desire for privacy—or the presence of that tall formidable figure at a nearby table? Ed was facing us; though he did it unobtrusively, he never took his eyes off his boss. He hadn't been so visible the night before. Had something happened to increase his concern about Larry's safety? I was considering this, and not liking the possibilities that occurred to me, when a man approached our table. Tall, fair-haired . . . My heart did not skip a beat. My heart would not have skipped a beat even if I hadn't recognized Foggington-Smythe.

"May I join you?" Without waiting for an answer he pulled out a chair and planted himself in it. "I felt I deserved a respite after spending the entire day answering idiotic questions from people who didn't bother doing basic research."

There was a resemblance to John, all right—that air of condescending superiority. John wouldn't have made a stupid remark like that one, though. He had too strong a sense of the ridiculous.

"They aren't scholars," I said. "Just tourists having fun. Why should they do any work when they have an expert like you to set them straight on every possible subject?"

Larry raised a hand to conceal his smile, but Foggington-Smythe only nodded gravely. "I suppose that's true." Then he turned to Larry, who, I suspected, was the real attraction. "Is it true that our schedule has been changed because the authorities learned that terrorists were planning an attack at Meydum tomorrow?"

Larry's jaw dropped. "Where did you hear that?"

"That's the rumor that is going around."

"To the best of my knowledge there's no basis for it," Larry said firmly. He glanced at the door of the saloon. "At any rate, we're under way now. Why don't you take Vicky out on deck and show her some of the sights?"

I didn't blame him for wanting to escape from Perry, or even for using me as a decoy. "Sounds good to me," I said agreeably. "Sure you won't join us?"

"Duty calls, I'm afraid," Larry murmured. "This may necessitate an alteration in my plans for the reception and formal opening of the Tetisheri tomb. I'll have to find out what's going on."

His staff fell in behind him as he made for the door, and Perry led me out.

The sun was sinking in a smoky haze. I couldn't see any of the sights Perry pointed out; I don't think he could either, but he indicated their location and went on to tell me all about them. I let the words wash over me; an occasional "Really?" or "How fascinating!" was all he wanted anyhow. The view was lovely. Sunset colors stained the rippling water and lights began to twinkle along the shore.

"Damn," Perry said suddenly. "Here comes the bride." He chuckled at his own wit, and went on, "Pretty little thing, but without a brain in her head; I suppose she wants to ask some fool question . . . Ah, Mrs. Tregarth. If you are in quest of information, perhaps you would be good enough to wait until this evening. I am lecturing on Egyptian literature but will take questions afterward."

It was as rude a put-down as I had ever heard, but Mary met it head-on. Smiling, she drawled, "How frightfully kind of you. It was Vicky I wanted to talk with, actually."

"Oh? Oh. Well, then—uh . . . Excuse me."

Mary gave me a conspiratorial smile. The breeze whipped her full skirt around her calves and molded her silk blouse to her body. "He's the world's most pompous ass, isn't he? I hope I didn't misinterpret your expression of glazed boredom, Vicky."

"You rushed to my rescue?" I inquired.

With a graceful gesture she invited me to walk with her, and we strolled on in silence for a while. Then she stopped, leaning against the rail, and turned to face me.

"I really did want to speak with you. To thank you for being so kind to Mother Tregarth."

"I just happened to be there."

"You did what I ought to have done." Mary's pretty mouth twisted. "I'm so squeamish; I can't stand seeing someone I love in pain. I hope you don't think badly of me. I'd like us to be friends."

It was not a relationship that held much appeal for me. A ghastly picture formed in my mind—the bride and the groom and the bride's new friend, in a cozy trio. I couldn't bring myself to slap her down, though. She had to tilt her head back to look into my eyes, and hers were big and wide and innocent. The irises were an unusual shade of golden brown; they glowed like amber in the sunset light.

"I admire women like you so much," she went on. "You're so intelligent and so capable—so in control of your life. Not like me."

"Well," I said. "That's very . . ."

"Inaccurate" was the word that came to mind. I substituted a feeble "kind."

"You wouldn't be intruding," Mary went on eagerly. "I wouldn't want you to think that. If we'd wanted to be alone together we wouldn't have joined a cruise like this one."

"Or invited your mother-in-law to come along," I said, before I could stop myself. Instead of being offended at my candor, Mary laughed.

"I needn't tell you it was the other way round. Poor darling, she's so devoted to John. She kept sighing and dropping hints about how lonely she'd be."

So her doting son had yielded and let her come along? That theory certainly cast a new light on John's character. When he had spoken of his mother—which wasn't often—it had been with detached, amused exasperation.

"John is a very private person in many ways," Mary went on. "And very reserved. He doesn't make a public show of his feelings. When we're alone . . ." She broke off with an embarrassed laugh. "I don't know why I'm saying these things. You have a way of inducing confidences, Vicky. I feel so comfortable with you."

"That's nice." I didn't trust myself to say more.

"I hope you don't mind my unburdening myself."

I minded. The last thing I wanted was to be the recipient of her confidences about her relationship with John. Had he suggested she approach me? Surely not; it was to his advantage to keep us apart. More likely she had picked me as a confidante because I was unattached, and closer to her age than the other women on the boat. I had wondered—oh, yes, I admit I had—

why he'd settled on a half-baked girl barely out of finishing school, but it was becoming clearer now. Adoration, that was what he wanted—unquestioning, doglike devotion. And money? It was one of his favorite things, and I had already noticed, as what woman wouldn't, that Mary's clothes had not been bought at Marks and Spencer.

"Not a bit," I said, lying in my teeth. "Uh—I've been admiring your earrings. They're excellent reproductions."

She accepted this as a tactful, if ungraceful, method of changing the subject. "Oh, they aren't copies. Second century B.C., according to John. He gave them to me."

Before I could stop her she had unfastened one and handed it to me.

I was almost afraid to touch it. The miniature head was only three-quarters of an inch high, but every feature had been molded with delicate accuracy. It was a classically Greek face, with the long unbroken line from the forehead to the end of the nose, but on its brow it wore an ornament that was not Greek—the horns and full moon of the Egyptian goddess Isis. A modern jeweler had added new wires. One wouldn't want to keep bending the ancient gold; it was almost pure, close to twenty-four karat.

Silently I returned it to her. I had never seen anything I coveted more.

"It's nice, isn't it?" Casually she replaced the earring.

"Gorgeous."

"He asked if I'd rather have diamonds," Mary said innocently. "But I prefer these. He has such wonderful taste."

"Uh-huh," I said. The enameled golden rose, invisible under my blouse, seemed to burn into my hide.

"There he is." Mary looked past me. "I guess it's time to dress for dinner. I'm so glad we had this talk, Vicky."

She didn't ask me to join them. I watched her hurry toward him; he stood waiting, arms folded, like the Emperor preparing to receive a humble subject, and then I turned to go—the other way.

There was no warning, not even a rush of running feet. He hit me hard and low, hurling me forward. I bounced off the rail with a force that knocked the breath out of me and crashed to the deck, derriere first, the back of my head a close second.

Bright specks darted through the blackness like pretty little shooting stars.

After a while I opened my eyes, and immediately closed them again when I saw a familiar face hovering over me. Then I opened them again. Not that familiar. It was Foggington-Smythe.

"Good old Perry," I croaked.

"Good," said good old Perry. "You know me. You'd better lie still, though; that was quite a crack on the head."

"She's not got concussion." John was sitting on the deck next to me. He was rubbing his wrist and scowling like a gargoyle on a cathedral. "I think I broke my arm," he went on bitterly.

"Of course," I said. "You were the one who knocked me down. I should have known."

"I think I broke my arm," John repeated.

It was like old times, me bruised and prostrate, John whining. "God damn it, what'd you do that for?" I demanded. I sat up and then grabbed the back of my head. "Ow."

Perry put a manly arm around my shoulders and squeezed. "Ow," I said again.

"I'll carry you to the infirmary," Perry announced.

"No, you won't. I don't have a concussion." I indicated John, who was still nursing his arm. "Carry him. I'll take his feet. We can drop him, heavily, several times along the way."

The corner of John's mouth twitched, but he said nothing. I saw Mary, pressed up against the rail, her hands over her mouth, her eyes wide and horrified. I saw the spattered dirt and fragments of pottery and the broken remains of the jasmine that had been in the pot. It had hit the deck in the exact spot where I would have been standing if someone hadn't knocked me out of the way.

"Oh," I said.

"Vicky, don't be angry with him." Mary knelt beside me and put her arm around me, from the other side. A pretty tableau we must have made. "It was my fault, I saw the flowerpot tottering on the edge and cried out. John acted instinctively, as any gentleman would."

I glowered at John. His eyelids fell, but not in time to hide the fury that had darkened his eyes to sapphire. I wasn't moved to apologize; at that point I wouldn't have given him credit for good intentions if the testimonial had come from the pope. "Oh, right," I snarled. "Thanks a lot. My head hurts worse than it would have done if that little bitty pot had landed on it and I've got a bruise on my bum the size of a soup tureen."

"It might have hurt you badly, Vicky," Mary insisted.

I staggered to my feet, assisted by Perry. "Worse than this? Oh, well. I guess I'll live. Excuse me. I've got to shower and change and find out who tried to brain me."

"You aren't implying that it was deliberate, I hope," Perry exclaimed.

"An unfortunate accident," said John. "Or a warning."

"Warning?" Perry repeated, staring.

"To enjoy life to the full while one can," John said sententiously. " 'Gather ye rosebuds while ye may.' This is a world fraught with peril; one never knows when the ax will fall. Life is at best—"

"Darling, please." Mary abandoned me and hurried to take his arm. "Vicky will think you're making fun of her."

"Oh, she'd never be mistaken about that," John said.

"Never," I agreed, and let Perry lead me away.

# Chapter Four

*i*

Terrorists, low water, or whatever, the change in schedule couldn't have been more welcome. It would give me a chance to collect my wits and nurse my bruises. I had exaggerated a trifle; the one on my butt was only the size of a salad plate. As I lowered myself very gently into a hot tub filled with bubbles I tried to look on the bright side.

The flowerpot wasn't a lethal weapon; even if it had landed square on the top of my head it wouldn't have done lasting damage. As John had unnecessarily and condescendingly emphasized, it had been meant as a warning. Not that there were certain individuals on the ship who wanted me off the ship—I had already known that—or even that they were willing to use violence to achieve that end. It was a little more subtle: a reminder that I wasn't safe anywhere on the boat, that "they" had access even to my room. That was where I had been standing when the pot fell—under my own balcony.

Too damn many people had access to my room. I let my toes float up to the surface of the water and studied them pensively, remembering the agitated faces of the staff members who had been interrogated. Perry had insisted I report the incident immediately, and Hamid, the purser, had hauled the obvious suspects into his office.

Hamid was in charge of the domestic arrangements on the boat, the civilian equivalent of the captain. A slim, handsome man of indeterminate age, he radiated an air of calm competence. I had already wondered if he might be Burckhardt's mysterious agent; he had keys to all the rooms and a perfect excuse to enter them. He could always claim he was checking up on his staff.

If he was in disguise, the disguise was excellent. In his crisp, tailored uniform, his hair graying attractively at the temples, he was the perfect model of an efficient hotel manager. And, I reminded myself, he wasn't the only one who had a key to my room. Until that moment I hadn't realized how many stewards there were. One replenished the liquor cabinet (he was a Copt, since handling alcoholic beverages might have offended Muslim sensibilities); another picked up and delivered laundry; a third cleaned and changed the beds. Hamid lined them up in a cringing row and questioned them in vehement Arabic. They protested their innocence volubly and passionately. The most obvious suspect was a kid named Ali, who was responsible for the overall cleaning, including the care of the flowers. He looked no more than eighteen—a graceful, smiling boy with the thick dark lashes many Egyptians have. He denied everything. Yes, he had watered the flowers and clipped the dead blooms; everything had been in perfect order when he left the room, he had made certain to replace the pots securely in the stand. He wrung his hands. Then he started to cry.

That was when I put an end to the proceedings. They were a waste of time, and I can't stand masculine tears. Ali cried even harder when I said I didn't blame him.

Hamid and Perry went with me to my room. As I had begun to suspect, there was nothing wrong with the flowers on my balcony. Every pot was still in place and firmly anchored.

The most logical explanation, proposed by a visibly relieved Hamid, was that one of the passengers in an adjoining room had been fooling around with the flowers. He would investigate, of course . . . I said fine, and got rid of him and Perry. He wouldn't investigate very hard, not with this lot of passengers, and I knew perfectly well that the pot had fallen from my balcony even it it hadn't originated there.

I blew bubbles off my hand and decided I had better start looking for some more crooks. The sight of John had thrown me off balance and distracted me, but he obviously wasn't the only malefactor on board. I had suspected that before; the flowerpot incident proved it. I had a perfect opportunity to investigate, since this was like one of those old-fashioned English country-house murder mysteries: all the suspects gathered together, isolated from the outside world. I would interview all of them, including the ones I hadn't had a chance to talk with; I would mingle and be charming and very, very clever. And very, very careful.

*ii*

Aside from the other distractions, such as wondering who was going to hit me next and with what, my luxury cruise developed another hitch. Mary wanted John and me to "make up." She began her campaign that night, leaving her chair and running to greet me when I entered the dining room. "We saved a place for you, Vicky. You'll join us, won't you?"

Short of knocking her down and walking over her, there was no way I could get away from the little hands that clung to my arm and towed me with remorseless goodwill toward a table. John was on his feet, waiting. No one had dressed for dinner that night, but even his casual clothes looked as if they had come from Savile Row—a white polo shirt with a discreet insignia on the breast pocket, the creases in his slacks so sharp they could cut you. He looked me over, from my cheap sandals to the imitation Hermès scarf tying my hair back, and then focused pointedly on my throat, where the locket hung from its heavy chain.

"How kind of you to honor us, Dr. Bliss. You don't appear to be limping; I hope that means the bruise you mentioned was not too extensive."

He gave my chair a shove as I lowered myself into it. I had expected something of the sort, so I was able to catch myself before the edge of the table rammed me in the stomach. "And your poor wrist," I said. "Not a thing wrong with it, I see."

It went on that way through five courses. John was as smoothly offensive as only he could be, his voice the exaggerated drawl I particularly hated, his conversation studded with stinging barbs. I thought Mary missed most of the double entendres, but when John commented on my locket—"So large and so *very* gold"—she flushed and said quickly,

"Now, darling, not everyone shares your tastes. Antique jewelry is one of his specialities," she explained to me.

"Oh, is it?" I said.

She was still wearing the Greek earrings. They glowed with a soft patina under the lights, and the tiny, exquisite faces had the same expression of aloof disdain that marked John's features.

"Isis," he said, following my gaze—or reading my mind, which wasn't hard to do under the circumstances. "Though she was an Egyptian goddess, her cult was quite popular in Greece during the Hellenistic period. Three hundred to thirty B.C."

"Thank you so much for telling me." I propped my chin on my hand and smiled sweetly at him. "They're lovely. Where on earth do you pick up such things?"

"Here and there," John said, smiling not so sweetly back. "I found that pair at an antiquarian jeweler's in New York. You may know of the shop; it's on Madison in the seventies."

Straight to the liver, that one. I did know of the shop. My golden rose had come from the same place.

I made one feeble attempt at criminal investigation during the meal, questioning them in guileless girlish curiosity about the other passengers. It wasn't very successful. John knew perfectly well what I was up to; smiling and suave, he gushed useless information. Mary was more helpful. She had already struck up acquaintances with most of the passengers. "The

Johnsons are from San Francisco," she said, nodding toward
the elderly couple I had seen with Jen the first night on board.
"He has something to do with the stock market."

"He is the dullest individual on board," John said. "With
the possible exception of his wife. His hobby, if you can
believe it, is miniature railroads."

And so it went, with Mary identifying people and John
making rude remarks about each and every one. When we
retired to the lounge for coffee I excused myself and went
out on deck for a cigarette. John didn't join me. However, I
had a nice chat with Mr. Johnson, who smoked cigars. He
was even more boring than John had claimed. Luckily Alice
joined us before he could tell me more about HO or HQ or
whatever; she had heard about my "accident" and was full of
questions.

"Dirty things, flowers," Johnson declared. "Why not imi-
tations, that's what I say. Wife likes the damned things,
though . . ."

A voice from the saloon suggested that the evening lecture
was about to begin, so we went inside. The assistant purser
was on the podium, making the official announcement of what
everyone already knew, and promising us varied forms of
amusement to make up for the change in schedule. One of
the passengers, a distinguished amateur ornithologist, had
offered to talk to us about birds, and Dr. Foggington-Smythe
would give an additional lecture, on Egyptian religion. In
three days' time there would be a grand Egyptian banquet
and cabaret, at which passengers and crew would entertain.
Prizes would be given for the best costumes; if we had not
already purchased Egyptian garb in Cairo, the staff would be
glad to help us concoct an appropriate costume, or we could
visit the excellent shop of Mr. Azad (who rose and smiled
ingratiatingly) to select from his stock of clothing.

"Sounds like fun," I said to Alice, who had signaled one
of the waiters.

"Chacun à son goût," said Alice enigmatically. "You want
coffee? I strongly recommend it. Perry's lectures are as effective as a couple of Valium."

I was glad I had taken her advice. Perry went droning on
about Isis and Osiris and Mut and a lot of other people with

improbable names; when he started discussing the differences
between pantheism, monotheism, and henotheism, my head
began to droop. I was saved from shame by Alice, who kept
pinching me.

There were not many questions. Nobody wanted to get him
started again.

The crew hauled away the screen and podium and our dance
band—a grand total of four—ambled in. Perry asked me to
dance, but I was able to use my bruises as an excuse for
refusing. As I hobbled toward the door I saw the Johnsons
solemnly gyrating; he was holding her at arm's length and
moving about as fast as a sluggish snail. The newlyweds were
not dancing.

*iii*

I had breakfast in my room next morning. From what I had
heard, room service was not usual on tour boats, but Ali
was now my best friend in the whole world and would—he
earnestly assured me—lay down his life for me anytime I
wanted. I told him I'd settle for a couple of boiled eggs and
coffee. He was back in record time, with an array of food
that looked like samples of the entire breakfast menu. I had
to push him out the door. Then I took food, coffee, and a pad
and pencil out onto the balcony.

The views were pastoral—green fields, water buffalo knee-
deep in the shallows, black-garbed women washing clothes
and keeping a watchful eye on the children in their bright
brief garments. I waved back at a group of kids who were
lined up along the bank waving and calling.

I didn't want to think about crime. Why the hell should I?
I had done what I was supposed to do. *All* I was supposed to
do. Maybe the flowerpot had been an unfortunate accident.
Maybe John didn't have a confederate on board. Even if both
those comfortable assumptions were wrong, there was no
reason to suppose I would recognize any of his henchmen.

I had met more crooks than I would have liked, but one is more than I would have liked. I made a list.

Some of the names on that list were out of the picture—dead, or in jail. The people in Rome who had been happily selling fake jewelry until I so rudely interrupted them were neither of the above. They had pinned the blame for that caper on John and were still leading la dolce vita, which just goes to prove that crime often does pay and that justice frequently doesn't triumph. However, that had been a purely local operation, run by amateurs; it was most unlikely that they had extended their activities abroad.

The group I'd encountered in Sweden were another kettle of fish. They were all professionals and cold-blooded as sharks: big stupid Hans, who wasn't really *bad,* just awfully good at obeying orders; Rudi, who was built like a ferret and had the same mind-set (kill things, kill lots of things); Max, who cut silhouettes as a relaxing hobby after a day of bumping people off; and their boss, Leif, the man who had been slashing at me with a long sharp knife before John removed him forcibly from my vicinity. No doubt about Leif's death; I had identified the body.

I had a couple of Max's silhouettes—souvenirs, presented to me by the artist himself. Mine had been fashioned of the traditional black paper, and very fine likenesses they were. Occasionally Max used red paper—for "a particular collection." He was a soft-spoken, harmless-looking little man, and he'd always been very pleasant to me up to and including the moment when I waved bye-bye to him just before they carted him off to the hoosegow. He had even ... Well, he hadn't actually thanked me for helping to get rid of his boss, not in so many words, but he had implied that Leif's death opened up new and interesting possibilities of advancement for him. "If I can ever do you a favor, Dr. Bliss," he had said ...

I had never met anybody who scared me more than Max. I hoped and believed he was still in prison. But in any case, Max wouldn't have collaborated with John if John had been the only other crook on earth. The antipathy was personal as well as professional. Max had absolutely no sense of humor and John drove him up the wall even when John wasn't trying to, and he often *was* trying to.

The Trojan gold affair ... I could forget about that one. All the villains were dead. Very, very unmistakably dead, including the head villain, who had fallen fifty feet onto a pile of rocks. John had been indirectly responsible for his demise, which had occurred in the course of one of John's nerve-racking, impromptu rescues.

For the first time I found myself wondering how John had felt about killing those two men. Neither had been deliberate, premeditated murders; he could reasonably claim self-defense or maybe justifiable homicide. But he had always insisted he disliked violence, even when it wasn't directed at him. Did he ever have bad dreams?

I shifted uncomfortably and then tore the list into a heap of unreadable scraps.

John's confederate couldn't be anyone I knew, so it must be someone I didn't know. (Brilliant deduction, Vicky.) I turned my attention to the passenger list.

I could now attach faces and personalities to most of the names. There were only thirty names in all—twenty-nine, now that Jen had left. I started to cross her name out and then stopped myself. She might not be on the boat, but she was not out of the picture. Difficult as it was to imagine her as a criminal mastermind, I couldn't dismiss the odd coincidence that had left her on the loose in Cairo.

After considerable thought I eliminated sixteen people. I wasn't credulous or prejudiced enough to think that old age put a person above, or below, suspicion, but a minimal degree of physical agility is one necessary qualification for a master thief—at least I'd have insisted on it if I had been hiring one—and a round dozen of the passengers had to be in their seventies or older. I also eliminated Louisa. Her name was a permanent fixture on the best-seller lists, so she didn't have to turn to crime to make a living, and she was unquestionably the real Louisa Ferncliffe. The picture that adorned all her book jackets had been retouched but it was recognizable.

Sweet and Bright were two of the good guys. So who was left? Blenkiron was too rich and too famous to be a suspect, but I hadn't eliminated his bodyguard or his secretary. I'd have to find out how long they had been in his employ. That was the sort of setup John specialized in, forging impressive credentials to gain access to a person or a place. Suzi? She was a little too good to be true. I was unacquainted with the social elite of Memphis, Tennessee; she could be a ringer. The unsociable German was another possibility. Somehow I'd have to get to know him better.

Mary and John made twenty-one. That left eight people I hadn't spoken with except to exchange names and casual good-mornings. I was inclined to eliminate them too; they were all members of an amateur archaeology organization from Dallas, and they were traveling together. They were also rich and not exactly spring chickens.

How about the staff? Alice and Perry were who they claimed to be. They knew one another and they were known to others, including Blenkiron. Could either be corrupted? In theory, yes. In theory Feisal was also corruptible. Or he could be in league with one of the fundamentalist groups who wanted to rid Egypt of foreign influence. Promoting a scheme that would arouse public indignation, riot, and insurrection was the sort of thing fanatics might do.

I seemed to be long on hypothetical motives and very, very short on actual clues, and all too well supplied with possible suspects. John's ally (or allies) might be one of the housekeeping staff or one of the crew. There was no way I could question them.

The hell with it. I got dressed and went up to the lounge to hear the lecture on birds. It would be a pleasure to hear about pretty, harmless things like birds. Bugs, that was what birds ate. Nothing wrong with killing bugs.

I had forgotten about owls. They eat a lot of things, including cute little mice and an occasional unwary kitten. There was an unexpected bonus, though; the lecturer turned out to be the unsociable German gent and he certainly knew a lot about birds. If he wasn't a genuine enthusiast, he gave a good imitation of one; he talked about the creatures the way another man might talk about his mistress. Long slim legs were mentioned, and delicate flushes of pink. Some birds, he was sorry to report, were rather secretive in their habits. He'd even brought a collection of slides, all two hundred of which he showed us. Oh, well, maybe it wasn't two hundred. It seemed like more.

A passion for birding would account for his presence on board. However, it did occur to me that it's easier to bone up on Egyptian ornithology than Egyptology or—as I knew to my sorrow—Islamic art. A clever man could learn enough about it in a few weeks to convince non-experts that he was one.

When questions were invited, I asked a lot. They were all stupid questions, the only kind I was capable of asking about that subject. He answered glibly and with assurance—if that proved anything. Unfortunately he decided my interest was so intense and my ignorance so abysmal that I deserved special coaching, and I didn't manage to shake him off until after lunch, by which time I knew more about the nesting habits of wigeons than I wanted to know—and I still wasn't sure whether he was on the level or not.

The sound of music struck my ears when I got off the elevator. Someone was playing the piano, and playing quite well. It was a stormy, violent piece of music—Chopin's "Revolutionary Etude."

He had his back to me and the music covered the sound of my footsteps. I couldn't resist. I moved close and spoke.

"How nice. You're playing our song."

His hands came down on the keyboard with a crash and he bent his head. I couldn't see his face, but his ear was bright crimson. After a moment he said under his breath, "Don't do that!"

"Where's your dear little wife?" I inquired.

He looked directly at me. His face was still flushed and his expression was so savage I stepped back. "Drop it, Vicky. Leave me alone."

There were a number of other people in the saloon, including an elderly German couple from Hamburg, Suzi Umphenour, and Sweet and Bright, their heads bent over a chessboard.

Recovering, I said softly, "You don't have to be so rude. Or do you?"

Several heads turned in our direction. John's hands went back to the keyboard, covering his next words with a series of emphatic but rather ragged arpeggios. "Apparently I must. Subtle hints are wasted on you. Excuse me."

He stopped playing and rose. I took the hint. As I walked away I heard a spatter of applause and the Frau from Hamburg called out in English, "Beautiful! Will you be performing for us at the cabaret?"

John answered in German. "Vielen Dank, gnädige Frau, aber nein." In the same language, pitched so I could hear, he added, "I try never to perform in public."

The phone woke me at the unholy hour of 6 A.M. next morning. It was my wake-up call. I grunted an acknowledgment into the phone and reached out a languid hand for the button that would summon my room steward. I was going to miss this kind of service when I got home and was wakened at about the same hour by Clara sitting on my face and Caesar licking any part of me he could reach. Neither of them would bring me coffee.

The response was slower than usual, and when I answered the tactful tap at the door it wasn't Ali. This man was darker-skinned and older and not so pretty.

"Madame wishes breakfast?" he inquired.

"Where's Ali?"

The fellow's eyes shifted. "I am here instead, madame. Mahmud is my name. What is it the lady wishes?"

I didn't pursue the matter. Maybe it was Ali's day off. I had just finished showering when Mahmud came back; slinging on my robe, I told him to take the tray onto the balcony.

The boat rocked gently at its moorings. We had reached El Till, as promised, and at seven-fifteen would disembark to visit the site of Amarna. My room faced west, so all I could see was the river and the opposite bank. It was a beautiful morning, as usual. I wouldn't need a jacket today. Already the breeze felt warm.

When we assembled in the lobby, Feisal began shouting directions. He seemed a little on edge that morning and reminded us twice, rather sharply, that we were to stay with the group and not wander off alone.

"That doesn't apply to me, of course," said Perry, edging up to me. "If there's anything particular you want to see—"

"It sounds to me as if the regular tour covers as much as I want to see."

And that was the truth. It was going to be a long, hot, tiring day. We were to spend the morning visiting part of the ruins of the city and a few of the nobles' tombs. We would then return to the boat for an early lunch, and the weaker vessels would stay on board while the enthusiasts returned for a visit to the royal tomb in its remote wadi and, if time permitted, a few more nobles' tombs.

I had a feeling that by lunchtime I would be tempted to join the weaker vessels. I had read about Amarna, and Perry's lecture the previous evening had brought my memories into sharper focus.

The site is a great empty plain shaped like a half-moon, with the river forming the straight side and the cliffs of the high desert forming the curve. Amarna had been the capital city of the heretic king Akhenaton. He was one of the most interesting and enigmatic of ancient rulers; I had seen dignified scholars turn purple in the face and threaten to punch one another out when they got to arguing about whether Akhenaton was a monotheist or a pacifist or an idealist or a crazy religious fanatic or a disgusting "pre-vert." The artistic conventions of the period intrigued me, but the best examples of the painting and sculpture were elsewhere—in museums and private collections—since the site had been thoroughly vandalized in ancient and modern times.

I was not looking forward to enjoying Perry's company all day, especially when we visited the city ruins. I knew what it would be like, since I've seen a number of archaeological sites: boring mud-brick walls, some as low as foundations, some as high as my head, in a confusing maze. The guide would say things like, "And this was the great reception hall," and we'd all gape at a square of dirt bounded by more of the bare brick walls and then he'd go on for hours pointing out things that had once been there but weren't there now.

Feisal interrupted my thoughts with a sharp, "Vicky, please don't dawdle," and I trotted obediently after him. Perry trotted after me.

"Has he got a hangover or what?" I whispered.

"He doesn't drink," Perry said. "Muslims don't—"

"I was joking. What is bugging him?"

"We're in Middle Egypt now," Perry said soberly. "This is

the area where terrorist attacks have been most frequent. But every precaution has been taken."

They sure had. The first thing I saw when I stepped out onto the gangplank was a truck full of soldiers. "An armed escort?" I exclaimed.

"If anything happened to a member of this group, there'd be hell to pay," Perry said. "Ignore them and be thankful they're here."

I tried to follow his advice. The view was rather wonderful, unless you were of the school that insists on things like trees and flowers and grass and babbling brooks. It was a beauty of line and subtle shadings of color, shadows that deepened from violet to blue-black, rugged rock walls turning from golden pink to paler silver as the sunlight strengthened. I wasn't awfully taken by our means of transport—a tractor pulling an open metal trailer with rows of benches—but I didn't suggest walking. Not with those grim-faced guys in uniform watching me.

The trailer proved to be just as uncomfortable as I had expected. I held on to the edge of the bench as we bumped along over a track that was barely distinguishable from the surrounding desert. I had managed to escape Perry, but when Sweet offered me a seat next to him (and, I hardly need say, Bright), there was no way I could refuse without rudeness. John obligingly shifted over to give me plenty of room. He also gave me a smile that indicated he was well aware I would have preferred another place.

"I haven't seen much of you lately," I said, turning my back on him and favoring Sweet with my most seductive smile.

"We were shy," said Sweet, giggling. "You are so popular, Vicky. With all the handsome young men following you we thought you wouldn't want to associate with two old bores like us."

Bright grinned and nodded. Could he talk? Maybe he had some painfully embarrassing speech defect, a bad stutter or a lisp.

We exchanged a few coy jokes—about their good looks and my irresistible appeal—and then I said, "I haven't seen Larry this morning. Did he stay on board?"

"My dear, he was first off the boat!"

"He has a schoolboy crush on Nefertiti," said John.

I would have ignored this, but Sweet leaned forward, including John in the conversation. "I thought Tetisheri was his dream girl."

"And Nefertari and Ti and all the other beautiful romantic queens of Egypt. He has succumbed to the legends and the portraits, all of which, one may reasonably assume, bore only a distant resemblance to their subjects."

Sweet nodded sympathetically. "It is not difficult to understand why a shy, sensitive man, a lover of beauty and of art, would prefer a dream to reality."

"Or why a man might prefer a woman who has been dead for four thousand years to certain of the living specimens," said John.

"Why, John, how cynical!" Sweet exclaimed.

Mary had heard; her lips tightened and color darkened her cheeks.

The trailer stopped and we climbed out. A hot breeze whipped the ends of my scarf across my face.

We were at the foot of the cliffs. High above I could see the entrances to the tombs. Once visitors had had to scramble up the steep, dangerous slope at the base of the rocks, but the need for tourist dollars and pounds, marks and yen had prompted the building of easier paths and several flights of steps. Straight ahead the trek began with a flight of long shallow stairs. Some of our party had already started up.

Perched on one of the steps was a figure wearing a pair of enormous sunglasses and the biggest, snowiest pith helmet I had ever beheld. He was surrounded by a pride of mewing cats and he was feeding them scraps which he took from the innumerable pockets of his khaki jacket. His comments, addressed to the cats, came to my ears like the tolling of a funeral bell.

"Do not push; it is rude. There is plenty for all. Ach, you are a bad Mutti; let the little ones eat first."

Behind me a voice said hollowly, "I don't deserve this. Admittedly I have not led a wholly exemplary life, but *no one* deserves this. Even Jack the Ripper or Attila the Hun . . ."

My sentiments exactly. I couldn't say so because my vocal

cords were paralyzed. Please, God, I thought, let me be suffering from sunstroke or schizophrenia or something harmless like that.

Schmidt looked up. His bushy white mustache flapped and his cute little pink mouth opened in a broad grin.

"Excuse me," John said, shoving me aside. He set off with that deceptively leisurely stride that could cover ground faster than a run. Intent on me, Schmidt didn't notice him at first; when he did, a look of rapture spread over his face. John reached him before he could bellow out a greeting and bent over him.

"Isn't that adorable?" The speaker was Mary. I had recovered enough to turn my head.

"Adorable," I repeated, in the same doom-ridden voice John had employed.

"That dear old gentleman feeding the cats." Mary slipped her arm in mine. "I should have thought of bringing some scraps; all the animals here are so neglected, so hungry." She let out a fond little laugh. Her eyes were shining as she looked at John, who had seated himself on the step next to Schmidt. John was doing the talking; Schmidt listened, openmouthed.

"John is so tenderhearted," Mary went on. "He loves cats."

That was news to me. John certainly didn't love Clara, who had disliked him on sight. She was an astute judge of character.

The cute little pussycats had given him an excuse to have a private and vital conversation with Schmidt, though. By the time we reached my boss, John had gone on ahead and Schmidt had finished serving breakfast to the pride. He heaved himself to his feet and let out the shriek the sight of John had aborted.

"Vicky! Grüss Gott, good morning, hello! I am so glad to see you!"

"What are you doing here, Schmidt?" I inquired. My voice was very calm.

"It was Fate, no less. I will tell you all about it later." Schmidt glanced at Mary and then back at me. His grin faded and he blinked rapidly. John must have told him. He'd have had to, in order to forestall any embarrassing references to former acquaintanceships. I wished to God I knew what other confidences had passed between the two.

I introduced Mary. Schmidt didn't say much; he was very
gallant with her, though, studying her pretty face intently.
They were almost the same height.

She excused herself, saying that her husband was waiting
for her. He hadn't waited; he was already some distance ahead.
She hurried after him.

"My poor dear Vicky," Schmidt said gently. He took off
his sunglasses and wiped his eyes. "Do not allow evil to enter
your heart, my child."

"What the hell are you talking about, Schmidt?"

"You are not in despair?" Schmidt peered up into my face
from under the brim of his hat. "Well. Perhaps you are not.
A woman with so many lovers as you—"

"Shut up, Schmidt," I said.

Schmidt paid no attention; he'd heard me say that so often,
the words just washed past his ears. "And it is not to be
expected that all your lovers would remain faithful when you
do nothing to encourage them and are, in fact, often very rude
to them. Nein, nein, do not deny it, I have seen it myself. I
only hope that Sir John did not marry this poor child on the
rebound, for that would not be fair to her. She seems a
charming young lady."

"Schmidt . . ." He waited expectantly; but I couldn't think
what to say. It was probably safer to say nothing at all until
I had had a chance to find out what pack of lies John had
told Schmidt. So I finished lamely, "I don't want to talk about
it."

"This is not, perhaps, the best place for an intimate conversation," Schmidt agreed. Feisal was bearing down—or up—
on us, shepherding the last and slowest of the group—a very
elderly English lady whose physical strength didn't equal her
zest for living.

Gallant as always, Schmidt whipped off his pith helmet
and bowed from the approximate region of the waist. That
part of him doesn't bend easily. I introduced them and Feisal
nodded. "Yes, Herr Doktor Schmidt; we were told you would
be joining us here. Willkommen."

"But how well you speak German," Schmidt exclaimed.
"You are our guide, my friend? Excellent! I have many questions. You can tell me—"

"It would be better, Dr. Schmidt, if you waited until we reach the tombs. The others are already far ahead."

"My fault, I'm afraid," Mrs. Blessington (she had told me to call her Anna, but I couldn't manage it yet) said cheerfully. "You young things are most kind to put up with my infirmities."

Her smile included Schmidt, who puffed up to twice normal size and exclaimed, "I will carry you! Yes, yes, it will be a pleasure, an excuse to hold a beautiful woman in my arms!"

He'd have tried it, too. I looked meaningfully at Feisal, who said quickly, "No, no, Herr Schmidt, that is not fair; I saw her first. Anna, if you will allow me—?"

Laughing, she allowed him. She couldn't have weighed much, she was all bones and skin and gumption; even so, the ease with which Feisal mounted the stairs was an impressive demonstration of muscle. Schmidt trotted alongside, offering to take over whenever Feisal tired. They seemed to be having a very good time, so I said, "I'll just run on ahead," and did so.

It was a long climb, up stairs and along winding paths, and the interval gave me time to think. The only positive aspect of the disaster of Schmidt was that in this at least John and I were on the same side. He didn't want Schmidt involved any more than I did.

On an earlier occasion John had somehow managed to convince Schmidt that he was an "undercover agent" of some variety, even though Schmidt was well aware that John had been trying to pull off an illegal deal involving antique jewelry when I first encountered him. John and Schmidt were perfectly matched: one the world's most accomplished teller of tall tales, the other happy to believe any lie so long as it was "romantic."

John wouldn't dare tell Schmidt he was on another "secret mission" this time. But Schmidt wasn't stupid, even if he was romantic. How could I, or John, possibly explain how we happened to turn up on the same cruise?

Coincidences happen. This was a pretty hard coincidence to swallow, but John might have been desperate enough to insist on it. He had only had about ten seconds to come up with a story that would convince Schmidt we weren't engaged

in some dangerous, exciting bit of undercover work, in which
Schmidt would of course want to participate.

Then another explanation occurred to me and a cold chill
froze the sweat on my heated body. I had read a mystery
novel once—one of Agatha Christie's, I think—in which the
abandoned fiancée, intent on revenge, follows her faithless
lover and his new bride on their honeymoon—a Nile cruise,
by another of those strange coincidences. Schmidt had
undoubtedly read that book or seen the film, he loved thrillers.
The chilly sweat congealed as I remembered what Schmidt
had said. Something about letting evil enter my heart?

John must know that story too. If he had dared imply to
Schmidt that I had pursued him and Mary out of jealousy I
would not only kill him, I would dismember him and strew
pieces of his admirable anatomy all over the boat. Mary could
try putting him back together, like Isis with Osiris.

Schmidt would fall for it, too. If he couldn't be James
Bond, he would settle for Hercule Poirot. Maybe . . .

The fact that for a few seconds I actually considered encouraging Schmidt to believe that fantasy as the lesser of two
evils should be sufficient indication of how dangerous the
little imp was.

"There you are."

I glared wildly at the tall blond individual who had taken
my arm. It was Perry. Peering into my face, he went on, "You
look a bit done up, Vicky. The climate can be difficult if you
aren't used to it."

I looked around. I had reached the top of the path where
a ledge stretched along the cliff face. The tombs opened onto it.
Several of our group were standing around fanning themselves
with their hats. From a nearby tomb, whose metal gate stood
open, came the sound of a voice lecturing. One of the local
guides, I assumed.

"You don't want to join the tourist types," Perry said condescendingly. "Let me give you a private, personal tour."

The robed and turbaned custodian of the keys flapped
toward us and unlocked another gate. I let Perry lead me
inside. There is some excuse for me, I think, if I wondered
whether he had an ulterior motive for wanting to get me alone.

If he did, he had no opportunity to act upon it. Schmidt

was hot on my trail. I started to introduce them, but Schmidt interrupted me. "I know this gentleman. Have I not told you, Vicky, that I never forget a face? It was at a symposium on Egyptian art, five years ago, in Rome. He spoke on Amarna portraiture. Grüss Gott, Dr. Foggington-Smythe. You may remember me—Schmidt is my name—"

"I remember you very well, Herr Direktor," Perry said coldly. "You took up the entire question period disagreeing with every point I had made."

Schmidt chuckled. "Yes, it was a very friendly professional discussion. I look forward to continuing it."

He did continue it. Before long Perry excused himself and fled. I may have been prejudiced, but I enjoyed Schmidt's commentary a lot more than I had Perry's. For one thing, Schmidt isn't afraid of expressing his emotional reactions. Some of the details—a group of blind musicians, a pair of vibrant, prancing horses—moved him so much he actually stopped talking, which was more than Perry had done.

After we had seen the tombs we all gathered around Feisal and one of his flunkies for a spot of refreshment. Drinking lots of liquids was a necessity in that climate; dehydration had felled a number of ignorant tourists. As I had come to expect from Galactic Tours, we were offered a variety of beverages as well as water, plus cookies and biscuits.

Schmidt was so happy. Friends, antiquities, and now food. He had been crooning to himself, and after we had collected our lemonade and cookies he burst into song. It is easier to let Schmidt sing than try to talk him out of singing, so I gritted my teeth and let him go on. " 'Frankie und Johnny waren Liebende,' " he bellowed. " 'Mein Gott, wie verstanden sie sich auf die Liebe!' "

Several of the more nervous passengers jumped spasmodically, and John, standing nearby, actually reeled back a few steps. Schmidt took his pained stare for fascinated interest. "It is old American Volk musik," he explained. "The gnädige Frau from Hamburg has told me what a fine musician you are, Sssss . . . Herr Tregarth; no doubt you are familiar with that song?"

John shook his head. For once, he appeared to be incapable of speech.

"Oh, but it is very well known. In English it goes, 'Frankie und Johnny were lovers, Oh, lordie—' "

"Ah, yes." John blinked.

"It is a most interessante variety of music," Schmidt explained. "Songs of the country and of the Wild West, blues and bluegrass . . . These are not the same, you understand; they have different roots."

"Bluegrass," John repeated blankly.

"Many are deeply and touchingly full of religion. Have you heard the one about the crash on the highway, when whiskey and blood mixed together?"

John edged closer. I had seen the same look on the face of a cat when a small energetic child cornered it—horrified disbelief mingled with unwilling curiosity. "Fascinating. Tell me more, Herr Schmidt."

I went quickly away. Not quickly enough, alas, to miss the next verse.

Eventually we retraced our steps to the waiting trailer, which was to take us to the next stop, the ruins of the Northern City. Schmidt caught up with me there, and Perry, who had been edging toward me, veered away. Feisal, counting heads, called to the stragglers to hurry up and urged the rest of us to take our places.

Schmidt gave me a hand up, which I accepted, and then turned to Mary. She was alone for once, and her anxious gaze was fixed on the upward path.

"So, he is slow?" Schmidt said pleasantly. "All the better for me, you will allow me to assist you into the seat."

"I don't see him." She shielded her eyes with her hand, ignoring the one Schmidt had offered.

Feisal turned. "He decided to walk. It isn't far, he'll be there soon after us. Get in, please, we only have forty-five minutes at the site."

Forty-five minutes was long enough for me, and even Schmidt wandered off after a while. I caught sight of him talking to a man who appeared to be an archaeologist—he was dressed sloppily enough—working in one of the areas blocked off to tourists. I didn't see John—not that I was looking for him—until we were almost ready to leave. Mary's face lit up at the sight of him, and she hurried to take his arm.

"Darling, I was worried about you. Where have you been?"

"Having a look round," John said vaguely. He caught my eye and added, "And avoiding certain people."

The hints were becoming less subtle. I took this one too.

In the space of a few hours Schmidt had managed to become best friends with most of the others. He was particularly taken with Suzi, whom he described, as I might have expected, as "a fine figure of a woman!" Safely surrounded by listening ears, I managed to stick to generalities during the ride back to the boat.

"Why didn't you tell me you were joining the tour, Schmidt?" I asked.

"I wanted to surprise you." Schmidt beamed at me.

"You succeeded."

"I wanted all along to come. I told you that."

"At some length."

"But duty came first." Schmidt was talking at the top of his lungs, inviting the interest and admiration of his newfound friends. "So to Amsterdam I went. But it was a fiasco, Vicky, the gentleman could not make up his mind, he kept putting me off, and anyhow he did not have anything of great interest. So finally I said, 'Vielen Dank, auf Wiedersehen,' and I put a call to the travel bureau and they said there had been a cancellation. I arrived last night in Minya, by the train, and hired a boat to carry me across the river first thing this morning, because I wanted to be here waiting for you. They were to bring my luggage to the boat later."

He turned to answer a question from Alice—whom, of course, he had met at some conference somewhere, some-time—and left me a prey to painful reflections. Apparently the travel bureau hadn't mentioned—why should they, after all?—that a space had been made available by the illness of one of the passengers. John had said Jen would be joining us at Luxor. Did this mean she wasn't going to, or had there been an earlier defection, another cancellation? I wanted, rather badly, to find out.

I didn't have the opportunity until after lunch. There was

barely time for a much-needed shower and change of clothing before the gong rang, and when I reached the dining room Schmidt was already seated, waving and yelling at me to join him—and Louisa. I might have known he'd latch on to her.

For once she didn't monopolize the conversation. She didn't have to, Schmidt talked of nothing but her wonderful books and how thrilled he was to meet the author he had admired for so long.

I think it was Mark Twain who outlined the three steps to a writer's heart: 1) tell him you have read one of his books; 2) tell him you have read all of his books; 3) ask him to let you read the manuscript of his forthcoming book. Schmidt did all three, and added the culminating compliment which Twain didn't mention: 4) know the names of all the characters in all the books and remember every detail of the plots.

Having noticed Louisa's shape, I was not surprised to see her stow away almost as much food as Schmidt did. Swollen with calories and pleased conceit, her face was not a pretty sight.

"Vicky is also a writer of romances," Schmidt said.

"Oh?" Louisa's smile turned sour. If I hadn't taken such a dislike to her I would have sympathized; she probably thought I was going to ask her to read my manuscript, give me the name of her agent, or recommend my book to her publisher. I was tempted to do all three, in order to annoy her, but dignity prevailed.

"I just do it for fun," I said modestly. "My heroine's adventures are too improbable for publication."

Rosanna's adventures weren't much more improbable than those of most romance heroines, including Louisa's, but they had got a little out of hand in recent years. It was Schmidt's fault; he egged me on. Nothing was too improbable for him so long as there were lots of sword fights and ripped bodices and heaving breasts.

Louisa dropped the subject of my manuscript with a thud and started to tell Schmidt the plot of her forthcoming book. She hadn't written it yet, so she didn't have a manuscript (see Twain, above, number three).

I excused myself, leaving Schmidt listening with prurient fascination to Louisa's description of her heroine's struggles with the lustful priest of Amon. I had some hope of waylaying John before the afternoon tour left. Instead I was waylaid, by Mr. Hamid the purser. I thought he was looking rather grave, and when he drew me aside I expected . . . well, I don't know what I expected, but it certainly wasn't what I heard.

"You remember young Ali, your room steward, Dr. Bliss?"

"Of course I remember him. He wasn't on duty this morning . . . Oh, good heavens. Don't tell me he's jumped ship, or whatever you call it?"

"That was what we believed, when he did not report for duty this morning. It would not have surprised me; if he was responsible for the accident of the flowerpot, his guilty conscience and fear of punishment might have driven him into flight."

That would have been bad enough, but I could tell by Hamid's frown that it was even worse. I didn't say anything. I suppose I had a premonition of what was coming.

"He fell, or jumped, overboard, sometime during the night," Hamid said slowly. "The body was found a few hours ago."

# Chapter Five

*i*

I must have looked as sick as I felt. Hamid took my arm and led me to a chair.

"You must not blame yourself, Dr. Bliss."

"I don't." One of my less convincing lies, that one. It didn't even convince me.

"It was an unfortunate accident," Hamid said gently. "He must have tried to swim to shore and been seized by a cramp or something of the sort."

The others were gathering for the afternoon tour. John was among them—with Mary, as usual, by his side.

"Tell them to wait for me," I said, rising. "I won't be long."

All I could see as I ran up the stairs was that kid's face—wet with tears as he protested his innocence, wreathed in smiles as he assured me of his appreciation for my kindness. Kindness! It couldn't have been an accident. Either he had been bribed to drop the flowerpot and later repented, or he had seen the person responsible. They had disposed of him as coolly and callously as if he had been a mosquito.

The note I scribbled wasn't very coherent, but I was pretty

sure it would get the point across. I put it in the safe and ran back to the lobby.

The others were heading down the gangplank when I got there, but Feisal had waited for me.

"Hamid said he had told you." His warm dark eyes searched my face.

"Yes."

"He should not have. It has distressed you."

"Of course it has! What kind of monster do you think I am?"

"I don't think you are a monster. That is why I did not want Hamid to tell you." He put a supportive arm around my shoulders. I leaned against him for a moment, and his grip tightened as a violent tremor ran through me. He didn't know I was shaking with rage, not distress.

"There is no need to mention this unhappy business to the other passengers," Feisal said.

I nodded. "I'm all right, Feisal. Let's go."

"Herr Schmidt is not yet here. He indicated his wish to accompany us."

A wild hope dawned in my heart. "We can't wait indefinitely. He's probably fallen asleep."

No such luck. Beaming all over his round pink face, burbling apologies, he emerged from the elevator, complete with pith helmet, sunglasses, bag, and a variety of objects that dangled from straps crisscrossing his torso. I identified a camera, a pair of binoculars, and a canteen among other, more arcane, impedimenta.

Fewer than half the passengers had taken advantage of the opportunity to visit the royal tomb. I was relieved to see that dear old Anna had declined; in fact, only the die-hards, all of them relatively young and vigorous, were there. After considering the other options—Sweet and Bright, John and Mary, Louisa, swathed in veils and trying to look mysterious, the German couple from Hamburg, Alice and Perry—Schmidt seated himself next to Larry Blenkiron and greeted him like an old friend, which, as it turned out, he was—or at least an old acquaintance, which is the same thing by Schmidt's standards. I wondered if there was anybody in the world of art and archaeology Schmidt didn't know. Ed Whitbread politely moved over so I could sit on Larry's other side. It was a touching demonstration of confidence, I thought—in my harmlessness, or in his ability to stop me if I attempted to assassinate his boss. I didn't doubt he could.

We went rattling off across the empty plain, followed by the armed escort. The sun high overhead bleached all the color from the sand; the only contrast was the brilliant blue of the sky above. The breeze of our movement felt like the blast from an oven.

Schmidt started reminiscing about the last time he and Larry had met, at a conference on preservation and restoration. From the stained glass of medieval cathedrals to the stones of the Colosseum, scarcely a monument in the world has escaped damage from fire and flood, pollution and traffic, and the mere presence of human beings. Larry, of course, was primarily interested in Egyptian monuments and he became more animated than I had ever seen him, his voice deepening with distress as he described the devastation of the tombs.

"The plaster, and the paintings on it, are literally falling off the walls. There has been more damage done in the last twenty years than in the preceding four thousand."

"But it is a wonderful thing you have done," Schmidt exclaimed. "To restore the tomb paintings of Tetisheri—"

"It's only one out of many."

"There is also Nefertari's tomb."

"The Getty people have done a splendid job with Nefertari," Larry agreed. "But if the tomb is reopened, the same thing will happen again."

"Then you support the idea of constructing reproductions?" Schmidt asked. "For the tourists to visit, while the original tombs are open only to scholars?"

"Yes." Larry caught my eye and smiled deprecatingly. "It does smack of elitism, doesn't it? Don't admit anyone— except me!" He shifted uncomfortably; the seats were hard. "It's too late for the Amarna tombs," he went on regretfully. "There's very little left. I admit the Egyptian government needs tourist dollars, but I regret what they've done here to make it easier for visitors to reach the royal tomb. Until they made this road through the wadi, it was a long, hard, three-mile walk."

"I hear that the Japanese are talking of building lifts to the nobles' tombs," Schmidt said.

They sighed in unison.

We had crossed the plain and entered a canyon or wadi that cut through the enclosing cliffs. They gave little shade; the sun was still high and the center of the road baked in the bright light. Seeing me swallow, Schmidt unscrewed his canteen and offered it to me. Gratefully I accepted it. I took a drink and gagged.

"Beer!"

"Aber natürlich," said Schmidt, retrieving the canteen. "Herr Blenkiron?"

Larry refused the offer. So did Ed.

There was an ice chest on the trailer. When it stopped we had drinks all around before starting on the last part of the trip. It was an easy walk along a narrower side wadi up to the entrance to the tomb. A short flight of steep steps led down. I could see a glow of light from the passage beyond, but it wasn't exactly dazzling.

Feisal gathered us around him and began lecturing. Schmidt wasn't looking at Feisal. He was looking at me. He had taken off his sunglasses preparatory to descending into the dimly lighted passageway, and his beady little eyes were worried.

Schmidt was one of the few people in the world who knew about the time I had been buried alive under a castle in Bavaria. That may sound melodramatic, but it's the literal truth; the tunnel had been blocked by an earthfall and I had to dig my way out. I had no tools, only my bare hands, no light except a few matches, and, toward the end, not much in the way of oxygen. I have avoided dark, confined underground places since. Even Schmidt didn't know that I still dream about it from time to time.

John knew. He knew because I had had the dream once when he was with me. He had held me while I choked and gurgled and made a damned fool of myself, clinging to him and pleading incoherently for light and for air. After I calmed down he had insisted I tell him the whole story. It would help exorcise the demons, he had said . . .

He was staring at me too. Over Mary's head his eyes, narrowed and unblinking, met mine. I looked away.

The others started down the stairs and Schmidt edged closer to me. "Vicky, perhaps you should not do this."

He was under the impression that he was whispering. Several heads turned, and Feisal came back to me. "Is there a problem, Vicky?"

"No problem," I said curtly.

Nor was there, not really. What bothered me was not claustrophobia in the classic sense: abnormal fear of narrow, confined spaces. As long as there was light and there were other people around, I was okay.

At least that's what I told myself.

It wasn't as bad as I had feared. There were lights at frequent intervals and modern stairs or ramps over the rougher parts of the ancient passageways. And people. Schmidt stuck close, bless his thoughtful little heart.

Egyptian tomb architecture has never been one of my passions in life. Sweet set out to prove it was one of his; he latched on to Perry, despite the latter's attempts to get away so he could come and tell me all about everything, and began babbling about changes in axis and angles of descent and comparisons with earlier and later types. He'd certainly done his homework. Alice and Schmidt were arguing about Minoan influences on Amarna art. Feisal's voice echoed weirdly as he mentioned points of interest.

There weren't many. The walls of the sloping passage were rough and unadorned. It had an eerie impressiveness, though, and by the time we reached the burial chamber everyone except Feisal had fallen silent.

There wasn't much to see there either, only a few scratches on the rough walls; but when Feisal pointed them out and described the scenes of which they were the scanty remainder, he managed to suggest something of the beauty that had once been there: depictions of the king and queen offering to the sole god they had worshiped, the sun disk with rays ending in small, caressing human hands; mourners, their garments rent and their hands raised in ceremonial grieving. Even with his eloquence I couldn't make out the details of the figure on the funeral bier. Feisal claimed these details proved it was a female figure.

"But I thought this was the king's tomb," the Frau from Hamburg said.

"We don't know the identity of the woman on the bier," Feisal answered. "It has been suggested she was—"

"Nefertiti!" Louisa swooped down on him, waving her arms. Her veils billowed like bat wings. "Yes, I feel it. I feel her presence."

She flopped down onto the floor and sat cross-legged, crooning to herself.

The others studied her in mingled disgust and embarrassment. Sweet muttered something derogatory about New Age mystics and Blenkiron's face was rigid with distaste.

"Odd how so many people go soggy over Nefertiti," murmured a satirical voice. Hands in his pockets, hair shining in the light of the bulb overhead, John glanced at me and smiled.

Feisal was the only other member of the party who was more amused than embarrassed. He had probably run into this sort of thing before. "It is not Nefertiti. She appears elsewhere in the same scene. One authority has suggested that this was her tomb, not that of her husband, but that viewpoint is not generally accepted. The unfinished suite of rooms leading off the downward passage may have been intended for her burial. We will visit them later, but first you will want to see the best preserved portion of the tomb, which was designed for one of the royal princesses."

Ignoring Louisa, he led us out the way we had come.

The others crowded after him. They weren't any more comfortable in that room than I had been, and I'm not just talking about the temperature and the close air. It was good sized—about thirty feet square, according to Feisal, and the ceiling didn't brush the top of my head. But somehow I felt as if it did, and the battered stone pillars looked as if they might collapse at any moment.

Whistling softly and irreverently, John stood studying the wall and Mary sidled up to me. "Are you as anxious to leave this place as I am?" she whispered.

"I don't know. How anxious are you?" I wiped the perspiration off my forehead.

"I suppose it's partly psychological," Mary murmured. "The reminders of death and decay and darkness . . ."

That was one of the words I didn't need to hear right then. Without replying I headed for the door.

I was determined to stick it out, though. The chambers we had visited in the mastaba tombs at Sakkara were above ground; the nobles' tombs at Amarna were cut into the cliff, but we hadn't gone down under, into the burial chambers, and I had always been able to see daylight in the distance. This was the most difficult place I'd encountered yet, and I felt I was going about conquering my phobia in a very sensible way. The hell with jumping back onto the horse; I'd rather start with a very small pony or a Saint Bernard, and work my way up.

One of Akhenaton's daughters had died young and had been buried in her father's tomb, in a suite of rooms located off the main descending corridor. The scene I had found particularly moving, that of the little body lying stiff on the funeral bed, with the grieving parents bending over it, could hardly be made out. Some vandal had tried to hack out a portion of the relief; the deep jagged incision had destroyed the upper part of the princess's body and other details.

"That's an example of why I dread increased accessibility," said Larry, who was standing next to me. "These reliefs were virtually intact until the thirties."

"But you cannot blame the poor devils of villagers," said Schmidt, the unreconstructed socialist, on my other side. "It is the European and American collectors who pay large prices for illegal antiquities who are responsible. I do not mean you, of course," he added quickly.

Larry laughed. "That's why my collection isn't very impressive. The best objects were acquired by museums and less scrupulous collectors before I got interested. Anyhow, I'm more concerned about preservation than collecting."

When we left the princess's rooms I noticed that John again hung back while Mary followed me. Had there been a lovers' tiff? I waited for her and gave her a friendly smile. I had, of course, no ulterior motive.

"Almost through," I said encouragingly.

"Oh, I don't mind." Her voice wavered a little, though. "It's been very interesting."

We started up the ramp. It seemed a lot steeper than it had when we descended. The last suite of rooms, the ones Feisal had said might have been meant for the queen's burial, was located about halfway up the incline. Indicating the entrance where the others were waiting, I asked, "Are you going to skip the final treat, or shall we participate?"

Mary glanced behind her. John was some distance away, taking his time. Couldn't the poor little wimp come to any decision without consulting him? What had he been doing down there alone? Perhaps there *had* been a quarrel and he was sulking, trying to make Mary feel guilty about hurting his sensitive feelings.

"I meant to ask you before," I said casually. "About Jen. How is she?"

"Much better. In fact—"

She stopped with a gulp. All of a sudden there he was, behind her, looming. "You startled me, darling!" she exclaimed.

"In fact," John said, "she's recovered enough to return home."

"You mean she's left Egypt?" I stared at him.

"This morning. She doesn't trust Egyptian doctors or hospitals."

"Then she won't be rejoining the tour?"

"No, she won't."

I looked from his self-satisfied smile to Mary's downcast face. Was that what the quarrel had been about?

"You sound pleased," I said.

"Oh, I am. She was a bloody nuisance," John said callously. "Now hurry along, girls. One would suppose, from the way you're dawdling, that you are enjoying this."

By the time we had finished examining a few more rough unfinished rock-cut rooms and listened to Feisal describe their possible function, everyone, even Louisa, was ready to call it a day. "I do not feel her presence," she intoned. "The beautiful one was never interred here."

"She's probably right about that," muttered Larry. "But for

the wrong reasons. Since when did she become an expert on Nefertiti?"

"I think she's making her the heroine of her new book," I said.

"Then why was she carrying on about missing Meydum?" Larry demanded. "That pyramid predates Nefertiti by over a thousand years."

"Historical novelists don't worry about little details like that," I explained, with certain guilty memories of my own heroine's activities. Having Rosanna hide in a broom closet to elude Genghis Khan had not been kosher, but it had entertained Schmidt, which was my primary purpose for continuing the saga.

Hot, thirsty, and coated with dust, we made a beeline for the ice chest and stood swilling down cold drinks. The late-afternoon heat was intense, but it felt refreshing after the confined airlessness of the tomb. Even in the shade I seemed to feel my skin drying and shrinking over my bones. It was the climate of Egypt, not the well-meaning but often destructive process of burial, that produced such excellent mummies.

Blenkiron wanted to see a few more tombs on the way back to the boat, but he gave in with smiling good grace when the others emphatically outvoted him. Mary let out a muted wail when he suggested stopping at the southern tombs. Schmidt, ever gallant, hurried to her and offered her his arm.

He'd held up well, but I was worried about him. The open-heart surgery he had undergone a few years earlier had, he claimed, made a new man of him. The new man looked to me just as unhealthy as the old one. His face was flushed with heat and exercise, but his smile was as broad and his mustache as defiant as ever. He was obviously having a wonderful time.

I let them and the others go on ahead. I hadn't had a chance to talk with John; huddling with him in an otherwise unoccupied tomb chamber might have inspired rude speculation. Maybe he was just as anxious for a private conversation. Maybe that was why he appeared to be avoiding Mary.

That theory was strengthened when he fell in step with me and said easily and audibly, "Enjoying yourself, Dr. Bliss?"

"Don't let's be so formal," I said, stretching my mouth into a tight smile.

"I'm trying, but my ingrained awe of academic titles makes it difficult." His voice kept dropping in pitch. "I don't believe I can possibly address Professor Schmidt as Anton."

"Try Poopsie," I suggested, losing it for a second.

The corners of his mouth compressed, holding back laughter—or a rude comment. The reference, to a particularly tense moment in one of our earlier encounters, might have inspired either.

I went on, in a hoarse whisper, "What did you tell him?"

"Why don't you ask him?"

"I intend to. But I want to hear your version. Quit stalling, the others are waiting for us."

I stumbled artistically, stopped, and bent over to examine my foot.

"Coincidence," John said, taking me by the arm as if to steady me. The flow of blood to my hand stopped dead.

"He'll never buy that."

"He'll have to, won't he?"

"Not Schmidt."

"I cannot be held accountable for Schmidt's unholy imagination. If you and I agree, what can he—" He broke off as Feisal and Larry hurried toward us. "Is it sprained?" he inquired, adding doubtfully, "Perhaps Feisal could—er—carry you."

The implication being that he couldn't, and that even Feisal might have some difficulty lifting my enormous body. I straightened. "I just turned it. It's fine."

My assignation with Schmidt was more easily arranged. We debated it at the top of our lungs as the trailer bounced noisily over the rough track. Schmidt wanted to meet in the lounge so we could share Happy Hour with all his newfound friends. That was reassuring; it suggested he had accepted the coincidence story and wasn't about to interrogate me about my real reasons for being on board. However, I figured I had better deliver a brief lecture on tact and discretion before I turned him loose on the world, and as I pointed out, he hadn't had time to unpack yet. We agreed that I would come to his room after I had freshened up.

After I had locked and bolted my door I went, not to the bathroom, but to the safe. The note was still there.

I stamped my foot and swore. That didn't accomplish anything, so I headed for the shower. Maybe my mysterious contact hadn't had a chance to retrieve the message as yet. Still, it was not an auspicious omen and the cool water sloshing over my heated body didn't settle the doubts that sloshed around in my heated brain. I was getting dressed when I heard the knock at the door.

Throwing on a robe, I hurried to answer it. "Oh," I said. "Hi."

Alice was certainly a fast-change artist. She was wearing a flowered print dress and white low-heeled sandals. "I thought you might need something for that ankle," she explained. "I've found this liniment very effective."

The bottle she offered me didn't look like liniment. Her hand covered the label.

"That's very kind of you," I said slowly. "Come in."

When I turned, after closing the door, she had settled herself in a chair, ankles crossed. The bottle, on the table beside her, proclaimed that its contents were hydrogen peroxide.

"You?" I squeaked unoriginally.

"I admit I don't look the part," Alice said coolly.

"How did you know I wanted to see you? You didn't get my note."

Her brow furrowed. "Which note?"

I produced it. "You were upset, weren't you," she murmured, after reading the hurried message.

"Of course I was. That poor innocent kid—"

"Come now, you aren't thinking clearly. Why do you suppose that note wasn't collected earlier?"

"My God." I dropped heavily onto the bed. "You mean Ali was—"

"An agent of the Egyptian security service." Alice's expression darkened. "Which I am not. I agreed to help out with this particular job because I care deeply about the protection of antiquities and because an increase in anti-foreign feeling here could affect my work and that of others. He was the man assigned to look after you; I was only supposed to pass on messages."

The news relieved one nightmare. Ali was just as young and just as dead, but at least he had been a professional, fully aware of the risks his job entailed.

"I didn't learn of his death until this afternoon," Alice went on. "I realized then that I had to talk to you, even though I had been told never, under any circumstances, to contact you directly. These people are stupidly obsessed with security, in my opinion, but to do them justice they may have been concerned with my safety as well as yours. I—"

"Holy shit, Alice!" I stared at her in horror. "I didn't think of that. And I should have. You'd better go. And stay far, far away from me in the future."

"Calm yourself, honey; I am not volunteering to take over Ali's job. I'm exactly what I seem to be—an aging, overweight archaeologist who's never fired a gun or taken a karate lesson. If you had to depend on me to protect you, you'd be a sitting duck. But we'd better discuss this situation and decide what to do about it." She reached into her shirt pocket. "Do you mind if I smoke?"

"No, go right ahead." I looked around for an ashtray. Alice laughed.

"That's a slip, Vicky. I don't know why you're pretending to be a smoker, but you'd better learn how to do it right. You haven't used the ashtray and you don't even inhale."

"It was not one of my brighter ideas," I admitted. "So what are we going to do?"

"Wait, I suppose." Alice frowned thoughtfully at her lighter. "They will have learned of Ali's death by now and will, one assumes, arrange for a replacement. The change of schedule worries me, though. My job was to pass on the information Ali gave me when I went ashore, but we've already skipped two of the scheduled stops and we'll miss a third tomorrow; I won't be able to communicate again until we get to Abydos."

"You have no other means of reaching the people in charge? Damn, that's stupid! What if there were an emergency?"

"There has been an emergency," Alice said wryly. "Two, in fact; the lines of communication have been cut in both directions. However, I've suspected all along that I was only a minor cog in the machinery—a backup, if you will, for the transmission of information. There must be at least one other agent on board—another professional, not a willing but incompetent amateur like me."

Wishful thinking? I hoped not. Burckhardt had used the plural when he promised me protection. "Who?" I asked.

"If I knew I wouldn't be talking to you." Alice rubbed her forehead, as if it ached. It probably did. She went on, "I gather from the spy thrillers I've read that this is standard procedure. Minimal contacts, maximum anonymity."

I'd read a few of the damned things myself. Ali had known me and Alice. If they had questioned him before they killed him . . . There wouldn't necessarily be any marks on his body. Up-to-date torturers have all kinds of neat scientific devices at their disposal, including drugs.

"It couldn't be Anton, could it?"

Her words made it as far as my ears but my brain refused to acknowledge them. "What?" I gasped.

"They'll have to replace Ali," Alice said. "Anton turned up this morning, out of the blue—"

"No! Are you crazy, or what? Schmidt isn't . . ." I stopped to catch my breath. "The timing is too tight, Alice. They couldn't have learned of Ali's death until early this morning. Schmidt was already in Minya."

"That's true." She stubbed out her cigarette and stood up. "No sense speculating, I guess. The situation won't become critical until we get back to Cairo, and surely we'll be contacted long before then—probably in Luxor. My advice would be to sit tight, play it cool, and be careful."

It was excellent advice and I had every intention of following it—if I was allowed to.

After she had left I stood stock-still staring at the closed door. My heart was pounding as if I'd run a mile. Her suggestion that Schmidt might be Ali's replacement was so far out that only a lunatic could believe it. Alice wasn't a lunatic, though. Did she know something about Schmidt I didn't know? Did other people know that same something?

Someone groaned. It had to be me; I was the only one there. "Impossible," I informed myself. All other considerations aside, such as the possibility that I was prejudiced, condescending, and easily manipulated by a cute little, shrewd

little actor, Schmidt couldn't have gotten from Munich to
Minya in three hours. I prayed with all my heart that the bad
guys were as familiar with plane schedules as I was. I didn't
want them to think, as Alice had done, that Schmidt might
be Ali's replacement.

The telephone rang. Schmidt, of course. The sound of that
fat, jolly, Father Christmas voice snapped me back into the
real world. "Impossible," I said.

"Was ist's?" said Schmidt.

"I'm on my way, Schmidt."

To judge by the image I saw in a mirror later on I must
have selected clothes that were more or less coordinated, but
I don't know how I did it; I was thinking of other things.

The opposition seemed to be a lot more efficient than our
group. They had fingered Ali, which was more than I had,
and disposed of him without scruple or delay. Why now? I
wondered. Just general tidiness, or had he been about to blow
the whistle on one or all of them? He'd have to have solid
evidence to do that—and they must have known he had it or
they wouldn't have taken the risk of committing murder at
this stage.

Despite the record he'd managed to build up while hobnob-
bing with me, John wasn't a killer. Admittedly that assessment
depended to some extent on his own statements, which were
far from reliable in other areas, but I was inclined to believe
him. He could reasonably claim self-defense in both the examples to which I had been an eyewitness.

Or defense of me.

The phone distracted me from that uncomfortable train of
thought. I didn't bother answering, since I assumed it was
Schmidt; I picked up my bag and headed out.

All prejudice aside, I couldn't visualize John knocking Ali
unconscious and holding his head underwater till he drowned.
That wasn't John's style. Apparently he had got himself mixed
up with a very nasty crowd. He had a bad habit of doing that.

Schmidt's room was on the top deck, the sundeck, on the
same side of the boat as mine. There were only four suites
on that level—the choicest of all, I assumed, since Blenkiron
had two of them.

Schmidt flung the door open before I could knock, and enveloped me in a huge hug. "At last! I was about to go in search of you. You are late."

"No, I'm not. We didn't settle on a time."

His room was a tad bigger and fancier than mine. A fixed screen separated the sitting area from the bedroom and there were two overstuffed chairs, plus a long comfortable sofa. The sliding doors stood open, admitting a cool breeze and a breathtaking view of the sunset-reddened cliffs.

"We will sit on the balcony and admire the scenery," Schmidt said, bustling around with glasses and bottles. "It is very pleasant, nicht? I have been on many cruise boats, but never one so luxurious as this."

Like mine, his balcony was fringed with flowering plants. I edged cautiously onto it, telling myself nobody could drop anything on me here; there wasn't another deck above this one. To my right I could see the prow—or maybe it was the stern—of one of the lifeboats. To the left a solid partition separated Schmidt's balcony from the one next door. However, it wasn't solid enough to muffle a voice as loud as Schmidt's, and when he shouted cheerfully, "Sit, sit, my dear Vicky, and we will have a pleasant chat," I said, "Who's next door?"

"Ssssir . . ." Schmidt caught himself. "Mr. Tregarth and his wife."

"Damn it, Schmidt," I said savagely but softly. "That's the precise reason I insisted on a private conversation. You've got to avoid slips like that."

"Ach, yes, yes, I know. But what is the harm this time? You know and he knows—"

"Maybe she doesn't."

"They have gone downstairs." Schmidt looked subdued. "You are right to remind me, though, Vicky. They have only been married a few weeks, and she is very young, very innocent. Perhaps he has not yet told her of his brave and perilous occupation. She is the sort of child one would wish to shield from the harsh realities of life, nicht?"

Down below I heard a rattle and clank that must have been the gangplank being drawn in. The boat began to move, gliding gently away from the shore. The eastern sky was darkening but the curving bay of cliffs glowed in reflected sunset light. A flock of egrets settling into the shallows looked like flying white flowers.

Schmidt was rambling on. "It may be that he will decide to retire from the service. A man of honor and of conscience would not wish to endanger his young bride or cause her a broken heart if he should—"

"It's a nice plot, Schmidt. Why don't you write a book? Now listen to me. You've never met him before. I've never met him before. Nobody has ever met anybody before. Can you remember that?"

Schmidt had taken advantage of the interruption to hoist his glass. Emerging from it, he fixed a stern eye on me. "Aber natürlich. And you, Vicky—do you promise me, on your word of honor, that you did not know he would be on this cruise?"

"I did not know," I said steadily.

"Not that you wouldn't lie to me if you wanted to." Schmidt ruminated. I drank my beer. It was some local variety—not bad, actually. Then Schmidt said, "And your heart is not broken? You would not revenge yourself on your faithless lover by betraying him to his innocent, trusting—"

"For God's sake, Schmidt!"

"Good," said Schmidt calmly. "Then we will have a pleasant holiday, eh, and enjoy ourselves. I have not been in Egypt for many years. This should be a wonderful excursion. I have long looked forward to making the friendly acquaintance of Mr. Blenkiron."

"And extracting a contribution?" I suggested.

Schmidt grinned. "It is my job, getting money from wealthy people. I am very good at it."

He was, too. Our museum is remarkably well endowed for such a small institution. "He gives money to many worthy causes," Schmidt went on reflectively. "Why not to us? Since your heart is not broken, you can help me do this. He is not such an ugly man, is he?"

"Shame on you, Schmidt. Is that any way to talk to a dedicated feminist like me?"

"Well, he is not ugly," Schmidt declared. "I would not ask

you to use your charms on a man who was disgusting to you. He is a woman hater, they say, but he said many nice things about you, Vicky, and asked many questions."

I long ago gave up hope of convincing Schmidt that it is not nice to seduce potential donors. He'd have done it himself if he had had the necessary equipment. I suspect this is true of most museum directors. "What did he say?" I asked, pulling my chair closer.

## ii

I had planned to sleep in next morning; it had been a long day, concluded by one of Perry's more boring lectures, but I was hauled out of bed at the crack of dawn by Schmidt, demanding that I join him on deck to watch the boat maneuver through the Asyut locks. Since I had already made the mistake of letting him in—the alternative being to let him go on yelling and pounding on my door—I scrambled into my clothes and let him lead me away.

The buffet on the upper deck offered tea and coffee and an assortment of pastries. I downed a cup of coffee while Schmidt wreaked havoc among the pastries, for, I presumed, the second time. It would have been unwise to admit it to him, but as the caffeine took effect I was glad he had awakened me. The sun was barely above the horizon and the air was fresh and cool. Ahead lay the massive barrier of the barrage; the traffic crossing the bridge atop it included buses, bicycles, and donkeys. The ship had stopped, waiting its turn to pass through. There was one boat ahead of us on this side of the lock.

Several other ships were already lined up behind us. Surrounding us and them, like minnows around a shark, were clusters of small boats filled with enterprising merchants, who were hawking their wares at the top of their lungs. I joined Schmidt and several of the others at the rail. Schmidt was yelling too, bargaining for a garment one of the merchants held up. It was a long robe, basically black but covered from shoulders to midsection with sequins, beads, and embroidery in pseudo-Egyptian patterns.

I was about to ask my tasteless boss how the exchange of merchandise and money could be made, since the little boats were a good thirty feet below us, when an object came hurtling through the air and landed with a splat on the deck.

I jumped back with the alacrity of a frog in reverse, and someone bent to pick up the parcel.

"You seem a trifle tense this morning, Dr. Bliss," John remarked. Turning with a gallant bow, he presented the parcel to Suzi Umphenour.

I had believed I was getting used to Suzi's outrageous outfits, but she constantly surprised me. This garment might have come straight out of a thirties' film starring Jean Harlow: bias-cut satin trimmed with marabou feathers at the neck and the cuffs of the flowing sleeves. The things she had on her feet were, I think, referred to as mules. How she had managed to get upstairs in them without breaking her neck I could not imagine. As she reached for the parcel she slipped and tottered. Several pairs of masculine arms, including those of Sweet and Bright, made hopeful grabs at her, but she managed to avoid them, and fell heavily against John. He had to detach both her hands before he could set her on her feet.

Giggling merrily, Suzi removed her purchase and held it up: a shift, very tight and very short, completely covered with gold sequins. There was, I regret to say, a matching cap.

"Oh, very smart," said John.

"It's for the Egyptian party tonight," Suzi explained, with one of her wide white grins.

"Ah, yes. I'd forgot. Perhaps I'd better get something for Mary. Advise me, will you, Suzi? Your taste is so impeccable." He offered her his arm.

Did I follow them to the rail? Certainly. I was going that way anyhow. I heard Suzi ask why Mary wasn't with him, and John's reply: "I persuaded her to sleep late. She had rather a restless night."

Plastic bags were landing all over the place. Schmidt had already retrieved one; tossing the hideous garment over a chair, he put money into the bag, knotted it tightly, and tossed it down. He had a good arm for a fat old guy; the seller snagged the bag without difficulty. Suzi's aim wasn't so good; her bag missed the boat entirely, splashing into the water, but it was neatly retrieved by the merchant using a long hook.

I didn't see what gorgeous garment John bought for his bride. I was too busy trying to keep Schmidt from buying not one but several for me. I did succeed in talking him out of one of the gold-sequined shifts. More of the passengers had come on deck to join in the fun. It would have been fun, I guess, if it hadn't been for my tense suspicious mind. Yet— I assured myself—it was an awfully sloppy method of exchanging contraband or delivering explosives. Especially when one of the boats down below was filled with men in black uniforms, who kept a keen eye on every transaction.

The party broke up when we started moving into the lock. It was a tricky maneuver, owing to the size of the *Queen of the Nile*; she filled the entire space, lengthways and sideways. The stone walls rose sheer on either side, broken only by a flight of stairs leading from the top to water level. Once we were in, even Suzi could have tossed a package into the hands of someone who stood on the steps.

The only person there, however, wore a black uniform and carried a rifle. There were more of them up above, lining the bridge that crossed the lock.

Schmidt tugged me away. "We will have breakfast," he announced.

In a meaningful manner I brushed the crumbs off his mustache. He chuckled. "That was not breakfast, only a little snack."

Since we were not going ashore that day, the service of food was practically continuous; the passengers had to be kept amused, and for some of them eating was a favorite sport. I kept Schmidt company while he stuffed himself, trying to decide how to occupy the long leisurely day. I am not ashamed to admit that Ali's death had put a damper on my enthusiasm, which had already been fairly water-logged. If Alice was my only ally, we were both in deep trouble. If she wasn't, why the hell hadn't the other person identified him- or herself? I had left another message in the safe; its tone was peremptory, not to say hysterical, but if I didn't get a response there was not a damn thing I could do about it.

As for the other guys, I was prepared to leave them alone if they did the same for me. I didn't want to learn anything or even look as if I had. If there was ever a time for retreating into the fort and concentrating on defense, this was it. And I was going to take Schmidt into the fort with me. If Alice could get crazy ideas about him, so could the other guys.

Schmidt had a lovely day. Usually he follows me around. This time I followed him, tight as a tick on a dog, and he was innocently delighted by my companionship. We tried on the ghastly garments he had bought, and although he assured me most sincerely that I looked wonderful in all of them (fond as I am of Schmidt, I was unable to return the compliment), I persuaded him to pay a visit to The Suq, as Mr. Azad's shop was called, to see if we could find something even gaudier.

Schmidt loved The Suq. He loves places where he can buy things, not only for himself but, bless his generous heart, for his friends and relations. The shop was small and crowded; the people who hadn't purchased their costumes from the aquatic merchants were looking for appropriate attire for the banquet that evening. Mr. Azad didn't have any gold-sequined shifts, but some of the robes were lavishly embroidered and trimmed with gold braid. With his smiling approval we carried an armful back to my room and tried *them* on. Schmidt adores trying on clothes and he likes even better watching me try them on.

After much consultation and much pirouetting in front of the mirror, Schmidt settled on the gaudiest and most volumi-nous of the robes. It was an ensemble, in fact; a long-sleeved floor-length caftan-type garment with a matching sleeveless robe, open down the front, that was worn over it. After he had tried three times to wind a long scarf around his head turban-fashion, I persuaded him he looked much more macho in a bedouin-type headdress.

By then it was time for Brotzeit—lunch. I don't even want to think about what Schmidt ate. I had hoped he would want to take a nap afterward, but he was full of beans (among other edibles) and raring to go. "You will not want to miss the lecture, Vicky. Herr Foggington-Smythe is speaking on the tomb of Tetisheri, and showing slides!"

"You haven't heard him lecture, Schmidt. He is the most boring—"

"But the slides, Vicky! Many have never been seen before. It is a complete photographic reproduction . . ."

I said I'd meet him in the lounge in ten minutes and he trotted off, after warning me not to be late and assuring me I was beautiful enough already.

I spent a few minutes putting on fresh makeup. Then I opened the safe.

My notes were gone, and something had been added. A nice shiny .45 automatic.

# Chapter Six

*i*

I grew up on a farm in Minnesota. Dad taught all of us how to handle a shotgun and a rifle; he didn't hunt, but he saw nothing wrong with discouraging varmints, including the human variety, when they attacked the livestock (including the human variety). A bullet was also the quickest and most humane method of dispatching a fatally injured or rabid animal. He hated handguns, though. He claimed they were cowards' weapons and more likely to get a person into trouble than out of it.

I suppose it's easy to take that attitude when you're six-five and built like a tank.

Inconsistent or not, I share his attitude. I picked the thing up with all due caution, and examined it with even greater caution. I can tell an automatic from a revolver, but that's about the limit of my expertise. This wasn't one of the few models I had handled. The safety was on and there was a full clip, but no extras.

The presence of the gun proved Ali had had a backup on board, which was good news. I only hoped it wasn't meant to convey a subtle message: "You're on your own, baby, don't expect me to rush to the rescue."

I can deliver subtle messages too. I put the gun back in the safe and closed the door. Anyhow, I couldn't carry the damned thing on me; my clothes were all lightweight cotton and linen, there was no place I could stash it where it wouldn't show. If I put it in my bag, either it would fall out at an inappropriate moment or it would sink to the bottom and I wouldn't be able to locate it in a hurry.

Dad was right. The damned things were more trouble than they were worth. I hoped.

Schmidt had saved me a seat in the lounge. By what was probably not a strange coincidence, the only other person at the table was Larry. He did seem pleased to see me. Schmidt's face had the bland, pink-cheeked innocence it wore when he was up to something. I knew what he was up to this time, and I wished him luck. I'm a loyal employee of the National Museum myself—up to a point.

"So they let you off for a few hours?" I said, glancing at the table where Larry's two henchmen were sitting.

"It's the other way around, actually," Larry said with a smile. "I had to order Schroeder to take a break. He's been on the phone to Luxor a dozen times, working on the arrangements for the reception."

"Mr. Schroeder is your secretary?" I asked.

"Executive assistant, rather. Haven't you met him?"

I shook my head. "I have," said Schmidt. "A very pleasant person. But shy, nicht?"

Larry laughed. "I wouldn't say that. But he's been pretty busy. These changes in schedule have been a damned nuisance. We've had to revise our own schedule for the reception at my place in Luxor, and for the formal opening of the tomb."

"It is true, then, that we will have the honor of being the first to see the tomb in all its new glory?" Schmidt asked eagerly.

"The first and possibly the last," Larry said.

"Aha!" Schmidt nodded and winked. "I thought that would be your aim. I am in full agreement, of course. But can you do that, mein Freund? The Bureau of Tourism will surely object to closing the tomb."

"I have an argument that may convince them. No," he added pleasantly but firmly, "don't ask, Anton. I'm saving it for a surprise. It will be announced at the reception day after tomorrow."

"I would not want you to tell me then," Schmidt announced, widening his eyes and pursing his lips. "I like surprises."

He was overdoing the cute stuff, and I tried to tip him off with a slight shake of my head. Schmidt only grinned.

The room had filled. Everyone was there, even Suzi, whom I had expected to prefer sunbathing over culture. Perhaps she had found she lacked an audience.

It was a long lecture, but for once even Perry's hopelessly pedantic delivery couldn't spoil the fascination of the subject.

The tomb had been discovered around the turn of the century by a famous husband-and-wife team of Egyptologists. It was an unusual combination in those days, when women weren't allowed to work in archaeology or any other serious discipline, and the excavators were also unusual in that they followed rigorous standards of recording and copying instead of the slash-and-burn, dig-'em-up-and-dump-'em techniques favored by many of their contemporaries.

Since color photography had not yet been developed, the only way of accurately reproducing the wall paintings was to have them copied by an artist. Howard Carter, known to the world for his discovery of Tutankhamon's tomb, began his career as a copyist. He did some nice work, but I believe I cannot be accused of prejudice when I claim that the greatest archaeological copyists of that period were women. The discoverers of Tetisheri's tomb had employed one of them, and she had copied the paintings with exquisite skill.

As Schmidt had mentioned a couple of dozen times, we were among the first people to see the photographs of the restorations. Larry had denied dozens of requests for permission to reproduce them. Even the *National Geographic* hadn't been able to talk him into letting them do a story.

Perry had had the bright idea of comparing three versions, slide by slide—first the painting, then a color photograph taken before the restoration began three years earlier, then the photograph of the same section as it now appeared. It was a fascinating and convincing demonstration of the hazards of accessibility, and an equally impressive demonstration of what expert restorers and pots of money could do. The paintings had deteriorated shockingly in only ninety years, but Larry's crew had returned them to their original beauty.

After the lights had come on and the shades had been drawn back, Perry started taking questions. I got up and headed for the deck. Larry followed me.

"In need of nicotine?" he asked, smiling.

I kept forgetting I was a smoker. I took out a cigarette, and said with perfect honesty, "I didn't want to spoil the impression. You've done a wonderful thing, Larry. I feel as if I ought to kiss your hand."

Schmidt was close on Larry's heels. "Sie hat recht, mein Freund," he said seriously. "The art lovers of the world owe you a great debt. I will not kiss your hand, but I would like to shake it."

A dark flush spread over Larry's face. He looked down and shuffled his feet like a bashful schoolboy. "Your praise means a great deal to me," he mumbled.

I was afraid Schmidt might take advantage of Larry's emotional state to start hinting about certain other things he could do for the art lovers of the world, so I changed the subject. "What happened to her mummy?"

"One of the unlabeled mummies in the Deir el Bahri cache is believed to be hers," Larry said. "I question the identification."

"On what basis?" Schmidt asked interestedly.

"It's a rather complicated question."

"Ach, ja, I recall reading about it." Schmidt leaned against the rail, his eyes bright with interest. Schmidt is interested in practically everything, and as I have said, he remembers practically everything he has ever read. "There is a papyrus— Amherst, I believe—dating from the twelfth century B.C., which describes the confessions of tomb robbers of Thebes. So many of the royal tombs had been robbed that priests gathered up the royal mummies, or their battered remains, and hid them in a secret place. This cache was found in the 1880s, after it, in turn, had been looted by local thieves. Some of the mummies were unidentified and none were in their original coffins—"

"You are very well informed," Larry said curtly. He turned, arms on the rail, looking out across the river.

I would have taken the hint, but Schmidt went gaily on. "A few years ago the University of Michigan undertook a complete X-ray examination of the royal mummies. There were some peculiar discoveries. For instance, the small wrapped mummy found with the body of a high priestess was not, as had been believed, that of her stillborn child, but a baboon! One of the little old queens was bald and had—what do you call it—teeth that stuck out—"

"Brotzeit, Schmidt," I interrupted. "Specifically, teatime. Why don't you get us a good table near the buffet before the others come out?"

The prospect of food can distract Schmidt from just about anything. He went bustling off.

"Are you having tea?" I asked Larry.

He shook his head. "I'm saving myself for the banquet this evening. Come to think of it, I ought to get a costume of some sort together. If you'll excuse me . . ."

I joined Schmidt. "They are still setting out the food," he complained. "There was no hurry. Why—"

"A gentle hint, Schmidt: if you want to win Larry's heart, don't talk to him about mummies. Especially the mummies of beautiful Egyptian queens."

"Ah." Schmidt thought it over. "Ah! Vielen Dank, Vicky, I should have realized. A romantic he is, nicht? He dreams of the lovely images, the paintings and the statues."

"That's my guess. Even at their best, mummies aren't romantic."

"Mmmm, yes. That is why he does not want to believe the little old lady, who is bald and sticking out of tooth like her descendant, is his dream queen. The head was broken from the badly damaged body—"

I let out a croak of protest. "Schmidt, I'm no romantic, but I am just about to eat. Knock it off, will you?"

I realized I was still holding the cigarette. I was about to return it to the packet when a lighter went off, so close to the end of my nose that I shied back.

"May we join you?" Mary asked.

Schmidt leaped to his feet and held a chair for her. I sucked on the damned cigarette, womanfully suppressing a cough. "Thank you," I said.

"A pleasure," said John.

I didn't doubt it.

"We were talking about Tetisheri," Schmidt explained. "Vicky did not want to hear about her mummy."

"Mary dotes on dead bodies," said John.

"Oh, darling, don't tease!" Mary's pretty mouth quirked with distaste.

Over the past days her skin had darkened from cream to pale gold, without so much as a hint of homely sunburn. She wore a white silk shirt with a scarf of burgundy and gold knotted loosely around her throat. The Greek earrings would have suited the ensemble better than the diamonds she was wearing—a carat and a half each, if I was any judge (and I am). At that they were smaller than the stone in the ring on her third finger. It overwhelmed the simple gold band next to it.

Schmidt was beginning to catch on to the idea that very few people enjoy talking about mummies. "You prefer the charming little statuette of the lady that is in the British Museum?" he said with a twinkle and a chuckle.

Mary glanced shyly at John. "I'm afraid I don't—"

"There is no need to apologize," Schmidt exclaimed. "A lovely young woman should not trouble her head with antiquities."

"Thanks, Schmidt," I said.

"In your case it is different," Schmidt said calmly.

I decided not to pursue that point, but I admit it was partly pique that inspired my next comment. "I've always loved that little statue. I was crushed when they decided it was . . . it was . . ."

"A forgery." Schmidt, oblivious to undercurrents, finished the sentence.

I tore my eyes away from John's face. He had raised one eyebrow, a trick of his I particularly dislike, and a faint smile curved his lips.

"What does it matter, if it is beautiful?" he asked. "A respected authority on Egyptian art said it was the most appealing and charming of the sculptures of that period. Has it lost artistic merit?"

"Ah, but you miss the point, my friend," Schmidt exclaimed. "The authenticity of the work . . ."

I was only too familiar with the arguments pro and con, including John's arguments. I'd heard them before, when I was about to blow the whistle on him and his scheme for substituting forgeries for valuable antique jewelry. They had been superb copies, almost indistinguishable from the originals. But one example of the counterargument had dangled from Mary's dainty earlobes the night before. I lusted after those Greek earrings, and I wouldn't have felt the same about copies, however accurate.

Mary reached for John's hand. The movement stretched the silk of her blouse across her arm; the fabric was so thin I could see the golden tan of her skin through it. I could see the dark spots too. There were several of them, spaced regularly. Not the sort of bruise you'd get from bumping into a piece of furniture or a door. More like the marks of fingers.

*ii*

Schmidt had taken a fancy to Mary, and vice versa. Who could blame her? He is awfully sweet, especially when he puts himself out to be gallant. John didn't want to leave us either. I wasn't sure what he had in mind. General aggravation, maybe. It certainly aggravated me when he turned Schmidt's attention from antiquities to country music. One question was enough. Schmidt was delighted to expand on the subject.

"Yes, yes, it is a most interesting type. I am indebted to Vicky for introducing me to it. I am thinking of taking up the guitar."

"It would be better than listening to you sing," I said rudely.

Schmidt had become impervious to my insults. He thinks I'm just teasing. (And maybe he's right.) "You sing, then. The one about the pillow that is dying."

"A moribund pillow?" John's eyes were as blue and innocent as forget-me-nots. "I must hear that one."

We ended up in the lounge, gathered cozily around the
piano. Schmidt plays a little, enough to pick out tunes. He
gave us all three verses of "The Sinner's Death," including
the dying pillow. ("A slight error in the reference of the
adjective," as John described it.)

There are a lot of bluegrass songs about prisoners and chain
gangs and sinners. Schmidt set out to prove he knew them
all. A sensitive man might have found that theme a trifle
awkward, but not John. His sense of humor is offbeat at best,
but that day he was in a particularly strange mood. He kept
egging Schmidt on. What Mary was thinking I could only
imagine. She certainly was not amused.

The lounge had emptied rapidly as soon as Schmidt began
singing. Since I didn't want to leave Schmidt alone—especially with John—I remained. In order to demonstrate my
cool I even joined in on a couple of choruses. I am rather
proud of my ability to slide from one note to the next. I was
giving my all to "Little Rosewood Casket" when I realized
that Schmidt had dropped out (he always breaks down during
"Little Rosewood Casket") and that John was singing harmony
in a flat, nasal tenor that bore a suspicious resemblance to the
voice of the great Sara Carter.

That brought me back to earth with a painful thud. We
had sung—a weird medley of Bach, German pop tunes, and
Christmas carols—to keep awake the night a blizzard trapped
us in the abandoned church. It was the most memorable night
we had spent together, and I include other occasions which
were memorable for quite different reasons. It was the night
of all nights I didn't want to remember.

The lyrics didn't help either. "Take his letters and his locket,
Place them gently on my heart . . ." I broke off in the middle
of a glissando. "We'd better go and dress for dinner, Schmidt.
It's getting late."

"One more," John pleaded, looking soulfully at me from
under his lashes.

"Yes, there is time. Let me think. Ah! Here is one you may
not have heard, it is the latest hit of the famous Road Sisters."

The song was "You're a Detour on the Highway to Heaven." A sample will suffice, I believe.

"When mama lay a-dyin' on the flatbed, She told me not to truck with gals like you; But you were just one more roadside attraction, And I went joy-ridin' jest for the view."

I cut Schmidt off after three verses and three choruses.

John's face was rapt. "My God," he said reverently. "That's magnificent. It's even better than the one about Jesus and the goal posts of life. How does it go again? 'Your curves made me lose my direction . . .'"

"Schmidt," I said, through clenched teeth.

"Yes, Vicky, we will go." Rising, he took John's arm. "'Mein' hand from the steering wheel strayed . . .'"

They went off arm in arm, voices clashing in duet. It was the most outrageous noise I have ever heard, and I have stepped on the tail of a cat or two in my time.

I caught Mary's eye.

"He's like that sometimes," she said, with a stiff, apologetic little smile. "So whimsical."

"Whimsical" wasn't the word I would have chosen.

*iii*

Getting Schmidt ready for the grand dinner and costume party was almost as bad as decking a bride out for the wedding. (Yes, I've been a bridesmaid. Twice.) It didn't take me long to dress. Schmidt, that sly little rascal, had presented me with three ghastly garments he had bought from the guys in the boats; one was too short, one was too tight, and the third was both, and all three were covered with multicolored sequins. I had already decided I wasn't going to appear in public in any of the three. I put on the simple blue-and-white-striped robe I had bought at The Suq and studied the effect. It might not be glamorous, but it was very comfortable and very simple: two rectangles stitched together at the shoulders and down

the sides, with open spaces left for the insertion of the arms.
Blue braid outlined the neck opening and a perpendicular slit
down the front.

I slung on all my fake gold jewelry and, after considering
the question for longer than it merited ("Take his letters and
his locket . . .") I fastened around my neck the chain that held
the golden rose. Too many people had access to my room
and that ornament was unusual enough and valuable enough
to arouse speculation. I tucked the pendant firmly down into
my bra so it could not be seen or dislodged, and proceeded
to Schmidt's room.

When he opened the door his pink mouth sagged in disap-
pointment. "Why didn't you wear one of your beautiful new
gowns? That is too plain, too large. It is ugly!"

I could have been equally insulting about his contributions
to my wardrobe, but my mother always told me it isn't nice
to criticize presents people give you. "I'm saving the others
so I can dazzle Gerda. Hurry up, Schmidt. Were you waiting
for me to button you up?"

"There are no buttons to button," said Schmidt, unamused.
"I have not decided what to wear. The gold-trimmed or the
silver? Or this, with red and green?"

"I thought you'd decided on the gold."

"I had. But now I think the silver. Ah, I have it! You will
wear the gold and I the silver."

"Nobody is going to believe we're twins, Schmidt."

Schmidt condescended to giggle. He was determined,
though, so I gave in. He retired modestly to the bathroom
with his ensemble while I changed. It took me about forty
seconds, after which I sat and cooled my heels for another
ten minutes. Finally I yelled, "What the hell are you doing,
Schmidt?"

The door opened. If I hadn't been sitting down I would
have fallen to the floor.

Flowing robes and a headcloth that frames the face and
hides a gent's bald spot make a very becoming, not to say
sexy, outfit; even short chubby guys look dignified. The only
trouble was Schmidt had dyed his mustache black.

That simple statement cannot convey how ridiculous he

looked. Schmidt has a fair complexion. It was now pink with sunburn. His eyebrows were still bushy and still white. The mustache was . . . well, let's say it was a serious mistake.

Did I say so? I did not. I said, "Ach, du Lieber! As we say in Minnesota, Schmidt, you're a sight for sore eyes."

Schmidt told me I looked gorgeous too, but he wanted me to let my hair down. I declined. He was still arguing about it when I opened the door, just in time to see his neighbors emerging from their room.

Mary looked about sixteen in another version of the basic caftan. Hers was pale yellow. It had little ribbons dangling from the bodice. The sleeves were elbow-length and the fabric was cotton, heavy and opaque. Nothing showed through it.

I'd expected John would let himself go—he specialized in disguises and he was something of a ham—but he wasn't even wearing a tux. Bareheaded, in his shirt sleeves and a pair of wrinkled khaki pants, he looked as scruffy as John was capable of looking.

The boots gave me the clue. "Ah," I said. "You're disguised as an honest, hard-working field archaeologist. Very original."

John was the only one who caught the veiled insult. He grinned, and Schmidt exclaimed, "Sehr gut! But you need a pith helmet, Ss . . . John. Have you not got one? Take mine. No, I insist, it will complete the ensemble."

Most of the other men had been unable to resist the chance to dress up. Only Ed Whitbread and the urologist-birder wore ordinary dinner jackets. Sweet and Bright sported enormous matching turbans, Herr Hamburger had a red fez set at a rakish angle, and Larry wore long robes of subdued brown. The women looked like a flock of bright birds. Suzi had crammed herself into the gold sequins, Louisa into one of the gaudy embroidered gowns. That would have been bad enough, since the seams were visibly straining, but she had topped it with a construction she must have made herself—a copy of the tall crown Nefertiti wears in most of her portraits. It looks great on Nefertiti. She has a long slim neck and no mustache.

We all milled around, admiring one another's outfits and exchanging compliments, and had a few drinks, and then were summoned to the banquet. I was getting very sick and tired of the newlyweds and I didn't feel up to watching Schmidt eat, so I approached Sweet and Bright and asked if I could join them.

My other reason for wanting to join them was foiled by Suzi, who decided to make the fourth at our table. Apparently she had set her cap for Bright; I decided he must be richer than he (or Sweet, rather) had implied. She didn't succeed in getting him to talk, but he grinned and nodded a lot, and kept trying to tear his eyes from her décolletage. It was, I had to admit, a remarkable sight.

I tried once to introduce an interesting subject, but when I mentioned Ali, Sweet frowned and shook his head. "Yes, I had heard. It is very sad. Too sad to think about on such an evening. Have you tried the couscous, Vicky? Delicious!"

I tried the couscous. I don't remember what else I ate; it was all delicious, but I couldn't remember the names even if I had been paying attention. As I wandered to and from the groaning board I caught glimpses of Schmidt, enjoying himself as only Schmidt can.

After dinner we retired to the lounge for coffee and entertainment. Almost everyone was a little tight by that time, and they entered into the contest for best costume with childish delight. Suzi tried to belly dance and Louisa struck a pose, arms raised and bent, à la Steve Martin imitating King Tut. The prize for best men's costume went to, of all people, Larry's secretary, who had apparently been persuaded to take the evening off. He looked very authentic in Arab costume, with dark glasses and an Ibn Saud mustache under his checked headcloth.

Our little musical ensemble had traded in their Western instruments for drums and pipes. They gave us a brief concert, and then Hamid, the master of ceremonies, made an announcement. We were in for a treat, it appeared. He would say no more, except that the dancer we were about to see ordinarily did not perform in public. This was a gracious gesture, a tribute to a particularly distinguished group of visitors.

Feisal walked out onto the floor.

I had never seen him in other than Western clothing. His robe was plain, light gray in color. He looked gorgeous just standing still. Then the band struck up, if that is an appropriate phrase, and he started to dance.

I knew belly dancing was a bastard form, and that the classic form of the art is performed only by men. If you think a man dancing alone looks effeminate, you haven't seen Baryshnikov or any of the other great premiers danseurs. In a completely different way, and in a completely different idiom, Feisal had the same power. I can't describe what he did. It involved movements of arms and body and head, sometimes graceful and gliding, sometimes forceful, almost abrupt. By the time he finished, every woman in the room was dry-mouthed and I was thinking things I would call sexist if a man had been thinking them about me.

Feisal stood still for a moment, acknowledging the applause with a slight inclination of his head. Then he held out his hands and gave us a brilliant smile. "Come, who will join me?"

Suzi was the first onto the floor. They glided around for a while; at least Feisal glided, holding her out at arm's length, only their hands touching. Graceful she was not, but she enjoyed herself hugely, flashing teeth almost as white as Feisal's, emitting peals of laughter when she tripped over her own feet. Sweet and Bright were the next to try it; they circled solemnly, waving their arms. The effect was not at all the same.

I decided I needed a cup of coffee. As I approached the dance floor, Feisal passed Suzi neatly off to Bright and caught my hand.

"All the ladies in turn," he called, towing me onto the floor.

There wasn't much I could do; he had a grip like a steel trap. I tried to be like a good sport, but I could feel my face turning red. I've always been self-conscious about my height. Even when they are clumsy, little women manage to look cute. Tall women just look clumsy, period.

"You are very graceful," Feisal murmured, steadying me as I stumbled.

"And you are very much a liar. I'll get you for this, Feisal."

He laughed, throwing his head back. His throat was smooth and brown, corded with muscle. "Have you been avoiding me? I have seen nothing of you."

"You've been busy. Oops. Sorry."

"Relax, don't fight me. You would do well if you were not so afraid."

As double entendres go it wasn't awfully subtle, especially when it was accompanied by a languishing look from those thick-lashed dark eyes. I laughed, and stumbled again. Feisal smiled. "Sorry. One gets into the habit. I have been busy, and social encounters on board ship present certain difficulties. We'll have some free time in Luxor; may I show you something of the city?"

"This is a hell of a time to ask for a date," I said, trying not to trip over my own feet.

"Think about it."

"I will. Now can I sit down?"

"Yes, certainly. It's time I gave Nefertiti a whirl. Doesn't she look frightful?"

I shouldn't have been out of breath, but I was. I decided what I needed was fresh air and time to regain my composure. As I headed for the open doors and the deck, I beheld an amusing little pantomime. Mary was on her feet, gesturing animatedly. I couldn't hear what she was saying, the music was too loud, but it was obvious she was trying to persuade John to dance with her. He kept shaking his head. She caught his hand and tugged at him, her face bright with laughter. He smiled and went on shaking his head. Schmidt had also been watching them. Ladies' man that he was, he sashayed up to Mary and offered his hand. They were heading for the dance floor when I went out.

There were no dark corners on that deck, but I found a spot between two lamps that was relatively shadowy and leaned against the rail. It was a glorious night; the breeze cooled my flushed cheeks, and the moon, three quarters full, cast a silvery path across the water. Lights from a village on the west bank sparkled through the trees and more stars than I could ever recall seeing brightened the sky. Romantic as all hell, that's what it was, and there I stood, alone in the moonlight, wondering which of the handsome men on board was planning to cut my throat, and when.

Feisal might be genuinely interested in my wonderful self. Tall blondes are popular in Italy and points east. He might also be an agent of the Egyptian security police. I'd have been quite happy to believe either and even happier to believe both.

He'd kept his distance until this evening. Had that been deliberate—a precaution, to prevent others from suspecting his real role? Proposing a rendezvous in Luxor might have been a way of reassuring me. It was all quite logical and completely unproven.

He walked like the fog, on little cat feet, so lightly I didn't hear him till he was right behind me. When I turned it was too late to get away. My back was against the rail and his arms, raised and ready, told me I wouldn't get far if I tried to run. The moon was behind him; it glimmered in his hair but his face was in shadow.

His hands gripped my upper arms and pulled me toward him. He was so quick, and it was such an unexpected, damn-fool gesture, I didn't react in time. I tried to raise my knee, but his body pressed mine against the rail, and my fists never made it as far as his face, they were caught between my breast and his as his arm went around my shoulders and pulled me close.

"If you're thinking of screaming, I'd strongly advise against it," he murmured.

"Damn you," I whispered. "What the hell do you think you're doing? Someone will see—"

He said something, in a voice so low and uneven I couldn't make out the words, as his free hand slid into the open neck of my robe. Screaming was no longer an option. There wasn't enough air in my lungs. The last of my breath mingled with his as his lips forced mine apart. I couldn't free them; his fingers had moved from my breast to twist through my hair, and the pressure of his mouth held my head in the hard cradle of his hand. I knew—I had thought I knew—the strength of his hands and arms and lean body, but never before had he used it like this, uncontrolled and mindlessly demanding. Not against me . . .

He let me go so abruptly that only the rail behind me kept me from falling, and stepped back, shoving his hands into his pockets. I felt like a swimmer who has been underwater too long—ears ringing, lungs straining, muscles limp. Gasping and shaking, I hung on to the rail until I got my breath back.

I can swear in several languages, but I couldn't think of any word in any of them that would be bad enough. "How long have you been married—two weeks?"

He turned slightly, lifting his shoulders in a shrug, but when he replied his voice was harsh and unsteady. "Monogamy is so dull. Why should I confine myself to one woman?"

"She's young and pretty and madly in love—"

"And wealthy," John said. "You don't suppose I paid for those vulgar diamonds, do you?"

Every negative emotion I had ever felt for him—anger, contempt, hatred, loathing—boiled up in a sudden flood. My Scandinavian ancestors were prone to berserker rages, but this was the first time I'd ever experienced one. I hauled my arm back and let fly.

It wasn't often I could catch John off guard, but I succeeded this time. The flat of my hand connected with a sound like that of a large dry branch snapping. The impact sent pain darting clear up my arm to my shoulder.

It felt wonderful.

As the roaring in my ears subsided I heard voices and laughter. The dancing must be over. People were coming out of the lounge. I didn't know whether any of them had seen us. I didn't care.

My evening bag had fallen to the deck. I picked it up, took out my handkerchief, and scrubbed my mouth. John had retreated into the shadow, his hand on his cheek. I threw the handkerchief down and walked away.

I didn't want to go through the lounge. I knew I looked like a Gorgon, my hair straggling, my lip dripping blood and my face set in a snarl. After blundering up a stairway marked "Crew Only" I reached the upper deck and made it to my room unobserved. I closed the curtains, then stripped and examined the damage. I ached in so many places it was hard to tell which hurt most. The reddened spots on my arms would be purple and black by morning. Nice, I thought. Mary and I could compare bruises.

I made it to the bathroom just in time. Kneeling by the commode, in the ultimate posture of humiliation, I faced the ugly truth. After the first split second that kiss had not been one-sided. If he hadn't held my arms pinned, they would have been around him.

And he'd found the rose pendant. It had been outside my dress when I reached my room. The movements of those long deft fingers, tracing the length of the chain to where the rose rested between my breasts, had been prompted by curiosity and amused malice. What a boost to his ego that must have been, to find another infatuated woman wearing his trinket.

One hard tug snapped the chain. I threw the ornament across the room, stepped into the shower, and turned it on full blast.

I didn't hear the pounding at the door till I turned off the water. It had to be Schmidt; nobody else would make such a racket. I might have expected he'd notice my absence and come looking for me. I swathed my dripping body and my bruises in a terry-cloth robe and went to open the door. He'd continue beating on it until I did.

He must have used shoe polish or some other water-soluble substance on his mustache. It had run, leaving long black streaks down his cheeks. He looked like Fu Manchu.

"Ah," he exclaimed, looking me over critically. "You have been sick."

"How did you know?"

"I know the look," said Schmidt. "Let me in. I will take care of you."

I sighed and stepped back. "I don't need you to take care of me, Schmidt, I just need to go to bed."

"Yes, that is true. We must be up at dawn, for the visit to Abydos. I will put you to bed."

I laughed and started to protest. The laugh was a mistake. It stretched my lower lip and the cut opened up again. Schmidt's face softened, and he said, in a voice he seldom used even to me, his favorite flunky, "You have done it for me, Vicky, when I was sick or hurting. Let me do something now for you."

I bent my head to keep him from seeing the tears that stung my eyes. "Okay," I muttered. "Thanks, Schmidt. Just don't suggest a glass of beer to settle my stomach."

"It is very good for a weak stomach," Schmidt said seriously. "However, I have something better. I will get it while you put on your nightgown. Unless you would like me to help you?"

He gave me a giggle and a leer and trotted out without waiting for an answer. I had time to change and hide the reddening bruises before he got back. He was so sweet and solicitous I swallowed the ghastly stuff he gave me without a whimper, and accepted a sleeping pill as well. After he had tucked me in he stood by the bed looking down at me.

"Do you want to tell me what is wrong?"

I turned my head away. "Nothing's wrong, Schmidt. I over-indulged, that's all."

"Hmph," said Schmidt.

"Good night, Schmidt. And thanks."

"Schlaf' wohl, Vicky. And do not worry. Farther along we will know all about whatever it may be."

He had deliberately garbled the quote to make me smile, so I smiled; he patted me clumsily on the shoulder and trotted out, leaving the bedside lamp burning. After he had gone I reached to turn it off. The rose pendant lay on the table, with the broken chain coiled around it like a tiny golden snake.

*iv*

I'd forgotten to leave a wake-up call, but Schmidt remembered. A good thing, too; I am not used to sleeping pills and I'd have snored on until mid-morning if he hadn't telephoned to say he was on his way down.

"Give me half an hour," I mumbled pathetically.

"Fifteen minutes."

Motivated by that promise or threat, I managed to get in and out of the shower and into my clothes before he arrived. I do not have transparent garments in my wardrobe—not for day wear, at any rate—so I had no trouble finding a shirt that covered the bruises, which were darkening as expected. Studying myself in the mirror I was pleased to find that the excesses—physical and emotional—of the previous night hadn't left visible marks, and when Schmidt insisted we go down to breakfast I agreed. I wanted John to see me smiling and calm, cool, collected, and contemptuous.

He wasn't in the dining room. Neither was Mary. The place was only half-full, so I concluded the others were breakfasting in their rooms. Alice was sitting with Feisal; they waved and I waved, and joined Schmidt at a table as far from Alice as I could get. The less we were seen together, the safer for her. She'd be looking for her contact when we went ashore. I wondered what disguise he'd assume—another tourist, a seller of souvenirs, a beggar? The setup was perfect for a seemingly casual encounter, the sites were swarming with people. He'd be there, I felt sure. The change in schedule must be known to the authorities, and after Ali's death it was imperative that they reestablish contact.

Schmidt stuffed himself with eggs and cornflakes and fruit and bread, and then proceeded to fill his pockets with tidbits. For the cats? "Yes," said Schmidt, when I asked. "And the poor dogs. Ach, Vicky, it is sad to see—"

Feisal interrupted the speech, stopping by our table on his way out to warn us we'd better hurry. "Don't forget a hat, Vicky. We are farther south, and the sun is hot."

I hoped that was a hint; but after I had dashed upstairs and opened the safe, nothing was there that hadn't been there the night before. Maybe it was a hint of another kind? And maybe it wasn't a hint of any kind. After deliberating for a few seconds I put the gun into my bag.

Most of the passengers had assembled. After all that time cruising, even the lazy ones were ready to go ashore. Schmidt had cornered Larry; ignoring his winks and nods, I joined Anna Blessington. She looked cute as a button, eyes bright in her wrinkled face, a broad-brimmed straw hat tied under her chin with a jaunty bow. The hands resting on her stick were mottled with age spots and twisted with arthritis. If she was a crook or a secret agent I'd turn in my Sherlock Holmes badge.

"Did you enjoy the party last night?" I asked.

"Yes, it was splendid, wasn't it?" She grinned, producing an even more astonishing set of wrinkles. "Especially Feisal's dancing. To think I am the only female whom he has held in his arms!"

"I'm thinking of spraining my ankle," I admitted.

"You don't have to resort to such painful expedients, my dear." She hoisted herself to her feet and reached, unselfconsciously, for my arm. "Just till we get down the gangplank, if you don't mind; it's a bit steep."

The ancient cemeteries and the temples that served them are in the desert; we had a long ride, through the cultivated fields and the town of Hammadi. The children were on their way to school; I was pleased to see girls among them, modestly clad in long-sleeved dark robes, their heads covered with white kerchiefs. Older women all wore black. Stalls along the street sold a variety of goods, from fruit and vegetables to cheap plastic dishes. After we left the town we drove through fields of cabbages and sugarcane. The road, paved but narrow, bordered a canal. We roared past donkeys loaded with reeds and rusty trucks loaded with pots and turbaned men riding bicycles, and another tourist bus.

The area outside the entrance to the archaeological enclosure was a modern disaster—rows of stalls selling film and souvenirs, a couple of coffee shops with rows of rusting tables and chairs outside. Feisal raced around like a Border collie, shepherding us into a compact group and assuring Suzi, who kept trying to break away and head for the souvenirs, that she would have a chance to spend her money after we had seen the temple. He lost Schmidt when we started up the ramp to the entrance. Looking back, I saw my boss surrounded by lean dogs and peremptory cats. Handing Anna over to Feisal, I went back to him.

"For heaven's sake, Schmidt, come on. Feisal has the tickets."

Schmidt had emptied his pockets of food. His stricken face was turned toward a child who sat on a low wall nearby. The kid's hand was out and he was whining for baksheesh. He had only one leg.

"Ach, Vicky—"

"I know, Schmidt. I know. Come on."

"One moment only . . ." He trotted toward the boy and

filled the outstretched hand with crumpled bills. That wasn't as generous as it sounds, since Egyptian currency consists mainly of paper money, the smallest being worth approximately ten cents. But I don't think Schmidt looked at the numbers on the bills.

He's a volatile old guy, though, and he cheered up after we got inside. There are those who consider the Abydos temples the most beautiful in Egypt, and I wouldn't argue with them. Some of the other tourist favorites—Dendera, El Kab, Philae—are better preserved, but they date from the Greek or Ptolemaic period, a thousand years later. Abydos is Nineteenth Dynasty, one of the high points of Egyptian art.

Schmidt hauled out his camera and took pictures of everything. Then he forced it on me and made me take pictures of him in front of everything. Then he forced it on Bright, who happened to be nearby, and made Bright take pictures of both of us in front of . . . well, practically everything. By the time we reached the inner courtyard he'd used up the first roll of film and retired behind a pillar to reload.

I took advantage of his absence to escape, not only from Schmidt's obsession with snapshots, but from the others. Feisal was lecturing. I didn't want to hear a lecture, I just wanted to look.

Some of the others had wandered off too. I saw Alice going up the steps that led into the Hypostyle Hall and John and Mary, hand in hand, following her. Bright and Sweet were nowhere around.

Perched on a low foundation wall of cut stone, I sat soaking it all in and trying not to think about what Alice might be doing. I sincerely hoped she was doing it, but I didn't want to think about it. After a while Feisal led the group into the pillared hall. I went on sitting. It was hot, but not unbearably so. The square pillars of the vestibule opposite were decorated with the mighty form of pharaoh being greeted by various gods. Exposed as these were, they had lost most of the paint that had once covered them. I tipped my hat so it shaded my eyes and relaxed. Gradually the voices of guides lecturing in six different languages faded into an agreeable background hum, and somehow I wasn't at all surprised to see that the reliefs were now bright with fresh paint, the king's body and limbs red-brown, his crown a soft blue, his collar and bracelets picked out with turquoise and gold.

One of the painted figures stepped out of the pillar. He wasn't wearing a crown, and his hair was pale gold, not black. Raising one eyebrow at me in distant acknowledgment, he turned and began removing objects from the wall. They solidified and took on dimension in his hands: jeweled and beaded collars, heavy bracelets, golden cups, bowls and containers . . .

"There you are."

I shook the sleep from my eyes and looked up. The figure standing over me wasn't wearing a white kilt and beaded collar but dust-colored pants and shirt. Larry gave me a tentative smile. "Sorry to disturb you."

"It's a good thing you did. I was about to fall over."

"Some of us are going to have a look at the Old Kingdom tombs," Larry explained. "Anton thought you might want to come along."

"The First Dynasty royal tombs? I thought nothing remained of them."

"Nothing worth visiting, no. But there are tombs of all periods here; this was one of the holiest places in Egypt, the legendary site of the tomb of Osiris. Last year an expedition from Boston located a new cemetery of Fourth Dynasty burials. Normally tourists aren't allowed, but I happen to know the chap in charge and . . ." He broke off, eyeing me doubtfully. "But perhaps only an enthusiast like myself would be interested."

He looked like a little boy whose mom has rejected his offering of a toad or a garter snake. Close your eyes and think of the National Museum, I told myself. The tombs must be mastabas, like the ones at Sakkara. The superstructures were all above ground. If anybody invited me to visit the sunken burial chamber I would politely decline.

"I'd love to," I said.

We were a select group, as it turned out. Ed Whitbread was present, of course; he trailed Larry and me at a discreet distance. Sweet and Bright had also joined us.

"Where's Schmidt?" I asked, turning to look back as we started off across the sandy wasteland.

"Feeding cats, I expect," Larry said. "Shall we go back for him? He may have changed his mind."

"He's easily distracted," I admitted. "Wait a minute, here comes . . . No, it's Feisal."

The sun was in my eyes or I wouldn't have made that mistake. Feisal soon caught up with us. He was frowning.

"Sir, the bus will be leaving in an hour. Where . . ."

Larry explained. "I'd have asked you to join us, Feisal, but I thought you had to stay with the group."

Feisal's scowl changed to a look of bright-eyed interest. It wasn't directed at me. I kept forgetting he was a trained Egyptologist. "They are now buying souvenirs and cold drinks. I haven't had a chance to see the excavations, so I will join you if you don't mind."

He fell tactfully behind, leaving me to Larry, who proceeded to tell me all about the Old Kingdom tombs. I must say it made a pleasant change to have a man flex his mind instead of his muscles to impress me.

It was also a pleasant change to leave the crowds behind. An ambitious "guide" trotted along with us until Larry dismissed him with a curt Arabic phrase. We had been walking for ten minutes when he gestured. "There it is."

I looked around for walls and cut stone. All I could see was a low mound up ahead. A sinking feeling came over me as I realized I had made a slight error. Anything that had been above ground in two thousand–plus B.C. would be under it now, buried by encroaching sand. I followed Larry up the slope of the mound, and cheered up when I saw below me, not a dark sinister hole in the ground, but a large pit open to the sky. It was paved with stone and there were a few stretches of wall, none of them over a meter high. In front of one such stretch squatted a tan bundle, which unfolded into a man.

"Sorry, folks, nobody is allowed . . ." he began. Then his narrow face relaxed. "Mr. Blenkiron! I heard you were in Egypt, but I didn't expect you'd honor us with a visit."

"Hope we're not interrupting anything." Larry offered me his hand and we scrambled down into the excavation.

Having lots of money makes one welcome in all social circles. The excavator would have kicked Cleopatra out of his bed to welcome the rich patron of archaeological excavations. He greeted Feisal by name, invited the rest of us to call him Ralph, and apologized feverishly for the fact that nothing particularly interesting was going on.

"The men are off today," he explained. "It's Friday. Pat will be sorry to have missed you; he's gone to Luxor to work at the library at Chicago House."

He showed us some of the reliefs. They were fragmentary but very beautiful, delicate low reliefs like the ones at Sakkara. He and Larry went off into a spate of technical discussion, and before long Sweet said he thought he and Bright would go back. Larry looked at his watch. "Yes, go ahead. Tell them we'll be along shortly. I'd like to have a quick look at the burial chamber."

He produced a huge flashlight from his pocket. "No need for that, sir," Ralph said proudly. "We've run a wire and stuck up a few lightbulbs. I'll turn them on, shall I?"

From the northwest corner of the pit, a gently sloping ramp led down. It was low-ceilinged but fairly well lit by a series of bare bulbs. I followed Larry and Ralph until we got to the dreaded, anticipated hole in the ground. The top of a rough wooden ladder showed at the edge of the shaft.

Somebody called from up above, and Ralph said, "Damn. I'd better go see—" He scrambled back up the ramp. Larry, already on the ladder, looked up at me and for once in my life I decided to be sensible instead of foolhardy.

"Sorry. I can't . . ."

I tried to keep my voice steady, but I didn't succeed. Larry looked startled. "Why, Vicky, I had no idea. Is that what was bothering you when we were in the royal tomb at Amarna? I thought you looked . . . We'll go back. I don't have to do this."

"No, you go ahead. I'll wait for you here."

"If you're sure . . ." His head sank down out of sight.

I thought the scream, high and piercing as a bird's call, had come from Larry until he echoed it. His startled cry was followed by a rattle and a crash. The lights went out.

There was daylight behind me, only thirty feet away—a

bright, heavenly square of brightness. I could crawl up the ramp . . . and leave Larry down below in the dark. The ladder must have broken. He had fallen from it—how far? I heard a faint groan. It died into silence.

Did I mention that I shared that tunnel under the Schloss in Rothenburg with two other people, both of them injured? One of them was Tony, once my Significant Other, still my cherished friend. The groan from the darkness shot me back into the past, and for a few horrible moments I lost track of where I was and *when* I was. I thought it was Tony down there, unconscious, gasping for breath. I had to go to him, help him . . .

I didn't. I couldn't. I rolled myself into a ball like a reluctant fetus and when the daylight behind me was blotted out I started to whimper.

# Chapter Seven

*i*

Hands took hold of me and tried to unwind me. I fought them frantically until it dawned on me that there was something familiar about that grip. "Tony," I croaked. "Oh, Tony, damn it, I thought you were—"

He slapped me, hard. After my head had settled back onto my neck I squinted up at him. It wasn't Tony. Of course it wasn't. Tony was in Chicago, not in that filthy tunnel under the Schloss. Neither was I. I was in Egypt in a filthy tunnel in a tomb, with . . .

"You bastard," I said feebly.

"How pitifully inadequate." John hauled me to my feet and propped me against the wall, out of his way. Leaning over the shaft he called, "Blenkiron! Speak up, don't be shy."

The voice echoed hollowly. "I'm okay. You'll have to get a rope. The ladder . . ."

"Hang on."

"What are you doing here?" I demanded.

John turned to me. I couldn't make out his features; the only light came from the top of the ramp and even that distant illumination dimmed as people crowded around the opening, spouting agitated questions and exclamations. I sensed, rather than saw, the movement when his raised arm fell to his side. I had hit him a lot harder than he had hit me. Apparently he had decided not to even things up with a second slap. Too many people watching.

"You have a positive genius for irrelevance," he remarked. "Come on, up you go; can you walk or shall I drag you?"

I couldn't walk. The roof was too low. So I crawled, as fast as I could, leaving John calmly discussing the situation with Larry.

I emerged from the opening to find myself in the middle of a fight, if one can use that word to describe an altercation between a fat elderly midget and a tall muscular man. Ed had Schmidt in a close embrace and Schmidt was pounding on his back and yelling in Mittelhochdeutsch, his favorite language for swearing.

"Cut it out, you little lunatic," Ed said. His breathing wasn't even fast. "Here she comes. Safe and sound."

He released Schmidt. Schmidt darted at me. "Vicky! Are you all right? I was trying to get to you—"

"Stop squeezing me, Schmidt. I'm fine." But I didn't try to free myself; it felt good to be held by someone who loved me. Over the top of Schmidt's head I saw other members of our group, in various poses of curiosity and concern. Feisal clutched Suzi's voluptuous form. Her eyes were closed, but I doubted she was unconscious; one of her arms was draped around Feisal's neck. Pale and shaken, Mary leaned against a wall. She wasn't as pale as the young archaeologist, who had just seen his hopes of a generous contribution go up in smoke. It is difficult to win the heart of a potential donor after he has fallen down a shaft.

"I don't understand how it could have happened," he insisted. "The ladder was perfectly sound, we've been up and down it a hundred times . . . Oh! Oh, thank God, Mr. Blenkiron. Are you all right?"

"Just a few bruises." Followed closely by John, Larry emerged from the tunnel. He was dusty and sweaty and disheveled, but he didn't seem to be damaged. "It wasn't your fault," he went on sheepishly. "The ladder is intact. I guess my foot slipped when the lights went out. And someone screamed—"

"Probably Suzi." Feisal lowered her unceremoniously to the ground. She promptly opened her eyes and muttered, "Where am I?"

Nobody told her.

"It's fortunate that no one was injured," said Feisal, in a voice that reminded me he was responsible for the safety and well-being of the group. Did they dock his pay for every tourist he lost? If so, he was already out a few bucks on account of Jen. Had she really left Cairo? I had only John's word for it and I wouldn't have relied on that if he had assured me the world was round.

Urged on by Feisal, we started back to the bus. Nobody asked why the power had failed. Apparently that sort of thing happened all the time. It was probably just an odd coincidence that it had happened after Vicky Bliss, the well-known phobic, had crawled down into a tomb. If I hadn't balked at the last minute I might have been on the ladder when it happened.

There were only two people who knew about my phobia. I thanked God I hadn't made an abject fool of myself in front of Larry; he had realized I was uncomfortable, but he wasn't aware of the disgusting performance I had put on. My vocal reaction had been in the form of whimpers rather than screams.

My eyes focused on John, who was ahead of us. Mary was clinging to his arm. They hadn't been part of the original expedition. They—and Suzi and the others—must have accompanied Schmidt. John could have managed it. A yank at the electric wire that snaked around the wall . . .

Another warning, designed to inflict emotional rather than physical damage. It was a low-down filthy trick to pull on a person under any circumstances; the circumstances under which John had learned of this particular Achilles heel made the trick even filthier.

Schmidt looked up at me. "You are very red in the face, Vicky. Is it the sunburn?"

"No, Schmidt. It's not sunburn."

## ii

The boat got under way as soon as we boarded. We were due in Luxor next day. I could hardly wait. By hell or high water, hook or crook, I was going to get myself into the presence of an actual living unmistakable policeman or a member of State Security Investigation, and demand to know what was going on. The situation was coming apart like a soggy paper towel and I must be losing my touch; I hadn't suspected Ali or spotted Alice until she declared herself. I was beginning to wonder about Sweet and Bright; if they were supposed to be protecting me they had screwed up at least twice. And I hadn't the faintest idea who John's confederates might be.

Not that my past record was all that good. On several memorable occasions I hadn't identified the criminal until he pointed a gun at me.

Alice and I managed to exchange a few words. They were, "I hear you had a little adventure, Vicky. Good thing no one was hurt," to which I replied, "Yes, isn't it," and to which she responded with, "Here's that book on the Memphis tombs I promised to lend you."

There were no messages written in invisible ink or spelled out by means of dots or pinpricks under certain words. What there was was a note, hastily scribbled in pencil and stuck in between the pages. "He was there. Promised we'll be contacted as soon as we get to Luxor. Said to lie low, take no action, stay in a crowd. Ali died of drowning. All bruises postmortem except for one on his face. Could have hit his head, knocked himself out, fallen overboard. Suggest you don't think about the alternative." There was a P.S. "Burn this and flush the ashes down the nearest convenience."

I would have done it anyhow. As I watched the ashes being sucked down with the swirling water I thought about the alternative.

After lunch Schmidt and I settled ourselves on the sundeck. Schmidt started writing postcards. He'd already sent them to everybody he knew and he couldn't understand why I wasn't doing the same.

"At least to your mama and papa," he insisted. "Here, here is a pretty one of the pyramids. And one of Cairo for Tony—"

I took them, to shut him up. It was a little difficult composing appropriate messages. "Having a wonderful time" was not only trite but untrue. As for "Wish you were here," I could only thank God they weren't.

Yet as I scribbled a witty greeting on Tony's card ("Hi! Guess where I am!") part of me, the selfish, cowardly part, wished he were. Here. This was the first time I'd been completely on my own, with no one to talk to, argue with, or fall back on. Schmidt hadn't been particularly useful during the Roman affair, but he had been aware of what I was doing, and toward the end of that business John and I had become reluctant allies. We had spent most of our time together trying to elude various people who wanted to kill either or both of us, but when you are running wildly away from killers it's nice to have company. John was awfully good at running away.

Stretched out in the chair next to mine, Schmidt had tipped his hat over his eyes and dozed off. His hands were clasped on his tummy and the ends of his mustache fluttered every time he exhaled.

The sight of him, vulnerable and lovable and harmless as a baby, was like a cold shower, clearing my head and bringing my thoughts into focus. I had to get Schmidt out of this. I had to get myself out too. I'd been a fool to consent to such a dangerous scheme—even if I hadn't realized how dangerous it was going to be—and an even bigger fool to go on with it after I spotted John. I had done the job I had agreed to do, and my mysterious employers hadn't kept their part of the bargain. They had let Schmidt get away. The hell with the Cairo Museum. I wouldn't have traded a square inch of Schmidt's bald scalp for the entire contents of the museum. The hell with security, too. I didn't have to flap around like a wounded duck until somebody condescended to contact me—or until somebody else drowned me in my bathtub and threw me overboard. As soon as we reached Luxor I'd call Karl Feder and hand in my resignation. I'd have done it that minute if it had been possible to make a direct call. I didn't trust anybody anymore, and that included the radio operator.

It was amazing how much better I felt once I'd made that decision. I could even enjoy the scenery. The cliffs of the high desert bounded the river on either side; even in bright sunlight they were a pale, ethereal pinky-yellow. At some places they rose sheer from the water's edge; elsewhere they fell back, leaving a narrow strip of cultivable land. Little clusters of brown mud-brick houses were framed by green crops and palm trees. Birds flapped and swooped and beds of blue water hyacinths glided past, floating flowery islands in the stream.

I waved back at a group of children gathered along the bank, but my mind kept wandering. The greatest difficulty would be to talk Schmidt into cutting the trip short. I toyed with wild ideas—a fake telegram announcing that the museum was on fire, or that a family member had fallen ill? No, that wouldn't work. He'd telephone and discover the truth. Anyhow, it would be cruel to scare him.

We were to be in Luxor for four days. There wasn't a prayer of getting Schmidt away until after he'd seen the famous tomb. I was rather keen on seeing it myself. Maybe, I thought hopefully, the cops were waiting on the quay at Luxor to round up the bad guys. Maybe John would call the whole thing off. Maybe Schmidt would get sick. A lot of tourists get sick. Maybe I'd get sick. Maybe I could pretend to be sick and insist that Schmidt take me home to Munich . . .

Maybe the mummy of Tutankhamon would rise up out of its coffin and blast the villains with a supernatural curse.

"Oh, hell," I muttered.

Schmidt stirred. "Was hast du gesagt?"

"Nothing."

How about faking a nervous breakdown? I shouldn't have any trouble doing that.

Schmidt pushed his hat back and sat up. "Brotzeit," he announced.

Sure enough, it was. The stewards were setting out the tea-things. Awake or sleeping, Schmidt always knows when it's time to eat. If he ever sinks into a deep coma I figure I can bring him out of it by waving a doughnut under his nose.

The passengers who had been elsewhere started to assemble. I was greedily collecting cookies when Perry joined me at the buffet. He was looking a little peaked, and when I recommended the chocolate wafers he grimaced and said he thought he'd better stick to tea.

"I noticed you didn't go ashore this morning," I said. "Are you okay?"

I hadn't noticed, actually—Perry was not one of those people who are conspicuous by their absence—but I thought it would be polite to say so. He hesitated. I decided he was torn between his desire for sympathy and his reluctance to admit he was no more immune to common weakness than any inferior tourist.

"Just a touch of stomach trouble," he said finally.

"There's a lot of it going around."

"It's never happened to me before," Perry said pettishly. "And I've eaten in places tourists are warned away from. Someone in the kitchen must have been careless."

There are some ailments that bring out the worst in people who don't suffer from them. I licked chocolate off my lower lip and took another big bite. "They say it happens to everybody sooner or later," I said heartlessly. "Several people have been sick. Anna, and the Hamburgers and—"

"Who? Oh." Perry laughed politely. "A joke. They're suffering from the usual tourist complaint. That's not my problem. I haven't actually—er—been sick, just a little queasy. My temperature is normal, but my pulse—"

"What are you lecturing about this evening?" I had intended to offer him a little sympathy with his tea, but I really didn't want to hear a list of unpleasant symptoms.

"The Valley of the Kings. That's where you'll be going tomorrow morning. But Alice has kindly offered to speak in my place. It is essential that I take care of myself. I must attend the reception tomorrow evening. Larry made a point of inviting me."

Everybody had been invited. An uncharacteristic wave of

kindness stopped me from saying so. Poor devil, he couldn't help being a bore. I wanted desperately to get away from him, but I couldn't think how to manage it without hurting his feelings. My eyes kept wandering. Schmidt had cut Larry out of the herd and Alice had joined them at their table. They seemed to be having a good time, laughing and talking animatedly. John and Mary were standing at the rail, their shoulders touching. Near them, but obviously not with them, were Bright and . . .

Just Bright. I realized I'd never seen one without the other. Where was Sweet? Could Bright be forced into conversation, lacking his interpreter?

Perry was rambling on about various boring things, all of which he claimed he could do better than anybody else. "Not that I couldn't handle the job, you understand. Anyone can be an administrator, but field archaeology and lecturing require special—"

"Right," I said, wondering vaguely what I had agreed with. "Shouldn't you rest now? You must take care of yourself."

As soon as he'd gone I made a beeline for Bright. No need for subtlety here; my first question was one anyone might have asked. "Where's your buddy? Not sick, I hope."

Bright considered the question. After a moment he nodded gravely. "Sick."

"I'm so sorry. Has the doctor seen him?"

Bright nodded and smiled.

"Is there anything I can do?"

Bright shook his head and shrugged.

"Are you all right?"

Bright nodded and smiled.

I had a feeling that if I kept asking questions the process would keep repeating itself. Nod and smile, shake head and shrug, nod and smile . . . The man wasn't mute, he had spoken. One word, in a soft hesitant voice, the voice of someone who has a painful speech defect, a lisp or a stutter, who has to choose his words with care.

Or someone who is trying to conceal the fact that he can't speak the language that is supposed to be his native tongue.

He had to risk it once more; he couldn't just walk away

without a word. His "Excuse me," was accompanied by
another smile and another nod. I watched him cross the deck,
nodding and smiling at people, until he had vanished inside.

I supposed he'd gotten tired of sitting with his sick friend
and came out for a breath of air and a change of scene.
Careless of him to risk it, though. The last two words had
been articulated with a precision no native speaker of the
language would employ. I had assumed he wasn't really a
manufacturer from Milwaukee, but I would have expected a
professional undercover agent to be smart enough to assume
a credible persona.

Yes, I definitely had to talk to somebody who knew what
was going on. I sure as hell didn't.

When I went back to Schmidt I found him entertaining
again. John was actually taking notes. "Hillbilly," he repeated,
writing it down.

"Das ist recht. It means—"

"I'm vaguely familiar with the term. Then the western
element—"

"Yes, the cowboys. A pessimistic group of individuals."
Schmidt illustrated the theme. "Do not bury me on the lone-
some prairie. There the coyotes (a variety of jackals, with
loud voices) howl . . ."

" 'And the wind blows free.' Yes, I've got that. It does have
a lugubrious quality, doesn't it?"

"But the most romantic are the prison and the railroad
songs."

I said, before I could stop myself, "Romantic?"

"All those dying pillows," John murmured.

Schmidt continued the lecture, with vocal illustrations. How
Mary stood it I could not imagine. She had to be tone-deaf
as well as infatuated. Finally I took pity on her and tried to
change the subject.

"Where is everybody? It's a beautiful day, you'd think there
would be more people on deck."

"On their dying pillows, no doubt," John said. "The pharaoh's curse has struck. The rest of us will probably be in the
same state before we reach Luxor."

"What do you mean?" I demanded.

"Hadn't you heard?" He turned slightly, facing me. "The

refrigeration apparatus has broken down. Perfect conditions for ptomaine."

I didn't bother to ask how he knew. Once such rumors start they spread quickly, especially in a small closed society like ours. By the time the group reassembled for drinks and the evening lecture, Hamid felt it necessary to make a public announcement.

It was true, as we had heard, that the refrigeration had failed and that efforts to repair it had been unsuccessful. However, there was not the slightest danger of food poisoning. As those of us who had experienced prolonged power failures knew, the freezers would remain cold for hours and we would be in Luxor by morning. Any food served that evening (and the chef, said Hamid, with one of his largest smiles, was preparing a veritable feast) would be perfectly safe.

When he finished there was some grumbling, most of it from our habitual complainers. Alice, who had replaced Hamid on the podium, added a few sentences of reassurance before beginning her lecture.

She was a much better speaker than Perry, enlivening the facts with personal reminiscences and funny stories. Cued by Schmidt's rumbling chuckles, I laughed in all the right places, but I have to admit I didn't pay proper attention. Just when I thought I had come to a sensible sane decision, something happened to make me question it. Could I have been mistaken about Sweet and Bright? The answer to that was depressingly obvious. The corollary was equally depressing. They were the only ones to whom I had spoken about John. Several little reels of tape were jostling around in my bag at this very moment. I hadn't left them in the safe. I kept telling myself there was nothing incriminatory on those tapes, only a series of rude remarks from John and feeble rejoinders from me, but I knew I was kidding myself. And I knew why.

And I knew it was high time I stopped behaving like a fool. John claimed he was opposed to violence, but either he had changed his views or he was mixed up with people who didn't share them. Ali had been murdered; I was as certain of that as if I had seen it done. I wasn't at all happy about the failure of the refrigeration either. Machinery is always breaking down—at least my machines are always breaking down—and this damage seemed, on the surface, quite harmless. But our schedule had already been altered once and this might necessitate an even more drastic change, if the coolers couldn't be repaired.

The lights went on, and I hastily rearranged my features into an expression of smiling interest. Alice started taking questions. As I might have expected, the first one was about the curse of Tutankhamon.

Pure coincidence, said Alice. Lord Carnarvon had cut himself shaving and blood poisoning had set in, followed by pneumonia. The others who had worked on the tomb with him had lived to ripe old ages. She reeled off names and dates with the assurance of someone who has been asked the question dozens of times before. Morbidly, I wondered whether tourists fifty years from now would be discussing the hideous doom that had fallen upon the passengers of the *Queen of the Nile*, and the sad fate of Victoria Bliss, cut off in her prime by an unfortunate coincidence.

Everybody went to bed early that night. We were supposed to disembark at six forty-five for our visit to the Valley of the Kings.

*iii*

The group that gathered in the lobby next morning was greatly diminished—only a dozen passengers, plus Alice and Feisal. Oh, and Perry. Sweet and Bright were not among them. John and Mary *were* among them. So was Suzi, somewhat to my surprise; I'd have expected her to spend the whole day primping for the grand reception that evening. Subtle questioning on my part elicited the information that the missing persons were all alive and undamaged; some were suffering from the conventional complaints, others had decided not to take the long tiring trek.

I had been tempted to skip the tour too. A hasty glance at

the itinerary had reminded me that several of the tombs we were to visit were described as "deep." I had acquired a violent aversion to tombs in general, never mind "deep" tombs. But when I called Schmidt, hoping against hope he would be suffering from tummy trouble, he informed me he was on his way to breakfast and demanded I hurry up. So I hurried. Schmidt was determined to go ashore and I couldn't let him go alone.

Before I left my room I collected the reels of tape and locked them in my safe.

The itinerary had reminded me of something else I had forgotten—the lay of the land. The modern city of Luxor is on the east bank of the Nile. The Valley of the Kings and the other ancient cemeteries are on the west bank. The boat had landed us on the west bank. It would then cross the river and moor, along with the other tourist steamers, and we would take the ferry across to rejoin the others in time for lunch. That meant I'd have to wait till afternoon before calling Karl or attempting to locate police headquarters.

The rising sun, behind us as we left the boat, turned the western cliffs an exquisite shade of deep rose. The air was cool and would have been fresh had it not been for a couple of dozen tour buses belching out pollution.

Feisal shepherded us toward one of them. As we stood in line waiting to climb on, I managed to draw Alice aside.

"I've decided to resign," I muttered.

"I'm about to."

I asked how.

"Someone will contact me this afternoon. Luxor Temple. I'm going to stamp my little foot and demand—" She broke off. The others had boarded the bus and Feisal was gesturing at us.

Schmidt had saved me a seat. He insisted I take the one next to the window so I could see the sights, which he described in a loud voice as we drove on. The man's memory was absolutely astonishing. By his own admission he hadn't been in Egypt for ten years, but he hadn't forgotten a thing.

The drive took about fifteen minutes, through the cultivated fields and across the barren desert. We were headed straight for the cliffs. Then a cleft opened up; the road curved and passed through, into the desolate valley where for centuries the kings of the empire had been buried. Schmidt rumbled on, spouting statistics and historical data.

Louisa, brooding among her veils, was sitting across the aisle. She interrupted Schmidt's lecture to say, "What of the tomb of the great queen Nefertari?"

"No, no, that is not on today's tour," Schmidt explained tolerantly. "It is in the Valley of the Queens, so called. Now this," he went on, without drawing breath, "this has changed since my last visit. The new parking place is some distance from the tombs, which is a very good thing since the buses caused much damage. This tram on which we will ride the rest of the way is electric . . ."

I wondered what the place looked like when tourism was at its height. It was bad enough now—a dozen buses, hundreds of people. As we got off the tram and trudged along a dusty path following Feisal, Schmidt said, in the loud mumble he thinks is a whisper, "How is with you, Vicky? Will it be too difficult, descending into the depths of—"

"That's why we're here, isn't it? I wouldn't have come if I couldn't handle it."

My sharp tone didn't offend him. Nodding sympathetically, he took my arm. "I will be next to you at all times. There will be bright lights, many people."

The first tomb was the easiest; it was also the one I didn't want to miss. Tutankhamon's tomb had been closed to tourists in the past. Like most of the others in the Valley, its wall paintings were deteriorating.

In itself the small tomb was relatively unimpressive. Unlike the long complex structures designed for royal burials, this one had only a flight of stairs and a single corridor, with a few rooms at its end. The accepted theory was that Tutankhamon had died suddenly at the age of eighteen, before he had had time to prepare his tomb, so it had been necessary to take over a tomb previously constructed for a non-royal person.

"Murder," said Feisal in a sepulchral voice, as we gathered around him. "Was that how the young king died? The fracture of his skull might have been the result of a fatal accident, but he had many enemies and no heirs."

The great stone box of the sarcophagus stood in the middle

of the room. Tut's mummy still lay there, decently hidden; it had been in ruinous condition. His golden coffins were now in the Cairo Museum. Involuntarily I looked at John, who was contemplating the sarcophagus with a look of pensive interest. Surely not even he would try ... One of the damned coffins was of solid 22-karat gold, weighing almost three hundred pounds. You'd need a block and tackle just to lift the thing. But there were hundreds of other objects, all easily portable, that would be worth his time and trouble. The four small rooms of the tomb had been stuffed with objects of artistic and historic value.

They were empty now, except for the sarcophagus and the poor, battered bones of the boy himself. Eighteen years old, childless, possibly murdered ... Schmidt pulled out his handkerchief and blew his nose. He's disgustingly sentimental.

We retraced our steps—twenty-five paces, I'd counted them—along the passage and up the stairs—sixteen of them, I'd counted them too. But it hadn't bothered me. Not with lights all along the way and Schmidt snuffling sentimentally beside me. After we had emerged into daylight the custodian swung the doors shut and locked them, to the audible annoyance of several loose tourists hanging around in the hope of getting in. The tomb must be officially closed. In this, as in other ways, our group had been favored.

Schmidt started fussing at me again when we reached the next of the tombs on our list, that of Amenhotep II. It was one of the ones the guidebook had described as "deep," and Schmidt kept insisting I ought not attempt it. He was talking loudly, as usual, and if there was anyone in the group who hadn't known about my phobia, they knew now.

"Don't be silly, Schmidt," I said. "I wouldn't miss it for the world."

Down, down, down we went, and if you think I wasn't counting you are dead wrong. The stairs led down, all the corridors sloped down, and just when I thought we had reached the bottom there was another flight of stairs—leading down, in case you are wondering—and another downward-sloping passage. The square pillars in the last room were painted and inscribed. That's about all I remember. I was too busy keeping an expression of insouciant calm on my face.

Other sources of discomfort aside, it was hot and close and very dusty down in the depths. By the time we started back up, Schmidt's face was bright red and I didn't like the way he was panting. Slowing my steps to match his, stopping frequently to rest, I forgot my own qualms in concern for him. I knew he'd never admit weakness and I could have kicked Feisal when he said solicitously, "Perhaps, Herr Doktor, you had better go to the rest house and have a cool drink instead of attempting the next tomb. That of Horemheb is the deepest in the Valley; the air is not good and the heat—"

Schmidt almost choked in his attempt to stop wheezing. Before he could protest I said, "I don't care what you do, Schmidt, but I'm copping out. Where's the rest house?"

Everybody voted for the rest house, so we returned to the entrance and got onto one of the cars of the tram. The sun was now high enough to bleach all the color from the cliffs, turning them a pale tan. Not that there was much color to begin with—only the clear blue sky overhead and the garish garb of some of the tourists.

Schmidt was on his second lemonade—he wanted beer, but I wouldn't let him have it—when Larry, with whom I had been discussing tomb reliefs, broke off in mid-sentence. With a murmured "Excuse me," he rose and headed for the door.

Schroeder, hat in hand, bald head shining with sweat, awaited him. I thought it was a little odd that the man hadn't joined us, and I wasn't the only one to wonder. Everyone stopped talking and stared. Everyone except John. After a quick glance at Schroeder he leaned back and lowered his eyes. He hadn't spoken since we sat down.

After a few minutes Schroeder left and Larry returned, shaking his head and smiling. "He takes his duties too seriously, as I keep telling him. Some unimportant detail about tonight's reception."

"How long has he been with you?" I asked guilelessly.

"Let's see . . ." He turned to the omnipresent Ed. "How long has it been? A couple of years?"

"'Bout that." Ed returned to his beer. He was not much of a conversationalist.

If Ed could remember when Schroeder signed on, he had

been with Larry even longer than two years. I reminded myself that I was no longer interested in details like that.

Schmidt polished off another lemonade and two candy bars, and announced he was ready to resume the tour. I was trying to think of a way of talking him out of it when Larry said, "It's too nice a day to spend underground. How about taking the path to Deir el Bahri, Vicky? It's in the bay south of here, over that range of hills, and the view of the temple from above is wonderful. The bus could pick us up there, couldn't it, Feisal?"

Feisal nodded and Schmidt exclaimed, "Good, good. An excellent idea! I will come too."

"But Herr Direktor," Feisal protested, "it is a long, hard walk. Forty-five minutes . . ." He eyed Schmidt's rotund shape dubiously and added, "Or longer."

What was more, Schmidt hadn't been invited. I didn't waste my breath mentioning this. The walk might be the lesser of two evils. It couldn't be more taxing for Schmidt than the hot dusty airlessness of the tombs.

"We'll take it easy," Larry said, with a reassuring nod at me.

"An enticing prospect," said John. "I'll join you, if I may."

"Yes, a walk would be lovely," Mary said eagerly.

"No." He turned to her. "It would be too strenuous for you, in your condition."

Mary's jaw dropped and a charming blush spread over her face. I don't know what my face looked like, but I'm pretty sure it wasn't charming.

"Anyone else?" Larry asked, after a moment of embarrassed silence. "All right, then, we'll see you all later."

Ed hadn't said a word, but I was not surprised to find him making up one of our party. He tried to give Schmidt a hand during the first and most difficult part of the hike, the steep climb up from the Valley, but was huffily rebuffed. Once we had reached the top, Schmidt mopped his perspiring brow and gasped triumphantly, "Ha! Such a fuss you make over a little walk. If you had climbed the Zugspitze and the Matterhorn . . ." His breath gave out, so he left it there, and we all looked impressed except John, who was grinning like an idiot.

We admired the view for longer than it deserved, to give

Schmidt time to recover, and Larry pointed out the locations of other tombs. Pale in the sunlight, the great pyramid-shaped peak called the Lady of the West rose over the valley it guarded.

The next part of the walk led across the rocky summit of the plateau. The path was rough but level, and Schmidt charged valiantly ahead. John kept pace with him. I started to quicken my step. Larry took my arm. "I want to talk to you, Vicky. That's why I suggested this."

I glanced over my shoulder. Ed was some distance behind, hands in his pockets.

"What about?" I asked.

Larry lowered his voice. "About a mutual friend. His name is Burckhardt."

I stumbled over a stone no bigger than a Ping-Pong ball. Larry's hand steadied me. "Sorry. You didn't know?"

"I don't know a damn thing," I sputtered. "That son of a polecat Burck——"

"Let's not mention the name again, okay? Don't get the wrong idea, Vicky." His face wrinkled in an attractive, deprecating smile. "I haven't been leading a double life, like some superhero in the comics. I was informed of the situation by the Egyptian government. They know how intensively I have worked for better relations between Egypt and the West, and how deeply I care about the wonderful antiquities of this country. The announcement I will make this evening . . . Well, you'll hear that in due course. The idea that someone could use this trip as a cover for activities designed to destroy everything I've worked for . . ."

"I understand."

"I know you do. And I can't tell you how much I—all of us—appreciate what you're doing. It was for your own protection that I was told not to contact you earlier. Now things have changed."

"That's why Mr. Schroeder came," I said. "To tell you—"

"That the refrigerating unit didn't break down, Vicky. It was a deliberate act of sabotage. It can't be repaired, it will have to be replaced. God knows how long that will take. The tour will have to be canceled. Hamid will make the announcement when we return at noon. You see what that means, don't you?"

My eyes were fixed on Schmidt, who was gesturing animatedly. A sound like the howl of a coyote drifted to my ears. I caught a few of the words; they had to do with heaven, mama, and train whistles.

"I'm not sure I do," I said slowly. "What alternatives will the passengers be offered—aside from a refund of the fare?"

"That, of course. But I expect most of them will choose to remain in Luxor for a few days, since this is the high point of the tour. Fortunately—or unfortunately, from the viewpoint of the tourism industry—there are plenty of hotel rooms empty. After that . . ."

He looked expectantly at me. "Some may decide to return to Cairo," I muttered. "Sooner or later everybody will end up in Cairo. Where the museum is."

"Yes. Vicky, have you any idea of who these people are?"

"Yeah." I gestured. "Him."

Schmidt and John had stopped, waiting for us to join them.

"Not Anton!" Larry exclaimed.

"Don't be ridiculous. Him." I couldn't pronounce his name.

"Mr. Tregarth?" Larry sounded almost as incredulous. He slowed his steps. "But he's a well-known—"

"Crook. I've encountered him before. I don't know who the others are; he's the only one I recognized."

"Surely he wouldn't bring his pregnant bride along." Larry looked shocked.

"Excellent cover, wouldn't you say?"

I heard John laugh. Schmidt had taught him a new one. A few words floated back to me: "When I woke up, I had shackles on my feet . . ."

"Come. Vicky, hurry, why are you so slow?" Schmidt yelled. "It is a glorious view."

"One more thing," Larry said quickly. "I want you to stay with me while you're in Luxor. I have a house here, you know—"

"Of course I know. You're holding the reception there, right?"

"Right. You'll be safer there than in a hotel. Anton too, of course."

Schmidt has twenty-twenty hearing. "What about me?" he demanded.

"I'll tell you later, Schmidt," I said. "It's a surprise."

Schmidt loves surprises. Beaming, he demanded that I admire the view.

The temple of the female pharaoh, Hatshepsut, lay below, its colonnades and courtyards sharp-etched by shadow and sunlight. It is probably the most graceful, perfectly proportioned structure in Egypt. I had looked forward to seeing it.

But not under these circumstances. Beside me, hands in his pockets, hair shining like silver-gilt, John was humming under his breath. " 'It takes a worried man to sing a worried song . . . I'm worried now—but I won't be worried long.' "

That's what he thought.

# *Chapter Eight*

*i*

Hamid waited until we had assembled for lunch before making the announcement. There was the usual chorus of complaints from certain parties, but the sputtering and shouts of "Outrageous" faded as Hamid went on to outline the alternatives. They were a good deal more generous than most companies would have offered.

That afternoon we would be transferred to the Winter Palace Hotel—all expenses paid, of course. After the prearranged four days in the Theban area, passengers who wished to do so could board another cruise ship for Aswan, where they would spend several days before sailing back to Luxor. They might instead opt to return to Cairo by air for a two-week stay at Mena House or one of the four-star Cairo hotels.

"What do you say, Vicky?" Schmidt demanded. "What shall we do? Me, I vote for Cairo. Aswan is sehr interresant, but except for the nobles' tombs—"

"We don't have to make up our minds this minute."

I couldn't take my eyes off John. His face was as bland and uninformative as an oyster as he listened to Hamid. I had

no doubt what his decision would be. He had known this
would happen; he must have had a hand in arranging it. Mary
was watching him too, her expression faintly troubled. She
wouldn't be consulted, but if I had been in her shoes (which
God forbid), I'd have had my own reasons for preferring
Cairo.

Shotgun wedding, I thought, savoring the ugly phrase.
Mary's daddy must be some guy. But he could never have
cornered such an expert at elusion if John hadn't had his own
reasons for embracing matrimony. The ripe, juicy chunk of
mango I was chewing tasted like sand as the inevitable calcula-
tions reeled off in my head. At least six weeks before she
could be sure, maybe longer—a few more weeks making the
arrangements for the wedding . . .

Months. It must have been going on for months. The same
months during which he had . . . visited . . . me. While I sat
there like some slack-jawed idiot in a country music ballad,
bein' true to my man.

I swallowed the loathsome morsel with a loud gulping
sound. Schmidt looked at me in alarm. "Was ist's? Are
you going to be sick? You cannot be sick now, we have
much—"

"I'm not sick, dammit! Stop fussing, Schmidt. Let's go
and pack."

My elegantly appointed room and pretty little balcony had
never looked more appealing. So much for that luxury tour
I'd been promised; I'd never had the chance to enjoy it. Mother
had always told me that if an offer seemed too good to be
true it probably was.

The prospect of being Larry's house guest offered some
consolation. (It would certainly impress my mother.) I'd seen
photographs of his Luxor establishment in some magazine;
it wasn't just a house, it was a whole estate, with beautiful
gardens and a swimming pool and all the other odds and ends
rich people consider necessary to happiness.

And I would be far far away from John and his pregnant
bride.

I am not a neat packer, and my mood that day was not
conducive to order and method; I tossed things at random

into the bags and put them by the door. After a final check of closets and drawers to make sure I hadn't forgotten anything, I opened the safe.

The reels of tape were gone.

I was squatting in front of the safe, fumbling in its interior in the hope of finding something—a gun, a message, a box of chocolates, anything to indicate interest—when the telephone rang. I snatched it up and yelled, "What do you want, Schmidt?"

"I'm afraid it's only me," an apologetic voice murmured.

"Larry?"

"Yes. You are going to accept my invitation, I hope. I intended to repeat it in person, but you left the dining room before I could speak to you."

He had meant it, then. A little quiver ran through me, a mixture of pleasure, relief, and renewed alarm. The situation must be serious if he was anxious to get me to a safe place without delay. "It's very kind of you. Are you sure?"

"I'm sure it's the best possible place for you."

He didn't have to spell it out. "All right," I said. "Thank you. What about Schmidt?"

"I've already spoken to him. He said he'd come if you did. So it's settled. We'll meet in the lobby in, say, half an hour?"

There was no point in hanging around my room, so I headed for the lounge. I expected to find Schmidt there, since Hamid had announced the bar would be open—a final farewell to the *Queen of the Nile*, for those who chose to take advantage of it. Schmidt hadn't chosen, but several of the others had, including Alice and Feisal, who were engaged in earnest conversation. I joined them.

"So what's going to happen to you guys?" I asked.

"All friends must part at last," said Feisal with a theatrical sigh. "We part sooner than I had hoped; but not for a few more days. I will remain with the tour here in Luxor."

"And after that?"

His smile was dazzling. "Something good, for me at least. I'm not at liberty to discuss it just yet. Are you coming with me to the Luxor Temple this afternoon?"

I shook my head. Feisal gave me one of those patronizing masculine looks. "Primping for the reception instead? I will see you later at the hotel, then."

He glanced at his watch and stood up.

"I won't be at the hotel. Larry has asked me to stay with him."

Alice gave me a startled look and then laughed. "Congratulations. You're the first single woman to be so honored in years."

"He'll be adequately chaperoned," I said. "Schmidt is coming too."

Feisal grinned. He was in a good mood, all right. "He is not the marrying kind, as you say. And he is too old for you. You haven't forgotten you promised to let me show you the night life of Luxor?"

"I'd like that. Thanks, Feisal."

"Till this evening, then." He went off, collecting Suzi as he passed her table. I heard her shrill voice raised in pretended protest as he led her out.

"Are you really staying with Larry?" Alice didn't wait for me to answer. Thoughtfully she went on, "You'll be all right, then. That compound of his could withstand a siege."

"How about you?"

"I'm out of it." Alice made no effort to conceal her relief. "They've asked me to accompany the group that will be going on to Aswan."

"Then you've talked to—someone?"

The lounge was emptying, but I was wary of specific references.

"Not yet. I'm supposed to meet—someone—at the Luxor Temple later this afternoon. But I can't imagine that my services will be required any longer. The people who—the people concerned won't be going to Aswan." She drained her glass and rose. "I was going to resign anyhow. I'm too old for this sort of thing. See you later."

I let her go on before I followed. She was undoubtedly correct. The passengers who opted for the Aswan cruise had to be innocents. The Cairo-bound crowd was the one to be watched.

The last of the shore-tour group was leaving the lobby

when I got there, to find my escort waiting—Schmidt, Larry, and the inevitable Ed. The open doors led, not to the gangplank but to the lobby of another cruise ship. We had to pass through it to reach the dock. Sometimes there were as many as five moored abreast, Larry said.

The car waiting for us looked as if it had been custom-built for a sheikh, and I felt sure the tinted glass was bulletproof. Ed rode up in front with the chauffeur, which left the three of us in splendid isolation in back. There was room for the sheikh's four legal wives and a couple of concubines.

The Shari el-Bahr el-Nil, familiarly known as the corniche, runs along the riverbank. It is a handsome boulevard with a tree-lined promenade on one side and on the other a fascinating mélange of ancient temples and modern hotels and souvenir shops. We passed the Winter Palace, where our fellow passengers were to stay, and went on for another mile or so before turning into a narrow driveway. The walls ahead resembled those of a fort. They were topped with wicked-looking coils of barbed wire, and the closed gates appeared to be fashioned of steel. They swung slowly open as the car approached.

I pinched Schmidt. "You know, Schmidt, I don't think we're in Kansas anymore."

It was like the sudden switch from black and white to Technicolor in the film. For the past mile we had driven past high-rise hotels and storefronts adorned with garish signs in Arabic and half a dozen other languages. Behind these grim walls were green lawns and flower beds bright with blossoms. Winding paths led between the trees to the buildings whose rooflines showed through the leaves. The main house was a low, unpretentious structure of pale brick. Two stories in height, it was roofed with red tiles and had balconies sprouting out from the upper floor.

Schmidt didn't answer. He was gaping in childish pleasure.

When we got out of the car a bunch of Munchkins descended on us. Two of them carried my bags up the stairs to my room, where a smiling, gray-haired maid was waiting to unpack for me. She expostulated when I insisted on helping, but I didn't want her to see the condition of my underwear. I finally got rid of her by allowing her to carry off an armful of garments to be pressed.

There was mineral water in a cut-glass carafe, and a bowl of fruit on the table, not to mention a vase of fresh flowers. I hadn't eaten much for lunch. Munching an apple (did they grow apples in Egypt? Did Larry have them flown in?) I wandered out onto the balcony.

I couldn't see the ugly walls; they were screened by careful plantings of shrubs and trees. Sprays of water shone with rainbow glints, soaking the thirsty grass. I could get accustomed to living this way. It wouldn't be any trouble at all.

Glancing down at my scuffed sandals and wrinkled skirt, I smiled wryly. I doubted Larry's intentions were honorable—or even dishonorable, in the conventional sense. This was business. I'd settle for that.

He had informed us that he'd be busy for the rest of the afternoon, and told us to make ourselves at home—explore the house, the grounds, take a swim, check out the library, ask for anything we wanted.

I lay down on the bed. Just for five minutes.

I was awakened by the sound of thunder. Blinking sleepily at the sunlight striping the floor with gold, I cleverly deduced it wasn't thunder. Someone was knocking at the door. Who else but Schmidt? Well-trained servants, as we sophisticates know, do not pound on doors.

"Come in," I called, stretching like a cat.

He came. Or was it another Munchkin? His robe, striped in green and purple, left his plump calves bare. His little pink toes stuck out of his huaraches.

"Why do you waste time in sleeping?" he demanded. "Already I have explored the house. You must see it, Vicky, he has some of the finest antiques I have seen—not antiquities, you understand, but Islamic art and furniture. But there is no time now. We are having the cocktails at the pool. Hurry and put on your bikini."

It struck me as a good idea. I fished my suit—it was not a bikini, I am a modest woman—out of the drawer and retired to the bathroom. Schmidt reached for a tangerine.

"Ah, that is very nice," he said approvingly when I emerged. "No, do not cover it up! You do not have a big stomach like mine, you do not have to—"

"Shut up, Schmidt," I said amiably, slipping into my robe.

He led the way unerringly down the stairs and along a shadowy corridor that ended in an inner court, with its own high walls. Hibiscus and roses bloomed with tropical luxuriance; jasmine twined over a pergola at one end of the huge free-form pool whose blue waters sparkled in the sunlight. Larry rose from one of the chairs under the pergola and hurried toward me.

He was wearing black trunks and I *think* he was trying to suck in his stomach. In fact he looked a lot fitter than most men of his age; but I'm afraid I wasn't paying much attention. Something else—someone else—had caught my eye.

He was poised, arms raised and knees slightly bent, on the diving board at the other end of the pool. He didn't look in my direction but I knew he had seen me; the pose was designed to show off his tan and the lean lines of his body, and he held it a little too long before he sprang and dived, slipping through the air and into the water as smoothly as a water snake.

I turned to Larry. "What the hell—"

I was so outraged I had forgotten Schmidt. Larry's raised hand reminded me. Schmidt was trotting toward the pergola, but if I'd gone on at the same volume he would have heard me.

"It's as difficult to get out of this place as it is to get in," Larry said quietly. "I'd rather have him here, where I can monitor his activities, than on the loose in Luxor."

"He's not stupid enough to make any false moves here," I insisted. "He knows he's under suspicion."

"Stupid, no." Larry's eyes were focused on John, who had pulled himself out of the water and was sitting on the edge of the pool. Schmidt came trotting up to him, waving a glass and calling out enthusiastic greetings. Smiling in response, John leaned back, supporting himself on his elbows. The movement stretched the muscles of his chest over the underlying structures of ribs and clavicles. He had lost weight—not much, he had never had much to lose, but those elegant bones were more visible now.

"Stupid, no," Larry repeated. "Arrogant, yes. If we give him enough rope . . ."

"His complexion is perfect gallows." I had proposed that once, as a fitting epitaph for John. Did they hang people in Egypt?

"I need a drink," I said.

John slid back into the water. Schmidt peeled off his robe, flung it aside with the panache of Arnold Schwarzenegger (whom he did not in the least resemble), pinched his nose with two fat fingers, and leaped into the pool. A fountain of water billowed skyward. Averting my eyes, I followed Larry toward the pergola. Mary was there, stretched out on a deck chair, half-hidden by sprays of jasmine, and not much else. Her suit was very French—a few patches and a few strings. In her case the effect was cute rather than sexy; she was shaped as delicately as a child. Not a bulge anywhere.

I forced myself to stop counting. Feeling like a big blond ox, I lumbered pergolaward and took a chair next to Mary while Larry busied himself with glasses and ice. Very cozy and informal it was, no servants, just a small group of friends.

"Isn't this lovely?" Mary said. "So kind of Larry."

"Uh-huh."

From the far end of the pool two voices blended—to use the term loosely—in song. Apparently they were delving deep into the historical roots of country music, for this was a real oldie. " 'If I had the wings of an angel, Over these prison walls I'd fly . . .' "

Not bloody likely, I thought. There was no way he'd get out of it this time. And nobody deserved it more.

*ii*

When I got back to my room I found that my freshly pressed clothes had been returned to the closet. They smelled faintly of jasmine.

It wasn't a closet, in fact, but an enormous gilded and painted cupboard, serving the same function as an armoire. My pitiful wardrobe occupied less than half of the vast interior.

The cupboard was lined with sandalwood, and like every other piece of furniture in the room it was old, beautiful, and probably extremely valuable. I examined the paintings appreciatively, wishing I knew as much as I had claimed about medieval Islamic art. Like orthodox Judaism, Islam avoids the use of the human form in art. These designs featured flowers, animals, and the ornamental Kufic script. An ornate grille, gilded and pierced so cleverly that the openings formed part of an overall pattern, covered the top half of the doors. A good idea that, in a hot climate; it allowed air to circulate among the garments hanging inside.

In contrast to the bedroom, the adjoining bath was completely modern. There was even a built-in hair dryer, and I blessed Larry as I worked on my dank locks. I'd been a fool to let my hair grow long, it was thick and heavy and took forever to dry. I promised myself I'd have it cut as soon as I got home.

We were to dine, en famille, with our host at seven-fifteen. The reception started at nine. I figured it would be pretty fancy, but the best I could do was my good old, slinky black cocktail dress. I had just slipped into it when Schmidt banged on my door. He was ten minutes early. I padded on stockinged feet to the door and opened it. Schmidt's face fell. He's always trying to catch me with my clothes off.

"You are ready," he said sadly.

"Not by a damn sight. Sit down, Schmidt, I've got to do my hair."

"It is very pretty hanging over your shoulders like that. Leave it so."

"It gets in my mouth when I eat."

In white tie and tails Schmidt looked like a portly penguin. He wandered to the mirror and began preening, straightening his tie and adjusting the ribbon that stretched diagonally across his chest. The ribbon was purple. I'd been with him when he bought it. I had talked him out of buying a medal to hang on it.

I decked myself out in my jewels, including the gold locket and *not* including the enameled rose. The locket had never looked tackier. Watching, Schmidt opened his mouth and then decided not to comment. He's tried several times to buy jewelry for me, and in that area, as in anything to do with art, he has superb taste. He also has more money than he knows what to do with. So why hadn't I accepted his gifts? Not because I suspected his motives. Schmidt loves me like a daughter and a friend. I suppose it was because I didn't want our friendship to be contaminated by expensive and one-sided presents.

I can be a damn fool at times.

At the top of the stairs Schmidt offered me his arm and we strutted down them with slow dignity. I knew he was seeing us, not as a cute little fat man and a tall gangly female, but as King Rudolf and Princess Flavia descending to the ballroom between rows of curtsying courtiers. In a sudden burst of affection I squeezed his arm. He squeezed back but he didn't look at me. He was smiling with regal condescension and matching his steps to the strains of the royal anthem of Ruritania.

I can't say that intimate dinner party was particularly enjoyable. Whitbread and Schroeder weren't present; I assumed they were supervising the final arrangements for the reception. Schmidt devoted himself to Mary, whose slim arms and delicate collarbones were exposed by a low-cut, blue chiffon frock that might as well have been printed with dollar signs. She was wearing a parure of sapphires and diamonds—earrings, necklace, and bracelet. The heavy bracelet weighted her narrow wrist.

For once John said very little. He seemed preoccupied; once or twice Mary had to repeat a comment or question before he responded.

Finally Larry looked at his watch. "We'd better go in. The guest will be arriving soon."

The grand salon occupied one entire side of the house. Words fail me when I attempt to describe it. (They fail me because I still don't know much about Islamic architecture.) The outside wall, the one facing the gardens, was a glorious hodgepodge of stained-glass panels and intricately carved wooden screens. The arches and pillars framing the windows were covered with antique tiles in shades of blue-green and coral.

The objects arranged in niches along two inner walls

weren't Islamic, but ancient Egyptian—a life-sized sandstone head of a pharaoh wearing the double crown, a small painted statue of a slender girl carrying a basket on her head, a wooden panel from a cosmetic box, with a charming painting of an ibis crouching, or squatting, or whatever ibises do. It was a modest collection for a man with Larry's money and taste. They were all good pieces, but none was what I'd have called outstanding.

I didn't have time to examine them in detail. Larry drew me to the door, where I stood for the next half hour helping him receive his guests. It was probably the high point of my social life. As I shook hands with the Minister of the Interior and allowed the head of the Egyptian Antiquities Organization to kiss my fingertips I couldn't help thinking, Wow, wait till Mom hears about this! Even the best of us (which doesn't include me) is susceptible to snobbery.

Our buddies from the tour were among the last to arrive. Suzi flashed her teeth at Larry and gave me a huge hug. Her diamonds left dents in my chest. Larry passed her on to a minister of something. I greeted Sweet and his silent companion, noted that Louisa's veils were already slipping, and pressed the flesh with the others. Among them was Feisal, resplendent in black tie and tails. He kissed my hand and winked at me.

"That's enough," Larry said, when the last of them had gone on. "Come and have some champagne. You've earned it."

Almost at once he was captured by some dignitary or other and I retreated to a relatively quiet corner. Sipping my champagne—with caution, since it has an unfortunate effect on me—I surveyed the room. "Our" crowd had gathered together, except for Suzi, who had found herself a general. Or maybe a colonel, I didn't know the significance of the insignia. He had several square acres of ribbons on his chest, and he seemed to be as fascinated by Suzi as she was by him. I spotted Ed, strategically situated by the windows opening onto the lawn, his eyes ceaselessly scanning the crowd. His tux had been cut by a good tailor, but it bulged in several places. At first I couldn't locate Schmidt. Then I saw him coming toward me, accompanied by a youngish man with a broad, open face that inspired a sudden wave of violent homesickness. My home town is full of people with faces like that. He had to be from Minnesota.

He had been born in Duluth, but that didn't emerge until later in the conversation. Schmidt introduced him as Dr. Paul Whitney, the director of Chicago House, the Luxor-based branch of the Oriental Institute.

"Skip the titles," Paul said, with a broad smile. (Oh, those lovely big teeth! Only in Minnesota . . .) "The place is swarming with doctors. Quite an occasion, isn't it?"

"I don't know what the occasion is," I admitted. "Larry said something about a surprise, but . . ."

"It's not that much of a surprise. We're a hopeless bunch of gossips here in Luxor. Larry is handing this place over to the Antiquities Organization and endowing it as a research institute specializing in conservation."

He took a glass from the tray a waiter had offered. So did I. What the heck, two glasses wouldn't hurt me.

"A most kind and generous action," said Schmidt. "I hope, my young friend Paul, that you are not out of joint in the nose concerning this."

It took Paul a few seconds to figure that one out. Then he laughed. "It's certainly a more impressive setup than ours. The Epigraphic Survey began in the twenties, and although we've tried to keep up-to-date, it isn't easy to get funding. There have been many new technological developments in archaeology, and the equipment costs a bundle. Everything here is state-of-the-art, from the computer setup to the laboratories. But no, our noses aren't out of joint. Quite the contrary. We're in the conservation business too, recording the monuments before they are destroyed."

Schmidt asked a couple of questions about the Temple of Medinet Habu, which had been one of the Survey's major projects, and in which I had only a vague interest. Actually, to be honest, I had no interest whatever. Seeing my wandering eye, Paul amiably changed the subject.

"If you have the time, Vicky, we'd be delighted to have you visit our humble establishment. Our library is one of the best in the country, should you care to use it."

I expressed my appreciation, adding that between Feisal,

Alice, and Perry I had already been stuffed full of information I'd probably forget within two weeks.

"They're all first-rate," Paul agreed. "Only the best for a fancy tour like yours. Oh, that reminds me—there is someone among your crowd I'm anxious to meet. You both know Mr. Tregarth, I'm sure. Can you point him out to me?"

"We will do better," Schmidt exclaimed. "We will present you. He is an old . . . er, hmm. We have become good friends during the voyage. Now where . . . Ah, there he is, talking with the Minister of the Interior."

If I'd needed anything else to complete my state of demoralization, that last sentence would have done it. The Interior Ministry controls, among other offices, that of State Security.

As we approached, the stout, coffee-colored gentleman with whom John had been conversing gave him a friendly slap on the back and turned away. John saw us coming. Eyebrow raised in polite inquiry, he awaited us.

Paul introduced himself; he was too eager to wait for Schmidt. "This is indeed a pleasure, Mr. Tregarth. The Director wrote to you, but I'm delighted to be able to express our appreciation in person."

"Appreciation," said somebody. Me, in fact.

John lowered his eyes modestly but not before I had seen the wicked glint in them.

"Mr. Tregarth was instrumental in restoring to the Oriental Institute an artifact that had been stolen," Paul explained. "One of his employees bought it, accepting the fraudulent documentation the seller presented, but when Mr. Tregarth saw it he recognized the piece and contacted us."

"How much did he take you for?" I inquired. Two glasses of champagne *had* been too many.

John's face lengthened into a look of noble suffering, but the glint was still there, and it was still directed at me. Paul said, shocked, "Only what he had paid for the piece, which was minimal. He wouldn't even accept a finder's fee."

"It was nothing," John murmured. "Anyone would have done the same."

I was spared further dramatics by Larry, who called for silence so that he could make his announcement. It was brief and quiet and modest, but bureaucrats can't do anything simply; everybody who was anybody had to make a speech. A couple of them embraced Larry, to his evident embarrassment. He concluded by presenting the new director of the new institute, a stocky, bearded young Swiss named Jean-Louis Mazarin. I had noticed him earlier, chug-a-lugging champagne. He had cause for celebration, all right. Jobs in archaeology are scarce, and this one was a scholar's dream. It was a fitting gesture of appreciation, said Larry, for Dr. Mazarin's supervision of the restoration of Tetisheri's tomb paintings.

Fitting, maybe; but not particularly tactful. I was surprised that the first director wasn't an Egyptian.

But not as surprised as I had been at Paul's gushing thanks. What was John up to now? He must have some ulterior motive, he always did. The most obvious explanation was that the Oriental Institute now owned a very well-made fake. Making them pay for it was a particularly nice touch.


The party was still in full swing when Larry edged up to me and invited me to come see his etchings. They were sketches, actually—the original hand-colored drawings of Egyptian sites made back in the 1830s by an artist named David Roberts. I'd seen countless reproductions of them on postcards and notepaper. Even the prints sold for hundreds of dollars at auction.

The main object of interest, however, was a man, short and slim and straight. He rose from his chair when we entered Larry's study, and although he was in civilian clothes you could see the invisible uniform. He cut Larry's introduction short.

"First names will suffice," he said, with a smile that came nowhere near his intent dark eyes. "Call me Achmet."

"I'd like to call you a few other names," said my champagne-loosened tongue. "What the hell's the idea of leaving me out in the cold without even a woolly scarf?"

"Sit down, please," said Achmet.

I sat. I imagine most people sat when Achmet told them to.

"I am sorry you feel that way," he went on. "We could not anticipate that our arrangements would be . . . disarranged."

"Ali was disarranged some too, wasn't he?"

His lips tightened. "He was murdered, yes. But you have nothing more to worry about, Dr. Bliss. Your part of the job is finished. Tregarth was the only one you recognized? You have not identified any of his allies?"

"Yes and no, in that order," I said shortly.

"Then there is no more for you to do." He sat back and spread his hands wide. "He will be under observation from now on. Enjoy the remainder of your visit to our country, and forget what has happened."

"Just a damned minute," I said, as he got to his feet. "I've got a few questions of my own."

"The less you know the better for you."

"Oh, that haunting old refrain! So I'm curious. What if he doesn't go through with it? He knows me. He knows—"

"That he is under suspicion?" Achmet stroked his neat black mustache. "I imagine he does. Your presence on the cruise would be enough to alert him to that."

"I told Burckhardt so at the beginning."

Achmet shrugged. "It does not matter. If he proceeds, and we believe he will, there is no way he can avoid being caught."

"What's he after?" I demanded. "I hope it's occurred to you, as it has to me, that the museum could be a decoy. While you increase security there, he may walk off with something else."

"Certainly it occurred to us." Achmet was halfway to the door. Obviously I bored him. He turned for a final word. "I told you to forget it, Dr. Bliss. Stay away from Tregarth, from the museum, and most especially from the offices of State Security."

"That's all very well and good. What if he—they—won't stay away from me?"

Achmet looked exasperated. At least I think that was the import of his frown. His face didn't appear to be capable of any more affable expression than annoyance. "Why should they bother with you? You have passed on the only information you possessed. Stop prying into matters that no longer concern you and you will be perfectly safe."

I returned his scowl with interest. "You guys were the ones who asked me to pry."

"That is true. We are very grateful for your assistance."

It was the most insincere thank-you I have ever heard, and I include a few I'd wrung out of John.

My memories of the remainder of the evening are somewhat blurred. People kept pressing champagne on me, and by that time I couldn't think of any reason to refuse. I had a little chat with Alice, who was looking quite elegant in sequins and chiffon; she had been told the same thing Achmet had told me: you're off the case, forget the whole thing. I vaguely remember congratulating Jean-Louis, the new director, but I don't recall what we talked about or how I got to bed.

I woke with a hangover, of course. Served me right.

The reopening of Tetisheri's tomb turned out to be another big occasion. I had expected a minister or two, but I hadn't realized there would be so many reporters or that security would be so tight. Our little caravan was accompanied by a military escort, and when we reached the site I realized there were no tourists around except us. Everywhere I looked I saw uniformed men carrying rifles.

Tetisheri's tomb is not in the Valley of the Kings or the Valley of the Queens. The royals and nobles of her dynasty had been buried on the slopes of a hill called the Dira' Abu'l-Naga. She was one of the last of her line to be buried in that cemetery; her predecessors had taken the choicer and more accessible sites in the flanks of the hill. The fact that hers was higher, at the back of a narrow cleft, had probably contributed to its survival.

We climbed the modern stairs that had made access to the tomb easier for the men who had worked on it for over three years. Naturally there were more speeches. Larry handed over a huge key to the minister, who unlocked the iron gates that had been built over the entrance. Everybody clapped, and Larry led the first party inside. All were government dignitaries. The rest of us commoners had to cool our heels.

While we were awaiting our turn I chatted with Paul Whitney. Only a few archaeologists had been invited, and according to Paul, plenty of noses were out of joint. "We all complain about the damage done to the tombs by visitors," he said with a wry smile. "But we except ourselves."

"So are you going to decline the invitation?" I asked.

"You've got to be kidding."

"I am."

I wasn't even worried about my claustrophobia. Compared to the more elaborate later tombs, this one was small and simple—a single flight of stairs, a short corridor, and two rooms. Only ten people were allowed in at a time, but the rooms seemed very crowded because we huddled together, elbows tight against our sides. We had been warned not to touch the paintings.

Carefully I edged up to one of the walls and squinted at close range. The ancient artists had covered the rock walls with a layer of plaster before applying the paint, and by the time Larry's people got to work, moisture and the formation of salt crystals had separated large sections of plaster from the rock behind it. The loose sections had been carefully removed and placed onto padded supports; then the rock wall had been cleaned before the plaster was replaced, using modern adhesives that wouldn't flake or dry or shrink as older types had often done. Not until that process was complete could the actual restoration begin—cleaning off the accumulated grime of decades, replacing tiny flakes of paint that had fallen to the floor or between the rock and the facing. The patience and skill required had been extraordinary.

After we emerged I found a convenient boulder and sat down, tipping my hat over my eyes. I must be getting used to the climate. The hot, dry air felt good. Yes, by God, I would do as jolly old Achmet had suggested—forget distractions and enjoy myself.

I could probably talk Schmidt into going to Aswan. It would be pleasant to cruise, without distractions. We could come back to Luxor later, after . . .

They'd be watching every move he made from now on, poised like cats by a mouse hole, waiting for him to commit the act that would condemn him to prison, or to a narrower and more permanent resting place. People have been shot while resisting arrest.

A pair of booted feet came into view and I looked up to see Jean-Louis. I wasn't sorry to have my train of thought interrupted.

"Do you have a cigarette?" Jean-Louis asked brusquely.

"I'm sorry, I don't . . ." Then I remembered that I did.

Reaching into my bag, I dredged out my cigarettes. The pack was almost full, but it was rather squashed. "Keep it," I added generously.

"That is most kind."

It wasn't, but I didn't say so. He must be a chain-smoker. The ground where he had been standing was littered with butts.

"So, did you enjoy the paintings?" he asked.

"I'm still dazzled. You've done a magnificent job. Mes hommages."

Between the mop of bushy hair and the beard I couldn't see much of his face, but he didn't respond to my smile. "It is only one small part of what needs to be done. That is what the work of the institute will be—preservation. A worthy cause, do you not think?"

"Unquestionably. As I said—"

"A cause worthy of sacrifice."

He appeared to be talking to himself rather than to me. I wondered if the guy was drunk. Surely not at this hour? His hands were shaking as he lit another cigarette from the butt of the first.

I could feel relays clicking into place. I don't know how society conditions women into feeling that they are obliged to console, reassure, and flatter melancholy males. I'd fought the impulse ever since I was old enough to recognize it, but I hadn't been entirely successful. I decided that Jean-Louis must be one of those unfortunate people who can't see the doughnut for the hole. Apparently he was brooding on the magnitude of the task ahead and questioning his ability to carry it out. The job would never be finished, not in his lifetime at least; there was too much to be done. That's true of a lot of things, though, including the achievement of social justice, universal peace, and a world in which there are no hungry children. It's no excuse to stop working toward those ends.

I said as much, larding the pompous speech with compliments, and gradually his face, or at least his mouth, relaxed. "It is true," he said thoughtfully. "And I am one of the few who can work effectively in this area."

"Uh—right," I said.

He went on to tell me how good he was at the restoration business and I went on to regret my womanly instincts. My wandering eye caught that of Larry, who had been watching us, and he responded to my unspoken plea for rescue.

"Come now, Jean-Louis, you're supposed to be mingling," he said.

"Me too," I said, rising. "I haven't had a chance to talk to our former shipmates."

Larry accompanied me. "Moody fellow, isn't he?" I inquired, when we were out of earshot.

Larry frowned. "He hasn't any reason to be moody right now. What did he say?"

"I'm afraid I didn't pay much attention."

"He was talking a lot. Unusual for him, he's not very sociable."

"He was fishing for compliments," I said. "Getting them, too."

Our shipmates greeted us with open arms. Sweet, who had apparently recovered from his bout of sickness, said slyly, "We were afraid you had deserted us, Vicky."

"I'd desert you too if I had the chance," Suzi said with a big grin. "How about wangling an invitation for me, Vicky?"

"I was only asked because . . . because of Schmidt," I said, fumbling for a reasonable explanation. "He and Larry are old pals."

"What about the Tregarths?" Suzi demanded. "They aren't old pals of Larry's, are they?"

"I've no idea what prompted that invitation," I said.

"Tregarth is good at pushing in where he's not wanted," said Perry, joining us.

"I can't get anyone an invitation," I said pointedly. "I wouldn't be rude enough to try."

"So what are your plans?" Sweet asked. "Will you be going on to Aswan with us day after tomorrow?"

I said I hadn't made up my mind. Some of the others were still wavering, but the majority had opted for the Aswan cruise. Including Sweet and Bright. Obviously I'd been wrong about them. But I still couldn't understand why Bright had lied about his origins.

"At any rate we will enjoy one another's company for a day or two longer," Sweet said cheerfully. "Are you coming to Karnak with us this afternoon, Vicky?"

The party was breaking up. Feisal began herding the group toward their bus and I returned to "my" stretch limo, but not before I had agreed to join the others that afternoon. It was pure reverse snobbism; I didn't want them to think I was too stuck up to mingle with non-billionaires.

There were five of us in the limo, not counting the chauffeur, but it wouldn't have seemed crowded if John hadn't been one of the five. At least I didn't have to sit next to him. I climbed in after Schmidt, and Larry took the seat beside me. Leaning back with a sigh, he loosened his tie.

"You must be glad it's over," I said.

Larry glanced at me and smiled sheepishly. "I hate ceremony and long speeches. I am glad to be done with that part of it, but it will be hard to leave Egypt."

I figured I'd done my duty as a sympathetic female, and I couldn't feel too sorry for a man who owned—if I remembered the newspaper stories correctly—six other residences, including a château in the Loire Valley.

"You can always build another house," I said.

"I have too many damn houses already," Larry said, with an uncanny impression of having read my thoughts. "No, I won't live in Egypt again."

"I'm sure they'll always have a spare room for a guest," said John.

He was referring to Jane Austen, but none of the others caught the allusion, or its implications. Nasty old Aunt Norris in *Mansfield Park* always had a spare room because she never invited anyone to stay with her.

Schmidt chuckled fatly. "For you, Larry, there will always be a spare room anywhere in Egypt. You have done the country a great service. When will you be departing, mein Freund? You must tell us when we are in the way. The ETAP hotel, I understand, is very fine; we can take ourselves there at any time."

Larry assured us we were welcome to stay as long as we liked. "The packers are coming tomorrow. It will take a while, since some of the ceramics and furniture are old and fragile, so there's no hurry. Have you decided on your future plans?"

He looked at John. John was looking at me. One eyebrow went up.

I remembered what Achmet had said. This seemed like an appropriate moment to indicate my complete disinterest in John Tregarth alias Smythe and all his works. "I'm going to Aswan," I said.

"But Vicky," Schmidt began.

"You don't have to come along, Schmidt."

"I will go where you go," Schmidt said, as I had hoped he would. Otherwise I'd have had to kidnap him and drag him away by force.

So that afternoon we went to the temple of Karnak. John and Mary decided to join us. I hadn't invited them. Schmidt had. Larry declined; he said he had work to do, and he'd seen the temple several dozen times.

We had to wait a few minutes for the rest of the group to arrive. Studying the crowds that filled the passage between the rows of ram-headed sphinxes, I said, "I can't imagine what this place is like when tourism is at its peak. Look at all those people."

"This is not an area where there have been attacks on tourists," Schmidt said, nodding encouragingly at Mary.

Mary's devoted husband wasn't so considerate of her feelings. Frowning slightly, he said, "Not precisely true, Schmidt. There was a bombing here a couple of years ago and another attempt earlier this season."

"Ah, but those attacks were in objection to what the fundamentalists consider the worship of the old heathen gods," Schmidt explained. "Some of these peoples"—his pointing finger indicated a group of unkempt visitors in ponytails and cut-off jeans—"the New Agers, you call them, hold ceremonies in the temple. We, we don't worship anything."

"We sure don't," I agreed. John grinned at me. Avoiding his eyes, I went on, "You're right about that bunch, Schmidt, they're all wearing amulets and crystals and earrings and junk. Why do they have to look so scruffy?"

"Their spiritual consciousness has elevated them above

earthly desire," said John, in a voice I knew well. "I should think you'd approve, Vicky; you dislike crass materialism and vulgar acquisitiveness, don't you?"

I was saved from replying by the arrival of our shipmates. Falling in step with Feisal I remarked, "You're looking very pleased with yourself, Feisal. Are you going to tell me about that good news you mentioned, or is it still a secret?"

"Not any longer." Feisal stopped and turned to face me. He thumped himself on the chest. "Greet, with proper respect, the assistant director of the institute."

I caught his hand and shook it vigorously. "Congratulations! I'm absolutely delighted."

Feisal kept hold of my hand as we walked on. "You'll help me celebrate, perhaps. I promised to show you some of the night life of Luxor."

"That would be great. But why are you guiding this tour?"

"I'm no quitter, as you Americans say. As soon as I get the last of this lot onto the plane in Cairo I'll come back and take up my new position. In the meantime I will carry out my duties like a good little soldier. All right, friends, gather around; the temple of Karnak is not one temple but a complex of temples, built over many centuries. The Avenue of Sphinxes . . ."

People wandered off as we proceeded, some to stop and rest, others to inspect a particular area in more detail. Schmidt and I had paused to look at an obelisk and he was lecturing me about the career of Hatshepsut—"one of the first feminists, Vicky, she should be of interest to you"—when I saw a familiar face that didn't belong to our group. A familiar beard, rather.

"I have been looking all over for you," Jean-Louis said grumpily.

"What for?" I asked. He certainly didn't look like a man who has finally found the girl of his dreams.

"To show you the temple, of course. Didn't you ask that I do so?"

"We are delighted to have you, of course," Schmidt exclaimed, before I could answer. Just as well; I would have said no, I hadn't. However, I was familiar with the habit some people have of believing in their own fantasies. I must have made a hit with Jean-Louis. That would teach me not to go around oozing sympathy.

He'd worked on the Aton Temple project for three years before leaving it to take up Larry's offer, and he knew Karnak as I know my own apartment. We finally managed to pry him away from that part of the temple and talked him into showing us boring tourist stuff like the Hypostyle Hall. "Impressive" is an overused word, but it's the only word for that cluster of mammoth columns. The only thing wrong with it was the tourists. One group had squatted in a circle and I recognized the seekers after truth we had seen entering the temple earlier. They were muttering to themselves and waving their hands. I heard somebody say something about auras.

"Cretins," Jean-Louis muttered.

"They do no harm," Schmidt said tolerantly.

Finally I decided I'd absorbed enough for one day and I cut Jean-Louis short in the middle of a translation of the annals of Thutmose III. He was reading the hieroglyphs off the wall. It was a wasted exhibition so far as I was concerned; how did I know he was reading them right?

Jean-Louis consulted his watch. "Yes, we must go. Mr. Blenkiron has sent the car for us, it will be waiting."

I spotted Suzi as we passed through the Hypostyle Hall. She waved and I waved back, but Jean-Louis didn't stop. I deduced that we were late. When we emerged from the last—or first, depending on which way you were going—pylon into the Avenue of Sphinxes, John and Mary were waiting. She looked done in. I didn't blame her; we had covered a lot of territory and still seen only part of the enormous complex.

That was when it happened. The force of the explosion threw me to the ground, or maybe it was Schmidt who threw me to the ground. He was on top of me when I got my breath and my wits back.

I decided I probably wasn't dead. I wished I could be sure about Schmidt. The plump pink hand lying on the ground near my face was flaccid and unmoving. I tried to squirm out from under him. People were screaming and there were sounds like firecrackers.

The weight on my back lifted. I got to my hands and knees, then to my knees. John was bending over Schmidt, shaking him. Schmidt's head rolled back and forth, then his eyes opened and he let out a anguished bellow. "Vicky? Vicky, wo bist du? Bist du verletzt? Ach, Gott—"

"You'll do," John said, stepping back. "Stop shrieking, Schmidt, she's not hurt."

"Speak for yourself." My shins and forearms had taken the brunt of the fall. Blood oozed from a few square feet of scraped skin. "What happened?"

Schmidt crawled over to me and enveloped me in a hug. "It was a bomb, Vicky. Terrorists, setting off bombs and shooting. Gott sei Dank, you are not injured."

I could see over his shoulder. The cloud of dust from the explosion was still settling. Other people had been bowled over but they didn't appear to be badly hurt, for they were moving and cursing. All except one. The bloody cavern where his face had been was framed all around by sticky wisps of hair.

# Chapter Nine

Mary had crumpled to the ground in a huddle of green voile and tumbled brown curls. John dragged her to her feet. "Let's get out of this."

"Shouldn't we wait for the police?" I squawked. I was trying not to throw up.

John didn't bother to answer. Towing his stumbling bride, he was already on his way, leading the retreat as usual. Schmidt tugged at me. "He is right, there may be more shooting. Come, we can do nothing here."

That seemed to be the general consensus. Screaming and shoving, people poured through the entrance. Their sheer numbers overwhelmed the guards, who appeared to be as shaken as the visitors. They were waving their rifles around in a disorganized manner, and one of them fired into the air. I think it was into the air. If it was intended to stop the stampede, it failed; the sound of gunfire made people even crazier. The crowd exploded into the parking lot, carrying us with them.

John materialized out of somewhere. He grabbed Schmidt by the collar. "This way."

Ed was standing by the car. When he saw us coming he opened the back door and motioned vigorously with the large, heavy, lethal object he was holding in his right hand. "In. Move it!"

John still had Schmidt by the collar. He heaved him in, gave me a hard shove, and followed close on my heels, scooping said heels and the legs to which they were attached in with him. The door slammed and the car took off.

We got our arms and legs sorted out eventually. Ed had gotten in front with the driver. The gun was no longer in sight. Mary crouched in the corner; her eyes were open, but they had a fixed, glassy stare. Her pretty frock was crumpled and dusty. Perched on the jump seat opposite, John ran his fingers through his disheveled hair. There wasn't a mark on him, or on Schmidt, who had cleverly managed to fall on top of me. I was bleeding all over Larry's expensive velvet upholstery.

I fully expected a visit, if not a reprimand, from the police. I should have known no such vulgarity would be perpetrated on a person like Larry. Schmidt was in my room trying to persuade me to let him wind yards of bandages around my scraped arms and legs when a servant knocked at the door and informed us that the master hoped we would join him on the terrace for drinks.

The others were already there. Mary had changed her dress. She was wearing white—and the Greek earrings. Larry began fussing over my injuries, but I cut his expressions of sympathy short. "Just scrapes and bruises. I'm fine. Unlike poor Jean-Louis. It was he, wasn't it? I couldn't . . . I couldn't be sure."

"So I have been informed. He was carrying identification, of course." Always the perfect host, Larry handed me a glass before dropping into a chair. He covered his eyes with his hand. "I dread telling his parents. They were so proud of him."

A tear rolled down Schmidt's cheek. "It is furchtbar— frightful, terrible. Just when he had attained his fondest dream. What will you do now about the institute, Larry?"

Impeccably groomed, gracefully lounging, John drawled, "Every cloud has a silver lining, they say. This seems to be Feisal's silver lining. Or are you going to appoint someone else as director?"

Even Larry had a hard time remaining courteous in the face of that outrageous speech. He answered shortly, "Feisal will assume the post, of course. He's on his way here now. We have a number of things to discuss, so I'll have to ask you to excuse me when he arrives."

"Have they caught the terrorists?" I asked.

"Not yet. Apparently there was a great deal of confusion. The police are rounding up—"

"The usual suspects," I murmured. From what I'd heard about the SSI, the usual suspects wouldn't have a pleasant time.

John put his glass on the table and stood up. "I think I'll have a swim. Anyone join me?"

Mary shook her head. Schmidt said doubtfully, "It does not seem proper."

Hands in his pockets, lips pursed in a whistle, John sauntered toward the house. His pitch was perfect. I recognized the strains of "The Wreck on the Highway." He really was exceeding himself in tactlessness that afternoon. There hadn't been any whiskey but there had been plenty of blood. And I hadn't heard anyone pray.

Larry reassured Schmidt—"After all, you hardly knew the poor man—" but Schmidt remained seated. I wouldn't like to imply that he was lacking in sensitivity, but I suspected mixed motives. He wanted more to eat and more to drink and more in the way of information. Browsing among the hors d'oeuvres, he peppered Larry with questions. Had anyone else been injured? Had a motive for the attack been established? Where had the bombs been placed, how had they been set off . . . Larry had no answers. A servant finally came to announce that Feisal was waiting in Larry's study, and Larry excused himself. Schmidt decided he'd have a swim after all and since I could not decide which alternative was less appealing—having a heart-to-heart with the pregnant bride or watching the pregnant bride's husband flex his muscles at me—I went to my room.

I didn't know the answers to the questions Schmidt had asked either, but my admittedly confused memories of the event raised a couple of others he hadn't asked. I had seen a big hole in the pavement and a lot of dust, but to the best of my recollection not a single column had toppled and nary a sphinx had been scarred. I had seen a lot of fallen bodies, but only one that was undeniably dead. The murder of a foreigner, and a foreign archaeologist at that, would raise a real stink. The usual suspects were in for a hard time. But maybe this time they were fall guys, not perps. (Note the technical vocabulary. We well-known amateur sleuths like to sound professional.)

I cannot say I felt particularly professional at that moment. What I felt was scared spitless, as my mother used to say, innocently unaware of the word the euphemism concealed. Bits and pieces of a theory were scuttling around in my brain like beetles with too many legs and shifty dispositions, darting for cover behind lumps of stupidity whenever I tried to swat one of them. The overall pattern was so preposterous I'd have laughed it off if anyone but John had been involved.

One thing stood out shining and clear though, and when I joined the others for dinner I was trying to think of a way of proposing it that wouldn't make matters even worse. Larry did not join us. He had sent his apologies, claiming he would be busy all evening. It seemed a heaven-sent opportunity for making my move.

"I feel guilty about taking advantage of Larry," I said, poking at a delectable fruit salad. "He's too polite to say so, but I'm sure we're making things more difficult for him. Not only is he getting ready to leave, but Jean-Louis's death will involve a good many additional administrative problems. What do you say we check out and move to a hotel, Schmidt?"

Usually Schmidt was agreeable to any activity as long as he could do it with me, but this time he looked mutinous. "We can give help and comfort to our poor friend—"

"I doubt you can give him the sort of help he needs," John said dryly. "I think Vicky's hit on a splendid idea. We'll miss you when you're gone, of course. Both of you."

If that wasn't a hint I'd never heard one. From the tilt of John's eyebrow I deduced it was also a quote from one of Schmidt's country ballads. Lots of them are about missing people after they've gone, and in most cases "gone" doesn't mean temporarily removed from the scene.

The meal dragged on, prolonged primarily by Schmidt,

who ate hugely of everything offered. Nobody else seemed to have much of an appetite. When we headed for the parlor for coffee, one of the servants drew me aside. "There is a gentleman to see you, miss," he murmured.

He was waiting in the hall. I didn't recognize him at first. He might have been dressed for a funeral, in a dark suit and somber tie, and his face was almost as gloomy.

"Feisal," I said in surprise.

His attempt at a smile wasn't very convincing. "I have been with Mr. Blenkiron. I thought—I hoped I might persuade you to come with me to a café."

I had a number of reasons for believing that might not be such a good idea. "I don't think so, Feisal. Not tonight."

He shifted his briefcase to his left hand and caught mine in a hard grip. His voice dropped to a whisper. "Please, Vicky. Only for a little while. It's not what you think; do you suppose I feel like celebrating? I have to talk to you."

There were also a number of reasons for believing it might not be such a bad idea. He saw I was weakening. In the same hoarse whisper he went on, "We'll go to the ETAP or the Winter Palace, wherever you will feel comfortable. Please?"

"Well . . ."

He practically dragged me to the door. I made a few feeble protests about freshening my makeup and getting my purse, which he overruled. I looked beautiful and I didn't need my purse, he would escort me home.

The last part turned out to be true, anyhow, if not in the sense I expected.

I was relieved to see a taxi waiting for us instead of Larry's mammoth car, and even more relieved to hear the words "Winter Palace" in the midst of Feisal's otherwise unintelligible order to the driver. We didn't go in the hotel, but sat on the terrace, which was crowded with people. I ordered coffee.

"Let's not waste time," I said. "What's wrong?"

"Can you ask?"

"I just did. It has to do with Dr. Mazarin's death, doesn't it? A nice step up for you."

He turned a queer shade of brownish gray. "You don't think I had anything to do with that?"

"I wouldn't be here if I did. But you are a member of one of the—er—revolutionary societies, aren't you?"

Feisal went a shade grayer. "If you'd like to see me hauled off to a detention cell, never to emerge again, speak a little louder."

"Sorry."

Feisal drained his cup and ordered a refill. "Forget politics, they've nothing to do with the present situation. I have a feeling you're well aware of that."

He stopped, watching me expectantly.

What little he had said confirmed my hunch. But although I was dying—make that "anxious"—to know more, I had no intention of blurting out my suspicions to one of the people I was suspicious of.

"Please continue," I said.

Feisal took out a handkerchief and mopped his forehead. "I'm taking an awful chance warning you, but I couldn't just walk away and leave you at risk. I'm going into hiding and so must you. I can take you to a place where you'll be safe."

I groaned. "Why do I do these things?" I inquired of the room at large. "You'd think by this time I'd have learned better. No, thanks, Feisal. If you'll excuse me, I'm going to go round the tables and panhandle a few bucks so I can take a cab—"

"Back into the lion's den?"

"You mean back into the frying pan. What you're proposing sounds a lot like the fire."

"I told you—"

"You haven't told me anything; you've just spouted vague threats. Appeal to my intelligence, Feisal. Give me two— hell, I'll settle for one—good reason why I should accept your offer."

Feisal groaned. We sounded like a pair of sick dogs.

"I was told to show you this." He opened his briefcase and took out a piece of paper.

There was no writing on it. It was a piece of plain black paper about eight inches square.

I felt the blood drain slowly out of my face, starting with my brain and backing up in my vocal cords. All I could do for a few seconds was gurgle horribly. Finally I managed to clear my throat. "Who gave you this? Larry? Max?"

"Who's Max?" Either he was honestly bewildered or he could have given drama lessons to Sir Laurence Olivier.

"He cuts silhouettes," I mumbled, staring at the piece of black paper. "For a hobby. His other hobbies are fraud, theft, and murder. Art and antiquities, those are his specialties. I thought he was in jail! I helped put him in jail! How the hell did he . . ."

I shoved my chair back and stood up. "I've got to get Schmidt out of there. If Max is one of them . . . Oh, Christ, of course, it has to be him! He was careful to keep out of my way, but I should have known, he was obviously wearing a wig the first time I . . ."

I wasted time fumbling under the table for my purse before I remembered I didn't have it. Feisal grabbed my arm as I started blindly for the street.

"Hold on a minute. You don't have money for a cab."

"I'll tell him to wait. Just long enough for me to collect Schmidt and my purse."

"I'll come with you. Wait a second."

He tossed a few bills onto the table and picked up his briefcase without relaxing his grip on me. I pulled away from him, and he said, "I sense you are now convinced of the danger. Come with me to the place I mentioned."

"Not without Schmidt."

There were several decrepit-looking vehicles lined up in front of the hotel. I opened the door of the first one—hoping it was a taxi—and got in. Feisal followed me.

"I'll go back for him after I've taken you—"

"No, you won't. Driver!"

Feisal enveloped me in a rib-cracking embrace and rattled off a string of directions to the driver. I didn't understand a word, but I was pretty sure he had not given the order I would have given. I tried to free myself. "Let me go, damn you!"

"Certainly," said Feisal, unwrapping his arms. I fell back against the seat and he socked me on the jaw.

* * *

He must have given me an injection of some kind, because it was morning when I woke up. Very early morning; the rosy hues of dawn fell prettily across the floor of . . . wherever I was. I didn't wait to examine my surroundings, but made a rush for the door. Somehow I wasn't surprised to discover that it was locked. The single window was blocked by ornate grillwork. It had been there awhile, rusty streaks stained the black iron, but it was still functional, as I discovered when I shook it. Had it been designed to keep people in or keep them out? I wondered. Whatever the original purpose, it would suffice to keep me in.

The rush of adrenaline subsided, leaving me shaking and weak-kneed. I staggered back to the bed and sat down.

After I had surveyed the room I had to admit that I had been shut up in worse places. The furniture looked as if it had come from the local equivalent of a low-budget outlet store, but it was clean and fairly new. In addition to the bed, the amenities consisted of a table, a lamp, and two straight chairs. On the table was a jug (plastic) full of water, a glass (plastic), a bowl (you guessed it), a bar of soap, a towel, and a paperback novel with the cover missing. I picked up the book. It was by Valerie Vandine. I threw it across the room.

There was only one door. I am not without experience. I was raised on a farm. I found what I was looking for chastely hidden under the bed.

After I had paced the room forty or fifty times I retrieved the book and started reading.

Voluptuous Madeleine de Montmorency was fighting off the villain for the second time when I heard a sound at the door. The book and my feet hit the floor simultaneously. There was nothing in the room I could use as a weapon, so I had to rely on craft, cunning, and my bare hands. Which left me, I had to admit, at a distinct disadvantage.

But when I saw the figure framed in the open doorway my clenched fist fell. Nothing my imagination had conjured up could equal that vision.

She was about three feet tall and about a hundred years old and she didn't have a tooth in her head. Black cloth covered everything except her face and her hands—the standard garb of a conservative Muslim female. She wouldn't wear a face

veil in her own house with only another woman present.
Baring her gums at me in what was probably not a smile, she
sidled into the room, and deposited a tray on the table.

Where I come from, punching old ladies simply isn't done.
My stupefied stare must have reassured her. Straightening to
her full height of three feet six, she gestured at the door and
twisted her bony wrist—once, twice, three times. I got the
message. Three doors, three locks, between me and freedom.

I was beginning to think maybe I could overcome my
conditioning about hitting old ladies—not hard, of course,
just a little tap—when she gave a sudden backward hop, agile
as an Egyptian cricket. (They are black and very large, and
they don't fly; they beam themselves from place to place like
Captain Kirk.) Before I could move she was out the door. It
closed with a slam and I heard the key turn in the lock.

I didn't swear. I was too dumbfounded to be angry. What
the hell kind of jailer was this? Where the hell was I? Who
the hell was responsible for this?

By the time I had finished the coffee and nibbled at a piece
of flat, unleavened bread I was pretty sure I knew the answer
to the last question. The situation had his distinctively lunatic
touch, including Grandma Moses. I wondered where he had
dug her up. So, fifty pages later, when I heard the key turn
in the lock again, I didn't bother assuming a posture of attack.
Where John was concerned, bare hands weren't worth a damn.
I'd need a water cannon to handle him.

The man who entered had the same swagger and the same
condescending smirk. It wasn't John. It was Feisal.

"Don't you have any Barbara Michaels or Charlotte Mac-
Leod?" I asked, waving the book at him. "I loathe Valerie."

Feisal settled himself comfortably in one of the chairs.
"Wrong cue. You're supposed to say, 'How dare you,' or
'What do you want with me?' so I can leer lustfully at you."

"Let's not bandy words," I said. "Who's the old lady?"

"My grandmother."

"You low-down skunk. You ought to be ashamed of yourself, dragging an innocent grandmother into this. Or is she
innocent?"

"Oh, quite. She thinks my interest in you is personal."

"Now wait a minute." I didn't believe him, but I thought

it might be a good idea to get up from the bed. I pulled out the other chair and sat down facing him. "A dear, old-fashioned Muslim granny wouldn't connive at abduction and rape."

"Certainly not." Feisal looked shocked. "She knows I'm irresistible to women. She thinks you're just playing hard to get. But don't worry," he went on, while I struggled to express my feelings, "much as I'd enjoy overcoming your maidenly scruples, you are perfectly safe from attentions of that sort."

"And why is that?"

Feisal sighed. "It's those years at Oxford, I suppose. The facade is only skin-deep but it sticks like glue. Besides, I have been told how many square inches of skin I would have removed if I so much as breathed heavily on you. He was quoting *The Merchant of Venice*, I think."

"He does quote Shakespeare a lot," I agreed. "How very gallant of him to be concerned about my maidenly scruples. Or is he saving me for later?"

Feisal folded his arms. "Vicky, you simply have to take this seriously. You are perfectly safe here. It's probably the only place in Luxor where you *are* perfectly safe. I'll supply you with additional reading material if you insist; just sit tight for a few days."

Emulating his cool, I folded my arms and stretched my legs out. "What's going to happen in a few days?"

"I'm not going to ask how much you know," Feisal began.

"I must know more than I think I know. What vital clue, observed but uncomprehended by me, prompted this rash act?"

Feisal's beautiful black eyebrows drew together, but he sounded more puzzled than angry when he spoke. "Astonishing. You really haven't a clue, have you?"

"I don't understand."

"Obviously not. So why don't you just relax and leave it to us?"

"Us being you and John? Boy, talk about broken reeds!"

I never did find out why so many Egyptians have such pretty thick lashes. Feisal's were as fuzzy as a toothbrush. They fell, concealing his eyes, and he said, "He got me into this. He promised he'd get me out."

"Oh, you poor, dear trusting man," I said, with sincere sympathy.

Feisal stopped trying to be cool. He scowled at me. "You really are an extremely irritating woman. I'm trying to save your life, at the risk of my own. If my part in this were discovered I would die a slow and horrible death."

"Where's Schmidt?" I demanded, ignoring this melodramatic remark. It might or might not be true, but at the moment I didn't give a damn.

"He's safe."

I figured it was now or never. Granny's vigilance would be relaxed now that there was a big strong man in the house, and at least one of the three doors was unlocked. Under the same illusion of macho superiority, Feisal might have neglected to lock the others. I sighed, smiled, shrugged, leaned back in the chair, hooked both feet under the rung of Feisal's chair and pulled.

The chair and Feisal combined made a very satisfying crash. As I had hoped and counted upon, the back of his head came into emphatic contact with the bare boards. I was already out the door when I heard him shout. The words were Arabic, but the tone was unquestionably profane.

I spun in an agitated circle, not knowing which way to go. There was a door at either end of the short corridor. I had a fifty-fifty chance of hitting the right one, so I went left.

Wrong choice. The door didn't lead to the street but to the kitchen. I found that out when it opened, to display a stove, a table, a sink, and Granny.

I should have such reflexes when I'm a hundred years old. Snarling toothlessly at me, she hopped back, reaching for something on the table. There were several things on the table: a pot, a bunch of onions, and a long knife. I didn't wait to see which one she wanted. I pushed her, as gently as circumstances allowed, and headed for the other door, followed by screams and curses. The latter came from Feisal, whose footsteps I could hear in the corridor.

Door number three wasn't locked either. My exultation received a rude check when I found myself, not on the street but in a walled enclosure. It was unpaved. Weeds, or maybe they were onions, stuck up from the dirt and there were a few chickens pecking disinterestedly at the ground. They scattered, squawking irritably, as I dashed for the gate. He hadn't bolted that either, the egotistical thing.

I didn't bother closing it behind me, nor did I stop to consider which way to go. Any way was better than where I was. I turned right this time and ran like hell, followed by renewed protests from the chickens and a lot of bad language from Feisal.

Back home they'd have called it an alley. It was narrow and unpaved and bounded by high walls—the backs of other such courtyards, I assumed. There was nobody around, not even a chicken, but not far ahead I could see people and cars and other hopeful signs.

I don't know how far behind he was when I burst out of the alley onto the street. He didn't follow me. I hadn't thought he would. He wouldn't dare drag me back fighting and yelling with all those people around.

I had no idea where I was. It had to be Luxor, but it didn't resemble the part of the city with which I was familiar. It looked more like one of the country towns we had passed through on our shore tours—one-story shops, street stalls, uneven sidewalks littered with debris. I walked on, ignoring the curious glances I got from passersby. This was definitely not one of the popular tourist spots. I was the only foreigner in sight.

I went on for another block or two, till my breathing slowed to normal speed. Still no sign of the river. The sun was no help; it was high overhead. I'd have to ask someone for directions. Luxor was a good-sized town, I could go on wandering in circles for hours, and I was in a hurry. Finally I saw what appeared to be a gas station, or rather two gas pumps and a shack roofed with rusty tin. A few men wearing T-shirts and jeans were lounging against the pumps.

I sidled up to them. "Corniche de Nil?" I said hopefully.

I got a pointing finger and a spate of Arabic, including what sounded like an improper suggestion. I said "Thank you," and turned down the street the finger had indicated. I had to ask twice more before I saw an open space and a gleam of water ahead.

I had found the river and the corniche and, a short distance away, a familiar tumble of pylons and columns—Karnak. But I was still a long way from my destination; I was tired and thirsty and I didn't have a piastre in my pocket.

I accosted the first tourists I met—a middle-aged couple strung with cameras, binoculars, and the other unmistakable stigma of the breed. He was wearing walking shorts and a shirt printed with sphinxes and palm trees; she was reading from her Baedeker.

There is no better way of getting money from people than by appealing to their prejudices. Tourists in Third World countries expect to be mugged, though from what I had heard that was more likely to happen in New York and Washington than in Cairo, not to mention Luxor. My appearance certainly substantiated the pathetic story I told.

They wanted me to go to the police. I applied the handkerchief the kindly lady had given me to my eyes. "No, no, I can't face it! I've got to get back to the hotel right away, my husband will be worried sick, I was supposed to meet him an hour ago, he warned me not to go off alone . . . There was a man . . ."

I got into the cab with ten pounds and the guy's business card. I had every intention of paying him back, and I would have too, if I hadn't lost the card.

The driver let me out some distance from the house. After I had paid him I was broke again; I suspected he had overcharged me, but I didn't feel like arguing with him. The river glittered in the sunlight and the sky was a pale clear blue. I walked slowly, trying to figure out my next move.

Had they carried or enticed Schmidt off to a "safe place" too? If he wasn't at the house I had no idea where to start looking for him, but there was reason to hope they would consider him harmless and not bother to imprison him. No doubt they had concocted a convincing explanation for my failure to return the night before. My escape had changed the picture, though. Feisal had had plenty of time to report it, and they would certainly expect me to turn up. John knew I wouldn't leave Schmidt in the lurch.

It all made sense to me at the time. So, I wasn't thinking too clearly. I was tired and hungry and thirsty and worried

sick about Schmidt. And even if I had known what I was
soon to discover, I don't know what I could have done about
it. Getting Schmidt out would still have been my first priority.

I had considered somewhat vaguely the minor problem of
how I was going to get past the gate or over the wall. It would
have to be the gate—I hadn't the time or the equipment for
climbing a wall topped with broken glass and barbed wire—
and I didn't suppose for a moment that I could enter without
identifying myself. My plan, if it could be called that, was
simple: get inside. After that . . . I had not the slightest idea
what I was going to do after that. Oh, well, I thought. Fortune
favors the brave and the meek shall inherit the earth, and,
more to the point, there was a nice little gun in my bag. I
might even have to use the damned thing—if it was still in
the wardrobe where I had left it, and if I could get to it before
I was caught.

When I reached the entrance I had my first piece of luck—
and high time, too. Two large vans and a pickup truck were
waiting outside the gate. The vans were closed, but the back
of the pickup was open. It was also full—of men, locals by
their clothing. Some were sitting down, others leaned against
the sides of the truck.

They were delighted to see me and not inclined to ask
unimportant questions. Or maybe they did ask questions. They
certainly didn't get any answers. I grinned ingratiatingly and
held up my hands. A dozen brawny brown arms assisted me
over the tailgate and a couple of the lads obligingly made
room for me when I indicated my intention of sitting down.
How true it is that language is no barrier to friendship! By
the time the truck reached the house we were close buddies.
Very close. I had to detach quite a few friendly arms before
I could get out, but they accepted my departure with grins
and shrugs and affectionate farewells.

With what I hoped was an insouciant smile, I strolled past
the packers and entered the house. Once inside, I stopped
being insouciant and ran along the corridor and up the first
flight of stairs. My only hope, if there was hope, lay in speed.
The servants probably weren't in on the deal, but if one of
the others caught sight of me I was dead meat.

I reached Schmidt's door unobserved—I hoped—and

turned the knob. The door wouldn't open. My brain wasn't working at top efficiency. All I could think was that they'd locked him in, that he was a prisoner. It took several important seconds for me to notice that the key was in the lock, and several equally vital seconds for my sweating fingers to turn it.

The room was empty. Not only was Schmidt not there, his clothes and luggage were gone too. I checked the wardrobe to be sure, but one glance had been enough; Schmidt can't occupy a room for five minutes without littering every surface with his possessions.

The hinges of the door had been well oiled. If I hadn't been looking in that direction I wouldn't have known it was opening again. I made a wild grab for the nearest hard object—a brass vase, intricately worked in enamel and silver.

John slid through the narrow opening and eased the door shut. He wasn't as neat as usual; his shirt was dusty and there was a cobweb in his hair. "Put that down," he said softly.

I brandished the vase. "What have you done with Schmidt? If you've hurt him—"

"He's left." John kept a wary eye on my impromptu weapon. "Of his own free will and under his own steam."

"I've figured it out," I said.

"Have you indeed?"

"Yes. How you ever expected to get away with a stunt like this . . ."

He was trying, with great difficulty, to control his temper. I knew the signs—the flexed hands, the taut muscles of the jaw. When he spoke his voice shook with fury but it was the same almost inaudible murmur. "For Christ's sake, Vicky, won't you ever learn? I don't know how you got in here—"

"Don't you? You were waiting for me."

"In that closet across the hall, to be precise. I was informed you'd got away, and although I hoped I was wrong for once, I had a strange foreboding you'd do something like this. Now get the hell out of here. If you can."

I gave him back stare for stare. My teeth were clenched so hard my jaws hurt. I had no intention of going out that door with John standing by, or of turning my back on him for so much as a split second. After a moment his hands relaxed and he lifted his shoulders in a shrug. "If that's how you want it," he said, and turned *his* back.

He couldn't have heard me; I was wearing sneakers and the rug was thick. He couldn't have seen me; there was no surface to reflect my movement. He just knew. His lifted arm struck mine with a jarring force that made me lose my grip on the vase. It clattered to the floor and I stumbled back, trying to elude those agile, reaching hands. I knew it was wasted effort but I went on squirming and struggling, even after he had pinioned my arms and clapped a hard hand over my mouth. He had lost the remains of his temper, his face was flushed, and he was hurting me. His nails dug into my cheek. I felt tears of pain and fury welling up in my eyes.

He took his hand from my mouth and relaxed his grip a little, but not enough to enable me to free myself. "You dim-witted twit, I'm trying to get you out of this. If you yell I'll squeeze your silly neck."

Since his fingers were now wrapped around my throat I didn't doubt he could—or would—carry out the threat. I took a deep breath and forced myself to relax, leaning against him. The angry color faded from his face and the corners of his mouth turned up.

"Don't even think about it," he murmured.

I wasn't thinking at all. His hand had moved from my throat to my cheek, long fingers twisting through my hair, tilting my head back.

I hate to think how I must have looked—lips parted, eyes half-closed . . . They weren't quite closed, though, and I was facing the door. The sudden alteration of my expression, from vacant acquiescence to shamed horror, was sufficient warning. He let me go and spun around.

She was wearing dark pants and a loose linen jacket that made her look like a little girl dressed in her big brother's clothes. Her hair was tied back with an amber-gold scarf. It matched the color of her wide, unblinking eyes.

"Why, it's you, Vicky," she said. "I'm so glad you've come back."

"If I had ever seen murder in a man's eyes . . ." I had read that trite phrase Lord knows how many times in Lord knows how many thrillers, and taken it for a figure of speech. It wasn't a figure of speech. I saw it now.

He moved so quickly I barely reacted in time, catching his upraised arm with both hands. "For God's sake, John!"

He threw me off with a single snap of flexed muscles, like a man dislodging a snake or venomous insect. I staggered back, slipped, and sat down with a thud. I didn't hear the shot but I heard him scream and saw him fall, his body curling into a hard knot of pain.

So that was what a silencer looked like, I thought, staring at the gun in Mary's dainty hand. For some reason I'd expected it would be bigger.

Her lips parted, and out came a string of obscenities that shocked me almost as much as what she'd just done. It was like hearing Dorothy cursing Uncle Henry and Auntie Em. Her pink mouth wasn't pretty now, it had the grotesque shape of a Greek Fury's, and her eyes were as opaque as coffee caramels.

"Damn him! Why'd he have to get in the way?" She turned those yellow-brown eyes toward me and the look in them made me shrink back. That pleased her. "Oh, well, it doesn't matter. He won't be going anywhere for a while, and you wouldn't leave him, would you? See what you can do for him. I'd hate to have him die. I have plans for you, Vicky dear, and it won't be nearly so much fun if John isn't there to watch."

The door closed. The key turned in the lock.

John sat up. "Missed," he said with satisfaction.

I stared at the spreading stain on his sleeve. "Missed?" I croaked.

"She meant to do a bit more damage than this."

He didn't have to elaborate. She must have known the only way she could stop him was to put a bullet in one or the other of us, and she probably didn't care which. If he hadn't pushed me away . . .

And if I hadn't interfered he could have stopped her, before she aimed and fired.

Out of all the questions boiling in my overheated brain I fished the least important. "Is she pregnant?"

"Not by me, at any rate." John didn't look up. He was

concentrating on rolling up his sleeve, and not doing a very good job of it.

"Are you trying to tell me you didn't . . . You never . . ."

"As you have had occasion to observe, my principles are somewhat elastic, but there are some things at which even I draw the line. All other considerations aside . . ." He glanced at me from under his lashes. "All other considerations aside, I'd as soon bed a black widow spider. If you don't believe me, and you probably don't, I can produce witnesses. Max and Whitbread took turns spending the night with us. Cozy little arrangement . . . Would you mind helping me with this? She'll be back before long, and it would not be a good idea for either of us to be here when that event occurs."

He had a point. I hoisted myself up and went to investigate the medicine cabinet. It was well equipped. You'd have thought they were expecting a small war.

I slapped some gauze and tape over the bloody furrow the bullet had left. "How are you planning to get out of this room?" I asked. "The door's locked."

"With these handy little devices you were clever enough to bring along." John plucked one of the pins out of my hair.

"Was that why you . . . Ow! That's the one with the hook on the end, it's caught—"

"One of the reasons." His fingers brushed my cheek in a caress so fleeting I might have imagined it. "You do it, then. I haven't had much practice at this, since I usually keep my lock picks elsewhere. Thank you."

He knelt by the door and started poking at the lock. "Maybe we should start thinking about where we're going after we get out," I said uneasily.

"The operative word, my love, is 'out.'" He seemed to be having some trouble, possibly because he was perspiring heavily, despite the comfortably cool temperature of the room. "Mary won't be pleased when she finds us gone."

"Is she in love with you?"

The pick slipped and rattled onto the floor. "Bloody hell," said John between his teeth. "Keep your grisly suggestions to yourself, will you? If I believed that were the case I'd cut my throat and be done with it. No . . ." Something clicked, and his fingers tightened. "Her motive is much simpler. She blames me—correctly, I must admit—for her brothers' death."

"Her brother . . ."

"Brothers. Two of them." After a brief pause he said resignedly, "The fat's deep in the fire now, so I may as well abandon reticence. Or have you enough clues to reason it out for yourself? Two brothers, a strong streak of homicidal mania, and those bright, empty brown eyes . . ."

It was true; I'd only known one other person with eyes of that unusual golden brown. When I first met him, in Stockholm, I had thought him a gorgeous specimen of Nordic manhood, built like a Viking, and tall—really tall. It's hard to find men who are six inches taller than I am. I had been prepared to overlook the fact that Leif's sense of humor was practically nonexistent, but when I found out he was Max's boss and one of the gang, I sort of lost my girlish enthusiasm.

John *had* been responsible for Leif's death. In this case my objection to murder had been overcome by the fact that Leif had been trying to kill me, and would undoubtedly have succeeded if John hadn't intervened.

"You didn't kill Georg," I said, watching his hands twist and press. "Or did you?"

"No. His cellmate did him in, rather messily, last year. However, since I was partially responsible for sending him away she has some justice on her . . . Ah. There we are."

He handed me the pins.

"Where are we going?" I asked. "I know—out. How?"

"Any ideas?" John peered cautiously through the slit in the opening door.

"My room. I want to get my purse."

"You won't need a purse if we don't make it out of here," was the depressing response.

"My room has a balcony. Someone is sure to spot us if we go through the house."

"Point taken. Come on, then."

My door was locked too. John left the key in place after he had turned it.

I offered him the lock picks. "If they find the door is still locked, they may not look in here."

"Once they discover we've gone they'll look everywhere."

He headed for the balcony. "You might have mentioned it's a thirty-foot drop," he said, returning.

"I assumed you knew." We were both whispering. Footsteps had passed my door without stopping, but I had a feeling they'd soon be back. "Knot some sheets together."

"Trite, but worth a try. Now what the hell are you doing?"

"Looking for my bag. Maybe I put it in the wardrobe."

I'd been expecting it, but I started convulsively when it came—a wordless, genderless shout of rage, hardly muted by the heavy door. The response was just as audible. "You two cover the doors. They may not have left the house."

I recognized that voice, though it had been several years since I'd heard it. I froze, my fingers clutching the strap of my bag. John grabbed me around the waist, trying, as I thought, to pull me toward the balcony. Instead he lifted me, shot me into the wardrobe, and closed the door.

And locked it. I couldn't imagine how, I hadn't seen a key or a keyhole, but when I shoved at the damned thing it didn't budge. Then I stopped shoving. I also stopped breathing. The door of the room had burst open.

Maybe they'd look under the bed first. The wardrobe would certainly be next, there was no place else to hide, and they were obviously thorough, well-organized chaps. And while they searched for me—and found me—John would have time . . .

He had time. He was as agile as a cat; he could have dropped from the balcony and taken his chances on breaking a rib or two. I would have risked it, given the alternative. He didn't. I stood there in the dark, wincing and biting my knuckles and calling myself names as I listened to what was happening. It didn't last long. They were three to one.

And one of them was Hans, Max's large, slow-witted associate. I discovered this after I had realized the interior of the wardrobe wasn't completely dark. The pierced openings in the grillwork admitted light. A couple of them were big enough to give me a clear view.

Fortunately I was too short of breath to cry out, or I might have done so when I spotted Max, less than two feet away from my wide blue eye. His bald head shone as if it had been polished. The heavy horn-rimmed glasses provided an additional distraction—he must have worn contact lenses before—but if I had ever gotten a long, close look at him I would have known him. "Mr. Schroeder," Larry's secretary, had found reasonable excuses for keeping out of my way.

One of Hans's ham-sized fists was wrapped around John's left arm. The guy who held his other arm was familiar too. Rudi always looked as if he wanted to murder somebody, and his expression hadn't changed. This time I deduced he wanted to murder John. Rudi had one hand pressed against his stomach and he was whooping for breath, but the gallant lad mustered enough strength to give John's arm a sharp upward and backward twist. John yelled, of course. Stoicism was not a quality he chose to cultivate.

"Gently," Max said gently. "That is his right arm, Rudi. He must be able to use it."

There was blood on his chin. (I couldn't help noticing that Hans was unbruised and unbloodied. John tried to pick on people who were smaller than he was.) Max took out a handkerchief, wiped his mouth, studied the resultant smear of blood with fastidious distaste, and threw the handkerchief on the floor.

"Where is she?" he asked.

John opened his eyes as wide as they would go. "Who?"

Rudi had got his breath back. His shoulder shifted and John let out a pained yelp.

"Stop it," Max said. He didn't sound as if he meant it, though.

"The balcony, I suppose," Max went on. "While you put up a gallant battle to prevent pursuit. Or was that the reason? I find it hard to believe that you would risk yourself even for her."

"I was dumbfounded myself," John admitted. "No doubt I did have another motive. I wonder what it could have been? You're such a profound student of human nature, Maxie, perhaps you can suggest—"

"Get him out of here," Max said shortly.

"What about the woman?" Rudi demanded. His eyes moved, scanning the room.

"The only woman in the house is my child bride," said John smoothly. "I wouldn't interrupt her if I were you, Rudi, old chap, she's probably sharpening her knives or dismembering a baby or—"

I knew Max would crack if he kept it up long enough. John must have known too. Max's backhand swing was—understandably—aimed at his mouth. It was hard enough to snap his head back and leave him hanging limp between the men who held him.

"Tie him up," Max said.

"But, Herr Max," Rudi began.

"And gag him. If he makes one more clever remark I may not be able to control myself."

I didn't want to watch, but I couldn't stop myself. Gnawing on my knuckles, I followed the proceedings with dry-eyed, unblinking attention. They tied his wrists and ankles and used the handkerchief Max had tossed onto the floor as a gag. There was more than a smear of blood on it when they finished.

Max watched too. His back was turned to me when he said coldly, "Take him away. I will stay here and search the room, just to be certain."

# Chapter Ten

My heart should have skipped a beat, or maybe my blood should have run cold. I didn't feel a thing. Except a distant primeval urge to lay violent hands on Max.

After the others had gone out he closed the door. Then he looked at the wardrobe and said quietly, "I am sorry you had to see that, Dr. Bliss."

"I'm sorry too." His statement had been so unexpected, not to say inapropos, that I answered without thinking. Why not? He knew I was there. Was he now going to apologize for dragging me out and turning me over to Hans and Rudi? And Mary?

"Do you have a watch?"

I was thinking about Mary and the look in her eyes when she said she had plans for me. "What? Oh. Yes."

"Wait fifteen minutes. Most of us will have left the house by then. If you take reasonable precautions—I suggest the balcony—you should be able to leave unseen. I beg you won't try something brave and foolish. You would only be caught again."

"Where are you taking him?"

Max clicked his tongue against his teeth. "Now, Dr. Bliss, you know better than to ask that."

"Max. Please. You said you owed me a favor—"

"I am doing you that favor. I would be in great trouble if it were known I had connived at your escape. Catch the first plane to Cairo and leave the country as soon as you are able."

"You know I won't do that." A sensible woman wouldn't have wasted her breath arguing with him. Vicky Bliss went right on talking. "You asked me a question once, remember? I didn't know the answer then. I do now. I love him, Max. Please . . ."

Max took a step toward me. "Are you crying?" he asked suspiciously.

"I would if I thought it would do any good," I said, sniffing.

"It would not. Honestly, I cannot comprehend why an intelligent woman like you should behave this way. You ought to be thanking me for . . . Stop that!"

"I can't," I snuffled. The conversation, between a courteous criminal and a weeping wardrobe, might have seemed funny to a detached observer. I was not detached, and Max was clearly uncomfortable. I couldn't figure him out. I never had been able to figure him out. Only in fiction do you find cold-blooded villains with one soft streak in their flinty hearts. But if he didn't mean to let me go, why had he sent Rudi and Hans away?

"Fifteen minutes," Max repeated. "There is no use trying to follow, they will have left the house by now. She is still here, however, and she would like nothing better than to get her hands on you. You can do him no good by allowing yourself to be recaptured."

He thought he was being so clever. I said, between gulps, "I can't get out. He locked me in."

"But there is no key. How . . . ." He came to the wardrobe. "Ah, I see. That is good, it will hold you just long enough. Auf Wiedersehen—or rather, good-bye, Dr. Bliss."

I threw a few more sobs at him as he walked to the door. His shoulders twitched but he didn't stop or turn around.

I waited a few minutes, just in case. When I tried the door again it opened without difficulty. The bolt was part of the carved ornamentation. It wasn't concealed, just inconspicuous, unless you were looking for it. I could have forced it if I had thrown myself against the door hard enough. Max had

NIGHT TRAIN TO MEMPHIS

saved me the trouble. It would have been a pity to damage such a beautiful antique.

John had pulled the bedclothes apart before he was interrupted. In case I haven't mentioned it, the sheets were linen, fine as silk. They knotted nicely. I took them out onto the balcony. My window overlooked the garden. I could hear sounds of activity at the back of the house—my friends the movers, I assumed. On this side there was no one in sight, not even a gardener, but I kept an eye peeled as I tied the end of one of the sheets around the wrought-iron railing. I slung my bag around my neck before I climbed over the balcony and took hold of the makeshift rope.

I have done some rock climbing and had become rather vain about my ability to lower myself smoothly down a chimney or rock face. I soon discovered that a bedsheet is not a good substitute for ropes and pulleys. My thigh muscles wouldn't work the way they were supposed to, the sheet kept stretching, and the bag kept banging against my chest. I didn't dare discard it, though. It's bad enough to be on the run. Being on the run sans money, passport, and other useful items complicates the problem even more.

I had to drop the last ten feet, not because the linen gave out but because my thighs lost the struggle. Scrambling up, I scuttled along the side of the house, ducking under the windows, till I reached the corner.

Two of the gardeners were at work on the flowers that lined the driveway. Kneeling, their backs to me and the house, they appeared to be weeding the beds. Their dusty faded robes blended with the shadowed foliage and their white turbans looked like cauliflower. There were no vehicles in the driveway. The gates at its far end were closed. So was the door next to the gates. I hadn't noticed it before, but I had anticipated it would be there, for the use of visitors who came and went on foot.

I had two choices. Well, actually, I had quite a few, but turning myself in didn't appeal to me and neither did trying to get over a wall ten feet high that was topped with barbed wire and broken glass. I could make a run for it or try to bluff my way out. I decided on the second alternative. The gardeners were bound to see me—I intended that they should—and they were more likely to stop a frantic fugitive than a casual stroller.

I stuck to the shrubbery as long as I could, but I was still ten yards from the gate when I had to leave the path and step out into the open. One hand in my pocket, the other in my bag, I strode briskly toward the gate. One of the weeders sat back on his haunches as I passed him and gave me a curious look. I gave him a pleasant nod and managed not to break into a run. My back felt exposed, as if it had been stripped not only of clothing but of skin. My neck muscles ached as I fought the impulse to look over my shoulder.

The pedestrian door was locked. I had expected that, but I had hoped there would be a simple bar or bolt. No such luck. There wasn't even a visible keyhole. The damned thing was probably electronically controlled, like the main gates. I heard the gardener call out; from the inflection it must have been a question. "Don't you know you're supposed to check out before you leave, you rude person?" or "What the hell do you think you're doing, lady?"

I strolled on without replying, but the next demonstration of interest was too emphatic to ignore. The bullet hit the steel panel of the big gate with a ringing crack. Obviously it was time I stopped fooling around. I took the gun out of my bag, squatted down, pressed the barrel against the metal box at the base of the nearest column, and squeezed the trigger a few times. The position was unstable and my legs were as unsteady as my shaking hands. The recoil toppled me over onto my back. The next bullet whistled through the empty space where my head would have been if I hadn't fallen over. The son of a bitch must be using a rifle. No hand weapon could have been so accurate at that distance.

The control box was a mess of smoking, ragged metal and the gate was ajar. So far so good, but I wouldn't get far unless I could delay pursuit. I looked back. The man with the rifle had stopped shooting and started running. He was still some distance away, but the gardener wasn't. I could see the whites of his eyes, so I stood up and pointed the gun in his general direction. He was no hero; with a yell he dived into the nearest bush. With an answering yell—I was beginning to lose my

famous cool by that time—I dived through the door and ran
. . . straight into a pair of grasping arms.

Eyes blurred, ears ringing, on the ragged edge of hysteria,
I punched him in the stomach. My fist bounced off a surface
as resilient as a beach ball. He staggered back, pulling me
with him, and we fell onto the seat of a waiting vehicle which
took off with a scream of tires and a stench of burning rubber.
The door flapped wildly until someone slammed it.

He'd fallen on top of me again. I stared up into the face
in such intimate proximity to my own and burst into tears.
"Schmidt! Oh, Schmidt, God bless you, what the hell are
you doing here?"

Schmidt's eyes were overflowing too, but only, as he was
careful to explain, because I had hit him in the solar plexus.
As soon as we had untangled ourselves he put an arm around
me and pressed me to his stomach. "Put your head on my
shoulder, little darlin'," he said tenderly. "All will be well.
Papa Schmidt is on the case."

That set me off again and Schmidt had to lend me his
handkerchief and tell me to blow my nose like a good girl.
The cab took a screeching turn into an alley hardly wider
than the one I had traversed earlier that day and went careening
along, scraping the walls on both sides.

"What's he doing?" I gasped.

"Eluding pursuit." Schmidt's happy grin stretched from
ear to ear and from mustache to double chin. Leaning forward,
he tossed a handful of bills onto the front seat and shouted
something in Arabic. The driver let out a whoop and roared
across an intersection filled with traffic. I shut my eyes.

"Schmidt." I had to raise my voice to be heard over the
roar of the engine and the screams of rage from the other
drivers, but I strove to speak calmly. "Schmidt, I think he's
eluded it. Wouldn't we be less conspicuous if he drove at
normal speed?"

"That is probably true," Schmidt said reluctantly. Another
fistful of money and another longish speech produced the
desired effect. "I have instructed him to drive us around the
city for a while," Schmidt said, settling back. "Now we can
talk, eh? What has happened?"

I told him. When my voice gave out he said gravely, "So he is a prisoner."

"Or dead."

Schmidt shook his head so vigorously that all his chins wobbled. "They won't kill him. Not yet. Vicky, you are not thinking clearly. Oh, I understand; your emotions are at war with your intelligence, your heart aches to rush to the rescue of the man you—"

"Shut up, Schmidt." I bit my lip. "I'm sorry, Schmidt. I didn't mean it."

"Ha," said Schmidt. "Well. I did not know what you told me, about the young woman. It explains the one thing that had confused me, however. Listen to me now, matters are more serious than I had realized, and we must act without delay. Late last night Sir John—"

"That's not his name."

"Well, I know that, but I have become accustomed to it. It suits him. Late last night he came to my room. He said that he had sent you away, for your safety, and that I too must remove myself from the house. So, following his advice, I announced this morning that I felt it best to take myself to a hotel. Larry made only token objections. He seemed distracted."

"I'm sure he was. Didn't he comment on my failure to return last night?"

"Oh, yes, he expressed concern and asked if I knew where you were. I was very clever," Schmidt said, puffing himself up. "I said that you were a grown-up woman and that this was not the first time you had gone off with a handsome young man."

"Thanks a lot."

"The important thing was not that he believed it but that he believed I believed it," said Schmidt. He added, smirking, "This facade of naïveté I assume is very useful. No one tried to prevent me from leaving. Ha, but they will be sorry, when they find how they have underestimated—"

"Schmidt," I said, trying to articulate through clenched teeth, "at some future date I will spend an entire day telling you how brilliant you are. Right now I'm in something of a hurry. Stick to the point. How did you happen to turn up today?"

"In the nick of time," Schmidt pointed out. "It was not a coincidence that I was there."

"I didn't think it was."

My teeth weren't clenched, they were bared. Schmidt said hurriedly, "Yes, I will tell you, if you will stop the interruptions. I went, as I had said I would, to the Winter Palace Hotel and checked myself in. I was eating Mittagessen when a waiter summoned me to the telephone. It was Feisal; he was calling me, he said, at the instruction of a mutual friend. You had foolishly run away from him—Feisal, that is—and he—the friend—feared you would return to the house of Larry Blenkiron. He—the friend—strongly advised that I should adopt evasive measures for my own sake and for your sake I should hover outside the gates and try to intercept you."

I had a sudden, insane mental image of Schmidt hovering over the house like the Goodyear blimp. Or a very well-fed angel. It won't be Heaven to Schmidt unless there is an unending flow of fattening food.

"You were too quick for me," Schmidt went on, frowning. "I was still hoping to see you come when I heard the guns shooting and knew they must be shooting at you or at Sss . . . at John. So I leaped from the taxi, telling the driver to be ready for instant departure, and was about to break down the gate when you emerged."

"Break down the gate," I repeated. "How did . . . Never mind. You're a hero, Schmidt. If you hadn't been there I'd never have made it."

"If it had not been for the foresight and noble sacrifice of John you would not have made it," Schmidt corrected. "So now we must rescue him, eh? Do you know where they have taken him?"

"They didn't take him anywhere." I stared at my hand. The knuckles were raw. "John managed to—to distract the other guys, they aren't awfully bright, but he didn't fool Max. Max knew there hadn't been time for me to get away. He figured I had to be hiding somewhere in the room. The wardrobe was the most obvious place. When he told them to tie

John up he was trying to mislead me, to suggest that they
intended to transport him some distance. Rudi even started
to question the order, but Max cut him off. John is still there.
So I've got to go back."

"Aber natürlich," Schmidt said.

"I had to leave him, Schmidt. I had to convince Max I had
fallen for his fabrication, and make sure the others knew I
was gone. My departure was a little more conspicuous than
I meant it to be," I admitted. "But now they'll be off guard,
they won't expect me to come back. If I'd hung around—"

"Stop it, Vicky." Schmidt stifled me with the handkerchief.
I blew my nose and mopped my face, while he continued
gently, "You do not have to convince me. To have acted
otherwise would have been folly."

"Sorry," I muttered. "I get nervous when people shoot at
me."

"Ha," said Schmidt. "Now be quiet and I will tell you
some things. Did you think I was so stupid I did not know
what you were doing? From the first I have known—known
more than you, Ms. Know-it-all. I told you I never forget a
face. The moment I set eyes on the secretary of Mr. Blenkiron
I recognized him for the criminous cutter of silhouettes."

"How could you?" I demanded incredulously. "You never
saw Max. He was in jail."

"And that is where I saw him, in the jail. I was curious,"
Schmidt admitted. "I am interested in the criminal mentality,
and what you had told me of him suggested he was an unusual
person. On the boat he kept away from you, but he did not
expect I would remember. As soon as I recognized him I knew
there was trouble brewing, which I had of course suspected as
soon as I saw Sir John. A coincidence, that you and he should
both be on that boat? You insult me to think I would believe
such a story."

"You pretended to believe it."

"Well, of course. My feelings were deeply wounded by
your lack of faith in me. But I forgave you," Schmidt said
magnanimously. "For the desperateness of the situation
became clear to me when I recognized that terrible man. The
one thing I did not know was the identity of the young woman,

but of course I realized that it was only a marriage of convenience and that his heart still belonged to you."

I started to say something sarcastic but I changed my mind. If his heart didn't belong to me, he had gone to considerable lengths for the sake of friendship.

"How'd you figure that out?" I asked meekly.

"From the way he did not look at you when he thought others were looking and the way he *did* look at you when he thought others were not. You," said Schmidt judiciously, "were more skilled at concealing your feelings. Had I not known better I would have believed you were adversaries instead of—"

"Yeah, right. Did John tell you what they're planning, Schmidt?"

"No, he did not have to tell me. I knew."

"How did . . . Oh, hell, never mind that now." I looked out the window of the cab. Palm trees, flower beds, the rippling river beyond . . . "First things first. Did you check out of the Winter Palace?"

"No. You see—"

"For God's sake, Schmidt! They know you're there; they'll be looking for you."

Schmidt let out a roar. For all his pretended calm, his nerves weren't in much better shape than mine. "Give me some credit for good sense, Vicky! If I had checked out they would only look for me somewhere else. Now they will wait for me to return. I left my luggage, but I have with me all we will need." He indicated the briefcase on the seat next to him.

"You're right, and I'm a fool," I said humbly.

"No, you are not a fool. You are fearing for the life and safety of the man you—"

I didn't want to scream at him but I knew I would if he said it, so I cut in. "I have the essentials with me too, but I've got to get rid of this gold-and-turquoise bag. It's too conspicuous."

"Now you are thinking," Schmidt said approvingly. He leaned forward and addressed the driver.

"I didn't know you spoke Arabic."

"I speak all languages." Schmidt twirled his mustache. "My Arabic is not good, however. Only a few phrases."

Following—I assumed—Schmidt's instructions, the cab stopped at one of the street markets, and Schmidt hopped out. He returned with an armful of souvenirs, including a new bag. This one was black, with the head of Nefertiti on one side and rows of hieroglyphs on the other. A good half of the souvenirs sold in Egypt have Nefertiti on them.

"Now where?" I asked, transferring passport, wallet, and a few dozen other objects into the new bag.

"The ETAP," Schmidt answered. "It is good that you have your passport; we will need them in order to register."

"Under our own names?"

"Unless you happen to have a false passport with you, we have no other choice," Schmidt said with pardonable sarcasm. "You know the regulations for foreigners. And don't tell me we should choose a less expensive hotel. When they begin looking for us they will look in the cheaper places, thinking that we would not be so foolish as to go to another four-star hotel. It is what you call the double whammy," Schmidt added.

I hated to get out of that taxi. I felt as conspicuous as a stoplight. However, I was less conspicuous at an expensive hotel, with other tall blond female tourists around, than I had been in the back streets of Luxor. Schmidt had had another bright idea, so, following his suggestion, I hung back, studying a rack of brochures, while he registered. The old boy was really in top form today—and I was not. If they tracked him down he could come up with a legitimate excuse for changing hotels, and my name would not be on the register. As he passed me, following the bellboy, he said loudly, "The fourth floor, you say?" I waited a few minutes before following. When I got out on the fourth floor Schmidt was waiting to lead me to his room. It was a nice room, with a balcony and twin beds. Not that I expected to occupy one.

"Good work, Schmidt," I said. "Now we have to—"

"Call the room service," said Schmidt, suiting the action to the word. "When he comes you will hide in the bathroom. Now close your mouth, Vicky, it looks very ugly when it is in that shape. I know the anguish that grips you, the frantic need to rush to the rescue of the man you—"

"No," I said. "I don't think you do, Schmidt."

"But it is important that we organize ourselves instead of running headlong into danger and inevitable defeat. How long has it been since you have eaten?"

I sat down on one of the beds. "I don't remember."

"We will be running and shooting and using much energy," Schmidt said with evident relish. "We will need all our strength and cunning. We must procure disguises. And weapons, and money, much more money, for bribes and for—"

"You can't come with me, Schmidt."

"But Vicky—"

"Come here, Schmidt." I patted the bed next to me. Pouting, Schmidt sat down. I put my arms around him—as far around as they would go. "You're the man I love, Schmidt. You're also about a thousand percent smarter than anybody I know, including me. Especially me. I will have something to eat and I will assume any disguise you can supply, and I will proceed with the utmost care and caution. But one person has a better chance of sneaking into that place than two." Especially when one of them was the size of Schmidt. I'd have cut my tongue out before saying it, though. I went on, "And one of us has to play backup. If I don't make it, you'll have to come in for me. That," I added quickly, "is a football term, Schmidt, not a literal suggestion. I mean—"

"I know the football," Schmidt sniffed. He had given me his handkerchief, so he wiped his eyes with the back of his hand. "You mean I must go to to the police. Why don't we do that now?"

"I can think of at least two good—" A knock on the door interrupted me. I dragged myself into the bathroom and splashed water on my face while I waited for the waiter to leave. The face needed a lot more than water, but I got the worst of the dirt off before Schmidt called me back.

"I know the reasons too," he said, waving me into a chair. "It will be hard to convince the police they must invade the home of so distinguished a visitor as Herr Blenkiron. Have you any proof, Vicky, of what he plans?"

"No." I put things in my mouth and chewed them. Swallowing wasn't easy, but I managed it. "That's one reason. The other . . ."

"Yes, I have thought of that too." For once Schmidt didn't appear to be enjoying his food.

Neither of us wanted to say it. Even supposing the cops could be persuaded to search the house, they might not find anything. It's easier to hide a dead body than a live one. John knew exactly what they were planning. They still needed him for one part of the scheme—I was pretty sure I knew what part—but they'd work around that rather than take the risk of letting him talk to the authorities.

"Another thing concerns me," Schmidt said, tactfully changing the subject. "Is there a possibility, do you think, that not all the police are honest?"

"It's a dead certainty, I think, that some of them are not. There are a few people in any security service in any country who can be bought." I put my fork down and stared dismally at my boss. "That's another little problem, Schmidt. I doubt that even John knows who is in Blenkiron's pay and who is unwitting. If we pick the wrong person . . ."

"Eat, eat," Schmidt urged. "Do not lose heart. We will not pick the wrong person because we will go straight to the tops—my old acquaintance, Dr. Ramadan, the director of the Cairo Museum, and my dear friend the Interior Minister, and the pleasant individual I met at a conference—"

"I'll leave it to you, Schmidt," I said. I couldn't eat, I couldn't think, I couldn't sit still a second longer. At that moment I was in complete sympathy with the people who want to censor films because of excessive, explicit violence. Obviously I'd seen too many of them; Technicolor images kept flashing across the screen of my mind. "Help me figure out how I'm going to get back in that place."

The main gate was out. They'd be guarding it closely, especially since I had wrecked the electronic controls. Once inside there was a chance I could mingle with the packers long enough to enter the house. If the packers were still there and if I could climb that damned wall and if my turban didn't fall off . . .

"Forget it," I said impatiently, grabbing the strip of white cloth from Schmidt after it had collapsed around my ears for the third time. "I can't put it on till after we leave the hotel anyhow. I'll cheat and use safety pins."

He'd had to make a quick shopping trip. There are dozens of shops and souvenir stands along the corniche; the only problem he'd had was finding a galabiya without sequins, embroidery, or bright braid. The one he'd brought back was plain gray. After I wadded it up and rubbed it in the flower box on the balcony and frayed the hem, it looked reasonably authentic. The white cloth was a cotton scarf designed for female tourists. My handsome tanned complexion came out of a bottle.

"What else have you got in there?" I asked, curiosity overcoming my raging impatience as Schmidt replaced the bottle in his briefcase.

"Contact lenses," said Schmidt. "Black ones and brown ones. Scissors. They are useful for many things. Dye for the hair—"

I declined the hair coloring. It would take too long to dry, and if it was the same stuff Schmidt had used on his mustache it would probably run.

"Traveler's checks," Schmidt continued. "And money. Take it, you may need it. I will cash more traveler's checks this afternoon. And take this also."

I put the cash into my pocket. The other offering was a knife.

"Where'd you get that?" I demanded. He must have brought the other things all the way from Munich, but he could never have gotten the knife through customs. It had a worn wooden hilt and a blade eight inches long. The edges shone.

"From the taxi driver," Schmidt said calmly. "He did not have a gun, but he—"

"Thanks." I was in no mood to be fussy. I was only sorry the taxi driver hadn't packed an Uzi.

I didn't get to use my pretty new bag after all. I filled my pockets with as many useful items as they would hold and fastened them securely with safety pins. Schmidt was talking—something about Cairo—but I cut him off. "Let's go."

I assumed my disguise in the taxi. Watching in the rearview mirror, the driver was so interested he almost ran over a bicycle and two Swedish tourists. Schmidt told him some story—something indecent, probably, because the driver howled with laughter and Schmidt blushed when I asked him what he had said.

He dropped me off and I waved bye-bye to him as the taxi headed back along the corniche. The arrangements had taken longer than I would have liked. The sun was sinking toward the cliffs of the west bank and the river reflected the glow of gathering sunset. It might have been more sensible to wait until after dark before I made the attempt. In fact, there was no question about it; it would have been more sensible.

Carrying my shopping bag, I shuffled along the broken sidewalk in my backless leather slippers. For once I was grateful I had feet as big as a man's. The women's slippers were gaudy affairs with turned-up toes and gilt trim. By the time I'd gone a few hundred yards my footwear was dusty and scuffed, like the shoes of the other pedestrians.

What I saw at the entrance to the institute made me duck into the first street leading away from the corniche. I had expected guards. I had not expected they would be wearing black uniforms. It was depressing confirmation of the doubts Schmidt and I had had earlier. Larry must have convinced the police he needed protection. If they were stationed all around the perimeter, I was in deep trouble.

By the time I had worked my way around to the back of the estate, blue shadows were gathering and my nerves were ready to snap. I had been warned away from the wall by one guy carrying a rifle and wearing a uniform, and there were apartment buildings facing it across a narrow street. Finally I reached a place where the buildings were replaced by a vacant lot, filled with weeds and tumbled masonry. The base of the wall was in deepening shadow and the mud plaster had flaked, leaving crevices between the underlying bricks. Nobody was around. It was now or never, and by that time I was about ready to whip out my gun and shoot anybody who tried to stop me. If, that is, there were any bullets in the gun. I couldn't remember how many shots I'd fired. Several.

I've never climbed anything as fast as I did that wall. At any second I expected to hear a shout or a shot. Hanging on by my toenails and one hand, I reached into the shopping bag slung onto my back and pulled out the pillow I had taken from Schmidt's bed. It helped some, but the barbed wire

ripped a gash in my long skirts as I swung my leg over. It
didn't do my shin any good either. I didn't try climbing down,
I just let go.

The ten-foot drop knocked the breath out of me and the
shrub through which I fell had lots of thorns. It was a nice
thick shrub, though. I blessed Larry's landscaper for wanting
to hide that ugly wall.

I had left my Nefertiti bag with Schmidt and was wearing
my own clothes under the galabiya. After gathering up the
odds and ends that had fallen out of my pockets I peered
through the branches and tried to figure out where I was.
The swimming pool—or, to be more precise, the surrounding
fence—oriented me. I pinned my turban back on and headed
for the house, skulking along in the shrubbery when I could,
dashing across the open spaces when I couldn't. It would be
dark before long, but if the movers had quit for the day . . .
Apparently the gardeners were about to do so. I spotted a
couple of them heading for a shed, rakes and spades over
their shoulders. Some of the others—the ones I particularly
didn't want to meet—must be away from the house, not
heading for another hideout as Max had tried to make me
believe, but searching for poor little me. They needed me.
Not for my sweet self, but in order to persuade John to carry
out his part of the deal.

And I needed John. Not only for his sweet self, but because
he knew the answers to certain vital questions. How far had
the corruption spread? How many people were in on the
scheme? One reason why I was reluctant to appeal to the
police, or the SSI, was that I felt certain some of them must
be involved. The man I had met in Larry's office, who had
insisted on the conveniently anonymous appellation of Achmet, had to be in Larry's pay. The purpose of that interview
was clear to me now; it had been intended to get me off the
case and convince me there was no need to contact anyone
else.

Until I spotted Max I hadn't been certain Larry was
involved. They could have done the job without his knowledge, though it would have been difficult. But Larry had lied
about how long his secretary had been with him. A year ago
Max had been in a Swedish prison. Larry had pulled the

necessary strings and gotten him out when he was needed.
It's terrifying, the amount of power money can wield. All the
complex aspects of the plot had been made easier by Larry's
influence and wealth. He probably owned the *Queen of the
Nile*—and the crew and the captain, and the engineer who
had dutifully demolished the refrigeration machinery. And
Jean-Louis and Feisal. It wasn't fair. Everybody was on Larry's side. Except John, who was, as usual, on his own side.
Not entirely, though; not any longer. I didn't dare think about
his reasons for defying the others, or the price he would
probably have to pay. I didn't dare think about a lot of things.
If I did, the defenses I had built up over the years would
crumble and fall, and I couldn't afford that kind of weakness
now.

As I approached the side entrance I heard voices. The
movers were working late, but one look told me this clever
idea wasn't going to work a second time. The man who stood
by the open door watching them pass in and out was wearing
European clothes. Though darkness was not yet complete,
the floodlights illumining the entrance had been turned on,
enabling him to see their faces clearly. They also enabled me
to see his features clearly. I had known him as Bright. I had
a hunch that wasn't his real name.

The floodlights served me as well, half-blinding him to
anything that was going on outside their glare. I sidled through
the landscaping until I reached the terrace. As I crawled on
hands and knees in the dubious shelter of the low walls, one
of my sandals fell off. Instead of replacing it I kicked the
other one off. Once I was inside the house, bare feet would
be quieter and quicker than those clumsy sandals.

I had come prepared to break the glass if I had to; one of
the useful objects Schmidt had pressed upon me was a roll
of tape. However, the French doors weren't locked. The parlor
was lighted but empty. After I had closed the door behind me
I relaxed a little, though I knew the feeling of greater safety
was mostly wishful thinking. There were places to hide,
behind draperies and furniture, but several of the pieces I
had seen before were gone—into one of the moving vans, I
supposed.

I wished I were more familiar with the plan of the house.

Somewhere, I felt certain, there were rooms not open to the general public, and I wasn't thinking of the kitchen and service areas. But if they were as secret as they had to be—underground, protected by every possible security device—access wouldn't be easy. I had decided I would investigate the bedrooms first.

My turban had come unhitched and my hands were too unsteady to deal with the damned thing. I tied it around my neck in a neat Girl Scout knot and padded toward the hall and the front stairs.

If the man who came down the stairs had been barefoot I would have walked right into him. He was wearing boots and his step was firm and confident; I heard him coming and ducked back into the parlor, praying that room wasn't his destination. He went the other way, heading for Larry's study. The door opened and I heard voices before it closed again.

Evidently a business meeting was in progress. There had been several voices, including a woman's soprano, considerably louder and shriller than her usual soft tones. I hadn't dared look to see who the latest arrival had been—Max? Larry?—but at least four of them were now in the office.

Lifting my skirts, I ran up the stairs. All the doors along the corridor were closed; lights in antique bronze sconces shone brightly.

A methodical searcher would have tried each door in turn. That procedure had its risks, however. It was too much to expect that all of them would be in Larry's study. If I opened the door of an occupied room the search would end then and there. I tried the door of Schmidt's former room first, and then that of my own. Both were dark. I had to turn on the lights to make certain nobody was there. It was not a very smart move, but I hadn't thought of bringing a flashlight. There were a lot of things I hadn't thought of.

Time was getting on. The meeting could break up at any moment. It occurred to me that maybe I ought to find a place where I could hide in case someone came upstairs. If I couldn't find him right away, if he wasn't in this part of the house, I would have to wait till after they had gone to bed before I resumed the search. Maybe I would be lucky enough to overhear a snatch of conversation: "Let us go to the cellar, which is reached by a flight of stairs next to the kitchen, and see how our guest (sneering laughter) is getting on.''

Fat chance. I had been associating with Schmidt too long even to imagine such a thing.

It was likely that he was in the cellar (if there was a cellar) or in one of the other buildings. Checking the bedrooms was probably a waste of time, but it had to be done and now was the best time, before the occupants of the house retired for the night. First, though, I needed to find a place where I could hide temporarily. The narrow unadorned door at the back of a shallow recess looked as if it led to another broom closet or a linen closet, so I tried it first. No one would be there.

Someone was, though.

It was a small room, only eight or ten feet square, with a single window. Shelves along two of the walls indicated that its original function had been that of storage, of linens or other household objects. The furniture consisted of a cot, a table, and a few chairs.

They hadn't even bothered to lock the door.

His head had fallen forward and his body sagged against the ropes that bound him to the chair. I hadn't dared hope I would find him in pristine condition. I had even braced myself for a little blood. But only the dark hours of nightmare could have prepared me for this. The stains covered his shirt like a macabre crazy-quilt pattern of rust and scarlet, some patches still wet and bright, some dried to ugly brown.

The sound I made was wordless, more like a bird's squawk than anything human, but John must have recognized my voice. His head lifted alertly and his face was set in a scowl.

"You again," he said, without enthusiasm.

"What . . ." His face was unmarked except for a swollen lip. I cleared my throat and tried again. "What did they . . ."

"It's called 'The Death of a Thousand Cuts,' or something equally picturesque. Lower percentages are employed for purposes of discipline or persuasion." The scowl became even more pronounced. "The primary subject of the interrogation was your present whereabouts. I ought to have told them not to bother, because you'd be sure to turn up before long. Christ Almighty, Vicky, wasn't one encounter with that ghastly woman enough? I have been trying for two days to get you out of here, and you keep coming back like a—a bloody boomerang!"

"You're the nastiest, most ungrateful bastard I have ever—" I began.

"If you're going to shout, at least close the door!"

"Oh." I closed the door.

"Dare I flatter myself that you came after me this time?" John inquired in his most poisonously polite voice. "Very good of you, I'm sure. All right, let's try the escape bit again. If we keep practicing we may get it right one day. I trust it occurred to you to bring along a weapon? Possibly even a knife? If you didn't, there's one on the table."

I had already seen it and was trying hard not to look at it. The blade was dark and clotted. Hoisting my skirts, I whipped out my own knife. I had wrapped a cloth around it as a makeshift scabbard.

A look of apprehension replaced John's scowl as I wobbled toward him. "Do please watch what you're doing. There are several essential arteries running down the extremities and your knowledge of anatomy—"

"I don't suppose it's as expert as hers." I had no doubt who had used that knife. His shirt was open and I could see some of the cuts, arranged in patterns as neat as cross-stitch.

I managed to free his ankles without slashing an artery and then crawled around behind the chair. When the knife touched his bare arm he made a profane remark and I snapped, "I'm trying to slide it down between your wrists. The rope is pretty tight."

"Oh, is it really?"

"If you don't stop twitching and complaining it will be your own damned fault if you end up with a spouting artery."

After the last of the ropes had fallen away John rose briskly to his feet and immediately dropped to his knees. Instinctively I reached for him. He flinched away from my touch.

"No. Just . . . give me a minute."

I stood looking helplessly down at him as he fought to control his ragged breathing. Sweat had darkened his hair and his wrists were ringed with ridged flesh.

"John," I whispered. "I, uh . . . I . . ."

"Well?" He didn't look up, but his shoulders straightened as if in expectation.

"I . . . I'm sorry."

"You're sorry," John repeated.

"Well, uh . . . It was very nice of you to lock me up in the wardrobe and . . . and all the rest. Of course if you had taken the trouble to mention at an earlier point in time that Mary was one of the gang and a closet sadist, none of this would have happened."

"Oh, well done," John said. "For a moment there, I feared that the Vicky I know and love had gone soft." He fumbled in his pant pocket. His hands were still numb; he managed to extract a small tin, but it slipped through his fingers when he tried to open it.

"Let me." I picked it up. "Though I think you need something a little stronger than aspirin."

"That *is* something a little stronger than aspirin. One of the white and two of the yellow, please."

I didn't like the looks of those pills. If they weren't illegal they were dangerous. Maybe both. This didn't seem an appropriate time for a lecture on drugs, however. "Can you swallow them without water?"

"I'll have to, won't I?"

After he had forced them down I said, "Maybe we'd better get moving."

"I couldn't agree more. Perhaps we ought first to discuss the method of escape you have in mind. I trust you do have a method in mind?"

"I hadn't gotten that far," I admitted.

"Hadn't you?"

We were both kneeling. When he turned his head his eyes were on a level with mine.

Neither of us spoke for a moment. Then he said, "Unless you were planning to tuck me under one arm and make a break for it, you'll have to contain yourself for . . . say, ten minutes. It will take that long for those pills to kick in. Until they do I might manage a slow crawl."

"Did they say when they'd be back?"

"No, they were not so considerate as that. Have you been here all this time? Not in the wardrobe, surely."

"No, I left. Thanks to Max. He knew I was in the wardrobe."

That shocked him into relative alertness. "What? How do you know?"

"We had a long talk. He sent Hans and Rudi out of the room before he spoke to me, and he obviously meant to let me get away, but he refused to tell me where they were taking you even after I . . . I . . . uh."

"You seem to be suffering from a speech disability," John remarked. "You, uh, what?"

"Are you ready to—"

"No. What did you do or say to poor old Maxie? Burst into tears? Tell him you . . . Oh, Christ," John said, reading my face as only he could. "You didn't! You didn't really give Max—Max, of all people!—the old Romeo and Juliet routine? Did you threaten to perch on my tombstone and drink poison? Did you promise you'd follow him to the ends of the earth and stab him before throwing yourself off the battlements, à la Tosca? I'm immensely touched that you should perjure yourself for me, darling, but my opinion of your intelligence has been sadly shaken. You'd have stood a better chance of softening a rattlesnake than that cold-blooded, cynical—"

The door opened just far enough to admit a man, and then closed as quietly. The man was Max.

"Ah," he said softly. "I thought I'd find you here."

My skirts were bunched up under me. I had to stand before I could get at my gun. Max watched interestedly while I fumbled in my pockets. John didn't move a muscle. His mouth was still open and his eyes were glazed. Finally I got the gun out and pointed it at Max.

"Don't call for help," I said.

"My dear Dr. Bliss, I had time to recite an entire sonnet while you were trying to locate that weapon," Max said. "Something by Shakespeare or Mrs. Browning, perhaps? I am not as familiar with your English poets as I would like to be."

John closed his mouth and cleared his throat, but he was not yet capable of speech. I said, "Turn around, Max."

"So you can strike me unconscious with the butt of the gun? I think not, Dr. Bliss. It would be painful for me and counterproductive for you."

John got unsteadily to his feet and took the gun from me. He squinted at it, and then slipped it into his belt. "Would you care to elaborate on that, Max?"

"My meaning should be clear," Max said. "I am going to help you escape."

# Chapter Eleven

It was fortunate John was too petrified to argue or make long-winded, sarcastic speeches. Time was running out on us. The meeting had broken up; people were dispersing, to dress for dinner—and for other purposes.

Max was waiting for Mary. He had told us what we were to do, but he wouldn't answer my questions. There was no time, he had said, and when I heard that shrill, arrogant voice outside the door where we stood listening, I understood. He had expected she would want to amuse herself for a while before she changed.

"Get out of my way, Max."

"No, I forbid it. You have done enough already."

"You have no authority over me!"

"Then I will appeal to someone who does." His voice hardened. "He will not allow you to endanger the entire enterprise."

She spat out a string of nouns and adjectives. I thought she was applying them to Max until he replied dryly, "I have no fondness for Tregarth either, but business must take precedence over personal resentment. He cannot be forced to carry out his part of the plan unless we hold a hostage as surety for his compliance, and he will be unable to carry it out if you go on playing your little games with him. I have locked the door and I will keep the key, so don't bother coming back after I have gone."

She stormed off, using language no lady should employ, and I heard the reverberation as she slammed her door. Max moved away without speaking to us. He'd already given us our instructions, and I couldn't blame him for minimizing the risk to himself. They probably kept Mary happy by letting her play with traitors and other expendable individuals before disposing of them. Her brother had been fond of knives, too.

Max had given me the key and told me to lock the door. My hand was clenched so tightly John had to pry my fingers loose one by one before he could take it from me.

"What are you doing?" I demanded in a hoarse whisper. "He told us to stay here."

"He told us not to attempt to leave the house for an hour," John corrected. "I'd prefer to wait elsewhere. I don't entirely share your blind faith in Maxie."

"Why is he doing this then?"

"God knows. But you can be certain it isn't because his heart was touched by an appeal to sentiment, of which he has none. Possibly he's come to think of you as a kind of mascot or good-luck charm. He's frightfully superstitious—look at those ghastly silhouettes of his. They aren't a hobby any longer, they have become an obsession." He unlocked the door and then turned to look at me. "Do you want your gun back?"

"No."

"Then get the knife. You left it on the floor by the chair. And don't put it in your pocket! Keep hold of it. Stay close behind me. If we're spotted and I tell you to run, do it, without one of those interminable arguments of yours, and without looking back. Is that clear?"

I nodded. His orders had been perfectly clear. Whether or not I would follow them was another matter.

"Come on, then."

Either he had explored the house more systematically than I had had the opportunity of doing or he had stayed there before. Instead of heading for the main stairs, he turned in the opposite direction. We had to pass several of the bedrooms, including Mary's, and if I had not reached a state of total emotional paralysis I would have dropped in my tracks when I heard a crash and an inarticulate shriek from her room. The cry had been one of rage. She must be relieving her feelings by smashing lamps, vases, and other fragile objects.

John's long, even stride didn't alter. He was moving more easily now. The end of the corridor was in shadow, there were no wall sconces near it. What I had taken to be a dead end turned out to be a door, painted the same neutral color as the wall. When he opened it I saw a landing with narrow, uncarpeted steps leading down, and another flight going up. It was lighted by a single bulb on the ceiling. I ought to have known there would be a separate staircase for the servants. Not that the knowledge would have helped. There would be people in that part of the house too.

I felt somewhat easier after John had closed the door, but when he sat down on the topmost step I said nervously, "What are you waiting for? The servants will be coming this way."

"No, they won't. Not for a while." Leaning back, supporting his weight on his elbows, he went on in the same subdued voice, "It's obvious that you have never seriously contemplated a career in crime. If you do, bear in mind that strict attention to schedules is vitally important. Human beings are creatures of habit, and the older they get, the more they insist on regularity. Blenkiron always dines at seven-fifteen. The servants will be preparing dinner for the guests and eating their own; they don't come upstairs to turn down the beds and so on until the guests have retired to—"

"John, if you don't stop lecturing and start answering questions I am going to scream."

"Ask a sensible question, then."

"How did you get involved with—"

"No, no. That is a reasonable question, I admit, but under the present circumstances it is less relevant than a number of others, and the answer would involve a prolonged explanation which you probably wouldn't believe anyhow. Try again, keeping in mind that our primary concern at this moment—"

"All right! Are we going to stay here until eight o'clock?"

"What time is it?"

"Seven-fifteen."

"How time flies when one is enjoying oneself," John murmured. "For the next half hour this is as safe a place as any. I've a little errand to do before we leave. You wait here while I—"

"No."

"It may be a bit tricky—"

"No. I'm not letting you out of my sight."

John studied me speculatively. I scooted back, out of his reach. "Oh, no, you don't. Not another sock on the jaw, for my own good."

"It's a tempting idea. But in this case it might do more harm than good. Besides, you'd probably hit me back. Come along, then. And don't forget what I told you."

The stairs ended at another closed door. When John eased it open I started; the voices sounded as if they were only a few feet away. They were. The room to our left was the kitchen. I could smell cooking and hear pots and dishes rattling.

John went the other way, moving as soundlessly as if he too were barefoot. I hadn't been in this part of the house and I had no idea where we were or where we were going, so I stayed close on his heels. When he opened the next door I did know where we were, and that encouraging old adage about the frying pan and the fire came back to me. Ahead was the main hall of the house, lighted like a stage by the hanging brass chandelier and a dozen sconces. The open archway to my right led to the parlor. Lights blazed from that room as well; in another forty minutes, give or take five minutes, Larry and his "guests" would be entering it. On my left was the staircase. I'd have preferred to stay in the illusory safety of the shadows cast by that massive structure, but John didn't pause. He walked unconcernedly past the foot of the stairs and entered the corridor that led to the library and Larry's study.

Apparently he had been right about the household schedule. We met no one. When we reached the study John's fingers pressed a switch and prodded a button, both concealed in the carving of the frame, before he turned the knob. So, I thought, this wasn't the first time he had enjoyed Larry's hospitality.

He was one of the world's most efficient snoops, but even he couldn't have discovered so many useful details in two days.

It was at this point that John's theories failed. I suppose it was something of a compliment to me that Larry had taken the precaution of stationing a guard in his study. Or, to look at it another way, it was something of an insult. Had he really believed I'd be foolhardy enough to return? Well, he had been right. And if I had been looking for evidence of guilt, this was where I'd have looked first.

The guard was the man I had known as Sweet. He was eating his supper off a tray, and he must have assumed his visitors were members of the household, familiar with the security system. That moment of misapprehension, brief though it was, saved our necks. Dropping his fork, he reached for his shoulder holster, but he was too slow. John had him covered.

"Get his gun," John said. "Go round behind him. Far around, if you'll forgive me for pointing out the obvious."

Sweet's expression didn't live up to the nom de guerre he had chosen. His eyes, unblinking as those of a reptile, followed me as I sidled to one side, giving him a wide berth. I was not looking forward to coming within arm's reach of him but I didn't have to. As soon as I had reached a point at which Sweet had to turn his head to follow my progress John hit him, not with the gun, but with his left fist.

"I didn't know you were ambidextrous," I said, removing my Girl Scout neckerchief and winding it around Sweet's wrists.

"I'm not. Bloody hell! That hurt."

"Stop complaining and help me. I need some rope."

"Sorry, I'm fresh out." Removing his belt, he used it to bind Sweet's ankles.

"We need a gag. Where's that nice, clean white handkerchief a proper gent always carries?"

"Never mind the gag." John went to the fireplace and began running his hands over the paneling next to it. "What time is it?"

"Seven twenty-five."

"Not much time. I hope to God I haven't forgotten . . . Ah. That's done it."

A section of the paneling slid aside under the pressure of his hands. I could see lights behind it; they must have come on automatically when the door was opened. "Go ahead," he said. "I'll fetch the unwanted baggage."

"Larry's quite a romantic, isn't he?" I remarked, starting down the stairs the open panel had disclosed. "Secret passages all over the place."

"There's a good and sufficient practical reason for this bit of romanticism." John followed me, towing "Sweet" by his feet. I am as a rule a tenderhearted person but I did not wince when I heard his head bounce from step to step.

There was no door at the bottom of the stairs. They opened directly into a large windowless room.

No wonder I hadn't been impressed with Larry's collection of antiquities. Here was the real collection—his own private collection, hidden away from all eyes but his. The room was softly lit and carpeted. The air was cool, the temperature and humidity carefully controlled to preserve the exhibits. They stood along the walls and rested in velvet-lined cases. The cases were open, so he could touch and fondle to his heart's content.

My eyes moved in dazed disbelief from one masterpiece to another. The lovely little statuette of Tetisheri in the British Museum was a fake, all right. The original was here. So was the Nefertiti bust—not the painted bust in Berlin, but the other, even more beautiful, that was—was supposed to be—in the Cairo Museum.

Had I been mistaken about Larry's ultimate intent after all? The contents of this room represented the greatest art theft in history. Getting them out of the museum and into this room was only half the battle. He was in the process of finishing the job—getting his prizes out of Egypt. Packed in among his household effects, they would pass through customs without a hitch. No one would be boorish enough to inspect the possessions of the great philanthropist, the man who had just presented Egypt with a multimillion-dollar institute. Wasn't this enough for Larry?

No. My original reasoning still held, tenuous and unsupported though it was. The convenient breakdown of the *Queen of the Nile*, the violent death of the new director of the institute, only a few hours after he had found a sympathetic and notoriously inquisitive listener in me, the precise timing of Larry's permanent departure from Egypt, his bizarre obsession . . . The collection I saw before me was a convincing demonstration of that obsession. Almost every object in the room depicted, or had belonged to, a queen or princess.

Many of the cases were empty, their contents already transferred to the wooden packing boxes that spoiled the neatness of the room. But there was lots left. A small head of an Amarna princess, a diadem of twisted golden wire set with tiny turquoise flowers . . .

John heard me gasp. "I wondered if you'd spot that," he said, dragging Sweet into a corner and turning one of the empty boxes over on top of him.

The diadem had been buried with a princess of the Middle Kingdom. I'd found a sketch of it in the workshop of the goldsmith who had been producing fake jewels for the gang in Rome. The original had been in the Cairo Museum, not the Metropolitan, as I had ignorantly supposed at the time. Obviously it wasn't there now.

"You . . ." I began. "You . . . You started this that long ago?"

"This sort of collection takes a while to build up," John said coolly. He joined me and studied the lovely thing with obvious appreciation. Then he shook his head regretfully. "Too large and too fragile. This will do the trick just as well, I expect."

The object he shoved carelessly into his pocket was a pectoral, its complex design dominated by a huge scarab of lapis lazuli. It had belonged to Tutankhamon.

John took my limp hand and led me up the stairs.

"Time?" he asked, closing the sliding panel.

"Uh . . . seven-forty."

"We may as well get into position, then."

"Do you know what Max has planned?"

"I've an inkling, yes. Don't tell me you haven't anticipated his intentions. You're the one who is supposed to be in charge of this rescue."

I snarled at him. The sight of that incredible collection—a good deal of which had probably come to Larry via John—

had made me remember what he was, and the sight of him,
bright-eyed and cheerful and higher than a kite in a March
gale, didn't relieve my apprehensions any. I had had more
than a nodding acquaintance with amphetamines and other
useful drugs during my days as a grad student. Sooner or later
he would crash, and to judge by the immediate effects it
would be a long hard fall. Some of the cuts were still bleeding.
The bright splashes of red looked like flowers against the
rusty stains.

He saw me staring at his shirt and misinterpreted my expression. "Lend me that peculiar garment you're wearing."

"What for?"

"For God's sake, Vicky, pull yourself together and stop
asking silly questions. It won't serve you as a disguise, not
with that mop of blond hair shining like a beacon, and you
can probably run faster without it. If, as I hope but dare not
expect, we get as far as the corniche, we'll have to catch a
taxi. Even a Luxor cab driver may be reluctant to pick up a
fare who looks as if he's been in a war."

"Especially these days," I muttered, stripping off the
galabiya.

It didn't suit him, but at least it covered the blood.

Max had instructed us to be ready at ten minutes to eight.
Once he had made his move—whatever it was—we could
count on five minutes, maybe less. If he hadn't acted by ten
after eight we were on our own, and he wished us the best
of British luck.

Either he had overestimated the appetites of his associates
or my watch was slow. We were crossing the hall, exposed
and fully visible from at least four directions, when I heard
them leaving the dining room. I almost ran over John, who
was in the lead, in my wild dash toward what could only
be described as comparative concealment. The first of them
entered the parlor as I ducked under the stairs.

Before I had time to catch my breath, Max acted. It wasn't
until later that I figured out what he had done; at the time I
was too confused to hear anything except a medley of shouts
and expletives, in various languages and various voices. People were running in all directions, some through the French
doors onto the terrace, others into the hall. Mary was among

the latter. I caught only a glimpse of her as she darted past. One glimpse was more than enough. That face would have looked appropriate under a head of writhing snakes.

Larry was right behind her. Instead of following her up the stairs he ran toward his study. Interesting, how basic instincts prevail in moments of crisis. Inconvenient, too. I didn't know how Mary planned to get through that locked door, but I didn't underestimate the little dear's cunning, and when she discovered she'd lost her new toy she'd be back. And so would Larry, as soon as he had found Sweet. And we were still in the house and the door was probably locked or guarded or both. I began to wonder if my girlish confidence in Max had been misplaced.

Even as this unkind doubt entered my mind I heard the door open. It must have been Hans who was standing guard outside, for Max called out in German. "Hurry! They went that way. After them!"

He followed Hans. When I started forward, assisted by a shove from John, the hall was empty and the front door stood open.

It was almost too easy. Max had directed the search toward the back of the house, which was where sensible fugitives would go—poorly lighted, thickly landscaped. It was even darker back there after Max shot out scme of the lights. I assumed it was Max, since none of the others would have been so helpful.

Almost too easy, I said. One dedicated soul had stuck to his post. His black uniform blended with the darkness. If he hadn't moved closer to the gate, drawn by curiosity, we wouldn't have seen him in time. The light glinted dully off the rifle barrel.

We froze in a puddle of shadow, knowing the slightest movement would betray our presence. There wasn't even a skinny shrub between us and the guard.

"Give me the knife." John breathed the words into my ear.

I didn't ask what he was going to do with it. I couldn't imagine what he was going to do with it. The guy was ten or fifteen feet away and there was no way of creeping up on him unobserved. The rifle wasn't slung over his shoulder, it was in his hands.

John's arm shot back and his foot hooked around my ankle, sending me sprawling to the ground. A bullet whined through the air over my head; when I got up, which I did with considerable alacrity, the guard lay face down and unmoving.

"Is he dead?" I asked breathlessly.

John straightened, the rifle in his hand. "Not unless he passed on from sheer terror. I can't throw a knife that accurately; it was only meant to distract him. Vicky, would you mind terribly if we postponed this conversation and started running? They'll have heard the shot, you know."

Running barefoot over a hard, broken surface is no fun. The first time I stubbed my toe John tossed the rifle away and took my hand. When I stumbled, which I did every two or three steps, he yanked at my arm and kept me moving forward in a series of staggering rushes. I stopped listening for sounds of pursuit, I stopped worrying about whether there would be another guard at the street; I could only think how much my feet hurt.

When we emerged, unchallenged, onto the brightly lit expanse of the corniche I was still preoccupied with my feet. "Slow down," I panted, trying to free my hand. "We made it."

"Not yet." He stopped, raising his arm. "Praise be to God and Saint Jude, there's a taxi. I do hope you have some money. I'm getting tired of hitting people."

The driver may have been dubious about picking us up but John didn't give him time to think about it. As the cab pulled away he looked out the back window and said something under his breath. I deduced that Saint Jude, the patron of hopeless causes, wasn't going to get a donation after all. Someone had seen us get into the cab.

After giving the driver directions John didn't speak again except to demand money, in the tone a bank robber might have employed. I handed over part of Schmidt's wad and sat nursing my sore feet. I wondered where we were going, but I didn't have the energy to inquire. After we passed the Luxor Temple the cab turned away from the river into the streets of the town and finally came to a stop.

"Can you walk a little farther?" John asked, helping me out.

"What's the alternative?" I stood on one foot. It only hurt half as much that way.

"Crawling a little farther."

But he put his arm around me and lifted me over the worst spots. The sidewalk was broken and littered. I was too busy watching where I stepped to notice my surroundings; when he turned into a doorway and knocked, I was only glad we had reached our destination. I was beginning to think the occupant wasn't home when I heard a rattle of bolts and chains. The door opened a crack. Then it started to close again.

John inserted his foot. "Open, sesame," he said.

It was the foot, not the request, that got the point across. The door swung open and there she was. She had drawn a fold of cloth across her face, hiding all her features except beady little black eyes. But I'd have known her anywhere.

"Hi, Granny," I said. "I'm back. Aren't you glad to see me?"

Feisal wasn't glad to see us either. After a prolonged and obviously profane monologue in his own language he threw up his hands. "In here," he snapped, opening a door. It was Granny's parlor, elegantly fitted out with shiny upholstered furniture and a television set and a rug covered with bright red roses. Granny let out a wavering howl of protest. I couldn't really blame her for not wanting two dusty vagabonds in her nice clean room. However, my bloody footprints blended with the red roses.

I collapsed into the nearest chair and stretched my legs. When he saw my feet, Feisal's face changed. "What happened?"

"Quite a lot has happened," John said.

Granny had slipped out of the room. Now she returned with her veil pinned firmly in place. She was carrying a basin of water, which she set down on the floor beside my chair. There was a dead fly floating in the basin; I pushed the body callously aside with my toes and slid my feet into the warm water. It felt wonderful. I smiled and nodded at the old lady. She ducked her head and muttered in Arabic.

"She is begging your pardon," Feisal translated. "She

thinks you hurt yourself running away from her. She says she didn't mean to frighten you."

I leaned over and touched Granny on her bowed shoulder. "Shoukran," I said. "That's all the Arabic I know, Feisal; tell her I owe her an apology and that I'm very grateful."

"She's not the only one to whom you owe an apology," said John, unmoved by this touching exchange. "If you'd stayed here as you were supposed to—"

"I did apologize to you. It's your own fault. If you would stop pushing people around and take the trouble to explain why you're doing what you're doing, instead of being so insufferably condescending, people might—"

"Enough!" Feisal exclaimed. "We have not the time to waste on recriminations. You promised you'd get me out of this mess, Johnny—"

"Johnny?" I repeated. "Isn't that sweet. How come you never let me call you Johnny?"

"I never allow him to do it either. It's only a crude attempt to soften me by recalling sentimental memories of our school days."

"Then I'll have to go on thinking of you as my blue eyes."

I thought he'd miss that one, but Schmidt's tutelage had been more extensive than I had believed. Spontaneous, unguarded laughter transformed his face, and my defensive barriers developed a few more cracks. I hadn't often seen that look.

"I'll never forget the pleasures we've both seen together," he assured me.

"What in God's name—" Feisal began.

"You don't want to know. The fact is, old chap, I can't get you out unless I can extricate myself as well, and the only way I can do that is to turn my coat and join the forces of law and order. Until our former associates are safely stowed away in a maximum-security prison neither of us is going to be out of this." He sighed. "Ironic, isn't it? Forced by circumstances beyond my control to become an honest man . . ."

"Don't let it bother you too much," I advised. "You can console yourself with the knowledge that it wasn't morality but self-preservation that drove you to that painful decision.

Clearing your name is going to be something of a tall order, though. How are you planning to go about it?"

"A good question." John rubbed his forehead. "How many of the local gendarmes are in Blenkiron's pay, Feisal?"

"Too many," was the blunt response. "He's got enough money to buy several medium-sized countries, much less a few poor devils who are trying to raise families on inadequate salaries. Some of them are honest, but I don't know which, and the honest ones think he's the greatest thing to come along since King Tut's tomb. If it's our word against his, we haven't a prayer."

"I've a little more than that," John murmured. "But I think we'll have to take it to Cairo—straight to the Ministry and the EAO."

"They'll be watching the airport and the train station," Feisal said soberly. "I assume they know you're on the loose."

"You assume correctly. We'll have to go by road."

"I don't own a car," Feisal said. "And don't suggest I steal one. I'm in enough trouble already."

"How much money have we?" John asked.

It added up to more than I had realized. Grimacing but game, Feisal contributed his hard-earned savings—a few hundred pounds Egyptian. John had only a few pounds in his wallet. Being broke when payment was required was an old habit of his, but in this case I refrained from caustic comment. He hadn't had a chance to pick up his luggage before we left.

"Schmidt will have money," I said. "He was going to cash more traveler's checks." John started to speak, but I cut him off. "I'm not leaving without Schmidt. We'll have to collect him before we go."

"Of course," John said, raising one eyebrow. "You didn't suppose I'd throw Schmidt to the wolves, did you? And before you burst into a fiery denunciation, let me remind you that it was I who got him out of that bloody house and into . . . I hope to God he's not still at the Winter Palace?"

"No. He—"

"Hold on." He handed Feisal the roll of bills. "You'll have to hire the vehicle, Feisal."

"They'll be looking for me too," Feisal objected.

"Not as assiduously as they will be looking for us. Try to

find one that has four wheels and some rudimentary brakes if you can. And don't dawdle."

Feisal went out, shaking his head. Granny, bless her heart, was still trying to make up for being so mean to me. She had been trotting in and out with trays and bottles.

"Now," John said, reaching for a beer. "Tell me what happened after Maxie sprang you."

"Should you be drinking alcohol?"

"I certainly shouldn't be drinking the local water. Please try to concentrate on essentials, my dear. We don't have much time and I need to know what's been going on. Where did you run into Schmidt? Obviously he didn't succeed in intercepting you."

"Obviously. But he was waiting when I came out." I gave him a brief synopsis of succeeding events to which he listened with amused and infuriatingly detached interest.

"Good old Schmidt. We'll have to get someone to present him with a medal and kiss him on both cheeks. He'd love that."

"I'll settle for getting him out of this in one piece. I don't trust him, John. If I don't turn up pretty soon he's apt to go looking for me. Trying to sneak into the institute disguised as James Bond, or—"

"I hardly think even Schmidt would do anything so useless. He must realize his best hope of helping you is to blow the whistle on Blenkiron. How much does he know?"

"Uh—"

John said something under his breath. Then he said it out loud.

"Dammit," I said defensively, "there wasn't time for a leisurely discussion! He said he thought he knew and I said I did too and then . . . Uh."

"What do you think you know?" John inquired very softly.

"Well . . . I assume Larry's using the *Queen of the Nile* to transport his loot. He had to get rid of the tour group so he could make a quick run, no stops, no delays. The reason for the changes in schedule really was concern about low water levels, he has to get through the locks—"

"The schedule wasn't changed. It was the one he intended all along."

"You knew—"

"No, I did not. Never mind that, it's a side issue. You are correct so far. Once the boat reaches Cairo the loot—how well you put it!—will be transferred to the airport. I'm sure I hardly need mention that Blenkiron owns one or two airlines."

"Or that the Luxor airport is too small for big cargo planes?"

"Clever girl."

"How long will it take him—"

The sound of someone at the door made me break off. It was Feisal. "A friend of mine has gone after the car," he announced. "He'll bring it by in an hour or so."

"We'd better be ready to leave when he arrives," John said.

He pulled the robe over his head. Feisal sucked in his breath. "You need a doctor. Or a hospital."

"Oh, right," John said. "I can see myself explaining how I absentmindedly walked into a sausage slicer. What I need is a clean shirt."

Dried blood had glued the fabric to his skin in a number of places. For once he resisted the temptation to overact, peeling the garment off with only a few manfully repressed groans. The full effect, which I now saw for the first time, was grisly enough to require no additional theatrics. Feisal winced and averted his eyes. Sympathetic he may have been, but I had a feeling that he was picturing himself in the same condition. I also suspected that John was well aware of the effect on his reluctant ally. A visual demonstration is worth a thousand words.

I didn't volunteer to administer first aid. I was outvoted. It wasn't the first time I had patched John up after a work-related accident. Some of the others had required more extensive first aid, but this was worse—deliberate sadism instead of random violence. The less said about that process, the better. John was obliging enough to make a lot of noise, which made it a little easier for me. A little.

"Now what?" I inquired, tossing the roll of tape and the scissors onto the bed. "I don't suppose you've got any wigs, fake mustaches, and miscellaneous disguises around, Feisal?"

John was still muttering profanely, but he couldn't resist

the chance to instruct the ignorant. He began, "The art of disguise—"

"I don't want to hear you lecture on the subject of disguise."

"Neither do I," said Feisal. "But she has a point. I could go out and get—"

"No time," John said. "As I was saying, the art of disguise depends on posture and mannerisms rather than crude physical alterations. Let's see what you've got on hand."

Fitting John out wasn't a problem; he and Feisal were about the same size. Feisal objected violently when John selected his best Cairo-tailored suit, but he was overruled. "I've got to look like a respectable businessman when I go in after Schmidt. Or are you volunteering for that little job?"

"No," Feisal said unhesitatingly.

"A wise decision. They'll be checking the hotels by now if they haven't already done so. I intend to be as unobtrusive as possible, but—"

"You'll have to dye your hair, then," Feisal said. After John's demonstration of what might happen to him if we were caught he was cooperating wholeheartedly, if not happily. "And your eyebrows."

"I don't suppose you have any boot polish?"

"I don't polish my own shoes," Feisal said haughtily.

"Do forgive me," John said. "I didn't mean to imply you did anything so vulgar. You'll have to wind me a nice neat turban, then. Dark glasses will look a little out of place at this time of night. The honored sitt your grandmother must have some kohl or other eye paint?"

I must say it was an education to watch him work. He didn't use much of the black stuff, whatever it was—just enough to darken his eyebrows and touch up those long lashes. He tanned easily; I had seen other Egyptians with skin as fair as his. Once the turban was in place, the difference in his appearance was astounding. It was partly a matter of expression—tight lips, outthrust chin, lowering brows.

"What about your beautiful, beautiful blue eyes?" I asked.

His response was automatic—"'I'll never love brown eyes again—'" and then he laughed shortly. "A truer word was never spoken. As for my beautiful blue eyes, I don't intend to stand still long enough for anyone to gaze deeply into them. Now what are we going to do about you?''

''Maybe Granny could lend me a robe and a veil.''

John shook his head. ''You're too tall to pass as an Egyptian female. It's male attire for you, I'm afraid. Your bonnie blue eyes are beyond my modest skill—''

'' 'You told me more lies than the stars in the . . .' Sorry. Don't take it personally. Country music does have a thing about blue eyes, doesn't it?''

Feisal was staring at us as if we had lost our minds. He was probably right. John had that effect on me.

''So far the score is tied,'' said John. ''As I was saying, we've got to do something about your hair.''

''Cut it off,'' I said, reaching for the scissors. ''Then Feisal can wind me a turban too.''

John took the scissors from me. ''Sit down. I'll do it.''

''I should have known you numbered barbering among your varied skills.''

His hands moved slowly from the crown of my head to the base of my skull, smoothing the tangled masses of hair and gathering them together. There was a long pause before he said, ''I've a better idea. A spot of cosmic cleansing wouldn't do you any harm.''

''What are you talking about?'' I tried to turn, but he closed his fingers around the impromptu ponytail and gave it a hard tug.

''Communing with the universe, awakening the collective consciousness of the world,'' John chanted. ''You're not quite grubby enough for a New Ager, but that's easy to fix.''

When he finished fixing it, I was a dirty blonde with a long lank ponytail and a distinct four-o'clock shadow. The dirt and the beard came from the garden, the single gold earring from Granny, and the collarless long-sleeved shirt from Feisal. Entering into the spirit of the thing, I demanded a crystal and a pair of cutoffs.

''We'll pick up some mystic insignia at one of the bazaars,'' John said. ''These types go in for scarabs and ankh signs and such. The shorts are out. Your knees aren't knobby enough.''

''You might have expressed it in more flattering terms,'' I said.

"Your legs, my darling, are masterpieces of sculptural elegance," John said agreeably. "Those appendages would grace an Aphrodite or a young Diana. Never could such marvels of slender rounded beauty be taken for those of a man. Your form, in short, is rare and divine."

" 'Philadelphia Lawyer,' " I said.

John raised one finger and made an invisible mark on the air. "One point for you."

Feisal's friend was a shy, retiring chap. As soon as we left the house in response to his signal on the horn, he slid out of the driver's seat of the car and walked away without looking back. If he wanted to make certain neither John or I could identify him, he succeeded.

As for the car, I had seen its likes before—in junkyards or abandoned in vacant lots. If it had been in good condition it would have ranked as a vintage vehicle; those tailfins had to be thirty years out of date.

"Good God," John said, staring. "Is this the best he could do? We won't get twenty miles in this wreck."

"I hope you won't think me rude," said Feisal, "if I remind you that you are in no position to be fastidious, and that you sound like a typical supercilious twit of a tourist. We underprivileged Third World types can't afford a new car every year, so we learn how to keep them on the road."

"Touché," John admitted. "After you, Vicky."

He handed me the basket Granny had pressed upon us. It was our only luggage except for Feisal's suitcase.

Feisal got in behind the wheel. "Where to?" he asked.

"The ETAP."

"Oh, wonderful. The big tourist hotels are the first places they'll look."

"Just drive," John said shortly.

Schmidt had given me one of his keys, "just in case." I hadn't asked, "Just in case of what?" I had had other things on my mind. As I crossed the lobby, trying to look as if I were focusing on auras instead of potential kidnapers, I wished I had asked. There was no need for him to leave the room except to cash his traveler's checks, which wouldn't take long, and every reason for him to stay put. Even if they located him they couldn't get at him unless he opened the door, and surely Schmidt wouldn't be foolish enough to admit anyone except . . . Except the room service? Someone imitating my voice?

John had gone ahead. He was waiting by the elevator when I got out of it. "What's wrong?" he asked.

I didn't ask how he could tell. He could always tell. "I'm having premonitions," I admitted.

"It's always best to assume the worst." He took the key from me. "Stand out of the way."

He gave the door a sharp kick and dropped to a crouching position. "That's what they do in the films," he remarked, straightening. "Futile, really, when you consider that most criminals use automatic weapons these days, but I suppose they believe it looks—"

"He's not here. Damn the crazy old idiot, where the hell has he got to now?"

The doors to the bathroom and closet stood open. The import of that didn't dawn on me until after we had investigated all possible hiding places; my morbid imagination was convinced we'd find Schmidt's crumpled body in the bathtub or under the bed.

"He must have left under his own steam; there's no sign of a struggle," I said. "If he's gone back to Larry's, looking for me, I'll kill him."

"He's not gone there," John said.

"What?" I spun around. He was bending over the desk. "How do you know?"

"He's left you a note."

The paper had been crumpled and then smoothed out. It was so badly stained by something brown and sticky that the words were barely legible.

"My dear Vicky," it began. (I translate; he had written in German.) "I have the proof we need. I will drop this off at your hotel and then proceed to the rendezvous we . . ."

"What is this?" I demanded. "What proof? He never mentioned it to me. What hotel? What rendezvous?"

"Calm down." John seated himself at the desk. "Let's see if we can figure out what he's up to."

"Maybe we'd better get out of here."

"No need for haste. They've already been."

"How . . ." I stopped myself. He was dying to show off; his half-smile and cool stare invited me to make a babbling fool of myself so he could patiently explain things to me. "Where was the note?" I asked.

John nodded graciously, like a teacher to a dull student who is finally getting the hang of it. "On the desk. Someone had smoothed it out."

"But Schmidt must have thrown it away. In the wastebasket or onto the floor, after he spilled food all over it . . ."

"Deliberately spilled food all over it," John said encouragingly.

"The implication being that he'd discarded the note because it was sticky and wet and illegible, and written another one." I began pacing the floor. "He expected they'd locate him sooner or later. I've been gone . . ." I looked at my watch. "Over five hours, and they had been looking for us since early afternoon. Time enough to inquire at every hotel in Luxor. He registered under his own name . . ."

"If he had the intelligence for which I am belatedly beginning to give him credit, he left this room shortly after you did," John said. "In disguise, if I know my Schmidt. Let's see. What would I do next? Stake myself out in the lobby. Hope you'd make it back before they located him. Be ready to move on in case they got here first. He'd already have cashed his traveler's checks and retrieved his passport."

"They did get here first."

"And found the discarded letter." John's eyes were bright with amusement and, as he proceeded to make clear, admiration. "You see what the little elf's done, don't you? This letter is not only a red herring, it is an attempt to protect you, in the event that you had been recaptured. If he's got the evidence that can convict them there's no reason for them to harm you. In fact, there is every reason for them to keep you whole and healthy so they can try to strike a deal: silence, or at least delay, in exchange for you." He paused, and then delivered the highest accolade in his repertoire. "I couldn't have done better myself."

"So you don't think he's gone back to the house?"

"Not our Schmidt. Whether you are a fugitive or a prisoner,

he can serve you best by remaining free." John returned to his study of the note. "I can't see anything else here. But I wouldn't be a bit surprised if he had . . . Wait a sec. What's this?"

"The sticky stuff must have spattered," I said, as he held up a blank page spotted with stains.

"The spots make a suspiciously regular pattern," John muttered.

"Try joining the dots," I suggested sarcastically.

John emitted a crow of triumph. "That's it! Look here."

Picking up a pen, he began to draw—not lines connecting the spots, but a series of parallel lines. Five parallel lines. They made the nature of those odd splotches plain. They were musical notes.

"No key signature," John muttered. "Let's assume it's the key of C and that there are no accidentals. Hard to indicate them, really . . ." He began to whistle. "Strike a chord?"

"Try to avoid puns if possible," I said critically. "No, it isn't familiar."

"How about this?" There was a slight difference. I assumed he'd thrown in a few miscellaneous sharps and/or flats.

"This is a waste of time," I grumbled. "Schmidt probably was trying to be cute, but if that's one of his beloved country music tunes you'll never figure out which song because there are only three or four melodies in the whole damned repertoire."

John dropped heavily into a chair. "My God. I should have known."

"What? What?"

He tried to give me the definitive version, but he was laughing so hard he couldn't keep his lips puckered. "If the Egyptians don't strike a medal for him I'll do it myself. And kiss him on both cheeks. He's taken the night train to Memphis."

# Chapter Twelve

The room had been stripped of all personal possessions, whether by Schmidt or by John's hypothetical searchers I could not determine. "They" became less hypothetical as we continued our own search; they had made quite a neat job of it, but I doubted Schmidt would have removed the mattress from the bed and then replaced it and the bedclothes. The searchers must have been men; they hadn't bothered to tuck in the sheets.

"Is there a night train to Memphis?" I asked, investigating the drawers of the nightstand.

"There's one to Cairo. Close enough." John returned from the bathroom. "Nothing there. What about the chest of drawers?"

"Only the souvenirs he bought today." The Nefertiti bag had been on top of the pile. I turned it upside down and shook it. "He's even taken the few odds and ends I left—cosmetics, sunglasses—"

"Chocolates, apples, and gingerbread?"

I didn't want to be reminded of the night in the abandoned church when we had "dined" on the odds and ends I carried in my backpack. Sooner or later I would have to deal with those widening cracks in my defensive walls, but not now, not when we were still four hundred miles from safety and Schmidt was someplace or other doing God knows what, and Mary was looking forward to renewing old acquaintances. I said shortly, "He might have left us some money."

"He wouldn't leave anything of value. The point of the message was to suggest that neither of you intended to return to this room."

"Obviously," I said.

"That's it, then. There's nothing else except a few travel brochures. I'll go first. Take the next elevator. I'll meet you at the car."

But when I got out of the elevator he was standing nearby, glancing at his watch as if waiting for someone who was late for an appointment. A slight sideways movement of his head drew my attention toward the registration desk.

I saw Foggington-Smythe first. He was bareheaded, and his face was set in a frown as he talked with the clerk. The clerk kept shaking his head. He was looking, not at Perry but at Perry's companion. From behind all I could see was white— fur coat, long evening frock, bleached hair.

I ducked behind a convenient pillar. John sauntered toward me and paused to light a cigarette. "Yours?" he asked.

"No. I don't think so. Yours?"

"At this point we must assume everyone who isn't for us is against us. Walk, do not run, to the nearest exit."

It was the only thing to do; I'd be even more conspicuous lurking in doubtful concealment. But I felt as if I were being followed across the lobby by a gigantic searchlight, and when someone barred my path I almost jumped out of Feisal's oversized sandals.

"Excuse me, young fella."

I looked wildly over my shoulder before I realized I was the young fella in question. The speaker was a gray-haired American wearing a bright red fez. He wanted to know where I had bought my shirt. Innocent creature that I am, I didn't realize that wasn't all he wanted until he suggested that we have a drink while we talked it over.

I was about to tell him what he could do with his drink— and his fez—when John, passing on his way to the door, swung his briefcase and caught me a painful blow on the leg. It was, as the poet says, a salutary reminder. I growled wordlessly at my admirer and scuttled after John.

By the time I reached the car I was running, and so was the engine. John shoved me in.

"You daft female," he said crossly. "What did you stop for? I think Foggington-Smythe may have spotted you."

"I can't help it if I'm irresistible to men," I said, falling across his lap as Feisal made an abrupt and doubtless illegal U-turn.

John set me upright. "In your present costume I have no difficulty at all resisting you."

"Crushed again."

"I am beginning to understand why so many people are so annoyed with you two," said a voice from the front seat. "Where's the Herr Direktor? Where are we going? What—"

"One question at a time," said John. "First, I suggest you get off the corniche. Take back streets whenever possible—"

"We have to go past the railroad station first," I interrupted.

"No, we don't."

"Yes, we do. I want to make sure Schmidt—"

"No, we don't."

"Stop it!" Feisal shouted hysterically.

"Right," said John. "Who's in charge here, anyhow?"

"I'm not winding my way through a maze of back streets, either," Feisal declared. "The sooner we get out of Luxor the happier I'll be."

John sighed. "That was certainly one of the most futile questions I have ever asked. Vicky, there's no use looking for Schmidt at the station. I—er—I haven't been entirely candid with you."

"No!" I exclaimed. "You, not entirely candid? I can't believe it. What little teeny tiny unimportant detail did you omit? Don't tell me, let me guess. There is no night train to Memphis, right?"

"There is no bloody train to Memphis, stop, end of sentence!" He caught himself in mid-shout and in the silence that followed I could hear every shaken breath. "I told you that," he went on, a few decibels lower. "What I neglected to mention, for a number of reasons, all excellent, is that there are several night trains to Cairo. Would you care to hear my ideas as to which one Schmidt is most likely to have chosen, or would you rather continue this unproductive exchange of insults?"

"I hate it when you talk like that," I muttered. "Go on."

"Egyptian trains," said John, in an even more maddening drawl, and with even more infuriating precision, "are of several types. Wagon Lits runs two overnight expresses, with sleeping cars, between Luxor and Cairo. They start at Aswan, in fact, but that doesn't concern us. One leaves Luxor at seven-thirty and the other at ten-thirty. Both times, I hardly need add, are approximate."

"You hardly need. How do you know the times?"

"I believe I mentioned earlier that strict attention to schedules is essential for one who wishes to succeed in my profession. That rule applies particularly to transportation. Really," John mused, "one day I must write a little handbook. Rule number one: As soon as you arrive in a place, find out how to depart in a hurry."

"Don't do that, John," I said very gently.

"Then leave off distracting me. As I was saying: Most well-to-do tourists who travel by rail take those trains. And that, my dear, is a very good reason why Schmidt, if I read his character aright, wouldn't have taken either. They have a further disadvantage in that they do not stop between Luxor and Giza, just outside Cairo. Once you're on that train you can't get off it for ten or eleven hours. If I were worried about possible pursuit, I'd prefer more flexibility."

"Makes sense," I admitted. "So what's the alternative?"

"I'm so glad you asked. The other night trains make several stops, but only one of them offers first-class travel. First class is fairly comfortable, even by your effete American standards. Second and third class are not, and even if Schmidt were prepared to endure the crowding and the heat, he wouldn't stand a chance of passing as a student or an Egyptian."

"So—"

"So, I think he intends to take the eleven P.M. train. It stops at Sohag, Asyut, and Minya. If he wants to confuse his trail he'll buy a ticket through to Cairo and get off at one of the above."

"Is that the last train?"

"There are others, after midnight. We have to assume he meant not only 'night,' but 'tonight.' The note had today's date."

"It's clever, but awfully tenuous," I said.

We had left the city center behind and the only light came from the headlights of approaching vehicles. John had withdrawn into the opposite corner. He didn't respond to my comment, but I could still hear him breathing and I didn't like what I heard.

"Are you all right?" I asked.

"Perfectly."

"Maybe you should take another of those—"

"I just did." He hesitated for a moment and then said, "If I should happen to fall asleep, wake me before we reach Nag Hammadi. We may have to reconsider our strategy at that point."

"What strategy?" I demanded. "If you have some plan in mind I wish you'd let me in on it. Are we going to try to intercept Schmidt at one of the places you mentioned, or do you intend to drive straight through to Cairo, assuming this decrepit hunk of metal can make it that far, or—"

Feisal interrupted me with a vehement comment in Arabic.

"What did you say?" I leaned forward.

"I'd rather not translate literally. There are corresponding proverbs in English, referring to domineering women."

I heard a muffled laugh from John. "Now, kiddies, don't be rude. The main north-south highway and the railroad tracks cross the river at Hammadi. If they are going to set up a roadblock, that's the obvious place. We'll have to reconnoiter before we try the bridge. There's nothing we can do about it until we get there, so stop quarreling and let me get some sleep."

I couldn't think of a response that wasn't rude, childish, or irrelevant, so I didn't say anything.

John was out before we'd gone another mile, so far under that he only muttered sleepily when I put my arms around his shoulders and drew him down so that he was lying across the seat with his head on my lap. Feisal had his foot down as far as it would go. The car shook alarmingly but the engine was surprisingly quiet.

There was a good deal of traffic. Egyptian drivers have a demoralizing habit of switching on their bright lights instead of dimming them as they approach another car. I tried not to cringe every time this happened, but I didn't succeed. Each approaching vehicle cast a brief, garish glow into the interior of the car. It might have been a delicately sculpted skull I held in the curve of one arm, the eye sockets dark hollows, the skin clinging tightly to the bones of cheek and temple. There was no softness of underlying flesh, except for the parted lips.

"Is he asleep?" Feisal's voice was barely audible.

I applied a gentle pinch to John's arm. He didn't respond, not even with a mutter of complaint. Not that that proved anything. Feigning sleep or unconsciousness was one of his favorite tricks. "They usually stop hitting you when they think you can't feel it," he had once solemnly explained, during one of his lectures on crime.

"I think so." I raised one hand and brushed at my cheek.

"I'm sorry I was rude. But you are being a little hard on him, aren't you?"

"He hasn't been exactly easy on me."

"Easy on you?" Feisal's voice rose. "He wouldn't be here if it weren't for you. He had no intention of going through with this business. He tried to talk me out of it. If you hadn't turned up out of the blue—"

"Just a minute," I said. "Let me get this straight. Are you implying . . ."

He did more than imply. He told me, brutally and directly. Feisal didn't like me very much just then. That made two of us.

"This particular project began over three years ago. Johnny had pulled off a few jobs for Blenkiron earlier, but this one was a lot more complicated, so Blenkiron hired the group represented by the man who calls himself Max. After the tomb restoration was completed and Max had served his time, Blenkiron contacted Johnny. Johnny said no, he wanted out. They'd have let him get away with it, I think, since he couldn't blow the whistle on them without accusing himself, if somebody hadn't come up with the bright idea of having him rob the museum at the same time Blenkiron was loading his prizes onto a plane in Cairo. Whether he succeeded or failed, the attempt would have served as a useful distraction."

"Very useful," I muttered. "Whose bright idea was it?"

"Can't you guess? Max is a businessman, he hasn't time for useless emotions like revenge—and that was what motivated the person who suggested the museum stunt. It sounded clever but there were a number of practical disadvantages, most particularly the difficulty of forcing a tricky devil like Johnny to go through with a job he doesn't want to do. Max was well aware of that and would have been more than happy to see Johnny out of it. Unfortunately, his group resembles certain other illegal organizations in that it is family-oriented, and the sole surviving member of this particular family is . . . You've seen what she's like. How easy do you suppose it was for Johnny, cooped up with that maniac day after day and night after night, listening to her obscene threats and knowing that if he laid a finger on her she'd retaliate on you?"

It was like hearing the other side of a long, hostile divorce case. Events that seem clear-cut and obvious from one person's point of view take on an entirely different aspect when you hear the other guy's version.

"They got you onto that cruise," Feisal went on. "Some kind of faked message planted on the body of a dead operative—I never knew the details. Johnny had cut off communication with you as soon as he realized what he'd got himself into. Jen was already at risk simply because they knew who she was and where she was; if he hadn't agreed to bring her along on the cruise as an unwitting hostage, they would have kidnapped her, or worse. He planned to get Jen away at some point during the cruise. Once she was safe, he could take care of himself. It never occurred to him that they'd bother with another hostage. I wonder if you can imagine how he felt that day at Giza when he saw you?"

I could imagine. I had seen his face.

He'd managed to get Jen out of their hands next day, improvising as only John could. And then Schmidt had turned up, and there were still two hostages. I remembered the consternation in his voice when he saw Schmidt at Amarna—and Mary's smile. Of course she had known who Schmidt was. She had probably memorized every detail of my biography, especially the episode in which her brothers had been involved.

"Why didn't he tell me?" I demanded.

"They made sure he never had a chance to tell you. Both of you were under surveillance every minute of the day and night. As a lovesick young bride she had a perfect excuse to stick closer to him than a cocklebur, and when she wasn't with him, Blenkiron or one of the others was with you."

The words stung like a snakebite, doubly painful because I felt I ought to have suspected some of it, at least. And there was worse to come. I knew what Feisal was going to say before he said it.

"That wasn't the main reason. I was present when they explained to him, in painstaking detail, precisely what they would do to you if you learned the truth, from him or in any other way."

"Okay, I get it," I said hoarsely. "You don't have to—"

"I'm going to anyway. You realize, don't you, that while the boat was on the river they had you completely isolated and in their power? The purported changes in schedule were nothing of the sort; they were known in advance to all of us except Johnny. They kept him off balance, made it impossible for him to make arrangements for his escape or yours. Blenkiron controlled the boat, the crew, and half the able-bodied passengers. And the doctor. The moment you became aware, or even suspicious, he'd have had you pumped full of drugs and locked in your cabin with a quarantine sign on the door. And there you would have stayed, inaccessible and helpless, until . . ."

"They tossed me overboard," I muttered. "Or would it have been something more—more inventive?"

"Much more inventive." Feisal's voice had softened a little, but he wasn't ready to let me off the hook yet. "And prolonged. They were prepared to deal with Schmidt in the same way if he became a nuisance. People are always falling ill, it wouldn't have raised questions if both of you had succumbed to some esoteric and ultimately fatal disease. Your only chance of survival depended on your remaining unwitting, and that meant your suspicions and your hostility had to be focused on Johnny. They promised him that if he'd cooperate you would be allowed to leave the cruise at Luxor with the other passengers."

"He believed that?"

"Of course he didn't. He's been moving heaven and earth to get you to a safe place without betraying information that would endanger you even more, and he's had to fight you as well as Blenkiron in the process."

Cursing under his breath, he swerved—to avoid some obstacle in the road, I assumed—and the car jolted along the shoulder for a few yards before he got it back on the paved surface. I steadied John's head with my other hand. "How far are we from Hammadi?" I asked.

"Another thirty or forty kilometers. Are you trying to change the subject?"

"Yes."

"You were full of questions a while ago. Here's your chance to get some of the answers you'll never get from him."

I didn't say anything. The events of the past week were unrolling in my memory like a foreign film I hadn't understood the first time I saw it. The captions Feisal had supplied cast a different light on every scene.

He had put on a pretty good act in public, but I might have noticed he never used a term of endearment or touched her if he could avoid doing so. In private . . . Knowing Mary as I now did, I felt sure she had enjoyed goading him into dangerous and ultimately futile outbursts of anger. The bruises on her arms were a graphic demonstration of at least one occasion on which she had succeeded, and she had retaliated, promptly and effectively. If Schmidt's loud concern about my phobia hadn't alerted her, my own behavior would have done so.

That incident had been a joint project—Larry getting me down into the tomb, Mary or one of the others bollixing the lights. John must have suspected something was going to happen, but he had been helpless to prevent it. All he could do was get to me as quickly as possible.

That wasn't the only time he'd managed to find an excuse to be around when he feared I might be in trouble. Seeing Schroeder-Max at the rest house had aroused his suspicions;

he had invited himself along on that stroll from the Valley to Deir el Bahri because he was afraid to leave me and Schmidt alone with Larry and Ed. And he had prevented Mary from accompanying us, not only because she was an additional threat to me, but because . . . Because getting away from her, by any means and for any length of time, would have been like a breath of clean air to a man trapped in a sewer.

But the memory that would haunt me longest was the one of that night he had followed me out on deck while Schmidt was dancing with Mary. By that time he must have been half-crazy with worry and frustration and disgust, and the necessity of hiding those emotions. No wonder he'd lost control of himself. But only for a few moments. Realizing we were being observed, he had deliberately provoked me into a demonstration that would prove we were still at odds, and that would get me off the deck, back into the comparative safety of my room.

There had been time, that night and on a few other occasions, for a brief private exchange. "Oh, by the by, Vicky, I'm not really married to that little bitch, this is a setup and you are in desperate danger, so when I give you the signal just trot off and go into hiding and stay there. And take Schmidt with you."

Of course I'd have obeyed, without question or argument. As would Schmidt.

Right.

Feisal slowed and pulled off the road. He turned, his arm over the back of the seat.

"What's wrong?" I asked.

"Nothing's wrong. I hope. We'll be approaching the bridge shortly, and I don't want to wake him yet. I don't suppose he's had a decent night's sleep since—"

"Stop it, Feisal."

"There's just one little point I want to emphasize. When he agreed to Blenkiron's proposal, his own survival wasn't part of the deal. It wasn't even mentioned. He was bargaining for your life, not his, and he was willing to let you go on thinking the worst of him if that would help to ensure your safety. I don't entirely blame you for doubting him, but if I understand the hints I've heard from various people he's put his neck in a noose for you before. Didn't it occur to you, even once, to give him the benefit of the doubt?"

Feisal's tactics had been as effective as a battering ram. The walls were down, and I was flat on my face in the rubble. I had a feeling that if I ever managed to hold my head up again I'd see something that would make that devastating experience worthwhile, but all I could think of at the moment was how much I hated Feisal. When you are crawling on your belly like a snake you like to have another snake along for company.

"So what have you done for your old schoolmate lately?" I demanded. "You'd still be cooperating with Blenkiron if Jean-Louis's murder hadn't cast some doubts on your own survival. The poor devil didn't tell me a damn thing; they killed him solely as a precaution, the way you'd get rid of a wasps' nest on your porch."

"Johnny was quick to point that out," Feisal said wryly. "And I admit it wasn't until then that I agreed to get you to a safe place. There was no way he could do it himself, they were watching him like a pack of vultures, and he was getting desperate. I don't claim to be any nobler than the next man, Vicky. Johnny did talk me into supplying you with a weapon some days ago. Hamid was one of us, I had no difficulty in getting at his keys. However—"

"However," said a remote voice, "you are going to be in great difficulty if you don't get moving again. What did you stop for?"

Feisal slammed the car into gear and pulled onto the road. "I thought you needed—"

"I could do with something to drink. And an end to idle gossip about things that are none of your damned business."

"How much did you hear?" I demanded, grateful for the darkness that hid my face.

"Quite a lot," John said.

"Are you lying?"

"I always do, don't I?"

I was in no condition to pursue the subject. "If you'll remove yourself from my lap I'll get you a drink."

"Country matters, lady?" I might have known he couldn't

resist that reference. A truck thundered toward us, the bright light and contrasting shadow giving his upturned face and tumbled hair the look of a cheerful scarecrow, but I was too familiar with the cadences of his voice to miss the signs. He sat up, yawning. I heard the rustle of cloth and a faint click. Time for two of those little yellow pills? How many more could he take before he started climbing the walls?

I bent over and rummaged in the basket Granny had packed. She must have emptied her larder. There was enough food for a dozen people—bread, boiled eggs, fruit, a six-pack of soda. I opened one of the cans and handed it to John.

"I don't know what this is—" I began.

"Neither do I. It tastes like battery acid. Never mind, it's liquid. Where are we?"

"A quarter of an hour from Nag Hammadi," Feisal answered. "I hope it was only a morbid fancy that made you mention roadblocks? If we don't cross here—"

"There are other bridges farther north. And, if memory serves, a road of sorts on the east bank?"

"Yes, to both. You didn't answer my question. What makes you think they might be waiting for us at Hammadi?"

"Foggington-Smythe followed Vicky out of the hotel. He was watching when we left."

"Why didn't you say so earlier?" Feisal demanded.

"Why should I? Either he saw us or he didn't. If he did, and if a lot of other equally unpleasant surmises are correct, they could be waiting for us at Nag Hammadi."

"But how—" I began.

"Oh, Christ, do I have to spell everything out for you? Use your head. Your guess is as good as mine as to what Blenkiron will and can do, but his resources are extensive. Always anticipate the worst, remember?"

He had edged away from me and was sitting bolt upright, staring straight ahead. Ten minutes, I thought. Give him that much, at least.

Feisal began, "What are we—"

I leaned forward. "How well do you know the roads?"

There was a perceptible pause before Feisal answered. "That depends on what roads you mean. The main north-south highway crosses the river at Hammadi and runs along the west bank from there to Cairo. There's a secondary road on the east bank, but parts of it haven't been completed."

"Where are the bridges?" I asked.

I was trying to buy John a little more time, but as Feisal expanded on the geographical features I found myself wondering how Schmidt meant to employ same. Damn it, I knew the old boy better than John did, I ought to be able to follow his thinking.

"So the next bridge after Hammadi is at Sohag? The train Schmidt took—might have taken—stops there, doesn't it?"

"That's right. It's about fifty miles from Nag Hammadi."

"And the next crossing is at Asyut."

"Right again."

"Asyut is the second train stop. After that there's only one before Cairo."

"Minya," Feisal agreed.

"That's where Schmidt stayed the night before he joined the cruise," I said thoughtfully.

John cleared his throat. "Are you suggesting he might have left some of his luggage there? My theories may have been a trifle exiguous, but that is really—"

"No, listen." The more I thought about it, the more likely it seemed. "Schmidt stocked up on spy stuff before he ever left Munich. He even had contact lenses made in various colors! He suspected this cruise was more than a simple vacation. Who would know better than Schmidt that I wouldn't try to pass myself off as an expert on a subject I know nothing about without good and sufficient reason? I'll bet he's been plotting and planning ever since he arrived in Egypt. He'd have done that just for the fun of it. He spotted Max immediately, and that confirmed—"

"Bloody hell," John said. "You mean the little elf's been on to us all along? Why didn't you tell me this?"

"There hasn't been time," I began.

"Schmidt is bad enough," John went on bitterly. "The two of you together . . . Feisal, stop the bloody car. No, not in the middle of the bloody road, pull over as soon as you can find a suitable place. Now then, Vicky, perhaps you can bring yourself to tell me precisely what Schmidt said to you and what you said to Schmidt before you sallied forth to rescue me. You did have sense enough to make contingency plans, didn't you, in case you were held up or Schmidt had to vacate his room?"

The medicine had cleared his head but it certainly hadn't improved his disposition. I realized, with only faint surprise, that we were back on the old footing. Nothing had really changed except my perception of him. He was the same person he'd always been—neither saint nor sinner, hero nor villain, but a bewildering and exasperating mixture of all of them. Human, in other words. Like me. We were more alike than I had wanted to admit—sarcastic, prickly, defensive, afraid of feeling emotion, much less expressing it. My other self, my dark angel, my dear, deadly companion, my . . .

"Take all the time you like," John said, sneering audibly. "We're in no hurry."

"Damn it, how the hell could we plan ahead?" I demanded. "I didn't know how long it would take me to get into the house, or where in the house you were. It might have taken me all night to locate you."

"All *night*?"

Feisal had turned off onto a narrow dirt road bordering one of the irrigation canals. I could see a dark glimmer of water below. On the other side of the road tall stalks of some kind of vegetation, sugarcane or reeds, blocked my view.

I didn't need John to tell me I must have been out of my mind to think I could ramble around the house for hours on end without being caught. I had been out of my mind. Since I couldn't think of anything sensible to say, I kept quiet.

"All right," John said. He sounded as if he were choking. "Perhaps this is not an appropriate moment to pursue that subject. We've got to come to a decision about where we're going next. God knows I'm reluctant to follow Schmidt along the chaotic pathways of his imagination, but I hate to think of the havoc he can wreak wandering through Egypt alone and uncontrolled."

"He's done better than we have so far," I said indignantly. "That message he left was damned ingenious."

"He's done better than you have, you mean," was the

unkind reply. "And on the basis of the ingenuity he has displayed thus far I'm willing to consider the possibility that he tried to give us additional information."

"Johnny," Feisal interrupted. "No one admires the precision of your syntax more than I, but could you possibly cut it short?"

"I'm thinking of those travel brochures," John said. "He wouldn't dare underline or circle a name, but the one on the top of the pile had been opened and refolded. The sites mentioned were all in Middle Egypt. Beni Hassan, Amarna—"

"Nefertiti!" I exclaimed. "She was on the top of the pile too. The bag he bought at the bazaar, with her picture on it—"

"Amarna," John muttered. "I don't see how ... He couldn't possibly ..."

"Johnny," Feisal began.

"Yes, right. We need more information before we reach a final decision as to our route. I don't suppose this miracle of automotive engineering possesses a radio? No, that would be too much to ask. Stop at the first café—or, even better, petrol station."

When we stopped, not far from the access road to the bridge, I withdrew into the darkest corner and covered my head with a scarf while Feisal got out for a man-to-man chat with the attendant and the other guys who were hanging around the pumps.

He wasn't gone long. When he came back I could tell by his expression he had heard something he didn't like.

John waited until Feisal had turned off onto a side road. "Well?"

"My career in crime is burgeoning," Feisal said sourly. "It seems I am now a kidnapper as well as a notorious terrorist."

"Who'd you kidnap?" I asked curiously.

"You, of course." Feisal made another sharp turn. "There's a taftish—checkpoint—ahead, on this side of the bridge. It's a safe bet they'll be watching for us." He spun the wheel again and the car squeezed itself into a narrow lane between walls that scraped the fenders. "We should pick up the eastbank road a couple of miles farther on." He let out a thin scream and slammed on the brakes. The rider of the donkey glanced over his shoulder and made a rude gesture. I assume it was a rude gesture.

"Bad luck, old chum," John said insincerely. "I had hoped they wouldn't get on to you so soon, but I suppose it was inevitable, when we all turned up missing at the same time."

"So Foggington-Smythe is in Larry's pay," I said.

"Not necessarily. He might have mentioned in all innocence that he had seen someone resembling you at the hotel."

"But I'm in disguise," I protested.

"He was studying your rear view," John said disagreeably. "I told you those jeans were too tight. Dare I inquire how Foggington-Smythe became so familiar with the contours of your—Christ! Feisal, watch out for that—"

A splintering crunch announced the destruction of a small shed.

"Don't distract me," Feisal said between his teeth.

The last few hundred yards of the detour ran along the top of a bank above an irrigation ditch. I think three of the wheels were on the path most of the time. We missed the guy on the bicycle, though.

Once we were back on the highway John cleared his throat. "Would you like me to drive for a while?" he asked tactfully.

I had been about to offer myself. Night driving in Egypt was something no sane tourist would tackle, but I figured I could do better than Feisal was doing at that moment. I think his eyes were closed.

Feisal hit the brakes. "Is there anything to drink?"

I handed him a can of soda. He slid over into the passenger seat and John took his place behind the wheel.

"So what else is new?" he inquired, returning to the road.

"They didn't get the license number, but they do have a description of the car. They aren't certain whether my motive for making off with Vicky was lust or politics or—"

"Kidnapping an American tourist for any reason is enough to stir things up," John said thoughtfully. "Did you abduct me too?"

"They know or assume we're all together, if that's what

you mean. Odd, now that you mention it; they were somewhat vague as to your precise role. It's been on all the news broadcasts. The government is appalled, shocked, and distraught. They will pursue the hunt with the utmost diligence and punish the perpetrator—" He swallowed. "Appropriately."

"Oh, very good," John said. "By accusing you of abduction they've enlisted the assistance of every honest police officer and worthy citizen, and they've left open the possibility that I may be a crypto-terrorist too."

"That's crazy," I exclaimed. "I can tell them—"

"You may not have the chance," John said.

We went on awhile in gloomy silence. A snatch of song drifted back to me from the front seat. "There's a girl from Minnesota, She's long and she's tall . . ."

I leaned forward. "She was from Birmingham, I believe."

"Wrong. Tennessee. One for me."

"I got the song right," I protested. "Anyhow, she wasn't a girl, she was a train."

"Half a point, then. Why don't you get some sleep? You must be tired. Heroic rescues take a lot out of a girl."

"The hell with that. I'm not going to sleep while you two big, strong intelligent men make all the decisions. Where are we going?"

Feisal chuckled. "She does have a strange charm all her own, doesn't she? I'm beginning to understand why you—"

"She grows on you," John agreed. "As for where we're going, that depends to some extent on what we encounter along the way, but I think we'll head for Minya. That must have been what Schmidt meant by his delightfully mysterious clues; it's the nearest stop to Amarna. The train he's taken doesn't arrive until seven in the morning and it may be late. If we can make it in time we'll look out for him at the station. If we miss him we'll check the hotels."

"How are you planning to get across the river?" Feisal inquired.

"I intend to avoid the bridges. They are the most logical places for roadblocks. We'll stay on the east bank until we reach Amarna and then take the ferry across. There are a number of advantages to that agenda; they will expect us to take the main road, and it's always a good idea to do what the enemy doesn't expect."

"Skip the lectures on crime, will you?" Feisal said sourly. "There's only one little problem with your agenda, Johnny. We can't get to Amarna from here."

"The road—" John began.

"Ends a few kilometers north of Asyut. They haven't finished it."

"There's a track, surely."

"There are a number of paths, yes. For donkeys and camels. If we follow the river, there's one point where the cliffs come right down to the water's edge. The car would never make it through."

"Hmmm. Then we'll have to think of another way, won't we?"

"It doesn't sound to me as if there is another way," I remarked. "We'll have to cross at Asyut and risk the roadblocks."

"Feisal is being modest," John said gently. "I'm sure he can suggest an alternative. He has friends everywhere. Knowledgeable friends. Right, old chum?"

"Damn it, Johnny, I haven't had anything to do with that crowd for years. It was one of those youthful enthusiasms—"

"I quite understand," John said, in the same quiet, very unpleasant voice. "No bright, idealistic lad or lassie can resist the lure of revolution. All the same . . ."

The silence from the front seat was practically deafening. It seemed to satisfy John, though.

I don't know how long I slept, but I was stiff and cold when I woke. The car had stopped and the view out the window next to me was so beautiful I forgot, for a few moments, that this wasn't exactly the time to enjoy the scenery.

The moon had risen. Now at the full, it hung over the cliffs like a silver balloon. In the cold, bright light the rocky ramparts looked like glaciers and the desert floor like new-fallen snow. I had never seen so many stars.

My window was closed, but the one on the passenger

side in front was partly open. I could hear their voices clearly.

"You won't need that," Feisal said.

"I hope not. Just so you and your friend understand that I'll use it if I must."

I shifted position so I could see. Feisal leaned against the front fender, his hands in his pockets and his shoulders hunched against the chill of the night air. John faced him, a few feet away. The moonlight was so bright I could see every detail.

"I don't doubt it in the least," Feisal said. He sounded more amused than apprehensive. "Amazing. I never thought I'd see the day . . . Now keep calm, Johnny. I wasn't objecting to the aim, only to the means. It's been five years since I went that route, and I don't know whether I can persuade, bully, or bribe Amr into lending us the jeep. We haven't much money left. Threatening him would be a serious error, however. Put the gun away, okay?"

"Give him this." John unstrapped his wristwatch.

Feisal took the watch. "All right, let's make the attempt."

They got back into the car. John turned and looked back at me. "Awake?"

"Yes. Where are we?"

"A few miles north of Asyut. Any further questions?"

"How—"

"Save them. And don't join in any discussion that may ensue. This is a conservative area. They don't approve of uppity women."

The huddle of low, flat-roofed buildings a few miles farther on might, if one were charitably inclined, be described as a village. No lights showed at the windows of the houses. There was a café; there is always a café, but even it was dark.

To give myself credit, which I am always inclined to do, I felt sure I knew the answers to most of the questions I might have asked. The individual in the house on whose door Feisal was knocking had to be a member of the organization to which he had once belonged—whatever that might be. Even experts in Middle East politics had some trouble keeping track of the various revolutionary groups and how their aims and methods differed. I wasn't familiar with the ramifications, but

I knew that many students had been attracted to the radical
movements because they promised an end to government
corruption and inefficiency.

That's what they all promise. And sooner or later, in the
Middle East or Ireland or the States, the noble aims are dis-
torted; violence inspires answering violence, and often the
ones who suffer most are the poor devils both sides claim to
be defending. The repressive measures of the State Security
forces had won a lot of waverers over to the revolutionary
cause, and I wouldn't have been surprised to learn that everyone in the village was a secret sympathizer. We were in Middle
Egypt now; the city of Asyut, across the river, had been
and probably still was one of the centers of rebellion—or
terrorism, depending on which side you supported.

The door finally opened and Feisal went inside. John had
gotten out of the car and was leaning against the door, hands
in his jacket pockets. I'd never known him to carry a weapon
before. I wondered if he really would use the gun—or if the
guy inside the house would shoot first.

Feisal was only gone for ten minutes. When he returned
he was accompanied by his—friend? He didn't look very
friendly. He had wound his woolen scarf around his head and
throat, but I could see his face clearly in the bright moonlight.

"It's all right," Feisal said, eyes fixed on John's right-hand
pocket. "He's agreed. He's not happy about it, but he has
agreed."

"Good." John took his hand out of his pocket and opened
the car door. "Come on, Vicky."

The sight of me didn't make the other guy any happier. He
let out a spate of low-voiced Arabic and began waving his
arms. I gave him an ingratiating smile. "What's he mad
about?" I asked.

"Everything," Feisal said. "I don't blame him. The situation has deteriorated, if that is possible. They're setting up
checkpoints on this side of the river now. And along the Red
Sea highway."

"That's encouraging," John said coolly. "They don't know
which route we've taken."

"They'll soon find out if we don't get moving. This way."

We followed our unwilling host to the back of the house,

where the jeep—or, to be more accurate, the rusting skeleton of a jeep—was parked. The doors were tied on with rope. I climbed over the side, noting, as I sat down, that there were a few springs left. One, at least.

Feisal dumped the luggage in on top of me and turned to John. "How much money have we?"

"A couple of hundred pounds. Why?"

"We're going to need more supplies. Water, blankets, petrol. No, don't argue, just listen. The moon will be down before long and I daren't risk driving this route in the dark. We'll have to hole up somewhere for the rest of the night, and probably all day tomorrow. I presume you don't want to arrive in broad daylight?"

John began, "It's only thirty or forty miles—"

"As the vulture flies. You've never done this. I have. You don't know this country. I do."

The moonlight drained all the color from John's face. It looked like bleached bone. I said impulsively, "You've got to get some rest before we go much farther, John."

He turned on me. "I told you to keep quiet."

"Keep quiet yourself. Feisal, how long—"

Feisal waved his hands wildly. "Don't ask. Don't ask any more questions, either of you. Leave this to me."

Our reluctant ally was becoming more reluctant by the minute, but—in exchange for all the money we possessed—he grudgingly produced a few jerricans of gas, a couple of blankets—taken off a donkey, to judge by the smell—several bottles of water, and a six-pack of what turned out to be fizzy lemon-flavored soda. Our departure was not marked by formal farewells. I started to say thank you, but the man just shook his head and trudged off.

After a few abortive coughs the engine started. The racket was appalling. It must have roused every sleeper who wasn't already awake, but not a light showed in any of the windows.

I popped the top of a can and poured half a cup of lemonade down my front when Feisal threw the jeep into gear. We went bouncing off across the plain; there may have been a track of sorts, but you couldn't prove it by me. I clenched my teeth to keep from biting my tongue and refrained from comment. I knew why Feisal was proceeding at such an uncomfortable speed. We had to get well away from the village and into hiding before morning, and the moon was setting. I had an unpleasant feeling I also knew why Feisal didn't want to drive in the dark, and that suspicion was confirmed when I saw we were heading straight for the cliffs that rose sheer ahead.

They call them wadis—canyons, cut by water, in the ramparts of the high desert. Flash floods and natural erosion have littered the uneven ground with rubble varying from pebbles to Chevy-sized boulders. The one into which Feisal drove, without slackening speed, was fairly wide at first, and there was a track of sorts through the center. The boulders weren't much bigger than toasters. We hit every one of them. I bit my tongue.

Before long the moonlight faded as the canyon narrowed and the cliffs closed in on either side. Feisal switched on the headlights. They didn't help much. One had burned out and the other was about to go. Feisal went on a little farther and then stopped, with a jolt that jarred my back teeth together. He turned off the lights and the ignition.

"That's it," he said. "The terrain gets rougher from here on. I don't want to break an axle."

"Rougher?" I croaked.

Our voices echoed eerily in the silence. It was so dark I couldn't even see their outlines, but I heard the springs creak when John shifted his weight.

"How much farther?" he asked, in a voice flat with fatigue.

"Irrelevant." Feisal sounded equally exhausted. "We can't go on tonight. Let's get some rest. Hand out a couple of those blankets, Vicky. You can curl up in the backseat."

"Curl up is right," I said. "I'd rather sleep on a rock."

Which was precisely what I did. Feisal cleared away some of the bigger boulders, leaving a space just wide enough for the three of us to lie down, huddling together for warmth. I expected John would make some rude comment about bundling but he didn't speak at all. He was trying to keep his teeth from chattering, I think. We were all shivering; the air was cold and the blankets were too thin to be much use. Without discussing the subject aloud, Feisal and I put John between us. He fell asleep immediately. Not even the hard ground and the stench of donkey and the cold could keep my eyes open, but as I drifted off I was thinking longingly of Suzi's great big furry white coat.

Against all the odds I slept for over six hours. It was the heat that woke me, the heat and a sensation of vague discomfort. When I pried my sticky eyes open I realized I had shifted position during the night; John's head was on my shoulder and my left arm, which was around him, had gone numb. He looked like one of the better-preserved mummies, skin stretched tight over cheekbones and forehead, eyelids shriveled and sunken, lips cracked.

I heard a gurgling sound and looked up through my loosened hair to see Feisal standing over me. His appearance wasn't much of an improvement over John's—or, I suspected, my own. Wiping his mouth on his sleeve, he offered me the bottle of water. I swallowed, or tried to—my throat was as dry as the sandy dust—and shook my head.

John slept for another half hour. When he opened his eyes I croaked out a cheery "Good morning." Removing himself from my limp embrace, he sat up and lowered his head onto his hands.

"Did I ever mention," he said, "that one of your least lovable characteristics is that you are so bloody cheerful early in the morning?"

"You're usually pretty bloody cheerful yourself."

He lifted his head. "On the occasions to which you refer I had excellent reasons to be—"

"Stop it," Feisal ordered. "Come and have breakfast, such as it is."

Water and dry bread, oranges and hard-boiled eggs was what it was. There was no way of heating water even if we had had coffee or tea with us, which we didn't. Chewing on the hard bread, I studied our surroundings: stony desert underfoot, steep rocky walls around. There wasn't so much as a blade of grass, much less a tree, dead or alive. The pale limestone of the cliff opposite dazzled in the sunlight.

"At least it's not raining," I said.

John gave me a look in which amusement and exasperation were mingled. Feisal was not amused.

"Pray it doesn't. We don't have much rain here, but when

it comes it comes hard and the water is all funneled through these wadis. A flash flood would be the end of us."

"Say something positive," I suggested.

"I'm trying my damnedest," Feisal said morosely. "All right, let's take stock of where we stand." Clearing a patch of sand with a sweep of his hand, he took a pen from his pocket and used the blunt end to sketch a rough map. "Here's the river, here's the wadi we're in. And this is the one we're heading for. It passes the Hatnub Quarries and comes out eventually into the Amarna plain near the southern tombs."

I studied the sketch doubtfully. "The two wadis don't connect."

"Not according to the standard maps, no. But it's barely possible to get a vehicle through," Feisal said, rubbing his prickly chin. "At least it was five years ago. I can't be more specific about the route because it's too hard to describe. If anything happens to me—"

"It will happen to all of us," John said evenly. "At this point you're the least expendable member of the party. More precious than diamonds, more precious—"

"Than gold," I said. "One point for me."

John grinned, or tried to. Feisal rolled his eyes.

"You two are a pair, I'll say that. Can't you keep your minds on essentials?"

Laughter is one of the two things that make life worthwhile. Another of John's sententious sayings, delivered one morning after he had demonstrated the importance of the other one. He was right on both counts. There are times when you have to laugh to keep from screaming, and if I'm in a tight spot I'd rather be with someone who makes bad jokes instead of big dramatic scenes.

"If anything happens," Feisal repeated, "keep heading west."

John's hand obliterated the sketch. "Forget that. Will we make it today?"

"We'll have to," Feisal said curtly. "With luck, sometime this afternoon. That's the next question. We don't want to come bursting onto the scene while the site is crowded with tourists and guides and guards, do we?"

"No," John agreed. "Let's set our ETA at nine P.M., when people will be inside eating and watching telly."

"We've missed Schmidt," I said.

My voice was steady, I think, but John said, with unexpected gentleness, "Don't worry about him, Vicky. I have a feeling we've both underestimated the old boy rather badly, and even if they catch up with him they won't harm him so long as we're on the loose."

"I hope you're right."

"I'm always right," John said firmly. "Anyhow, we can hardly be said to have missed him when we don't know for certain where he is or what he's up to. Pray that he's gone on to Cairo. If he can convince someone in authority to search that boat we'll be in the clear."

"The boat won't be there yet, will it?" I asked, mopping my sweating face with my sleeve.

"I shouldn't think so. But you can be sure Blenkiron has moved up his schedule. He'll load and be under way as soon as he possibly can, and the *Queen of the Nile* is capable of a pretty fair turn of speed. If she travels night and day and Blenkiron uses his influence to get her through the locks without delay, she could reach Cairo in a few days. We—or Schmidt—must get there before the boat does."

He reached casually into his pocket and took out the Tutankhamon pectoral. Glowing with soft shades of gold and turquoise and coral, it covered his entire palm. The giant blue beetle that dominated the design held a sun disk of carnelian in its raised pincers.

Feisal caught his breath. "From Blenkiron's collection? Good thinking, Johnny. That should be enough—"

John shook his disheveled head. "It should be enough to capture the attention of the museum authorities, certainly; that's why I—er—borrowed it. But once Blenkiron is out of the country with his collection, it will be my word against his as to where this came from. Eventually they may discover that the other objects are forgeries as well, but things move slowly in this part of the world and bureaucrats in any part of the world are reluctant to take action. And while they are discussing and debating and arguing and speculating, we will be wasting away in a dungeon cell. If we're lucky."

"I like you better when you're being frivolous," I said.

"I don't." Feisal hoisted himself to his feet. "We'd better get started."

Even after seeing the terrain I wouldn't have believed it would take six hours to cover less than thirty miles. I suppose it could have been worse. Nobody got bitten by a scorpion or a cobra and the jeep held together, except for one of the doors, which Feisal wired back on. We only had two flat tires. Smaller canyons opened up along the way and sometimes it was impossible to tell the main wadi from a dead end. We went for almost a mile into one of the latter before Feisal realized his error. He had to back out. As the sun rose higher it beat straight down into the canyon and the temperature kept climbing. We were all sticky wet and itching with sweat when we reached the end of the first wadi and found the steep slope ahead completely blocked by fallen boulders.

"Is there a way around?" I asked.

Both of them turned to glare at me. Feisal had taken off his shirt; perspiration ran down his face and puddled in the hollows over his collarbones. It was a pity I was too hot and tired to enjoy the view, because he did have a great body. John had chosen not to display his.

"No, my dear," said Feisal, baring all his beautiful white teeth in a snarl. "This is it. The only way. There must have been a minor quake or a flash flood since I was last here."

He got out and began fumbling among the miscellany of rusted tools in the backseat. I didn't ask any more questions. The options were obvious even to me: either we abandoned the jeep and proceeded on foot, or we tried to clear away enough of the debris so we could go on.

It would have been a formidable job even if we had had proper tools and if the weather had been comfortable. With only a tire iron as a lever, and a temperature in the high nineties, and our supply of water running low . . . I remember thinking sympathetically of Sisyphus, the guy in the Greek legend who had been condemned to spend eternity pushing a big rock up a hill. As soon as he got it to the top, it rolled back down again.

When we stopped for a rest, Feisal mopped his forehead with what had once been a white handkerchief and was now a filthy rag. The sun had moved farther west and there was some shade. We passed the water bottle around and sat there wheezing. Even John was too far gone to make jokes. His shirt was soaking wet and not all the liquid was sweat. The bullet wound must have opened up again. As if he felt my eyes on him he raised his head and gave me a hard stare, daring me to speak. I didn't.

"A little more should do it," Feisal said, after a while.

"Do you really think so?" I asked.

"I really do." He took my hand and turned it, inspecting first the scraped palm and then the broken nails and bleeding fingers.

"Those are not the hands of a lady," I said. "Guess I won't be invited to the Junior Cotillion."

"You're number one on my list," Feisal said softly. He raised my filthy, bloody hand to his lips.

John stood up. "I hate to interrupt this tender scene, but could we please get on with it?"

When Feisal called a halt there were still a lot of rocks on that slope. We all climbed into the jeep and Feisal backed off, to get a good running start, and then gunned the engine. I closed my eyes, and kept them closed while the jeep jounced up and over the ridge and then began to descend.

The descent wasn't as steep as the ascent, but it was just as bumpy. When we reached relatively level ground Feisal picked up speed and I opened my eyes.

He was watching me in the cracked rearview mirror. "The worst is over," he yelled. "Not long now."

"Don't look at me," I yelled back. "Keep your eyes on the—you should excuse the word—road."

Experience is broadening, all right; never again would I complain about any road surface, anywhere. Compared to what we'd been through, this stretch was a piece of cake. I now had leisure to realize how hot it was. The air was bone-dry; I could feel my skin stretching and cracking. After approximately an hour Feisal pulled up and turned off the engine.

"Almost there. People come this way occasionally, so we'd better lie low until dark."

Stretched out on the hard ground, we finished the water. I was bone-tired but not sleepy; I waited till John had dropped off, or passed out, whichever came first, before I spoke. "He can't go on much longer."

"I know. But there's nothing we can do for him now. Get some rest, Vicky. You worked like a hero today."

"What's going to happen when we reach Amarna?"

"He's got something in mind, but don't ask me what. He told me where to go and what to say, but he did not condescend to explain further." Feisal stretched out with a long, heartfelt sigh. "At least we can be sure no one has followed us. Only an idiot would attempt this route. Don't worry, love, we'll bribe or bully someone into helping us."

"We haven't any money."

Feisal's long fuzzy lashes were drooping. He opened his eyes a little wider and grinned at me. "We'll sell something. You, perhaps. A woman who can work that hard should fetch a good price."

I let him sleep. I tried to, but I couldn't, so I lay still counting John's breaths and watching the sky darken and the stars brighten against the night.

Finally Feisal stirred. "Did we finish the water?"

"There's some fizzy lemonade. I've been hoarding it."

"Well done. All right, let's do it. Johnny?"

"I told you not to call me that," said a grumpy voice from the darkness.

"I assumed you'd prefer it to 'blue eyes.' Someday perhaps one of you will explain those esoteric comments to me."

"A cold day in hell, perhaps," John said.

When we emerged from the widening mouth of the wadi the moon was shining down on the plain of Amarna. Lights twinkled among the dark bank of trees along the river.

Nobody felt like cheering. Not yet.

"Head north," John said. "I suggest you follow the cliffs as long as possible. Less chance of our being observed."

"If people don't know we're here, they're deaf," I remarked.

"Back to your old form, I see," John said. "Perhaps you'd prefer to walk. It's only six or seven miles."

I said no more.

Feisal proceeded at a slower speed, and if I hadn't had

other things on my mind I might have enjoyed the scenery.
The cliffs enclosing the plain were icy-pale in that eerie light,
checkered with shadow where crevices and canyons broke
their ramparts. One deeper, darker opening might have been
the entrance to the royal wadi which we had visited earlier.
After we crossed the road that led from the landing to the
tombs, Feisal stopped and shut off the ignition.

"That's the village, over there." He indicated a few lights
along the river.

John didn't move. "We'll wait here."

"What are you up to now?" Feisal asked.

"Taking reasonable precautions, that's all. Three people
are more conspicuous than one, especially when two of them
are obviously foreigners. Someone must have heard us. You
can have a look around and withdraw if there's trouble. The
house you want is on the northeast corner of the village.
There's a brickyard on one side and—"

"I know, you told me." Feisal hoisted himself out of the
car and stretched. "I'll signal if it's safe to proceed and wait
for you on the edge of the cultivation. Six flashes and then
two at ten-minute intervals."

He started off. John watched him for a few minutes and
then climbed over the side of the jeep. "Get out."

"What for?"

"I would love to live long enough to see you respond to
a sensible suggestion without asking why. A little exercise
will be good for you."

I got up, stretching. "Oh, God. If this is what it feels like
to be eighty, I'm not sure I want to live that long."

"I'm sure." John steadied me as I climbed arthritically
over the side of the jeep.

We settled down next to a rock outcropping a few hundred
yards away. "This isn't very comfortable," I grumbled,
squirming around in the hope of finding some surface that
wasn't littered with sharp pebbles.

"It's flat and it's in shadow. Oh, for Christ's sake. Here."
He took off Feisal's jacket and spread it on the ground.

"Aren't you cold?"

"No."

"Have you got a temperature?"

He moved away from my outstretched hand and sat down a few feet away, his back against a rock. "It will certainly begin to rise if you don't stop asking meaningless questions."

"How about a few meaningful questions?" I handed him one of the cans of soda.

"Such as?"

"Were you really planning to rob the Cairo Museum?"

"Good God, no. I've already robbed the damned place twice, why should I do it again? A man's reach should exceed his grasp, don't you think?"

"Stealing an entire tomb is certainly a challenge."

"Your sympathetic understanding touches me more than I can say." He opened the can and drank deeply before going on. "It isn't the entire tomb, you know. Only a few selected walls."

"I still find it difficult to believe. How he hoped to get away with it—"

"Oh, he'll get away with it," John said calmly. "Unless we can stop him. It's a pity, in a way. This might have been the high point of my distinguished career. You can see why the idea appealed to me."

"When did it start appealing?"

John settled himself more comfortably. "My first arrangement with Blenkiron concerned the princess's diadem. You ought to have noticed the anomaly of that item during your encounter with my friends in Rome. All the other jewelry we—er—replaced was Renaissance or later in date, and it was all in private collections. The diadem was in the Cairo Museum, and only a fanatical collector would want an item that could never be displayed. You might have postulated a man like Blenkiron—obscenely wealthy and totally unscrupulous—when you saw that."

"Don't hassle me, John. I'm trying very hard to be nice."

"Are you? Sorry, I hadn't noticed. As I was saying, the beauty of my arrangement with Blenkiron was that I only had to liberate the objects from the museum. They stayed in the country, so there were no nerve-racking encounters with customs. The only exception was the Tetisheri statuette. He was so besotted with it he insisted on carrying it around with him. However, smuggling antiquities into Egypt isn't as difficult as smuggling them out."

"So the one in the British Museum is a fake."

John chuckled. "Ironically enough, Blenkiron's is probably a fake as well. It wasn't only the analysis of the paint that cast doubts on the one I removed from the B.M.; there's something a bit off about the hieroglyphs. I wouldn't be at all surprised to learn that the first one was manufactured by the great-grandfather of the little old forger in Gurnah who made the second one for me. Manufacturing forgeries is an old tradition there."

"How did you find him?"

"It's a long story," John said. "Reaching back into the mists of the past, and replete with details Schmidt would undoubtedly find extremely romantic."

"Then don't tell it now. The British Museum must have been a real test of your skills. Their security measures are pretty good."

"I shan't respond to your subtle hints, darling, so don't bother asking how I did it. Trade secrets, you know. However, I will say that the theatrical plots concocted by writers and producers of thrillers are completely unworkable, especially the ones that depend on esoteric equipment. The more complicated a gadget, the more likely it is to break down just when you need it."

He paused for refreshment before going on. "The idea of stealing Tetisheri's tomb came to Blenkiron soon after the Getty people began working on the other queen's tomb—that of Nefertari. It was really rather a clever idea. Restoring the reliefs was precisely the sort of philanthropic endeavor people had come to expect of him, and it gave him a perfect opportunity to have them copied. There was even a suggestion that a replica of the tomb might be made, in order to satisfy tourists without endangering the original. If at any point his activities had been discovered he could claim that's what he was doing, as a boyish surprise for his good friends in the EAO. It was a monumental job, of course, but as Feisal pointed out, Blenkiron's rich enough to buy all the expertise he needs."

"And the experts," I murmured. "Poor Jean-Louis."

"That was one of the most difficult aspects, actually," John said. "You'd be surprised how many honest scholars there are. They had to be approached very, very carefully. But there aren't many positions in archaeology open, and there are a lot of poor, overeducated devils like Mazarin and Feisal seeking employment. Mazarin wasn't the one I would have chosen. Instead of admitting his own venality he had to convince himself he was guided by noble motives. Such men are dangerous. Their consciences are never at ease, and they are apt to crack under pressure. I told Blenkiron that. He ignored my advice, and now you know why. He was prepared from the first to remove inconvenient witnesses."

"Is that why you tried to pull out?"

"It was certainly a consideration. However, Max was an even stronger deterrent. If you recall, he was already vexed with me when we ran into one another in Sweden. I had advised Blenkiron not to hire him for this job and Max knew it. He took my refusal to work with him personally, I'm sorry to say. He's such a sensitive chap."

"How did he learn your real name?"

I had caught him off guard. The empty can crumpled in his hands. "That's not—"

"You've been controlling the direction of this conversation. Now it's my turn. How did they find you? Max didn't know who you were before. He kept calling you Smythe."

John didn't answer. I knew he must be feeling rotten or he'd have been able to come up with a facile lie. Not that I'd have believed it. I knew the answer.

"It was through me, wasn't it? Max knew you weren't dead. He knew my identity. *She* knew it, from him. When she set out to track you down she started with me. They must have been watching me for months, hoping—expecting— you'd turn up. All they had to do then was follow you home."

John tossed the crumpled can aside. "What difference does it make?"

"None at all," I said morosely. "It's just the last goddamn straw that broke . . . Look! Isn't that a light?"

John caught my arm as I started to stand up. "It's a light, certainly. One of several. Hold on."

"You think it's not Feisal?"

"There hasn't been time for him to reach El Till, much less have a look around. They're coming this way. Oh, dear, oh, dear," John said. "I always expect the worst, but I loathe having it happen."

# Chapter Thirteen

"They got him," I whispered.

"Or he turned us in?"

"He wouldn't do that! Would he?"

"One would certainly hate to think so." John's voice was so soft I could scarcely hear it. "There are other possibilities, I suppose . . ."

"The hell with other possibilities! We have to assume the worst, as you keep telling me. What are we going to do?"

"You may do as you like," said John. "I am going to—er—lie down."

And he proceeded to do so, though "fall over" would have been a more accurate description.

He looked rather peaceful with his head pillowed on his bent arm but when I touched his cheek he didn't move. His skin was burning hot.

In a way, it was a relief to have no more choices left. I covered him with the coat and brushed the hair away from his temple. "Good-bye, John," I whispered. "I love you."

I stood up.

His hand wrapped around my ankle and brought me thudding to the ground. "Where the hell do you think you're going?" he demanded.

Sand is a lot harder than it looks, and this variety of desert is littered with rocks. By the time I recovered my breath it was too late to get away; he had rolled me over onto my back and was lying across me.

"You low-down skunk!" I gasped. "You did that on purpose!"

"Is that any way to talk to the man you love?" His voice was almost back to normal; I knew the slight unevenness was due to suppressed laughter. "I'm deeply hurt that you would think I'd resort to a childish, melodramatic trick like that one."

"John, are you crazy? Those people out there—"

"There's plenty of time. Were you really going to dash out and lead the hunters away from me, risking capture and a fate worse than death?"

His lips were hot and dry. At first. I wrenched mine away. "You're not crazy, you're delirious. Let me go. It's the only sensible course of action."

"No, it's not."

"Yes, it is. Stop doing that."

"No, it's not. Why should I?"

"Because . . ." I had lost my grip on the conversation, not to mention the whole situation. "Look—"

"I can't. I'm busy."

"They won't do anything to me," I said, giggling insanely. I do that when I'm upset, and his lashes were tickling me. "I'll tell them—"

"It is not a sensible idea," said John, "because that may not be the police. And if it isn't, and if they catch you, I'll go after you and then we'll have to repeat the whole tedious performance."

"Would you?"

"I told you not to ask silly questions. Say it again."

"I love you."

"That's what I thought you said." He lifted himself on his elbows, freeing my hands. I wrapped them around the back of his head and drew his face down to mine.

I was a trifle distracted, however, not only by the unnatural heat of his skin but by a far-off sound. Turning my head I murmured, "We'd better stop this."

"Discretion would seem to suggest a more responsible

course of action." Instead of moving, he kissed the corner of my mouth. "Vicky, I couldn't tell you the truth. I couldn't even let you begin to wonder. They had me so boxed in—"

"I know. Feisal told me."

"I must have missed that part. I hope he portrayed me in a favorable light?"

"You came out looking like Sir Galahad and me like something that had crawled out from under a . . . Oh, God. John—"

"Sorry. Did I hurt you?"

"Yes. Do it again. No! No, don't, we've got to—"

"I did hurt you—that night, after you danced with Feisal. While you were laughing and giving him languishing glances, *she* was leaning against my shoulder, watching you, and smiling, and saying things under her breath . . . Schmidt turned up in the nick of time. I couldn't have kept my hands off her much longer. And then when I saw you—you'd been so cool and indifferent, I thought you didn't care, and . . . But that doesn't excuse what I did. Can you—"

"John," I said desperately, "isn't that a dog I hear?"

"Probably. There are dozens of them around and they howl at . . . Oh." He lifted his head and listened. "You mean *a* dog, as opposed to dogs in general. Damned if I don't think you're right. That puts a different complexion on things. We might elude human searchers but man's best friend is another matter. I'm beginning to detest the bloody creatures. First that diabolical hound of yours—"

"Get up this minute!"

The lights were closer now. Three separate beams—flashlights, I thought. Not the police, then. They'd have more effective equipment, and they'd be making a lot more noise.

"How could they know we'd end up here?" I demanded.

"Good question." John got to his feet. Another outburst of canine commentary floated across the desert, and John echoed it with an outburst of profanity. "My brain seems to have crashed. We'd better get into hiding. It may not be necessary, but—"

My brain wasn't working any better than his. It had gone back to basics, driven by the same primitive instincts that move all hunted creatures. "Right. Hide. Where?"

"I know a place. I hoped we wouldn't have to resort to it since I know how you feel about—"

"Oh, no. Not a tomb. I can't, John, I really can't."

"Not a tomb. We couldn't get into them anyhow; they've all got locked gates. Come on."

The surface under our feet cracked and crunched with every step. The shadows through which we moved weren't dark enough; the rocks between us and the plain weren't thick enough or hard enough. If John hadn't kept shoving at me, I might have sat down on the ground and waited in fatalistic acceptance like some poor cornered rabbit. In a way it was worse for me than it would have been for the rabbit. I knew exactly what would happen if we were caught. I had seen what Mary could do when she was just amusing herself. She'd be really annoyed by now.

The face of the cliff was weathered and uneven; I saw a dozen crevices big enough to offer concealment, but every time I headed mindlessly toward one, John pulled me on. I could have handled a nice shallow crevice, no problem. I had a feeling he had something less comfortable in mind. He seemed to know where he was going. How? The question, like a lot of others, ran through my head and out the other side, without hanging around long enough to inspire an answer.

After passing around a low ridge he headed for one of the openings in the cliff. The moon was down but those impossibly bright stars cast enough light for me to see how dark the opening was. Really dark. Very, very dark. He had to drag me though it. The space beyond was devoid of light but not of sound. Things squeaked and flapped. The blackness moved.

I flung myself at him, clutching at his shirt. Not such a smart move, that one, but there was a wall behind him; otherwise we'd have both fallen to the ground. His breath went out in a sound that would have been audible a long way off if compressed lips hadn't contained it. Then his arms closed around me and his mouth brushed my ear.

"Hang on, darling, it's just a cave and a few miserable bats. Lazy little buggers, they ought to have been out before this."

"Oh, God," I whimpered. "I'm sorry. I'm so sorry. I hurt you."

"No, you didn't." That was a lie if I'd ever heard one, and I had heard plenty of them from John. "Listen to me, Vicky. I doubt they know about this place but the dog may be able to lead them here. If that happens, there's another way out. A tunnel."

"I can't—"

"Yes, you can." We had both been whispering; he was barely breathing the words now, his lips against my ear. "Rest a minute. Catch your breath."

I tried to pull away from him, so my weight wouldn't press against his chest, but he tightened his grip. His lips moved across my cheek.

"Show me where the tunnel is," I murmured.

"In a minute."

It seemed to go on longer than a minute. Then he said softly, "This way," and drew me with him toward the back of the cave. "Here. See it?"

"I can't see a damned thing."

"Feel it, then." He guided my hand.

"Got it. How did you know about this place?"

"There's an old family . . ."

He didn't have to warn me to stop talking. Sound carries a long way in the quiet desert night. The footsteps were still some distance away, but they were coming closer.

His hand moved to my shoulder. I resisted the pressure. It wasn't difficult.

"You first," I said.

"I'll follow."

Another lie. Adrenaline and a mix of other hormones had given him a temporary burst of strength, but I doubted he could stand erect without the support of the wall against which he was leaning.

Sometimes my instincts work better than my so-called brain. The one that gripped me now superseded fear and even self-preservation. My hands were icy-cold but absolutely steady. His were neither. I got the gun out of his pocket while he was still fumbling for my wrist.

The dog was right outside. I heard its quick, excited panting, then a slither of rock and a muffled expletive. The uneven contours of the entrance brightened.

I got my finger around the trigger and aimed, bracing my wrist with the other hand.

The dog let out a sharp, peremptory bark. The man with it cleared his throat.

"Uh—Dr. Bliss? Mr. Tregarth? Are you there?"

It wasn't Max's voice. It was a voice I had never heard before—slow and hesitant, with a pleasant Southern accent.

John's hand closed over mine and pushed my arm down. The voice went on, "Uh—I haven't had the pleasure of meeting you, Dr. Bliss, but—uh—if you're there, you, uh— Damn it, Fido, are you sure this is the right place? Stupid dog . . ."

Fido (Fido?) barked indignantly. "Oh, well, then," the voice said. "I feel like a jackass, but if you say so . . . Uh. You remember me, Mr. Tregarth—Keith Kendrick, from UCal? Uh—how are you?"

I started to laugh.

"Do come in," John said. "You'll have to excuse Dr. Bliss; she does this sometimes."

Giggling maniacally, I shielded my eyes against the brilliance of the light. Behind it was a tall, thin man with sandy hair and an embarrassed smile. The dog at his heels looked like one of the pariah dogs that hang around the villages, but it had a collar and its tail was flailing furiously.

John cleared his throat. "Dr. Bliss, may I present Dr. Kendrick?"

"Vicky," I gasped. "Pleased to meet you."

"Call me Keith."

I made an effort and managed to stop laughing. "How did you know we were here?"

"He told me, of course. He's been expecting you."

"Feisal?" I asked doubtfully.

"Not Feisal," John muttered. "I'm afraid it wasn't Feisal. I'm afraid . . . I don't think I can stand this."

"We did run into Feisal," Kendrick said. "While we were looking for you. He expected you'd be here before this, and he was getting worried, so we went out—"

"He?" I began waving my arms. "I don't think I can stand this either. He who?"

Kendrick shied back. I'd forgotten I was still holding the

gun. "Uh—Dr. Bliss, if you wouldn't mind putting that away
. . . He's coming. Don't get excited. I think I hear him now."

There was no "think" about it. He was coming at full
speed, tripping over and running into things. When he burst
into the cave he was too out of breath to speak; he grabbed
me and hung on, wheezing.

"Schmidt," I gasped. "Schmidt, is that you? Thank God
you're all right! What are you doing here?"

"But why should you be so surprised?" Schmidt let me
go. "I told you I would be here. Guten Abend, Sir—John, I
am so very happy to see you again!"

He rushed at John, grabbed his hand, and began pumping
it up and down. John gave him a bemused smile. "Amarna,"
he mumbled. "You left those clues. The brochure and the—
the—"

"The bag, yes, I knew you clever ones would know what
they meant. What else could they mean?"

"Amarna," John repeated. "Right. Clever ones."

"Stop shaking him that way, Schmidt," I said. "He's not
. . . he's not feeling well."

"Ach, my poor friend! You have a fever, ja? We will return
at once to the house. Here, I will support you." He turned
and yanked John's arm over his shoulder.

It was too much for poor John. I don't know whether he
was shaking with chills or with laughter, but he managed to
make it back to the jeep, where Feisal was waiting, before
he keeled over.

Our arrival at Keith's house wasn't exactly inconspicuous.
He and Feisal had to carry John in, and Schmidt wouldn't
shut up. But nobody came out of the neighboring houses to
ask what was going on. Sometimes it's safer not to know
what is going on.

The house had only two rooms. The one into which Keith
led us was obviously his bedroom. It contained a camp cot, a
few boxes, a table and chair—both draped with miscellaneous
male garments—and a lamp. "I wouldn't have been able to
afford such comfortable quarters if it hadn't been for Mr.
Tregarth's generosity," Keith said. "I hope he's not seriously
ill. What can I do?"

The place didn't look comfortable to me. It didn't even look sanitary. But it was a lot better than we had any reason to expect. I asked for water, and was pleased to learn that John's generosity had also provided plenty of the bottled variety. Feisal went off to deal with the jeep and Keith went for more water, and Schmidt hunkered down beside me and watched while I unbuttoned John's shirt and started peeling back the tape.

"He has been wounded?" He was genuinely concerned, but I detected an underlying note of enjoyment. Wounds are so romantic. In Schmidt's favorite form of fiction they are usually in the arm or the shoulder and after biting his lip and muttering, "It's only a scratch," the hero goes back to fighting four or five opponents barehanded.

"You could say that." I lifted the cloth.

"Lieber Gott," Schmidt whispered. "Who has done this?"

"I'll tell you later. It's not as bad as it looks, Schmidt," I added, as tears of sympathy rolled down Schmidt's sunburned cheeks. "Something else must be causing the fever. Maybe ... . Maybe a good night's sleep is all he needs."

John opened one eye. "Was that . . ." The eye rolled toward Schmidt and then closed. "It was. I thought I was dreaming. I hoped I was dreaming. Schmidt, what have you—"

"Ruhig sein, my poor friend," Schmidt said. "All is well. You are safe with—"

"All is not well." John raised himself on one elbow. "What have—"

"Rest and sleep," Schmidt insisted, trying to push him back down.

"No, have something to drink. You're probably dehydrated." I shoved Schmidt away and held a glass to John's lips.

"Yes, that is probably better," Schmidt agreed.

"Oh, Christ. Will you two stop picking at me like dogs over a bone? I'll submit to your infernal attentions as soon as Schmidt tells me what wild story he gave Kendrick."

" 'Richard is himself again,' " I remarked.

"Richard is a hell of a long way from being himself. Which is lucky for you. Schmidt—"

"Why, I told him the truth, of course."

"Oh, God." John collapsed back onto the hard pillow.

"That you had discovered a plot directed against the museum and were on your way to Cairo to disclose it, with the villains in hot pursuit," Schmidt went on.

"In those exact words, I suppose." He let out an involuntary sigh as I began wiping his face with a wet cloth. "Well, it could be worse. You didn't go into detail?"

"I told him no more than that," Schmidt said indignantly. "It is an old rule of espionage, the need to know. Besides, he would have thought me verrückt if I had told him the entire truth. And now you must rest. Perhaps a sleeping pill, eh? I have with me—"

"No pills," I said. "He's taken too many already."

Feisal and Keith returned at that point. "How is he?" the latter asked, squatting beside the bed. "God Almighty. How did he—"

"A slight accident," John said. "I'm prone to them. Especially when I'm in the company of certain people."

"If he's complaining he's back to normal," said Feisal. He shoved a heap of garments off the chair and sat down.

"You all look as if you could use a drink," Keith said. "I've got a bottle of bourbon."

"And there is beer," Schmidt offered. "I brought with me—"

"Beer, of course," I said. "Where there's Schmidt there's always beer. Sorry, boys, but we are not going to have a party. Everybody out. He needs to rest."

"Just . . . one more thing." John's brief burst of energy was fading. He forced his eyes open. "Schmidt. How did you get here?"

"Why, by the train of course. My cryptic message to you—"

"Was received and deciphered," John said gravely. "Which train?"

"It left Luxor at six in the evening. It tore my heart in two to leave you, Vicky, before I could know whether you had succeeded in your courageous rescue, but I felt certain you would, and if you did not, I could serve you best by going for help as quickly as possible. So—"

"You left the hotel shortly after I did." I was beginning to understand what was on John's mind, and to share the wild curiosity that kept him conscious. "I suppose you were . . . disguised?"

"Aber natürlich. They might have been watching for us at the station. Would you like to see how I disguised myself?"

"I can hardly wait," John murmured.

Schmidt rummaged among the articles on the table. He was too pleased with himself simply to display the garments; he had to put them on—a long, dusty black robe, a headcloth of the same color, and an opaque veil that covered his face from the bridge of his nose to the end of his chin.

"I wore also my contact lenses," said the chubby little Egyptian woman in a muffled voice. "They made my eyes water very much because the windows of the car were open and there was a great deal of dust and sand. Such a useful costume, eh? I did not even have to cut off my mustache, though I would have done it, Vicky, if . . . What is wrong?"

"He's fainted," I said. I didn't blame him.

He felt cooler after I had sponged him off, and he had passed from unconsciousness to what seemed to be normal sleep. After washing the parts of me that showed, and a few that didn't, I went into the next room, where the party was in full swing.

Schmidt jumped up from his chair. From *the* chair, I should say; there was only one. "Beer or bourbon, Vicky?"

"Neither. I . . . Oh, what the hell. Bourbon."

"You should rest too." Schmidt assisted me into the chair and patted me.

"I will. After we've decided what to do next."

"At the moment our options are somewhat limited," Feisal said dryly. He was sitting cross-legged on the floor. In his rumpled, dusty clothes, his face dark with a day's growth of beard, no one would have known him for the well-groomed young professional of the *Queen of the Nile*. "We'll have to stay here till Johnny's fit again. When will he—"

"How the hell should I know?" I took a swallow, shuddered, and took another one. "Sorry, Feisal, I didn't mean to snap at you. If he's not better—a lot better—by tomorrow,

I'll get him to a doctor. You may have to help me; if he's conscious he won't go voluntarily. Then you and Schmidt will have to proceed without us. It would probably be best for you to separate; that doubles the chance that one person will get through."

Feisal gave me an odd look and nodded, without comment. Schmidt said, "But, Vicky—"

"Shut up, Schmidt." The bourbon was great stuff. My brain was really clicking; I felt like a combination of Einstein and Ms. Super Spy, ready for anything. "We can't stay here long. For one thing, Keith could get in deep trouble if the cops find out he sheltered us."

"Once the truth comes out he will be a hero." Schmidt twirled his mustache and added happily, "Like the rest of us."

"*If* the truth comes out. Please don't argue, Schmidt, I figure I'm good for about ten more minutes and although I'm dying to hear about your train ride and why Keith is indebted to John and how the hell we all ended up here where none of us expected to be, all that can wait. The whole village must know we're here. Sooner or later someone will turn us in; any group of people has a few potential informers. I'd rather take my chances with the police than with—with the other guys. If they locate us first . . ."

I raised the glass to my lips. It was empty. No wonder I was starting to feel so peculiar. "I am not drunk," I said. Slowly and with dignity I slid from the perpendicular to the diagonal. I think it was Feisal who caught me.

I woke twice during what would have been the night if I had gotten to bed at a decent hour. On both occasions the room was light; on both occasions I found myself on my knees beside the bed, fumbling at John's face, before I came fully awake. The first time he felt hot so I sponged him off, getting only an irritable mumble as thanks. The second time he was shivering, so I covered him up, and then returned to the rug some kind soul had put beside the bed, promising myself I'd just rest for a few more minutes . . .

The next time I woke up the temperature had risen a good forty degrees. My clothes were sticking to me and my mouth

felt like a desert path along which a lot of camels had passed.
Keith stood in the open doorway, a tray in his hands.

"Oh, sorry," he said. "I was just getting him some coffee."

John was sitting up trying to look debonair, which isn't
easy for a man who is unshaven, dirty, half-naked, and in
somebody else's bed. I have to give him credit; he almost
carried it off.

"You look very fetching," he remarked. "If you ask me
nicely I might even share my coffee with you."

I sat up, observing for the first time that the garment sticking
to my sweating body was a white robe trimmed with gold.
Schmidt must have stopped at the shops on his way to the
station. I hoped it was he who had undressed me.

"I'll—uh—I'll just get another cup." Keith retreated.

"Tactful lad," John said. "Aren't you going to come here
and soothe my fevered brow?"

I crawled to the bed and touched his forehead. "It is warm."

His hand slid up my arm inside the loose sleeve. "So are
you. So is the climate of Upper Egypt."

"You look terrible."

His fingers tightened, drawing me closer. " 'Love looks
not with the eyes but with the mind.' "

"The mind has very little to do with it," I said wryly.

"If I were as ill-mannered as some people," said my
beloved, "I would point out that you aren't at your best just
now either. But you're my darling, you're my sunshine, and
I won't stop loving you when your hair has turned to silver.
Can you say less?"

"No fair. That's at least two different songs."

"Answer the question."

"What question?"

I hadn't supposed we'd be left alone for long, and I would
have bet money on the identity of the next visitor. John let
go of me and I sat back on my heels.

"Ah," said Schmidt, pleased. "You are feeling better."

"I hope you aren't going to make a habit of this, Schmidt,"
John said.

"No, no. Don't mind me. Just go on with——"

"Give me the coffee, Schmidt," I said.

Schmidt did so and then seated himself. "If you don't want

to make love some more, then perhaps we should talk, eh? Yes, that is best. You must save your strength, my friend. Making love is weakening to the vital forces of even a man who is in perfect health, and making love with a woman like Vicky—''

''Uh—right,'' John said. ''If you don't mind, Schmidt, we ought to turn our attention to more pressing matters than my vital forces. What's been going on in the great outside world? I seem to have wasted the day in slothful slumber.''

''It was not wasted,'' Schmidt assured him. ''You needed to recover your strength. Perhaps we will be able to go on tomorrow morning. Assuming, of course, that you and Vicky do not—''

''Shut up, Schmidt,'' I said automatically.

I would have liked to give John a hand with his toilette (without engaging in any of the debilitating activities Schmidt had mentioned) but the only way I could get Schmidt out of the room was to take him out.

It was later than I had realized. Schmidt had the right idea; John needed another night's rest before we could continue our journey and we needed clothes, nourishment and, above all, more information before we decided how to proceed.

Feisal had gone out in search of the last. Keith was brewing something on a two-burner hot plate; when he asked if I was hungry I said I'd wait for the others.

''I'm sorry we descended on you like this,'' I added. ''We'll try to make it up to you.''

Keith turned down the burner and squatted beside my chair. I remembered now where I had seen him—talking to Schmidt, the day the tour visited Amarna. Schmidt would, of course, view that brief encounter as the beginning of a beautiful friendship. What were friends for if not to help their friends in an emergency? Maybe this development would cure Keith of talking to strangers.

''I have to admit I thought Dr. Schmidt had lost his marbles when he turned up with a wild story about robbing the Cairo Museum.'' Keith glanced at Schmidt, who was sitting on the floor next to the rug where the dog lay. The dog's tail was flopping up and down and Schmidt was talking to him in German. ''But when he said Mr. Tregarth was meeting him,

I figured it was all right. I hope I didn't offend Mr. Tregarth when I mentioned his generosity, he asked to remain anonymous when he offered to support my work here for an additional month."

"He's a very modest man," I said. "When did he do that?"

"About six weeks ago. I had permission to work here, but I only had enough funding for a month, with strict economy. Now I can finish my survey."

I let him tell me about the survey, nodding and smiling at appropriate moments. I don't believe in coincidences; it was reassuring to know that this wasn't one. John's "generosity" had been nothing of the sort. Having been informed of Blenkiron's plans he had realized he would need all the allies he could find, and he had had to pick someone who already had the EAO's permission to work at a given site, since official permission wasn't easily or quickly achieved. He must have planned to leave the cruise at Amarna, and he had undoubtedly prepared a plausible story to win Keith's cooperation. My arrival had put an end to that scheme; he hadn't even bothered to approach Keith during our visit. But Schmidt had, and nice indiscreet Keith must have told Schmidt about his generous patron, and Schmidt had assumed that when he indicated Amarna as our meeting place, John would go to Keith.

As he had. So far Schmidt was way ahead of the rest of us. He had known exactly what he was doing. I still didn't know what I was doing.

Tiring of Schmidt's attentions, the dog wandered over to inspect me. He was a nondescript creature, like all the other pathetic strays, except that his ribs weren't showing and he seemed to trust people.

"What happens to him when you leave?" I asked, scratching Fido behind his ear.

"He's not mine. One of the Egypt Exploration Society people adopted him a couple of years ago—they come out for a few months every winter—and the custodian looks after him when they're away. He must prefer Boston baked beans to rice, though, because he's been hanging around me since I got here. I'm afraid that's the main course tonight," he added with a grin. "My commissariat isn't extensive."

I assured him I shared Fido's passion for baked beans.

"I'll get to it, then," Keith said, unfolding himself and rising. "Feisal should be back any minute. I hope Mr. Tregarth is better. I've never seen injuries quite like those. It's almost as if someone deliberately . . ."

"I don't think you want to know the details," I said. "It's not because we don't trust you."

"That's okay. The less I know, et cetera. Here's Feisal," he added. "Baked beans coming up."

Schmidt rushed to greet Feisal. "Sehr gut, mein Freund, you are safely returned. What is happening?"

"It could be worse," Feisal admitted. "The whole damned village knows we're here, of course."

"How did you explain our presence?" I asked. I know small towns; gossip is a favorite sport and personal questions aren't considered rude, just friendly.

Feisal ran his fingers through his dusty hair and squatted down on the floor. "I said I'd been hired to drive a couple of Kendrick's archaeological friends, who had come to visit him for a few days. Nobody questioned the story, but the sooner we move on the better. How's Johnny?"

Johnny made his appearance at that point. "Anything else of interest?" he inquired.

"Not much. I didn't want to ask questions about the kidnapped American tourist and nobody brought it up. You know villages; they're more interested in local scandal than in issues of national importance. Turn on the radio, Kendrick, and let's see if we can get a news broadcast."

We were eating dinner—Keith had also opened a couple of cans of beef stew—before the news came on. It was, of course, in Arabic, and I had to wait for a translation, but I could tell by Feisal's lengthening face that it would not be good news for us.

"They know we've changed vehicles," Feisal said, switching off the radio. "Amr reported the jeep stolen. Damn him!"

"One can't blame him for protecting himself," John said. "And his friends and family. So they know we're on this side of the river?"

"They seem to have lost track of us," Feisal admitted grudgingly. "We might have doubled back, getting through the checkpoints before they found out about the jeep, or struck out into the desert. But we can't use the jeep any longer, they've got a description and the number."

"Can we buy another car?" I asked.

John glanced at me. He didn't say anything, but I knew that look, and I realized that once again he was one step ahead of me. If he had planned to leave the cruise here, he must have made arrangements for transport away from the site.

After a brief pause—I give the guy credit, it was very brief—Keith cleared his throat. "You can take my Land Rover. I guess it's the least I can do, since it was your money that paid the hire fee."

John's faint smile faded and he said bluntly, "You're too intelligent not to suspect by now that you've been set up, Kendrick. I didn't expect matters to develop as they have and I'm sorry about taking advantage of you, but not sorry enough to let you off the hook. We've got to have that vehicle. I don't think you'll get in serious trouble over this. If anyone—police or otherwise—learns we were here, don't try to be clever or heroic. Tell them we robbed you, lied to you, or held you up at gunpoint—any story you like. We'll back you up."

"Let's hope it won't come to that," Keith said. "I don't understand what the hell this is all about, but as my granny used to say, you've got to trust somebody sometime. You will let me know what happens, won't you?"

"You'll hear it on the news broadcasts," John said. "One way or the other . . . All right then, we'll be on our way in the morning. Feisal, you and Schmidt take the Land Rover. You'll look very innocent with your dear old mum in the backseat. Vicky and I will wend our way to Minya and—"

Feisal shook his head. "It won't wash, Johnny."

"There's a greater chance . . ." John began.

"I agree. We'll have to divide forces. But neither of you speaks Arabic. Schmidt does."

"Only enough to swear and tell dirty jokes," I said.

Schmidt blushed. Feisal said, "That could be enough. No, Johnny, I'm sorry, but Vicky goes with me or with Schmidt. It had better be with me. That way there'll be one able-bodied man in each party."

"Listen, you male chauvinist," I began.

Schmidt was as indignant as I. "Ha! You think I cannot

defend myself and protect Vicky? I, the finest swordsman in Europe?''

I patted his hand and made appreciative noises, but I was watching John and I saw his face change as he met Feisal's steady stare. ''Feisal is right,'' he said slowly. ''This is a better arrangement all round. He knows the roads, and if Vicky slumps down in the backseat she can wear one of those conveniently concealing female garments, and remain modestly silent. I hope that won't be too great a strain, Vicky.''

''Oh, go to hell,'' I said angrily. ''If you think I don't know why Feisal suggested this you are sadly mistaken. Women and children into the lifeboats first, right? They'll be watching the railroad stations, and you're the one Larry wants, and you aren't able-bodied, and—''

Schmidt had taken my hand in his. He squeezed it and said gently but firmly, ''They are in the right, Vicky. Think with your head instead of your heart and do not make this more difficult.''

It wouldn't be any easier for John or for Schmidt than for me, I knew that. They'd be as worried about me as I would be frantic with apprehension for them. But they were right, damn them. Larry would be just as pleased to have me as John. If they catch you, John had said, then I'll come after you. So would Schmidt, the little hero.

They took my silence for agreement. Feisal got to his feet. ''The market is still open. What are we going to need?''

Schmidt had cashed all his traveler's checks, so we had money to burn. After Feisal had left, shopping list in hand, we settled down to wait. Keith declined my offer to help with the dishes so I joined John on the floor and Schmidt started singing to the dog.

Don't ask me why. I guess singing calmed Schmidt's nerves. The dog loved it. So did John. ''Let's have 'Detour on the Highway to Heaven' again, Schmidt,'' he suggested.

The third verse—''If you ever get out of the fast lane—'' fascinated Keith to such an extent that he squatted down on the rug next to the dog and requested an encore. Under cover of Schmidt's (and the dog's) howls, I said softly, ''You rotten cheat. You already knew those songs.''

''I am acquainted with the entire spectrum of western

music," John said modestly. He put his arm around me and I leaned against his shoulder.

"Then why did you pretend you'd never heard them?"

"I hadn't. Not as Schmidt performed them. I have been waiting all my life to hear him sing 'It Wasn't God Who Made Honky-tonk Angels.'"

Schmidt was explaining to Keith about traveling melodies. "You will find the same tune used for many different songs. The one I have just sung to you is the same one used for that tender love song, 'I Am Thinking Tonight of My Blue Eyes . . .'"

"Don't sing it, Schmidt," I begged.

"No, not our song," John agreed. He was shaking with amusement. "How about 'Great Speckled Bird' instead, Schmidt?"

"Ach, ja, that is right. Do you know that one, Keith? The large spotted bird is the church, you see. 'The other birds all flopped around her . . .'"

John's face took on a look of unholy glee. "I'm going to get him a guitar. No—a harmonica."

I hid my face against his shoulder. I was laughing. Laughing so hard I cried.

Feisal and I left at dawn. Schmidt and John would wait till later, when there were more people around, before they took the passenger ferry. Schmidt was the cutest little sheikh you ever saw. Since he had to do whatever talking might be necessary he had to wear male clothing, and since his accent was a trifle peculiar we had decided he had better be a tourist from some other Arab-speaking country. He was crying, of course. He held out his arms and I gave him a hearty hug.

"See you in Cairo, Schmidt. Take care of yourself."

"Yes, yes." Schmidt straightened his shoulders and wiped his eyes. "Fear not, Vicky. I will protect your lover with—"

"Shut up, Schmidt." I kissed him and turned to John.

Schmidt's dye wasn't as sophisticated as the hair coloring my female friends use; it had left John's hair flat and dull. His eyes were startlingly blue in the tan of his face.

We had not weakened John's vital forces the night before;

in fact I had hardly had a moment alone with him. There had been too much to do, and at Schmidt's insistence he had taken something to make him sleep.

"Take care," I said.

"And you."

We shook hands. It was an absurd thing to do, I suppose. But with Feisal and Schmidt looking on, and the black garments muffling even my face, anything more demonstrative would have been still more absurd. Feisal grinned and shook his head and murmured something in Arabic. Schmidt blinked furiously.

Since the section of the east-coast highway north of Amarna wasn't finished, we had to take the car ferry across to the west bank. (Feisal had turned pale when John asked if there wasn't a roundabout way, like the one we had taken to reach the site, and John had tactfully dropped the subject.) Once we reached Minya we would cross back to the east bank; there were fewer towns and less traffic on that side, and we could make better time.

I huddled down in the backseat and tried to look senile, while Feisal got out to chat and smoke with the other early birds. The crossing took only five minutes, and nobody approached me.

My thoughts weren't good company. Had some potential danger been overlooked, some precaution forgotten? John's temperature had been about normal that morning, as nearly as I could tell without a thermometer, but he was a long way from healthy and some of the deeper cuts weren't healing the way they should. Since Schmidt was a sheikh, with all that oil money in his pocket, they could at least travel comfortably. John was supposed to be his secretary or companion or something (Schmidt had turned purple with embarrassment and fury when Feisal made a ribald comment about one alternative). John was wearing poor Keith's one white shirt and best suit, and he would speak only German, at which he was fairly fluent.

But theirs, as I had known, was the most dangerous route. Once they reached the opposite bank they would have to hire a car or a taxi to take them to Minya in order to catch the train, and there was a good chance the police would have the railroad station under surveillance. Given the best possible scenario—if they weren't caught or delayed or forced to seek an alternative route—they couldn't hope to reach Cairo before afternoon.

Feisal had estimated it would take us at least six hours, even if none of the above disasters occurred. We were to meet the others at the central railroad station, where the giant statue of Ramses II marks the center of the square; there was enough traffic, pedestrian and vehicular, to provide reasonable cover. Five P.M. was the hour designated for the first attempt at a rendezvous; we'd try again every two hours until we met, or . . . until something else happened.

If either party reached the city earlier, it was not to wait for the other. John's instructions on that point had been clear and forceful. "The sooner we notify the authorities, the safer everyone will be. Schmidt will get in touch with his friends in the EAO and the Ministry. Vicky—"

"I'll put through a call to Karl Feder. He got me into this, damn him, and he can damn well get me out."

"All right. If you can't reach him or if anything whatsoever goes wrong, head straight for the American Embassy."

Feisal and I hit our first little problem when we approached the bridge crossing to the east bank. Traffic was backed up for half a mile and as Feisal slowed I heard him cursing quietly and monotonously under his breath. I leaned forward and he interrupted his monologue long enough to mutter, "Shut up and cover your face. And pray."

He called out a question to a man standing in the back of a pickup ahead of us. I didn't understand the answer (or the question) but I knew what it must have been. Traffic was moving, though very slowly; I could see the uniforms and the rifles up ahead.

I turned myself into a black huddle, trying to look seven inches shorter. In my extremity the only prayer I could remember was "Now I lay me down to sleep," which was, I devoutly hoped, inappropriate. I bowed my head and concentrated on breathing.

It took over twenty minutes to get through that half mile. I knew better than to look up, even when the car stopped and

I felt rather than saw a man right next to me. After a moment, during which I didn't breathe at all, and a brief exchange in Arabic, the Land Rover began to move.

Feisal went on for another ten or fifteen miles and then pulled off the road. Turning, his arm over the back of the seat, he gave me a strained smile and said hoarsely, "How about something to drink?"

I fumbled in the basket at my feet and got out a bottle of soda.

"If we have to do that again I am going to die," I informed him.

Feisal drained the bottle and tossed it out. "They're still looking for the jeep, I think. They didn't even ask for my papers. If they don't find out we've changed vehicles we should be all right. Relax and enjoy the scenery."

"Ha," I said.

One of these years I hope to travel that road again when I'm in a proper state of mind to appreciate the view. That day I wouldn't have noticed the Great Pyramid of Giza unless it had been in the middle of the road. Feisal drove like a man fleeing justice, but then so did everybody else. I had to hold my voluminous garments with both hands to keep them from flapping in the breeze from the open windows. He was in front, I was in back; there was no possibility of conversation, so I clung to my veils and closed my eyes. Twice we were slowed to a crawl by construction, three times by accidents. All three appeared to be minor; what blocked the road were the crowds of gesticulating debaters discussing the incident.

I hadn't slept much the previous night. When I awoke after a nap I hadn't meant to take we were on a wide street lined with shops and teeming with traffic. Straight ahead two slender, delicately carved towers rose into the sky.

I leaned forward and poked Feisal. "Where are we? Is that a mosque up ahead?"

"No. It's one of the city gates. Dates from the eleventh century. I took a roundabout route." His voice cracked. "We made it. Praise be to God, we made it!"

"Praise be to God," I agreed heartily. "What time is it?"

"Half past twelve. Do you want something to eat?"

"I want to get out of this tent," I grumbled. "I want a shower and a drink with ice in it and a change of clothes. But I'll settle for being here in one piece."

"You may as well divest yourself of that ensemble if you can do it gracefully and inconspicuously," Feisal said. "You'll be no more noticeable in Western clothes now. I'll find a café and we'll have a bite while we discuss our next move."

I was too stupefied by heat, drowsiness, and disbelief to argue, but by the time he stopped and I had—inconspicuously, I hoped—removed my tent and veil, I had had second thoughts. We were in the heart of the city by then and there were a number of young people around, including some foreigners. I cleverly deduced that Feisal had picked a spot in the university area.

"We shouldn't take time for this," I objected, as he helped me out. "I need to make that call to Karl Feder."

"Munich is in an earlier time zone, isn't it? He's probably out to lunch." Feisal led me through a doorway curtained with strings of beads and found a table. The place was hot and dark and noisy and full of flies; people were talking in a mixture of languages, and a radio was blaring Egyptian pop music in the background. "What do you want to eat?"

"I don't care. Anything. Something with ice in it."

"No ice, not here. It's made of the local water."

He ordered in Arabic. Then he said, "I'm going to telephone my father."

"Are you sure that's a good idea?"

"My mother will be out of her mind," Feisal said simply. "I have to let her know that I'm safe and innocent of the charges."

If he had presented any other argument I might have disagreed, but that one hit me where I lived. I knew what it was like to wait hour after hour and day after day for news of someone's fate, fearing the worst. Boy, did I know.

"Come to think of it, my mother is probably not very happy either," I said guiltily. "Does the whole world know I've been abducted?"

"Count on it," Feisal said, grimacing.

"Yeah. It's the kind of story reporters love. Damn! My dad's probably on his way to Cairo right now. Well, they'll have to wait a few more hours, I can't put through an international call from a public phone."

The food arrived—chunks of meat and pieces of pepper and onion, on little wooden skewers.

"It won't take long," Feisal said. "I'll be right back."

It was two o'clock. Three more hours to wait. At least three. If they weren't there at 5 P.M. . . . I tried not to think about it.

When Feisal came back he was smiling. I hadn't realized how tired and old he had looked until I saw that smile.

"It's all right," he announced, settling into his chair. "He wants us to meet him."

"Your father?"

"He started out ordering me to turn myself in. But when I explained, told him you were with me and that you'd confirm my story, he said he'd be willing to listen."

"Damn nice of him. Look, Feisal, I'm not sure—"

"It's okay, I tell you. A friend of his is away on business, Father has the key to his apartment, which is not far from the train station. We can hole up there, use his telephone to call Munich and your parents and, if you like, the Embassy. That's much safer than the central telegraph office. You can have that shower and maybe even a drink with ice in it."

"Where does he want us to meet him?" I asked doubtfully.

"Ezbekiya Gardens. It's not far from his office. He didn't want us to go there or to the house."

"The police have probably got both places staked out."

"He hinted as much. Have you finished?"

I sat in front with Feisal this time. He was in a very happy mood, relaxed and smiling. He kept pointing out sights—mosques and museums and parks. The traffic was horrendous and parking seemed to be hit or miss. I wouldn't have considered the place where Feisal stopped, in between a barrow piled with cauliflower and a little old lady who had apparently set up housekeeping on the curb, as a legitimate spot, but he waved my comments aside.

"God willing we won't be coming back to the damned car anyhow. We've got a couple of blocks to walk."

"Okay."

"Vicky."

"What?"

"Just in case . . ." He hesitated. "I'm sure it's all right. But stay a couple of hundred feet behind me. I'll talk to him, get the key to the apartment. Wait till I wave or call to you before you join us."

He didn't give me a chance to reply. He started walking.

I followed, close enough to keep him in sight, but no closer. What he had suggested was only a sensible precaution; his father might be under surveillance and unable to shake it.

Crossing Cairo streets is a death-defying procedure. The street on the west side of Ezbekiya Gardens is a wide, very busy thoroughfare, and I lost sight of Feisal for a few seconds while I tried to avoid being run down by taxis, buses, and trucks. Reaching the other side breathless but intact, I caught sight of him standing by a little kiosk. The gardens were large; they must have arranged to meet at that precise spot. Hanging back, per instructions, I saw a tall gray-haired man approach Feisal. He was wearing Western clothes, and even at that distance I noted the resemblance. They stood talking for a while; then the older man threw his arms around Feisal.

Any father might embrace a returning prodigal son, and Middle Eastern males have no hang-ups about expressing affection physically. Not until I saw the crowds disperse, like hens when a fox enters the chicken yard, did I realize what was happening. Feisal saw the foxes too. They were hard to miss—four of them, carrying automatic weapons. He twisted away from the arms that tried to hold him, and gave his father a shove that sent him staggering back.

"Run," he yelled. "Run, Vicky!"

He wasn't trying to escape. He was just trying to warn me. He was standing perfectly still when they cut him down. I heard the rattle of weapons, and I heard him cry out, and saw him fall. Another, shriller, cry echoed his. It came, I thought, from Feisal's father.

People were screaming and running and I ran with them, blindly. My throat ached with rage and horror and grief. What sort of man would turn in his own son? I hoped it had been the old man who had cried out. I hoped he was suffering. Maybe he hadn't expected they would fire without so much as a preliminary warning. But he ought to have known, he ought to have trusted his son, given him a chance to explain . . .

I threw myself in front of a taxi, pried myself off the front fender and wrenched the door open. "The American Embassy," I gasped. "Shari Latin America."

I'm as patriotic as the next guy, but the sight of the flag had never affected me as it had that day. The farther you are from home the better that star-spangled banner looks. I marched up to the door with my chin held high and demanded entry.

It's nice to be famous. As soon as I mentioned my name I was passed from flunky to flunky till I ended up in an office few tourists see. There was a flag there too, and behind the big mahogany desk hung a picture of the President. I had voted for him and I had always thought he had a nice friendly smile. It had never looked friendlier.

"Dr. Bliss? Dr. Victoria Bliss! Thank God! You have no idea how relieved I am to see you." The man who hurried to meet me didn't resemble my idea of an ambassador. He was too young and his hair wasn't gray. He sure was glad to see me, though. He invited me to call him Tom, and took both my hands and shook them, and went on to tell me exactly how relieved he was.

"The ambassador's in the States, which left me holding the bag, as you might say. A hostage situation is a diplomat's worst nightmare."

"Gee whiz, I'm really sorry to have upset you," I said.

He flushed, and I gave myself a mental kick. I was getting to be as bad as John, making smart-ass remarks when I should be trying to gain his support and attention. It was imperative that I remain calm. If I lost my temper or broke down he'd think I was just another hysterical female, and I'd never convince him in time that my wild, improbable story was true.

"I'm sorry," he said, with a smile so charming it must have been one of the qualifications for the job. "Our primary concern, of course, was for your safety. Sit down. No, I insist, I won't ask you any more questions until you've had a chance to catch your breath." He went to the desk and started punching buttons. "Joanie, will you come in here, please? Joanie's my assistant, she'll take care of you."

"But I want you to ask me questions! There's been a mistake. I was never—"

Joanie must have been waiting for the summons. By that time everybody had heard of my arrival, and they were all wild with curiosity. She was older than her boss. Being female she would of course rise more slowly up the diplomatic ladder.

"You have to listen to me!"

Joanie put her arms around me. "Sure we will, honey. Don't worry about a thing. Come along with me, I'll bet you'd like to freshen up some."

If she hadn't had gray hair and a lined, motherly face I might have resisted. There was shock on that pleasant face as well as sympathy. It gave me some idea of how awful I must look. I suddenly realized, as well, that I had to go to the bathroom. (I know, that's not "romantic." But it's true.)

"All right," I said. "Five minutes. I'll be right back, Tom. Don't go away."

Joanie was very kind. She even offered me some of her makeup, and after I'd seen the wild face glaring back at me from the mirror, I accepted. I wouldn't have listened to anything that came out of a face like that.

She only asked me one question. "Did he hurt you, honey? He didn't . . ."

It was the wrong question. I thought of Feisal, making jokes and worrying about his mother and falling, falling and screaming, trying to warn me with what might have been his last breath. I turned on her like a madwoman.

"Hurt me! He was . . ." It was the wrong tense, too. I threw her lipstick wildly at her. "Damn it, why I am I standing here doing stupid things to my stupid face? Maybe he's not dead. Maybe he's . . . just dying and being tortured and—"

"Take it easy, honey."

"And don't call me honey!"

I thought I had behaved quite rationally and reasonably until Joanie escorted me to a small room that was obviously an infirmary or clinic. Another motherly gray-haired woman, wearing a sweater over her white uniform, rose to greet us.

"So this is the young lady. Welcome home, my dear. We're all so relieved to see you."

I felt as if I were being smothered in cotton candy. They

closed in on me, one on each side, and Tom entered, barring my way to the door.

"How is she, Frances?" he inquired, rubbing his hands and smiling. He thought the worst was over. He was in for a shock.

"I haven't had a chance to look at her. If you'll just sit down, Miss Bliss—"

I started to argue. Then, belatedly, I realized what I had done. Defending Feisal had been a bad mistake. Hostages sometimes end up identifying with their captors, and when the captor is young and handsome and the hostage is female . . . I made a last desperate effort to control myself, but in retrospect I admit I didn't succeed very well.

"What are you going to do?" I demanded, backing away from the nurse. "I won't have any shots. I hate shots."

"Just your blood pressure and pulse," the nurse said, as she would have spoken to a child. "No nasty shots, I promise."

"All right." I let her push me into a chair and fixed Tom with what I intended to be a firm, unhysterical look. It must have been more like a wild-eyed glare. "You stand there and listen to me."

"Believe me, Dr. Bliss, there are a number of people who want nothing better than to listen to you. But," he added, with the first touch of kindly consideration he had displayed, "I'm damned if I'm going to let them at you until I'm sure you're okay. I called your—uh—your friend. He's on his way."

"My friend?" A wild hope dawned. Had Schmidt and John made it? If they had caught the 10 A.M. train . . .

"Yes." Tom smiled. "He's been calling every hour on the hour."

"Normal," the nurse announced, unwinding the blood pressure cuff. She sounded disappointed.

"I told you so. Now—"

"Open wide."

She propped my mouth open with a stick and peered in.

I don't suppose it would have made any difference. The whole business only took a few minutes. But if I had had a chance to ask one question . . .

I had forgotten that I wasn't the only important American

in Egypt. I had forgotten it takes only sixty minutes to fly from Luxor to Cairo. They brought him directly to the clinic. Well, wouldn't you escort a distraught millionaire into the presence of the fiancée he has lost and just recovered?

When I saw him I jumped up, spilling the glass of water the nurse had offered and the little white pills she was trying to persuade me to take. There was no place to go. The room had only one door. When he caught me in his arms I tried to fight free.

"Darling, it's all right!" he exclaimed, holding me tight. "Oh, Vicky, I've been so worried. Don't talk, sweetheart, just let me hold you."

Calm, reasoned behavior might have saved me, though that is questionable. It was also impossible. I couldn't stand having him touch me. Instead of expensive aftershave and fresh linen I smelled sweat and blood; instead of his smooth well-groomed face I saw the gaping hole that had been Jean-Louis's face, and Feisal falling, and John slashed to bloody ribbons by the people this man had hired. I struggled and screamed and tried to bite. I can't blame them for thinking the emotional collapse they expected had finally occurred. It took two of them to hold my arm rigid so the needle could go in. The last thing I heard was Larry's voice. "My poor darling. God bless you, all of you; I'll take care of her now."

# Chapter Fourteen

Right back where I'd started.

So I thought, when I woke up to find myself in a large room furnished with antiques. I felt quite calm and relaxed. That's one thing to be said for tranquilizers. They leave the recipient very tranquil.

Deep down under the layers of fuzzy pharmaceutical comfort a small section of my brain was trying frantically to get my attention. Think, it was screaming. Do something! Don't just lie there, get me out of this!

There had been time for him to take me back to Luxor. Night had fallen; the windows of the room were dark. But this wasn't one of the rooms in Larry's Luxor house. The furniture was old but it was not as well-cared-for as Larry's antiques; the gilt was chipped and the mattress of the bed on which I lay smelled slightly musty. Either Larry had a pied-à-terre in Cairo, or he was staying with a friend. (He had so many of them.) This wasn't a hotel room. There was no television set, no room service menu—and no telephone.

And no bolt and chain on the inside of the door. The door was locked from the outside. Was I surprised? No. But I was sorry that frantic little voice had shaken me out of my comfortable stupor.

The windows were not locked. They led onto a small balcony, and I stood there for a few minutes, letting the night breeze cool my face. A few lights showed through the branches of the trees that were, I was sorry to see, on the same level as the balcony and too far from it to offer a means of egress. The ground was a long way down. There was no familiar landmark in sight—no towers, no high-rise hotels, not even a pyramid. The house must be in one of the suburbs.

The adjoining bath had once been palatial. Now the tile was chipped and the marble discolored. The water ran rusty. After it had cleared a little I splashed water on my face and hands. Then I went back and sat down. There weren't that many alternatives.

By that time the fuzz was gone, and I was in a state of abject, disgusting panic. The past hours hadn't been comfortable; I had been scared most of the time, scared to death and out of my wits some of the time, but this was worse—like having a chair pulled out from under you just when you think you can finally sit down and relax. To do myself justice it wasn't the thought of Mary's plans for me that made my mouth go dry and my hands shake. John and Schmidt could be tucked away in neighboring rooms, with Mary busy at work on one or both. Feisal could be dead.

It wasn't courage that got me to my feet, it was desperation. I had to find out. The truth might be less painful than the things I was imagining. It couldn't be worse.

I banged on the door. After a moment I heard the sound of a key in the lock, and the door opened. He didn't point a gun at me. He didn't have to. The guard was Hans, my old acquaintance, the one with the face like a giant sheep and the physique of a giant, period. Hans even had muscles on his ears, and he was almost seven feet tall.

The Egyptian sun had been hard on his fair complexion. His cheeks were red and peeling. "Guten Abend, Fräulein Doktor," he said politely. "Also, Sie sind aufgewacht. I will tell them."

Ten interminable, dragging minutes passed before there was a response. My aching muscles relaxed when I saw Larry. I didn't like him a lot, but I definitely preferred his company to that of the lady. Ed followed him, carrying a tray. He didn't make a very convincing waiter.

"Shorthanded?" I inquired, as Ed put the tray on the table and retreated to the door, where he stood with his arms folded, looking bored. This sort of thing was all in a day's work for him, I supposed.

"You have disrupted my plans rather badly," Larry admitted. "But only temporarily. Would you care for something to drink?"

The bottle of mineral water hadn't been opened; the seal was intact. Larry watched with unconcealed amusement while I inspected it.

"You really haven't much choice," he pointed out pleasantly. "You might go on a hunger strike, but you can't do without water long in this climate."

Courteous as ever, he forbore to add that there were other, less comfortable means of controlling me. "So what are your plans?" I inquired.

Larry settled back in his chair and studied me with an approving smile. "You are quite a remarkable woman, Vicky. Would it surprise you to learn that when I informed the Embassy we were engaged to be married, I found the idea not entirely displeasing?"

"Let's just be friends," I suggested.

Larry laughed. "Your heart belongs to another? Think about it, Vicky. It would be one way out of our present difficulty."

"Where is he?"

He didn't ask whom I meant. "You don't know?"

"We separated this morning." There was no harm in telling him that much; he must know Feisal and I had traveled together. It was a reasonable assumption that John and Schmidt would have done the same.

"I thought you might have. You had, of course, arranged a meeting place in Cairo? Never mind, we don't need that information. We've taken the necessary steps to inform him that you are my guest. He should be arriving anytime."

They hadn't caught him. My face must have registered relief. Larry shook his head. "Don't get your hopes up, Vicky. There's a guard under your balcony and every door is being watched."

So it was to be an exchange—or an offer of one. They couldn't afford to let me go. John must know that.

"How did you get in touch with him?"

"My dear, your lovely face has been on every television program in the country this evening. I gave out the press release myself. I'm sure he's seen it, he'll have been following the news closely. You are suffering from shock and physical and nervous exhaustion at the villa of the chairman of the Egypto-American Trading Company. He spends most of his time in the States, but he was happy to offer a refuge to you and your solicitous fiancé."

And when I fell off the balcony or slashed my wrists my solicitous fiancé would say I'd committed suicide in a fit of clinical depression. They'd add that to Feisal's account too.

"What about Feisal?" I had to force myself to ask; I dreaded the answer.

Larry dismissed the minor question of a man's life with a wave of his hand. "Forget about him, he's no longer a factor. Schmidt and Tregarth are the ones who concern me, and they ought to concern you as well; you're in no danger unless they refuse to cooperate. No, don't interrupt, let me finish. Why should I want to harm you? Once I'm out of the country there's no way you can prove anything, and without that pectoral you haven't a leg to stand on."

He took my appalled silence as a sign that his arguments were beginning to have their effect. Leaning forward, his eyes intent, he went on, "You've gone to a great deal of trouble and endured a great deal of danger and distress to stop me. Admirable, no doubt, but very foolish. Why risk your life to prevent me from doing something so harmless? The antiquities I have acquired will be cared for and preserved more carefully than they would have been in their original locations. What I've done is an act of rescue, not desecration."

I knew the arguments. They have been used by every looter, archaeologist, or thief, from the beginning of time, and unfortunately they have some merit. There wouldn't be much left of the Elgin marbles if they had stayed on the Parthenon. I don't buy those arguments, but I didn't feel like arguing with Larry.

I had seen eyes like his once before—in the face of a

shabby, shy little man who had tried to smash a statue of Diana in our museum. The guards had got to him before he did much damage, and I had had a chance to talk to him later, when he was in police custody. He had been very polite and soft-spoken when he explained that God had told him to destroy the heathen images. He couldn't understand why we couldn't see his point of view.

The little man and Larry had opposite aims, but they had the same mind-set. A kind of mental constipation, if you will excuse the homely metaphor—a block of solid conviction through which no counterargument can pass.

Larry turned with a frown when the door opened. We'd been getting on so well; he felt sure I had been about to agree with him.

Her hair was tied back with a soft scarf that matched her pale blue dress. It was like a child's pinafore, with wide shoulder straps and big pockets in the gathered skirt, and she looked about sixteen. The Greek earrings shone bright against the masses of her dark hair.

"Has she got it?" Mary's voice was crisp and not at all childish.

"We haven't discussed that," Larry said. "I doubt it, though. Please go."

"You promised me . . ."

"No, I didn't. Get out and leave this to me."

She divided a malignant glance between the two of us and slipped out.

"That woman is getting to be a damned nuisance," Larry muttered. "I think she's a little crazy."

"You know, Larry, you might have something there. Why don't you fire her? You hired her."

"No, I didn't. My original arrangements were made with her brother. A very competent man."

Competent, sane Leif. I remembered the last sight I'd had of him. The knife with which he'd been slashing at me was still in his hand when John dragged him down under the icy water.

Larry's frown smoothed out. "Well, it won't be much longer. I will certainly sever my connections with the organization after this. I hate to do it because they've done excellent work for me in the past, and at the start she was quite efficient. Some of her ideas were brilliant, in fact—like planting that message with the dead agent to get you on board as a means of making Tregarth behave himself."

"Oh," I said. He seemed to expect some response, but congratulating him on that brilliant idea was more than I could manage.

"Her organization handled that matter, and very well, too." Larry went on. "She's been acting strangely the last few weeks, though, and one can't put up with that sort of thing. It's inefficient."

"Right," I said, swallowing.

"I need that pectoral, Vicky," Larry went on. "Do you have it?"

"What . . . Oh." In the fascination of following Larry's mind along its monster-haunted byways I had almost forgotten the Tutankhamon jewel. "No, I don't have it. Didn't you search me?"

Larry looked uncomfortable. "Only in the most respectful fashion. Mary wanted to . . . Of course I couldn't allow that."

"Thanks," I said. And I meant it. The idea of those soft little hands on me made my skin crawl.

"It's a very large object," Larry went on. "I don't believe I could have missed it. Anyhow, I didn't suppose Tregarth would trust you with it. He has it, doesn't he?"

"Unless he is a lot dumber than I think he is, he's stowed it away somewhere safe by now."

"So we decided. Well." Larry rose. "He'll turn it over to us in exchange for you. So you see, Vicky, you haven't a thing to worry about. Is there anything I can do to make you more comfortable?"

His departure would certainly have that effect but it wouldn't have been tactful to say so. I shook my head.

"Have a little rest," Larry said kindly. "I'll let you know as soon as we hear from him."

Mary wasn't the only one who'd gone around the bend in the last few weeks. Or had Larry always been this way, determinedly unconscious of the deadly results of his "harmless" schemes? Maybe they were all like that, the presidents and chairmen and commanding generals who sat in their fancy offices and gave orders to "engage targets" or "cut the work force." They never saw the suffering, bleeding bodies those orders affected.

I didn't have a little rest or eat any of the food on the tray. It wasn't very appetizing—dry sandwiches and a wilted salad that probably contained a whole colony of healthy typhoid germs. That suggested there were few or no servants in the house. Larry might not have his full crew with him. Some of them would have to stay with the boat. Mary and Hans were here, and that probably meant Max and Rudi were also with Larry. How many others?

And what the hell difference did it make? I couldn't get out and there was no way John could get to me without being caught.

I went onto the balcony. Down below—far down—I saw a stone-paved terrace without so much as a shrub to break one's fall. Rudi was down there too. At least the shape in the shadows, slim as a weasel, looked like his. To complete the picture of total disaster, the railing of the balcony swayed under the pressure of my hands. No point in trying the old bedsheet routine even if Rudi hadn't been lurking. Those rails wouldn't support the weight of a healthy six-foot female.

I was inspecting the bathroom, hoping to find a used razor blade or a nail file, when I heard the bedroom door open.

"He's on his way. He telephoned a few minutes ago."

Her eyes glowed. Little flecks floated in them like the dead insects in amber. My heart couldn't sink any farther; it was already trying to shove through the sole of my shoe.

"So," Mary went on briskly, "we must get ready to receive him, mustn't we. Sit down in that chair. Not the big carved armchair. That one."

It was a straight chair, the seat and back covered with faded gold brocade.

"No, thanks," I said, backing away. "I'd rather stand."

"If you prefer it this way." She turned to the door. "Hans. Come in."

Hans's face wasn't capable of displaying subtle emotion, but I got the impression that even he was beginning to wonder about little Mary. "Aber, gnädige Frau, Herr Max hat mir gesagt—"

"From whom do you take your orders? I'm not going to hurt her," she added unconvincingly. At least it didn't convince me. Poor bewildered Hans shrugged, setting off a miniature avalanche of muscles, and advanced on me.

Just for the look of the thing, I picked up a bowl from the table and heaved it. To my surprise it hit him square on the chest. Not to my surprise it didn't halt his advance.

So I sat down in the chair and Hans took the cord Mary had foresightedly brought with her, and he tied my wrists and ankles. He worked with slow deliberation. The knots weren't painfully tight. Hans didn't get any jollies from hurting people. He just killed them.

"Larry isn't going to like this," I said.

"Larry knows I'm here." Mary assisted Hans out the door and closed it. "My darling husband is an ingenious swine, and as I pointed out to Larry, it would be foolish to take unnecessary chances."

"Are you really married?"

"Bell, book, and candle." Mary leaned against the table, hands in her pockets. "Not for long, though," she went on conversationally. "I regret that, in a way. I shall hate wearing black. It's not my color. And sharing his bed was quite an interesting experience."

"Oh, come off it," I said. "You're wasting your time with that routine, Mary. He could hardly stand to touch you. It was always you hanging on to him, instead of—"

I wouldn't have believed a soft little hand like that could hit so hard. When my ears had stopped ringing I said, "Did Larry authorize beating me up?"

"He took my knife away." Mary's voice deepened and the golden eyes glittered. "But he can't object to this. A few bruises will have a persuasive effect on John. You've got him trained like one of Pavlov's dogs. I don't understand how you accomplished it—"

She examined me curiously, from head to foot and back again. I could see her problem; the idea that any normal man could resist a cuddly little cutie in favor of a six-foot Amazon with a sarcastic tongue and the disposition of a hedgehog absolutely baffled her. To be honest, it baffled me too—not that he could resist Little Miss Mary the Ripper, but that he had stuck with me so long.

With an abrupt movement she pulled the lovely little Greek heads from her ears and flung them at me. "These were meant for you, you know. I made him give them to me. Did you enjoy seeing me wear them?"

"I did wonder. They aren't your style."

"But they were clearly a love token, weren't they? Something distinctive and different, carefully chosen for a woman who would appreciate them." Her thumb caressed the gaudy diamond on her finger.

I knew what she intended and I was contemptibly relieved when she decided to try a little mental torture first. "Wouldn't you like to know how your other friends are faring?"

I shrugged. "You haven't got Schmidt or you would have said so. Feisal . . . I assume Feisal is dead."

"Oh, no," Mary said softly. "He's still alive. He may never walk again, but that won't concern him after they hang him for treason." The tip of her little pink tongue showed between her parted lips. She was having such a good time she didn't even hear the voices outside.

There's a poem about a highwayman who came riding, riding, up to the old inn door. The soldiers used his sweetheart as a decoy, tying her to a chair with a rifle pointed at her breast. She managed to get one finger around the trigger, and when she heard him coming she pulled—"and warned him with her death."

I always wondered why she didn't just yell.

Oh, well, maybe he couldn't have heard her over the pounding of his horse's hooves. Or maybe it didn't fit the meter. I didn't have a rifle at my breast. Anyhow, John knew the soldiers were there.

I threw my head back and opened my mouth and screamed. But the name I called was not that of my lover. "Max! Hey, Max!"

John was the first one through the door, but Max was right behind him. It wasn't until much later that I understood the significance of that sequence.

The Pavlovian conditioning didn't seem to be as strong as

Mary had believed. After a few steps John stopped. He had only glanced at me; his eyes were fixed on Mary.

"More melodrama," Max said in exasperation. "How weary I am of this! You were forbidden to come here, Mary. Mr. Tregarth is willing to cooperate. You will only irritate him if you persist in this nonsense."

"I am already irritated," John said. His eyes returned to my face. "Are you—"

"Fine, just fine," I said, stretching my mouth into a smile. My cheek hurt. "I do hope you have a couple of aces up your sleeve, because if you haven't, this was not one of your brighter moves."

He was still wearing Keith's suit, but he had washed the cheap dye out of his hair. Avoiding my eyes, he remarked, to the room in general, "She tends to babble when she's nervous. Mary does affect people that way. Get her out of here."

Blenkiron was the next to arrive. "Damn it," he exclaimed. "Mary, I told you—"

She laughed contemptuously. "What a conveniently bad memory you have, Larry."

"Well, I certainly didn't give you permission to . . ." He couldn't even say the ugly words. "I'm sorry, Vicky. I told her to stay with you but I never authorized . . ."

"Swell," I said. "So how about untying me?"

Nobody reacted to that naive suggestion. Mary backed off a few steps and Max said, with poorly concealed exasperation, "Can we now discuss the situation in a reasonable way? You have the pectoral, Mr. Tregarth?"

"You know I haven't," John said. "You watched Rudi search me."

"Where is it?"

"None of your damned business. Now, Maxie, don't lose your temper. That pectoral is my ace in the hole. You don't suppose I'll meekly hand it over without getting something in return, do you?"

"Need I ask what?"

"Surely not. And please don't insult my intelligence by suggesting you'll turn her loose after I deliver the goods. I want her out of here and safely back at the Embassy. As soon as she telephones to say she's there, and the ambassador confirms it, I'll get the pectoral for you."

"We could force you to tell us," Max said.

"You could certainly try," John said agreeably. Leaning against a chest of drawers, hands in his pockets, he was putting on a pretty good imitation of languid self-confidence, but the tension that vibrated along every nerve was evident to me at least. He was trying very hard not to look at me.

"But it's not the most efficient method of attaining your ends," he went on. "You know me well, Maxie; do you suppose I give a damn about the museum or the tomb or any bloody antiquity on the face of the earth? I'll even go through with the robbery, if that's what you want."

"You will?" Blenkiron said eagerly. "But you said—"

John raised an eyebrow. "I didn't object to robbing the museum. The thing that put me off a bit was a strong suspicion that I wouldn't survive the attempt. I'm willing to take my chances with the ordinary security system, but I object to being shot or stabbed in the back by one of my purported assistants."

Max looked a little embarrassed. "I was against that," he said. "I felt sure you would expect something of the sort and there really was no need—"

John cut him off. He was looking at Max, but I knew he was aware of every move Mary made and every breath she took. She was the most unstable and unpredictable factor in the structure of mutual self-interest he was building with such agonizing deliberation. I was afraid to move or speak for fear of shaking it. And I knew why he wouldn't look at me.

"There was no need," John agreed. "You're a businessman, Max, and Mr. Blenkiron's sole concern is making off with his pretty toys. My sole interest is my survival and Vicky's. My proposal will accomplish all those admirable aims, but you will have to make up your minds without delay. Herr Schmidt has an appointment with the director of the museum in"—he glanced at the cheap watch that had replaced his— "in an hour and a quarter. If he hasn't heard from me before he leaves his present location he will take the pectoral with him and then, if you will excuse a cliché, the die will be cast. There's barely time for Vicky to reach the Embassy providing she leaves within the next five minutes."

Max's eyes narrowed. "We must discuss this. It requires consultation."

"It's your own fault," John said. "You oughtn't to have selected such a remote hideout. Cairo traffic is difficult at any time of day or night."

Maybe there was something to that business about auras. I could almost see the taut lines of tension crisscrossing the empty air like a cat's cradle of colored yarn. The strain of manipulating them was beginning to tell on John; his nonchalant pose hadn't changed but his face was beaded with perspiration.

"It sounds reasonable to me," Blenkiron said slowly. "So long as we have Tregarth, the others won't risk—"

"You fools," Mary said suddenly. "Can't you see what he's doing?"

She had been standing quietly, hands folded and head bowed. It was her old pose of sweet submissiveness and the men, bless their chauvinist hearts, had dismissed her from consideration. But I had been afraid of this, and so had John. He straightened, taking his hands out of his pockets, but before he could speak Blenkiron said angrily, "Be still. You've already caused enough trouble."

"You sentimental idiot!" She took a step forward. Her hands were empty, clasped and twisting. "Too fine-minded to hurt a woman, is that it? And you, Max, you're getting soft too. I'm afraid I won't be able to give you a favorable efficiency report on this job. Are you really stupid enough to let him hypnotize you into giving up the one thing that will force him to cooperate? I'll show you how to get what you want. Hold on to him, Max."

She didn't wait to see him comply with her order. It would never have occurred to her that he might not.

Who needs a knife when she's got diamonds? They are harder than steel. She had twisted the ring around and when her hand struck my face the stone opened up a long stinging cut.

When I opened my eyes John had her by the throat. I

could see her, mouth gaping in a struggle for air, her cheeks darkening.

Max hadn't moved.

John could have snapped her neck with one twist of those long skilled hands. When he released his hold she crumpled bonelessly to the floor, but she was still alive. I heard the rattle of painfully drawn breath. John's hands fell to his sides. I couldn't see his face; his back was to me.

Max sighed. "You surprise me, Mr. Tregarth. Mr. Blenkiron, I think perhaps you had better run along."

Larry's features were drawn with disgust and horror. "Yes, yes, perhaps I had," he mumbled. "The boat will be in shortly; I'll just go down to the dock and ... You'll make the—the arrangements, Max?"

"Don't concern yourself, Mr. Blenkiron. I'll handle everything."

"You're a very competent man, Max. I leave everything in your hands. Vicky, I—uh—you'll be fine. I hope we meet again under more—uh—pleasant circumstances."

The door closed.

John turned. His color was bad and perspiration trickled down his cheeks, but his voice was cool and ironic. "A pity we didn't have a basin of water to offer him. Don't do anything you might regret, Max. It's over, you know."

He stepped back, closer to me, as Max came toward him.

"I know," Max said calmly. Stooping, he lifted the unconscious woman and carried her toward the bed. Instead of putting her down he went on, out onto the balcony. When he came back his arms were empty.

It was done with such quiet unhesitating efficiency I didn't understand what had happened until John moved, violently and jerkily, and then jolted to a stop.

"That's settled," Max said. "I had hoped you would take care of it for me, but evidently I overestimated you. It doesn't matter; the onus won't rest on me. If you two will wait here for—oh, an hour should be long enough—you can proceed on your way. Whitbread has gone with Blenkiron, and Rudi and Hans will accompany me, so you need not worry about being disturbed."

John cleared his throat. "You mean you—"

"I am a professional, Mr. Tregarth, and I don't understimate your intelligence. When I learned that you and Herr Schmidt had reached Cairo unscathed I knew we had lost. He would, of course, go straight to the authorities. His reputation is such that they would be forced to listen to him and, however reluctantly, act on his accusations. They would be hammering at the door by this time if they weren't hoping you could get Dr. Bliss out safely."

He waited for confirmation. John nodded dumbly. "So," Max went on, "I requested Mr. Blenkiron to settle our outstanding account, and made plane reservations. He has not my experience; I fear the unfortunate man doesn't realize that there will be a reception party waiting for that boat to dock." He glanced at his watch. "I really must be off. Oh, do forgive me, Dr. Bliss. No doubt Mr. Tregarth would find it easier to release you if I returned his pocket knife."

John had recovered enough to catch the knife, though his movements lacked their usual smoothness. "Thank you. I trust there won't be any—onus—directed at me either?"

"Only insofar as my employers are concerned." John started to protest and Max went on smoothly, "You must realize that I can't accept the responsibility without incurring a reprimand, at the very least. I take pride in my record and don't want to see it blemished. You are at liberty to tell the police whatever you choose. You needn't worry about retribution; from a financial viewpoint this affair has been a success for us and we haven't time to waste on personal grudges. We won't bother you if you stay out of our way."

"That, I assure you, is my greatest ambition," John said. He had cut the ropes around my ankles. Now he moved behind me and freed my arms. I just sat there. Joining in that conversation would have strained even my gift of repartee.

"And mine," Max said. "I don't like you, Mr. Tregarth. I hope never to see you again. Good-bye. Good-bye, Dr. Bliss."

"Good-bye, Max," I said. "I can't bring myself to thank you, but . . ."

"You owe me nothing." He hesitated briefly, and then an odd little smile stretched his thin mouth. "I wish you good luck. If you gain what you clearly desire, you will need it."

I sort of hoped that maybe, once we were alone, my hero,

the man who had risked all to save me, would sweep me into
his arms and hold me close, murmuring broken endearments
the way they do in romantic novels. John just stood there
staring blank-faced at the closed door. So I got up all by
myself. My legs seemed to be working all right, and I thought
I was in full possession of my senses until I realized I was
heading blindly for the balcony.

John caught my arm. "No, Vicky."

"She could be—"

"No."

He touched my cheek. I had forgotten about the cut until
his fingertip traced a line from my cheekbone to my jaw. I
don't know who moved first. His arms went around me with
bruising strength, but he was shaking from head to foot and
he didn't resist when I guided his head onto my shoulder.

"That's more like it," I murmured. "John, don't. You
couldn't have stopped him. He tried every trick in the book
to get you to do it for him."

"He almost succeeded. God. It was so close. Too close . . ."

"Kiss me."

"What? Oh. Right."

"Better now?" I asked after a while. My voice wasn't very
steady.

Neither was his. "Yes, thank you, I am experiencing temporary relief. Suppose we postpone further treatment? I can't
stand this ghastly place much longer."

"Is it safe to leave?"

"Oh, I should think so. Maxie's a man of his word—when
it suits him to keep it."

"Are we going to keep ours? To give him an hour?"

"I didn't give him my word. However, annoying Max
would not be a sensible move on my part. I shan't turn him
in, but there's no reason why we have to wait out the time
here."

"Okay. Wait just a minute."

The earrings were hard to see against the complex pattern
of the rug. I finally found both of them. One of the wires was
broken.

"It can be repaired," said John, over my shoulder. "Though
I shouldn't think you'd want them now."

"Are you kidding? They're the most beautiful things I've ever seen."

"How did you know I meant them for you?"

"She told me. That just made me want them more."

"Vindictive little creature, aren't you?"

"Vindictive, yes. Little, no." The light ran softly along the tiny golden faces. I closed my fingers carefully around them. "Over twenty centuries they have probably been in worse hands. And ears."

The house was uncannily quiet and as eerie as a mausoleum. Dust covers shrouded most of the furniture and our footsteps echoed in the silence. It was hard for me to believe the place was really deserted; I kept expecting someone to jump out at us from the shadows huddling in those vast, high-ceilinged rooms. When we reached the door without meeting anyone John let out his breath.

"There are television crews and newspaper reporters all around the house," he said. "I would offer to carry you out in a fainting condition, but appealing to the tender mercies of the press might not be as effective as making a run for it."

"We'll run," I said. "I won't even ask where."

"That's an encouraging sign. Stay close."

He put his arm around me and opened the door.

The limo was big and black and long. As we raced toward it, hotly pursued by assorted newspapers, the door opened. John tripped a reporter and pushed me into a pair of waiting arms.

"Hi, Schmidt," I said. "I had a feeling you'd be here."

When I woke next morning it wasn't morning, but afternoon. I was lying on my side, facing the window, with my back to John. I could tell by his breathing he was still asleep, so I lay still, enjoying . . . enjoying the fact that I could hear him breathing and that I was doing the same.

The scenery wasn't bad, though. Few hotels in the world can boast such view: the Great Pyramid of Giza, golden in the late sunlight, seeming so close it might have been right outside the bedroom window. Trust Schmidt to come up with the fanciest suite in one of the most elegant hotels in the country, on short notice and during the height of the tourist season.

We hadn't arrived at Mena House until 4 A.M. Our first stop, at John's insistence, had been at the hospital. The legal process which would clear Feisal might take some time, and the least we owed him and his family was to tell them at the earliest possible moment that it was under way.

It required a call to the minister to get us past the guards who were still on duty, and when I saw Feisal's father I felt so sorry for him I couldn't hold on to my anger. His mother was there too; they were sitting side by side on a hard bench in the corridor, and her arm was around his bowed shoulders. They both broke down when Schmidt told them the good news and everybody except John the imperturbable started crying and hugging one another indiscriminately. Feisal was under deep sedation, but when I kissed his cheek and whispered in his ear I think he heard me.

It had been John's suggestion that I be allowed to see Feisal. ("If anything can rouse him it will be a woman.") When I suggested that so long as we were there he might let a doctor have a look at him, he glowered and made a pointed remark about other kinds of therapy, but with Schmidt's assistance I managed to bully him into giving in. There would be time for another kind of therapy later. And I wanted to make sure he was in fit condition for it.

After that we had to talk with a lot of people who wanted answers to questions we hadn't figured out how to answer yet, and I had to droop and pretend to feel poorly so they would let us go. And later . . . He was out cold the moment his head hit the pillow. That's what you get for being thoughtful.

I changed position, trying to make as little noise as possible. His head was turned away; I could see only one side of his face and the curve of his cheek. I had always admired those cheekbones, but this one was too tightly shaped, and although his mouth was relaxed and his breathing even, a chill of superstitious terror ran through me when I saw how drawn his face was even in sleep.

The one visible eye opened. It held an expression of mild interest.

"Oh, you're awake," I said brightly.

"I am now. You were breathing on me."

"Sorry."

"Are you? I'm not." He turned over and gathered me in.

"The doctor said—"

"The subject was not mentioned. I carefully refrained from bringing it up."

His lips moved from my temple to my ear and were heading south when I said, "I don't think this is such a good idea. You look awful and you're too thin and—"

His lips touched mine and I threw caution to the winds and kissed him back so hard he let out a grunt.

"I knew you didn't mean it," he said complacently. "The men of my family are notoriously irresistible to women. Well, not my father; by all accounts, particularly those of my mother, he was a dull stick in every way. But Granddad was quite a lad in his time, and my great-grandfather has become something of a—"

"I don't want to hear about your great-grandfather. I love you. Did I mention that?"

"I wouldn't object to hearing it again." But he held me off, and he was no longer smiling. "It took long enough to wring it out of you. What were you afraid of?"

There were too many answers to that question, some obvious, some not. He had to know most of them.

I tried to pass it off. "You know me. Independent, bull-headed—"

"And afflicted with bad dreams."

"Oh, God. Did I . . ." I had. It was coming back to me. "I'm sorry."

"That's all right. You stopped crying and babbling when I got hold of you. Was it the old nightmare?"

"Yes. Uh—no. Not that one."

"I thought not. You went on like Lady Macbeth."

"Blood and . . . roses." I remembered now. So that was why I hadn't waked completely. "How embarrassing. My subconscious isn't awfully original."

His mouth relaxed. "I am willing to overlook a few minor flaws in a woman who is so talented in other areas."

"Are you sure you feel up to ... Damn it, don't laugh! That wasn't intentional."

"I should hope not. Trite *and* vulgar."

I was only conscious of the movements of his hands and lips until he started violently and lifted his head. "Oh, Christ! Isn't that—"

It could only be. Schmidt was humming like a drunken bumblebee. I didn't recognize the tune. Nobody could have recognized the tune.

"It's all right," I murmured tenderly. "I locked the door."

"I can't." He sounded like a nervous virgin. "Not with Schmidt out there. I haven't fully recovered from the time he broke the door down just when I—"

"He was laboring under a slight misapprehension." I drew his head back to my breast. "He won't break this door down. He's very romantic."

"Then he'll be listening at the keyhole," John mumbled. "I've become very fond of the little imp but I draw the line at providing him with vicarious entertainment."

"Try to rise above it," I suggested.

"That *was* deliberate. Well, perhaps with a little of the proper sort of encouragement . . ."

"How's this?"

"A step in the right direction, certainly. Do go on."

"More precious than jewels, more precious than gold," I murmured. "John, if you don't stop laughing, Schmidt will think we're telling jokes and want to come in."

I figured we could count on half an hour. It didn't seem that long, but it was actually forty minutes later when Schmidt raised his voice to a level that could not be ignored, even by me. Trust Schmidt to select an appropriate air with which to serenade us. This one was about a cold-blooded hoodlum named Pretty Boy Floyd. Folk music, like Schmidt, glamorizes outlaws; according to the lyrics of the ballad, Pretty Boy was a misunderstood martyr who had given Christmas dinners to families on relief.

"I'll head him off," I said, removing myself from John and the bed, in that order. "Stay there and rest."

"I don't need to rest. I was just getting warmed up. Are

you going to put on some clothes or have you decided to reward Schmidt for refraining from kicking the door in?"

"I don't have any clothes," I said bitterly. "Except that filthy, wrinkled, disgusting outfit I have worn day and night for too long. I will not put it on. I'm going to burn it first chance I get and dance around the bonfire."

"Widdershins," John suggested. "Have a sheet, then. You don't want to get the old chap too worked up."

He watched interestedly as I wrapped the sheet around me and tried to figure out how to keep it there. "I'm afraid you haven't got the hang of it. Why don't you come over here and let me show you?"

"Some other time."

"Excellent suggestion."

Schmidt had enjoyed himself with "the room service." I've never seen such a spread—everything from pastries to salads and from coffee to champagne. And, of course, beer.

"I did not know whether you would like breakfast or Mittagessen," he explained, pulling out a chair. "So I ordered both. How is Sir John? How do you feel? Did you have a pleasant time making—"

"Yes, thank you."

"You look very glamorous."

I pushed my tangled hair back from my face. "I look very terrible. I don't even have a comb. I need clothes, makeup, a toothbrush—"

"There is much to do," Schmidt said, around a mouthful of pâté. "We must organize ourselves."

"What's happened since last night?"

"I will wait to tell you until Sir John joins us. Perhaps I should go and—"

"No!" I shoved Schmidt back into his chair. "He'll be out in a minute."

Knowing Schmidt, he was. He was more kempt than I, though he was wearing the same grubby clothes. After submitting with only a faint grimace to Schmidt's embrace, he joined us at the table.

"Eat, eat," Schmidt crooned. "And I will tell you the news."

The *Queen of the Nile* had docked at midnight. After the briefest of inspections the authorities had ordered the hold sealed, arrested the entire crew, including my shipmates Sweet and Bright, and carried a protesting Larry away.

"Not to prison, though," Schmidt said. "It is a great embarrassment to all concerned. Not only is he an American citizen, but he is a powerful man with many friends. I do not know what will be done with him."

"Nothing," John said cynically. "At worst he'll end up in an expensive nursing home till he recovers from his fit of temporary insanity. The fact that it went on for ten years will be tactfully ignored. What about the others?"

"That is what we must discuss." Schmidt's round face was unusually serious. "For you, my friend, are one of the others and even the dangers you have incurred in order to redeem your initial—er—error will not save you if the truth comes out. Feisal too must be cleared of blame. We are three intelligent people; I feel certain we can invent a scenario that will achieve those ends."

If the situation hadn't been so serious I would have enjoyed listening to those two concoct a plot. The greatest collaborators of fiction couldn't have done better; Schmidt's inventive imagination had been developed by years of reading sensational fiction, and John had always been the world's champion liar.

Getting Feisal off the hook was the easiest part. He hadn't been involved with the restoration of the tomb and he could reasonably claim he had suspected nothing until after Jean-Louis's death. His activities thereafter warranted a medal, not a prison sentence. If all four of us told the same story and stuck to it, it would be hard to prove we were lying.

"What about Larry?" I asked.

"It will be his word against ours," Schmidt began.

John shook his head. "Forget about Blenkiron. His wisest course is to say nothing and admit nothing. There will be a behind-the-scenes deal made, in order to avoid embarrassment all around. Egypt will get its treasures back and will accept with proper appreciation the gift of the Institute for Archaeological Research, and the blame will be placed on the shoulders of Max's crowd—and on mine."

"No, no," Schmidt said energetically. "I have it all worked out, you will see."

Max and the boys had made their getaway. Three men of their descriptions had boarded a plane to Zurich shortly before midnight and were now believed to be somewhere in Europe. A rather large territory.

"They will not be caught this time," Schmidt said. "Which is all to the good. They will say nothing about you, John, and Blenkiron cannot accuse you without admitting things he will not wish to admit. So far as anyone else knows, you and Vicky met for the first time on the cruise. Neither of you had any reason to doubt Herr Blenkiron's intentions until I expressed to you my suspicions—"

"Oh, so you're going to take the credit for discovering the plot, are you?" I inquired.

"But I did discover it," said Schmidt.

"Oh yeah?" I caught John's eye and smiled self-consciously. "I never did get around to asking you how much you knew, Schmidt. I assumed—"

"You assumed I was a stupid old man," said Schmidt calmly. "And you did not ask because you were crazy with fear for the man you—"

"I think that point has been made, Schmidt," I said. "So tell me now, okay?"

"It was ratiocination of the most brilliant," Schmidt explained, twirling his mustache. "Though I will confess that the truth did not dawn until John told me that Herr Blenkiron was a criminal and that I must leave the house. Mind you, he told me no more than that. It was while I was eating my lunch at the hotel that I put the pieces together. The crime, I deduced, must be theft; for what other reason would Herr Blenkiron have in his employment a person like—er—like Herr Max? And what was it that a rich man could not buy, that he must steal it? The death of M. Mazarin was the ultimate clue. He was killed, not by the explosion but by a bullet. A coincidence, that the only one to die was the man who had directed the reconstruction of the tomb? I did not think so. And when I remembered the way in which the reconstruction was carried out, and the sudden ending to the tour, and all the other suspicious circumstances ... Voilà, Eureka! So you see it spells Fröhliche Weihnachten; we are heroes, and everyone will live happily ever after."

Exhausted by this creative effort, he paused to eat a croissant.

"Very well done, Schmidt," John said, "but you've overlooked one little detail. Vicky has already dutifully informed her mysterious superiors—and thereby, I feel certain, Interpol and every police department in Europe—that I am the dashing Robin Hood of crime they have sought so long in vain."

Schmidt choked, emitting a fine spray of crumbs. "Vicky! Did you do that? How could you?"

John gave me a kindly smile. "I don't hold it against you, darling. You will wait for me, won't you? Seven to ten years should do it, unless they make the sentences consecutive, in which case you may have to hire a wheelchair when you meet me at the prison gates."

"No, I'll hire Max and Hans to break you out. I've always wanted to be a moll."

"A what?" Schmidt demanded.

"Gun moll," I said abstractedly. "Like Bonnie and Clyde."

"It is not amusing," Schmidt grumbled. "How can you joke about such a disaster, such a tragedy—"

"Shut up, Schmidt. Just let me think. I told . . . That's right, I told Sweet and Bright. They knew anyway, they're part of the gang, nobody is going to believe . . . And Larry Blenkiron."

"And?" John had stiffened.

"That's all. Oh, damn. The tapes. They've got the tapes. But you didn't say anything—"

"They don't have the tapes. Feisal picked them up and handed them over to Larry. I was there when he destroyed them. You're sure you didn't mention me to anyone else?"

"I didn't tell Alice. She was the only person who identified herself to me. I don't know to this day who the other agent on board was, if there was one. Am I a great spy or what?"

"I can't believe this," John muttered. "It's too easy. There must be something we've overlooked."

"Very good," Schmidt said. He gave me a forgiving smile. "I should have known that in the struggle between love and duty your heart would triumph over your—"

"Shut up, Schmidt," I said.

"So, then, how does it stand?" Schmidt bit into a pastry and chewed, ruminating. "I see only one remaining difficulty. Are you prepared, John, to play the grieving husband? For if her part in this comes out it will be the knot that unravels the tangled skein of the truth."

"Very literary, Schmidt," I said. "I don't know what the hell it means but it sounds good."

"It is obvious, what it means," Schmidt said indignantly. "The forced marriage, his knowledge of the plot, his earlier connection with her brothers—all these things will become known, together with your acquaintance with John, and your reputation, my dear Vicky, will be in ruins."

"Do you think I care about my reputation?"

"I care," John said shortly. "Honestly, Vicky, I'm beginning to worry about you. Anyhow, Schmidt is right; the whole implausible story hangs on her innocence. Unless ... How about claiming I was unaware of her criminal connections when I married her? They aren't exactly public knowledge."

"But how could you have remained unaware of them?" Schmidt didn't like this version; he saw where it was leading, and he wanted the credit for unearthing the plot.

John grinned at him. "That's the point, isn't it? I'll leave the medals to you, Schmidt. I don't doubt that Max and his employers will appreciate our keeping her name out of it. That's another consideration. So when I marched in there last night I was hoping to rescue her as well as Vicky?"

"Yes, yes, that is it," Schmidt said eagerly. "The villains foully murdered her. Both of you saw it."

"No," John said. "She was dead when I arrived. Vicky saw nothing."

"That is easier, yes," Schmidt agreed. "The less one admits to knowing, the fewer lies there are to remember. Do you find any other holes in the plan?"

"Not at the moment," I said. I couldn't believe it either.

"Good. Then we will go shopping." Schmidt scraped crumbs off his mustache and bounced up. "You cannot come, Vicky, not wrapped in a bedsheet, so I will select for you a suitable wardrobe."

"Oh, God. See here, Schmidt—"

"I'll go along," John said. "And try to control Schmidt. I believe I can claim to have a reasonably good idea of your size."

He was smiling as if he didn't have a care in the world. But he hadn't eaten much and he had never spoken her name.

# Chapter Fifteen

## i

The following days are something of a blur. We spent most of the time trying to elude the press and the rest of it talking with various officials. Occasionally I'd catch a glimpse of a mosque or a suq and once I actually saw the gates of the Cairo Museum as the limo passed it.

While John and Schmidt were shopping I called Mother and Dad and told them the reports of my nervous breakdown had been greatly exaggerated, but not as exaggerated as the story of my abduction and the news of my engagement. Despite her all-around relief, Mom was a little disappointed to find out that I wasn't engaged to marry a millionaire. She was tactful enough not to say so, however. I managed to talk Dad out of flying to Cairo. My call had caught him just as he was about to leave for the airport.

It was a nerve-racking interlude, and not just because I kept wanting to punch out the ghouls who followed us with cameras and microphones shouting questions. The worst were the questions that focused on John's supposed bereavement. They would have been cruel and contemptible if he had really cared about her. Under the circumstances they verged on emotional assault and battery, and I don't know how he kept his temper. Mine came close to cracking more than once.

Even more nerve-racking were the interrogation sessions. Everybody from the CIA to Interpol to the SSI to the Salvation Army seemed intent on questioning us. It was tantamount to walking, not a tightrope, but a spiderweb strung over a pond full of piranhas. My head ached trying to keep track of the lies we'd invented.

One encounter stands out in my mind.

Following Schmidt's advice, I had refused to be questioned except at the Embassy and in his company. John was there that day too. Everyone understood why we stuck together—or at least they thought they understood. Clichés, good old clichés—we had suffered together and survived together, and so on ad nauseam.

I had been expecting this particular meeting and had braced myself for it, so when Burckhardt rose to greet me I didn't slug him or spit in his face or even throw anything at him.

"You son of a bitch," I said, slapping his outstretched hand aside. "How you have the gall to face me after screwing up the way you did—"

John and Schmidt descended on me murmuring soothing comments, and forced me into a chair. "No, I will not be quiet," I shouted. "I'm just getting started. God damn you, Burckhardt, if that's your name, which I doubt, you and your security measures and your smug superiority and your total indifference to ordinary human decency almost got me killed. And furthermore . . ."

I hadn't planned it that way, but my explosion turned out to be the smartest move I could have made. By the time I finished telling him what I thought of him he was too nervous to think straight.

"We know now," he said, when I gave him a chance to talk, "that the individual referred to in the message was the man you had encountered in Sweden."

"Max," I snapped. "That was the name I knew him by. And no, I didn't recognize him. He kept out of my way and he didn't look at all the way I remembered him. The others— Hans and Rudi—weren't on the boat."

Burckhardt fumbled through his notes. "Dakin and Gurk—"

"Who? Speak up, Burckhardt, I'm bloody sick and tired of stupid questions."

"Uh. You knew them as Sweet and Bright."

"Oh, right. I'd never seen them before. I thought they were two of your people." I added, in case he'd missed the point, "You and your goddamm obsession with security! It's no wonder the poor effed-up world is in the state it's in, with people like you behind the scenes manipulating policy."

"Now, Vicky," Schmidt began.

"Shut up, Schmidt. And you too, Burckhardt. I've answered the same questions fifty times and I'm not going to answer any more. And you can tell Karl Feder that when I get my hands on him—"

"Yes, yes," Burckhardt said quickly. "Would you like—uh—perhaps a glass of water?"

"I am not hysterical," I shouted. "I am . . . I am leaving! Yes, leaving! Now."

"I think no more questions?" said Tom the diplomat, trying to sound firm and professional.

I rounded on him. "Yes, and what about you? You're supposed to be looking out for my rights."

"I am, I am," Tom said quickly. "Herr—uh—Burckhardt, I don't believe it would be a good idea to continue. Not at the present time."

"Not at any time!" I informed him. I was beginning to enjoy myself. "I am leaving. But before I do, I want to ask Burckhardt a question for a change. Just out of idle curiosity, who was the incompetent jerk who was supposed to be protecting me?"

"It was not her fault," Burckhardt muttered. "She obeyed orders. She was told not to—"

"She?"

"Would you like to speak with her? She asked for a chance to express her congratulations and apologies personally, but I did not think that advisable."

"You wouldn't." I wanted to get the hell out of there, but curiosity got the better of me. "Where is she?"

In the next room, of course. That's where these people live,

in the next room—peeking through keyholes and eaves-
dropping on private conversations.

I didn't recognize her at first. I didn't recognize her the
second time I looked either. Close-cropped sandy hair, a tailored suit ... Not until she flashed that wide toothy grin did
enlightenment dawn.

"Suzi?"

She didn't come any closer. "I wanted to express my regrets
personally, Dr. Bliss. I failed you, and I feel very bad about
that. None of us had the slightest suspicion of Mr. Blenkiron;
I assumed that when you were with him you were okay."

Her voice was quicker and harder than Suzi's, with a flat
Midwestern twang instead of a Southern drawl.

"Criminy!" Surprise had numbed my brain. Then I remembered something. "You were at the hotel that night—with
Perry."

She nodded, no longer smiling. "Trying to find you and
Herr Schmidt. Foggington-Smythe knew nothing about my
real purpose; I took him along as camouflage. You saw me?"

"I saw you. Since I didn't know whose side you were on
I ran. All the way down the goddamn Nile!" Renewed rage
choked me. "That awful trip—scared out of my mind—
worried about—thirst and exhaustion—fever—Feisal lying
in that damned hospital with his legs full of bullet holes—
get out of my way! I'm going to kill him!"

Burckhardt retreated behind the desk and John caught me
by the arm. "You'll excuse us, gentlemen and madam. She's
been through a lot lately."

He and Schmidt towed me out. Suzi moved quickly to open
the door for us. Her back was to Burckhardt and when she
caught my eye she rolled hers and made an expressive face.

Then ... Then her eyes moved, slowly and deliberately,
from me to John. He had drawn my arm through his and his
hand covered mine. He shouldn't have done it, I shouldn't
have let him do it, but things like that happened occasionally;
it was so hard to be on guard every moment.

Involuntarily I started to pull my hand away. His fingers
tightened, holding mine fast, warning me not to react; but
she'd observed both movements, and she tilted her head and
widened her eyes, and there was Suzi again, and I knew as

clearly as if she had spoken aloud that she was remembering
a conversation between me and Larry the day at Sakkara.
"He's not so young," I had said, without thinking, and Larry
had asked if I had known him before.

She looked me straight in the eye and smiled. "Good-bye,
Dr. Bliss. Good-bye, Mr. Tregarth. Good luck—to both of
you."

Funny, how everybody kept wishing me luck.

I began to believe we might get away with it after all. In
fact there were rumors about ceremonies of honor and assorted
medals. Feisal was going to be the new director of the institute
and I didn't doubt for a moment that he'd be standing on
his own two feet when he assumed the position. He was
recuperating much faster than the doctors had expected; when
I leaned over to kiss him good-bye the last time we visited
him, he pulled me down onto the bed and into his arms, and
John had to detach me by force.

"You'll come back, won't you?" Feisal asked. "And let
me show you Egypt without distractions?"

"I hope so," I said. And to my surprise I found I meant it.

All in all, things were looking up. I wasn't even dreaming.
But John was.

He always quieted as soon as I touched him. But the night
before we were to leave I forced myself to wait and watch
while he thrashed around and groaned, and finally a few words
became audible. He might have said more, but I couldn't
stand it any longer, and when I took hold of him he woke.

He lay quiet in my arms until his breathing was back to
normal. Then he said, "There is one misapprehension you
may harbor that I would like to correct. I am not one of those
sensitive overeducated aristocrats who writhe around in a
frenzy of guilt because they have been responsible for bringing
a sociopath to his or her well-deserved end."

"I suspect they occur only in fiction," I said, trying to
match his precise, detached tone.

"Oh, quite. There's no one so bloody-minded and selfish
as your overeducated aristocrat. No doubt you've noticed
that."

"John—"

"I'm sorry I woke you. It won't happen again."

Before long he drifted off to sleep. I didn't.

We said good-bye at the airport next morning. Schmidt and I were leaving first; John's plane took off an hour later. He was wearing a sling, for the effect, he claimed; but that unimportant overlooked bullet hole wasn't healing the way it should and I thought that morning he had a touch of fever. I told myself not to worry. Jen would nag him till he saw a doctor.

The sling matched the black armband on his left sleeve. The suit hung a little loosely, but it was beautifully tailored and he was the picture of an English gent manfully suppressing personal sorrow. For the benefit of the photographers he bowed over my hand and allowed Schmidt to slap him on the back. "Three friends, brought together by chance and bonded in tragedy." I read some of the newspaper stories later. They were very mushy, especially the tabloid versions.

I had sworn I wouldn't look back, but of course I did. He raised his hand and smiled, and then turned away.

"Do not weep, mein Kind," Schmidt said. "You will see him soon again."

"I'm not weeping." I wasn't. Two tears do not constitute weeping. I knew there was a chance I wouldn't see him again.

## ii

A couple of weeks later Schmidt and I were walking along the Isar. In the rain. It was Schmidt's idea. He thinks walking in the rain is romantic. I did not share his opinion, and I remembered those bright hot days in Egypt with a nostalgia I had never expected to feel. The river was gray as steel under a steely sky. Fallen leaves formed soggy masses that squelched under our feet. My hair hung in lank dank locks that dripped onto my nose and down my neck. I had meant to have it cut. Why hadn't I? I knew why.

"This was a stupid idea," I grumbled. "I'm cold and wet and I want to go back to work."

"You have not done five minutes' work in the past week," Schmidt said. "You sit in your office, all alone in the tower, staring at your papers and accomplishing nothing. You are the stupid one. Why don't you telephone him? He is in the book."

"Schmidt, you devil!" My foot slipped and I had to grab at Schmidt to keep from falling. He grinned and grabbed back. "You didn't call him, did you?"

"No, what do you take me for?"

"An interfering, nosy—"

"I called the information in England to get the number," Schmidt said calmly. "It would be only courteous of you to inquire after his health."

"He's all right." I kicked at a wad of sodden leaves. "You know that. Jen called you too."

"Oh, yes, very touching," Schmidt said with a sniff. "The dear old Mutti thanking us for our kindness to her little boy. Herr Gott, when she began to talk about his tragic loss and the virtues of that terrible young woman I was hard-pressed to hold my tongue."

It hadn't been pleasant. Jen hadn't been awfully pleasant either. She'd said all the right things but I had had a feeling she wasn't too happy about some of the newspaper stories. None of the reporters had had the bad taste to come right out with their prurient suspicions but there had been references to my youthful blond beauty (every female in stories like those is beautiful) and John's tender concern.

He had told me once his mother wouldn't like me.

"He must be getting very tired of being fussed over," said Schmidt.

"He'll put up with it only as long as he chooses. Schmidt, can we go back now?" I sneezed.

"No. We have not yet said what must be said. But I do not want that you should catch cold. We will go to a café and have coffee. Mit Schlag," Schmidt added happily.

He had whipped cream on his coffee and on his double serving of chocolate torte and, by the time he finished, on his mustache. It was a warm, cozy little café, with low ceilings and windows covered with steam that blurred the gloomy weather outside. Schmidt wiped his mustache and leaned forward, elbows on the table.

"Now, Vicky. What is wrong? It is good to talk when one is in distress, and who better to listen than Papa Schmidt, eh?"

He'd missed a speck of whipped cream. It might have been that homely touch or his worried frown, or the comfortable intimate ambience, but all of a sudden I knew I was going to talk till I was hoarse.

"I love you, Schmidt," I said.

"Well, I have known that for a long time," Schmidt said complacently. "But it is good to hear you say it. Have you found the courage now to say it to him?"

"Uh-huh."

"With more enthusiasm than that, I hope. And he loves you too. So of what are you afraid?"

"Funny," I said hollowly. "He asked me the same thing."

"And what did you say?"

"Something stupid, I guess. It's a stupid question, Schmidt! Loving someone condemns you to a lifetime of fear. You become painfully conscious of how fragile people are—bundles of brittle bones and vulnerable flesh, breeding grounds for billions of deadly germs and horrible diseases. And loving a man like John is tantamount to playing Russian roulette. He can't help being the way he is, he'll never change, and that life-style doesn't offer much hope for a long-term relationship, does it? I've been fighting my feelings for a long time, longer than I wanted to admit, because I knew that once I gave way it would be all the way, no holding back, no reservations. That's the way I am. And he . . . It's not just physical attraction . . . Are you laughing, Schmidt? So help me God, if you laugh at me—"

"But who could not laugh? You, of all people, so prim and proper with the poor old gentleman. I was not always old, Vicky, and I have not forgotten what it is like to feel as you do. But I still do not understand what is holding you back."

"It's not me, damn it! It's John. He's gone all sentimental and noble and self-sacrificing on me. I saw it coming and I hoped I was wrong, but I couldn't think of anything that

would change his mind, he's so arrogant and stubborn, and
he'd have called me by now if he meant to, it's been almost
two weeks, and having her call instead was a deliberate
sign—''

Schmidt whipped out his handkerchief. ''Weep, my dear
Vicky. Break yourself down. It will relieve you.''

''Thanks, I think I will.''

He moved his chair closer to mine and put his arm around
me. He felt as comforting and soft as a huge pillow, and warm
besides. When I finished blubbering I saw there was another
cup of coffee in front of me, with a double order of Schlag
on it. Schmidt's ideas of consolation are based on whipped
cream and chocolate.

''So,'' said Schmidt in a businesslike voice. ''That is better.
We can seriously discuss the problem. I will accept your
assumption that this is how he feels, for you are in a better
position to know than I. Can you explain why he should feel
so? For surely now your position is safer than it has ever
been. He is not under suspicion by the police and you have
an excuse for enjoying an acquaintance that began openly
and legitimately.''

''John Tregarth isn't wanted, no. But Sir John Smythe and
a couple of dozen other aliases are, and not only by the police.
Max assured us he held no grudge, but John obviously didn't
believe him, and how many others like Max are there crawling
around in the woodwork? That's what has him worried,
Schmidt. Not just worried—terrified. I thought he was feeling
guilty about *her* until the night before we left Egypt, and then
. . . It was me he was having nightmares about. He was reliving
that awful hour with Max and the others, and dreading what
would happen—not to him, to me—if he didn't pull it off.
He kept repeating, 'It was too close,' and he didn't mean
coming too close to murder, he meant . . . Oh, hell. Do you
understand what I'm saying?''

''Yes, I understand,'' Schmidt said, frowning. ''It is
very—''

''If you say romantic I'll slug you.''

'' 'Touching' was the word I had in mind. More than touching. Beautiful! Yes, yes, it is what I would expect from such

a man. He fears to endanger you, and so he will stay away. Is that what you want?"

I had resigned myself to a long poetic tirade. The direct question startled me into the truth. "No."

"But he may be in the right," Schmidt said. "He knows more than you of the possible dangers."

"He has no right to make that decision for me. God damn it, Schmidt, it's the same old macho crap you guys always try to pull and it's not based on chivalry but on pure selfishness—tuck the little woman away in some safe place so *you* won't have to worry about *her*. What about *us* worrying about *you*? If you follow me."

"Oh, I do," said Schmidt. "I follow you very well."

My eyes fell. "Touché, Schmidt. I know; I've done the same thing to you. But in this case—in both cases—the damage is already done. Once you care about someone you're wide open, and the worst part of it is not knowing. Something awful could happen to him anytime, it could be happening at this very moment, and I might not even know about it for days or weeks or . . . You know what I did yesterday? I bought a goddamn London newspaper and read the goddamn obituaries! I can't live that way, Schmidt, and he has no right to expect me to, and no, I'm not going to call him because this is his problem and he's got to come to grips with it and if he can't admit the obvious, basic fact—"

I broke off. I had run out of breath. Schmidt was nodding and smiling, and there was a calculating look in those beady little eyes of his.

"Schmidt," I said. "I already owe you more than I can ever repay and I am deeply grateful to you for inducing this emotional orgy, even if you did enjoy every maudlin moment of it. But if you call him and repeat this conversation—"

"Now, Vicky, would I do such a thing?" He took out his wallet. "Come, we must return to the museum. To work, to work, eh? I trust you will be more efficient in the future."

It went on raining. Day after day. Three days, to be precise. I didn't mind. At that point I'd have considered sunlight a personal insult. And the bad weather kept me occupied. Cleaning up after Caesar was a full-time activity.

He and Clara had been glad to see me. Not that Clara admitted it. In fact, she spent a full day displaying her displeasure at my absence. She'd walk into the room and then sit down with her back to me, glancing over her shoulder now and then to make sure I was aware of how she was ignoring me. And she talked. There is nothing noisier than an irritated Siamese. Finally she condescended to get on my lap and after that I couldn't get rid of her. I fell over her every time I climbed the stairs and she slept on my head instead of at my feet. With her tail in my mouth.

Caesar's delight at my return was more openly expressed. Thanks to the incessant rain he was able to coat himself with mud whenever he went out and he was determined to share this pleasure with the one he loved best. If it hadn't been for them and for Schmidt . . .

But I was feeling more suicidal than ever that gloomy Thursday evening. The drive home, through misty rain and fog, had been a nightmare of traffic and fender benders. Caesar had found something dead in the garden when I let him out, and he had rolled in it. Clara had decided she didn't care for the brand of cat food I had been feeding her for a week. I had just bought a whole case of it.

I had been too depressed to change my wet clothes or my muddy shoes. I was sitting on the couch, elbows on my knees, chin on my hands, dank hair dripping down my face, when the doorbell rang.

Schmidt looked like Father Christmas with an armful of parcels and a red scarf wound around his double chins. The bottle sticking out of one of the bags appeared to be champagne.

"Coming to cheer me up, are you?" I inquired sourly.

"Do not be rude, you know you are glad to see me."

"Yes, I am. Hi, Schmidt."

"Grüss Gott," Schmidt said formally. "Help me unpack these things. We are having a party."

"I hope 'we' means you and me." I followed him to the kitchen. So did Caesar and Clara. They knew Schmidt. When he began unloading his parcels I realized he'd been shopping at Dallmayr's, Munich's legendary gourmet deli. "I don't want anybody else."

"I have invited another guest," Schmidt said. He was trying not to grin but he couldn't hold it back, and I knew before he went on what he was going to say. "I think you will be glad to see him, though."

Slowly I followed Schmidt back into the living room, and there I stayed—rooted to the spot is the phrase, I believe—while he went into the hall. Was I thinking, in that supreme and critical moment, of how god-awful I looked? Of course I was. I had allowed myself to imagine such a meeting. In that fantasy I was attired in robes of filmy white, and my (freshly washed and carefully brushed) hair fell over my shoulders. Trust Schmidt to pick a moment when I resembled a charwoman on her way home from work.

But I didn't really care.

However, I managed not to throw myself at him when he entered the room. His hair was damp and a little too long; it curled over his ears. I swallowed and said, with typical graciousness, "You didn't have to come."

"I tried to stay away," John said. "It was for your sake, my darling; I'm not worthy of you, but your image has been enshrined in my heart. Aren't you going to stop me before I perpetrate any more assaults on English prose?"

He was smiling, but it was an oddly tentative smile, and if I hadn't believed the word could never apply to John I would have said he looked a little shy.

"I'm not going to do anything till Schmidt leaves the room," I mumbled.

"Why not?" Schmidt inquired curiously.

"Why not, indeed," I agreed. "Damn good question, Schmidt."

Mine is a small living room. One step was all it took.

"Sehr gut," said Schmidt's voice from somewhere in the rosy pink clouds. (I hate to mention those clouds, but as I have already admitted, my imagination runs to clichés.) "I will now open the champagne."

"No bandages," I whispered. "Are you really all right?"

"What are you doing, counting ribs? The area is still a trifle sensitive, so if you wouldn't mind—"

"You're so thin. Did Schmidt call you, after I threatened to kill him if he—"

"You've lost a bit of weight yourself, haven't you? Here—and perhaps here—"

"He did call you."

"When he did, I had been sitting staring at the telephone for over two hours. Trying not to ring you. Are you angry with him?"

"No. What did he say?"

"My ears are still burning," John said wryly. "Even my dear old mum's lectures never attained that level of surgically accurate analysis. Vicky . . ." He put his hands on my shoulders and held me away. "We must settle this before Schmidt comes back and breaks that bottle of champagne over our bows. I thought it quite likely you'd never want to set eyes on me again."

"I told you I loved you."

"Yes, but—"

"Weren't my demonstrations convincing?"

"Oh, that. You couldn't help that, you were powerless to resist. I've been told Great-Granddad had to beat them off with a club. Darling, stop doing that and be serious for once."

"Me?" I stopped doing that.

"I know. It's your fault, I don't behave this idiotically with anyone but you." He took my face between his hands. "Seriously, Vicky. I did try to stay away. If you hadn't—"

"Will you marry me?"

His eyes widened with horror. "Certainly not! Are you out of your mind?"

"Well, what's a girl to do? If you won't ask me—"

"You don't suppose I would insult your intelligence by asking you to marry me, do you?" John demanded indignantly.

"How about a dangerous liaison, then?"

It was the wrong adjective. His eyes darkened and his fingers pressed painfully into my temples. "I haven't guts enough to go through this again, Vicky. If I had survived and you—and you hadn't, I would have put a bullet through my head."

"I'm told that drinking yourself to death is more fun," I said.

"Oh, God. Won't you allow me a single moment of high drama?"

"I owe you one for spoiling my big scene at Amarna."

"You're incorrigible." He pulled me into his arms. "And irresistible. All right, then—"

"Sweetheart! You've made me the happiest woman in—"

"I wouldn't marry you if you were the last woman on earth," John said. "But we'll give the other a try. And make frequent offerings to Saint Jude. My darling, are you certain this is what you want? It may be years before—"

The swinging door to the kitchen opened and Schmidt's head appeared. "Do not concern yourselves, my friends. Schmidt is working on the problem."

The head vanished, to be followed by a thump, a burst of profanity, and a series of frustrated yelps from Caesar. Schmidt had blocked Caesar's path but he had overlooked one little thing. John yelped and clutched his leg. "Bloody hell!"

I looked down. Clara had bit him on the ankle.

"Eight years," Schmidt said. His ingenuous face fell. "Unless it is petty theft—"

"There's nothing petty about my activities," John said. "Let me think . . . Italy."

It was a charming domestic scene. Schmidt was sitting at the table, his papers spread out before him, his pen poised. He had stripped to his shirt sleeves in order to work more efficiently, and with the glasses perched on the end of his nose and his face set in a frown of concentration he looked like a conscientious little accountant. An old Roy Acuff tape was playing; when one of his favorites came on, Schmidt joined in. His rendition of "The Prisoner's Lament" was particularly soulful.

Schmidt had graciously allowed me to retire in order to change and wash my face. My wardrobe doesn't run to diaphanous robes, but I did the best I could, and I tied a red ribbon around my hair. As I had hoped, the ribbon had the appropriate effect on John. His eyes widened, but all he said—all he had time to say, before Schmidt was with us again—was, "Once you've made up your mind you don't hold back, do you?"

Caesar was snoring under the table with his head on Schmidt's foot. Clara was in the kitchen. I had bribed her with the extravagant remains of Schmidt's feast, but she was still complaining. Every time she yowled John flinched.

He was recumbent on the couch, coat and tie off, shirt open, like a weary husband at the end of a hard day's work. I sat on the floor next to him. It is a sufficient indication of my state of mind that I had assumed that position without even thinking about it. Now and then his hand touched my hair, so lightly that no one except a woman who was totally besotted would have felt it. It ran through every nerve in my body.

"Italy," John repeated thoughtfully. "It's been almost three years since I did anything in Italy."

"Ah, sehr gut," Schmidt exclaimed. He made a notation. I turned my head. "Rome?"

"Right. What a memory you've got."

"Now then." Schmidt shuffled papers. "We have nothing in Norway. Sweden is next. Was your last, er, hum, adventure in Sweden the one in which Vicky was involved?"

"That doesn't count," John said, stretching comfortably. "They never pinned anything on me."

"How about Leif?" I suggested.

"Always looking on the bright side, aren't you?" He tugged lightly at the lock of hair he had wound round his fingers. "They can't prove I did it. Anyhow, it was self-defense."

"Very good, very good." Schmidt beamed. "And you have committed no, er, hum, actions in the U.K.?"

"Nothing we need worry about," John said somewhat evasively. "There's an old adage about fouling one's own nest."

"And the States?"

"No."

"What about that artifact the Oriental Institute fondly believes it got back?" I asked.

John looked shocked. "It's the original. How can you doubt me?"

Schmidt peered at his notes. "So we have ... Germany, Italy, France, Egypt, Turkey, and Greece. Hmmmm. Nothing for two years, anywhere?"

"I've been busy," John said defensively.

I rose to my knees and turned to face him. "Two years? Then last winter, when you fed me that line about a nice honest job and turning respectable . . . It was the truth?"

John smiled sheepishly. "Hard to credit, I know. I did lie about the cottage in the country. I can't afford it yet. Everything's gone back into the shop. Really, the difficulty of starting an honest business in today's world, what with taxes and endless forms to fill out and all those regulations—"

"Oh, John." I took his hand and carried it to my cheek. "Did you go straight for me? I think I'm going to cry."

"You dreadful woman, how dare you make fun of me?"

"Why didn't you tell me?"

He looked as embarrassed as if I had accused him of bigamy. I sat back on my heels. "You didn't want to prejudice my decision, was that it? John, if you don't stop being so damned noble I'll dump you and get myself a more interesting beau."

He grinned, but Schmidt was deeply moved. "You should not joke about such things, Vicky. It will not be so long after all; six years at the most, perhaps only five."

It wasn't that simple. The statutes of limitations with regard to art thefts are subject to interpretations that vary from country to country and even judge to judge—and they are constantly changing. And it wasn't the police John was primarily worried about. Schmidt knew all that as well as I did. He was just trying to cheer us up, bless his heart.

"I suppose I could give some of them back," John said, like a sulky little boy offering to return the candy bars he had swiped from the corner grocery. But I saw the gleam in his eye, and when Schmidt said eagerly, "That would be wunderbar," I said, "Not if you have to *steal* them back. Aren't you in enough trouble already? Honestly, John, I think you just enjoy taking things, never mind why."

Unobserved by Schmidt, who was considering this new angle, John's index finger curled around my ear.

"There's always a chance of time off for good behavior," he said brightly. "I've been very virtuous of late. Mending fences, so to speak. The Oriental Institute isn't the only institution that thinks kindly of me. Innumerable little old ladies have promised to mention me in their prayers, and several starving orphans—"

"It's getting late," I said, catching my breath. "You must be tired, Schmidt."

"Tired? No! We are celebrating, are we not?" The damned tape chose that moment to start a new song, and Schmidt jumped up, bouncing on his toes. "Come, Vicky, we will dance, nicht?"

"It's not a polka, Schmidt."

"Well, do you think I do not know a polka when I hear it? I waltz as well as I do the polka and the Schuhplattler and the samba and the rhumba."

He offered his hand. Smiling, I let him pull me to my feet. At that point I'd have agreed to anything the little guy wanted, even if he wouldn't go home. At least it wasn't a samba.

Schmidt clasped me in his arms and off we went, just as I had expected: one two three hop, one two three hop ... I was helpless with laughter, trying to figure out what outré combination of steps Schmidt was doing, when he stopped and stepped back, beaming. John caught my hand and swung me into the circle of his arm.

There were so many things we had never done together. Gone grocery shopping, walked in the rain ... Walked, period. Usually we were running. Planted daffodils, played pinochle, gone to the opera, washed the dishes ...

I wasn't surprised to find he was a good dancer, light on his feet, with a strong sense of rhythm. I thought I was doing pretty well myself until a voice murmured tenderly into my ear, "Stop trying to lead."

Laughter loosened my muscles and he spun me in an extravagant circle, adding, "For now, at least. We'll argue each case as it arises."

There is no more sickeningly saccharine, swoopingly sentimental piece of music than "The Tennessee Waltz." Over John's shoulder I caught glimpses of Schmidt smiling and nodding and swaying more or less in time with the music. Then I didn't see him anymore because I had closed my eyes and stopped trying to lead.

When the tape clicked off and I opened my eyes Schmidt was gone. I heard the front door close softly.

John inspected the room with a wary eye.

"She's in the kitchen," I said. "Could I interest you in a game of pinochle?"

He always knew what I was thinking. "Tomorrow. After we've walked the dog and done the washing up. I'll even attempt to establish a truce with that man-eating cat of yours. At the moment, however . . ."

"You can lead."

"I intend to. This time."

He took the ribbon from my hair.

There would be a next time. And at least one tomorrow. I'd settle for that. One is all any of us can count on.